P9-DTO-138

Praise for *The Bad Immigrant*

"A clever, compassionate and swift-paced exploration of identity, race, and belonging. In prose that is both witty and sharp, Atta draws the reader into an unforgettable tale of an immigrant family finding ways to live their own versions of the American dream. A brilliant, brilliant book."

—Chika Unigwe, author of *Better Never than Late* and winner of the 2012 Nigeria Prize for Literature

"Atta humorously and honestly executes the story of the Karim family as they try to make sense of the elusive American dream after winning the visa lottery. A hilarious, painfully candid, and thoroughly captivating read."

—Bunmi Oyinsan, author of *Three Women*

"An outstanding book from an exceptional author in which words seamlessly build on one another to erect a towering tale of compromise, tenacity, and hope, interlaced with wittiness and keen observations about culture and human character."

—Benjamin Kwakye, author of *The Clothes of Nakedness* and winner of the 1999 and 2006 Commonwealth Writers' Prize (Africa Region)

"This is such a powerful tale. Sefi Atta introduces us to a Nigerian family that has just arrived in America and renders their lives so effectively, so compellingly, that soon enough we find ourselves feeling their joy and pain, and we discover that by rooting for them we are also rooting for ourselves. An essential read."

—Tope Folarin, author of *A Particular Kind of Black Man* and winner of the 2013 Caine Prize for African Writing and 2021 Whiting Award in Fiction

Also by Sefi Atta

Everything Good Will Come (2005)
News From Home (short stories) (2009)
Swallow (2010)
A Bit of Difference (2013)
The Bead Collector (2019)
Sefi Atta: Selected Plays (2019)

THE BAD IMMIGRANT

Sefi Atta

Interlink Books
An imprint of Interlink Publishing Group, Inc.
Northampton, Massachusetts

First published in 2022 by
Interlink Books
An imprint of Interlink Publishing Group, Inc.
46 Crosby Street, Northampton, MA 01060

www.interlinkbooks.com

Library of Congress Cataloging-in-Publication Data
Names: Atta, Sefi, author.
Title: The bad immigrant / Sefi Atta.
Description: Northampton, Massachusetts : Interlink Books, an imprint of Interlink Publishing Group, Inc., 2021. | Summary: "An account of an immigrant family's struggle and the lessons learned about diversity"
Identifiers: LCCN 2021021331 | ISBN 9781623719050 (hardback)
Classification: LCC PS3601.T78 B33 2021 | DDC 813/.6--dc23
LC record available at https://lccn.loc.gov/2021021331

Printed and bound in the United States of America

To my husband Gboyega Ransome-Kuti
and our daughter Temi, for the journey

"If there is one secret I'd like to share
It's that we are what we dream
Or what we fear."

—Ben Okri
"As Clouds Pass Above Our Heads"

DREAMS

I was never keen on the idea of coming to America; my wife Moriam was, though. She was the one who submitted our entry for the green card lottery through the Diversity Immigrant Visa Program. She then convinced me to leave Nigeria after we found out we had won. I had my doubts from the very beginning—for one, about my job prospects. But Moriam didn't give up until she had made her case. I'd just turned forty and she was approaching. We'd been working for years and were barely getting by. She was a nurse and I was a public relations manager. How would we put our children, Taslim and Bashira, through secondary school? she asked. And to what end? Private universities were expensive; state universities provided substandard educations and students took longer to graduate because of government-employee strikes.

Moriam knew how to get to me. I'd taught literature for a while at a state university in Lagos and would have been happy to continue to. I went into banking in the late eighties because it was the only industry in the private sector where I could earn a decent living. At the bank where I worked, I was in charge of press releases and other external communiqués. The boredom of my daily routine almost killed me, but my paycheck kept her happy. At the military hospital where she worked, nurses fled overseas as soon as they got plane tickets and visas. They held meetings to pray about winning the green card lottery. She had some job security as a government employee and we lived in a two-bedroom flat on Lagos mainland. What would happen when she eventually retired? she went on. How would we pay our rent? She would have to beg for her pension, as government workers did. I was guaranteed to lose my job once I reached a certain age, and I had no other skill but an ability to write. No, she said, there was no future for us in Nigeria. We would end up poor if we stayed there.

I couldn't stop her. No one could. She filled out our immigration application forms and arranged our medical tests and interviews at the US Embassy. Her father was a retired army officer and she prided herself on being efficient. To raise money for our journey, she traded gold jewelry and sold our furniture and other belongings, including our Peugeot, which, despite severe wear and tear, fetched several times what I'd bought it for secondhand. I went along with her plans only because of the educational opportunities for our children. I found out about American schools and examinations and contacted an old colleague of mine, Osaro, who taught at a college in New York.

Osaro and I had both got our PhDs from the University of Ibadan. He was a lecturer when he left Nigeria. Now, he was also a published writer. I was honest about my situation when I spoke to him; I wasn't one to pretend I was doing well back home to prove a point. Our economy was yet to recover from a dictatorship. We'd recently held our general elections after fifteen years of military regimes and who had we elected as president? A former head of state, a soldier in mufti, under the watch of UN inspectors, as the rest of the world congratulated us on our peaceful transition to democracy. I decided that Nigeria's return to democracy only meant that any corrupt, incompetent individual could legitimately run the country from then on, so perhaps it was time for us to leave.

We arrived at John F. Kennedy Airport in the summer of 1999. My cousin Ismail met us there. I was surprised to find him gray-haired, although, with his height and pressed shirt and trousers, he looked somewhat distinguished.

Ismail was not my favorite relative, having borrowed money from me and never bothered to repay it, but he had agreed to let us stay with him temporarily. He worked as a financial planner in New York and lived in New Jersey. He was divorced and his only child, Hakeem, lived with his ex-wife, Sondra, in Los Angeles. He was my senior by a few years, and despite his acquired American accent and mannerisms, would expect the usual Yoruba courtesies. So I'd asked Taslim and Bashira to greet him appropriately and Moriam to call him Brother Ismail.

"In America," he said, as he drove us to his house, "every opportunity is given to immigrants to make it, wherever they are from. Those who don't take advantage of the opportunities are not meant to be here. They might as well get in their banana boats and paddle back home. They're failed immigrants. Now, those who persist and succeed are true Americans. But! But! They were born in the wrong countries."

I wished he would be quiet, so I could take in the sights without having to make conversation with him. I'd only ever been overseas once before, for my master's degree at the School of Oriental and African Studies in London. Queens was all overpasses and construction sites. On either side were towering tenements with zigzag stairs and dwarf buildings with cluttered balconies. Occasionally, a billboard or graffiti on a wall caught my eye. Summer in New York was hotter than I'd expected and I found it hard to pretend I was interested in what Ismail was saying, meanwhile. Everyone was protected under the Constitution, he assured us. Class distinctions would eventually become extinct. The homeless people we saw along the way had no excuse. They were drug abusers and alcoholics—lowlifes, essentially. I was barely nodding as we crossed the upper level of George Washington Bridge and passed the exit to Fort Lee.

Ismail lived in a town house that was the model home of a development. It was made of red brick and stucco. He gave us a tour, which was far too long, and threw in the odd brag. He said his kitchen had granite countertops not ordinary laminate. The furniture in his living room was some expensive brand. He didn't have a television there because that would be in bad taste. He did have a wide-screen television in the den in the basement, only to watch basketball games and pay-per-view boxing matches, and the wet bar there was custom-made.

He had not changed. When we were young, all he ever talked about was making money and living large. He was enterprising by nature but lacked, what I would call in English, a certain maturity. He was like a little boy showing off his toys. Yet he had become finicky, the way I imagined an old man who had lived on his own too long would be. At the front door, he'd made us take off our shoes. I hardly touched a cushion in the living room and he stopped to adjust it. I was nervous about how our children would cope in his house, as they both had a tendency to be untidy. Moriam cautioned them in his presence, "You make a mess in this place and it's me you'll answer to."

She decided they should share the guest room in the basement. In the den, Ismail handed Taslim the remote to the television and told him he had access to more channels than he'd ever seen in his life. In fact, we'd had satellite in Nigeria, but cable was new to our children. Taslim tried to figure out how to change channels, tensing his lips with each press of a button.

"It's my turn," Bashira said, after a moment.

She was timing him. She was convinced that Moriam and I favored him. Even if we gave them the same amount of water to drink, she would check Taslim's glass before drinking from hers. I'd warned her several times that she was in danger of being permanently miserable if she kept monitoring him to see if he were getting a better deal.

Taslim refused to hand over the remote and she turned to me and said, "Daddy?"

I shook my head. On another day, I would have had more sympathy, but we'd traveled overnight, six and a half hours of which we'd spent in Frankfurt.

"Switch off the television," Moriam said.

"But I haven't had my turn," Bashira said.

"I won't tell you again," Moriam said.

Taslim was only too happy to obey. He was almost seventeen and Bashira had just turned fourteen. They would never have behaved that way back home.

I was guilty of indulging our children, having been raised by a father who wouldn't hesitate to use a cane to discipline me. When I was their age, if my father found me watching television, I was in big trouble. The television in our house was for my parents to watch the news. My father was a headmaster and believed children were better off reading books. I never resented him for being strict; I only wanted Taslim and Bashira to be freer around me. Moriam felt I was spoiling them. Her mother was the disciplinarian in her family. Her father would order her to carry out military-style punishments like push-ups and squats. He did the same for fun, so Moriam didn't take him seriously. Over the years, she and I had clashed over how to raise our children. "They have to fear you, Lukmon," she would insist. "Otherwise they won't respect you." I would say our different ways of parenting balanced each other out. Moriam threatened more often than she followed through. I rarely made idle threats.

Ismail and I left the basement and returned to the living

room on the ground floor, which had dark-brown leather sofas and wood side tables. To me, the room appeared sparse, as if he couldn't afford to furnish it fully, but he said the idea behind the decor was minimalism, a new interior design trend. I couldn't decide if he had forgotten how much information flow there was from America to Nigeria, or if he just assumed I was as naïve as an American would be, first time in Nigeria.

He continued his civics lesson, telling me the Founding Fathers of America were brilliant men. The Constitution was a document of pure genius that had stood the test of time and was not to be tampered with. Flaming liberals had deceived him before, but he was a diehard conservative now.

I wondered why he would suggest America was a forward-looking country, only to keep harking back to its Constitution. Then I remembered that Ismail had business savvy rather than intellect. I assumed one necessitated the other but had often felt inept in the presence of successful businessmen I'd encountered in banking.

He further contradicted himself when I asked if America were ever likely to have a black president, since it was such a progressive country.

"A black president?" he asked. "In this country? That will never happen! That will ne-ver happen in a million years! They will have a Hispanic president before they have a black one. They will have an Italian president first. Listen, Americans will elect a white woman as president before they elect a black man. The Oval Office is historically white Protestant territory. They barely allow Catholics in there. The American dream has to end somewhere for everyone. We have to be grateful for what we have."

"I would be grateful for anyone who can run Nigeria," I said.

The American dream was nothing compared to the Nigerian one, where a halfwit could take over the whole government and make Nigerians wonder if our independence was worthwhile.

"Forget that useless country," he said. "Just be happy you're here. Actually, you look fresh for someone who has come straight from the jungle. Not a white hair on your head and you're still trim. Your wife must have been taking good care of you. She must have been cooking with some of that pure, unadulterated palm oil. Is that the secret?"

"It must be."

"She has to cook for me."

"Definitely."

Moriam was an excellent cook and didn't mind catering to my relatives, and Ismail's kitchen had to be the most over-equipped and underutilized kitchen we'd ever seen.

RELATIVES

When American men said they couldn't boil an egg, they usually didn't mean it literally; I did, and every good Nigerian wife knew that to win her in-laws over she had to cook for them. I didn't have to tell Moriam that.

On our first night, Ismail ordered Chinese takeaway, or "takeout," as he called it, but she got into a minor exchange with him when he said it was the best in Passaic County. She thought the rice was soggy. She would never put up with a badly prepared meal, no matter how expensive or elaborate. Overall, she felt that the Chinese food she'd had in Nigeria was better than the takeout Ismail had ordered, but he remained adamant.

"They probably gave you rat meat to eat in Nigeria and called it chicken," he said.

"No one would do that and get away with it," Moriam said.

"How would you know?" he asked.

"Naijas like chicken. We would know the difference."

"Naijas eat bushmeat," he said.

"Yes," she said, with a shrug.

"What do you think bushmeat is?" he asked. "Grasscutter! Also known as greater cane rat!"

They both got on my nerves. He had an annoying habit of laughing at his own jokes and she was in the habit of getting into arguments she could easily ignore.

Before we went to sleep, I asked her if she would take charge of the kitchen while we were staying at Ismail's house and she said, "I thought he prefers Chinese takeout."

"Come on," I said. "He wants to eat Nigerian food."

She also held on to grudges. Even a simple concession that Ismail was not smart would be too much for her.

"He should go back to Nigeria if he misses the food there," she said. "I didn't come to America to be his cook."

"Don't be wicked."

"How am I being wicked?"

"With everything he's doing for us?"

"Doesn't he owe you money?"

I regretted telling her that. She might use it to blackmail me. Not that she would ever repeat it to him, but she would constantly threaten to.

I'd never had to persuade Moriam to cook before. Even if we didn't have enough food, she made the best of whatever we had. In her family, they ate as if they were breaking fast every day. In mine, we'd only been allowed excesses on Muslim holidays.

We heard a loud rumble and I reached for my reading glasses on the bedside table and slipped them on. The noise was the air-conditioning system adjusting automatically as Ismail had said it would. I pointed at the vent and indicated that we should whisper because Ismail's bedroom was next to ours.

"He's saving us money by letting us stay here."

"Your cousin boasts too much."

"How?"

"Don't pretend you don't know. He boasts too much and he abuses Nigeria."

"Weren't you the one who wanted to leave?"

She knotted her black silk hair scarf. She was in an old nightgown, which she found comfortable and I found off-putting because it resembled a maternity gown. Of course, she was annoyed with me as well, for not taking her side.

"He thinks he's better than us," she said.

"I don't care what he thinks," I said.

"Seriously, Lukmon, your cousin annoys me. Seriously. I'm not playing here."

Ismail and I were paternal cousins. Our families were identified by our fathers' first names. I was an Ahmed-Karim and he was a Rasaq-Karim. The Ahmed-Karims ended up in academia and the Rasaq-Karims in business. Their father had owned an electronics shop in Abeokuta city, where we had all grown up. There was a longstanding rivalry between the Rasaq-Karim and Ahmed-Karim children. They thought they were superior because they were relatively well-off. They had air conditioners when we had fans. They had a stereo system when we had a record player, and so on. We were snobbish with regard to education. Our father was respected as a headmaster and we did better in school.

For a Nigerian family, mine was average, with two parents and four children. I was used to being around bigger families, but Ismail's father had three wives and so many children it was hard to monitor them all, or control them. You couldn't get into a fight with a Rasaq-Karim brother without the rest attacking you. They were hefty boys raised on goat meat and they called me "Herbivore" because I was built like one, sometimes shortening it to "Herbie," to imply I was a wimp. I wasn't physically combative and was targeted by neighborhood bullies. I could easily have floored them with insults, but I wasn't that sort either, so I walked around like a mini Jesus until I was old enough to defend myself. Until then, all I had were elder sisters to back me, which also called my father's manhood into question. My Uncle Rasaq couldn't understand why my father wouldn't just marry another woman who would bear him more sons.

My father never earned enough as a headmaster to afford a polygamous lifestyle, if he'd ever considered one. My mother, dear woman, believed her only duties were to take care of our family and teach Koranic lessons. Under her tutelage, I learned how to write the Arabic alphabet and recite *Al-Fatiha*, the opening *surah*, and short *suwar* like *Al-Kauthar*, *Al-Ikhlas* and *An-Nas*. I was no smarter than my sisters, but she gave me special attention because I was a boy. My sisters and I attended the primary school where my father was headmaster. They stayed on in Abeokuta for secondary school, while I was sent to Mayflower School in Ikenne, probably the only secular school in Nigeria, run by Tai Solarin, an avowed socialist and humanist. At the age of seventeen, I left Mayflower for the University of Ife and graduated with a degree in English, after which I was awarded a Commonwealth Scholarship for my master's degree in London.

Moriam and I met during my PhD at the University of Ibadan. She told me she'd wanted to study biochemistry but opted for nursing. I suspected she said that so I wouldn't think she wasn't intelligent. But she was—in ways I wasn't, in ways that mattered. She knew how to handle people and get whatever she wanted from them. She was a natural at bargaining. If she were not a nurse, she would probably have been like her mother, who was a jewelry trader and millionaire at a time when the naira was four to the dollar.

We met at one of those impromptu parties in dorms called arrangees. The drinks came from a whip-round. The girls who showed up were questionable. There was one with mosquito-bitten legs and another with a lazy eye I found sexy after enough beers. Moriam stood out when she walked in—small in stature, with a pretty face, but frowning as if she had been tricked or coerced into making an appearance. I loved troublesome-looking women. I was drawn to them. If you approached one, it could go either way, but once you had their attention, they were yours.

I gave her a few raps, as the slang was, back then, and she seemed open. I was just glad that a fine chick who hadn't been passed around was talking to me. She later said she talked to me only because she thought I was a nice guy. Why women assumed I was nice, I never knew. They mistook my silence for shyness. I was usually thinking about how to get them to go to bed with me.

Moriam found my sense of perspective warped. She was convinced I got it from studying in London. I was just easily amused by absurdities, which she dismissed as childishness on my part. But I marked my territory before she knew what was happening. I had her cooking *efo* stew for me, with bushmeat and stockfish, on an electric hot plate, against campus regulations. She was concerned I was too thin. My friends would say she'd done a juju number on me. I would laugh and say it was the other way around.

Her family was polygamous. Her father had two wives and there was a lot of infighting between them, mostly over money. Moriam's mother got tired of the fracases and left. She continued to buy and sell gold jewelry from Italy, sometimes traveling there with Moriam, who was her firstborn. Moriam had attended Command Children School in Ibadan while her father was in the army. After her father retired, her mother supported her through nursing school. Her father was from Kwara state and her mother from Lagos state. She looked exactly like her father, so much that I assumed she was adopted when I met her mother.

Her mother, whom we called Alhaja, was enormously fat with a gold cap on her side tooth. The day I met her, she warned me that if I so much as touched Moriam, I was destined to marry her. I didn't know if she meant she'd consulted an oracle, but it was the joke between Moriam and me until Moriam got pregnant, despite the precautions she took. I couldn't believe it. She apparently couldn't either because she'd walked around for two months convinced she had an irregular cycle. My family was disappointed. I was their studious son and quiet brother. The Rasaq-Karims had a good laugh at my expense, though they stopped calling me Herbie from then on. Alhaja just widened her eyes at me and asked, "Are you satisfied?"

Perhaps I would have been better off marrying a woman I was more compatible with, but I did what was right and married Moriam. Her father was laid-back about the whole affair, which may have been the result of his fondness for schnapps. He attended our wedding, where he was relegated to a figurehead because Alhaja had paid all the expenses. He was a Civil War veteran and when Taslim was born, would entertain him with war stories. He would tell Taslim how he'd eaten lizard flesh to stay alive in the bush, and how he'd drunk a rough-and-ready Guinness stout made from palm wine and coffee granules. Taslim grew up believing war was fun. The man was basically an alcoholic, though no one ever said that. Moriam would only say he drank too much.

I put my arm around her to pacify her over her argument with Ismail. Normally, I would tell her she didn't know how lucky she was because I would never put up with bad behavior from an ugly woman.

"What?" she asked, moving away.

"Nothing."

"I hope you're not trying to be silly."

"Of course not," I said.

Anything further than a hug would be bad manners as we were in Ismail's house. She was appropriate in that way. Despite her annoyance with him, she'd packed up the remnants of his Chinese takeout and put them in the fridge, and supervised Taslim and Bashira, who had cleaned up.

"How come he never remarried?" she persisted.

"Ask him."

"Don't you two discuss these things with each other?"

"No."

"He must have done something terrible to that woman."

"How would you know?"

"I'm sure he did. Why did she leave him? Think about it. There isn't a woman in the world who would leave a man and take her son with her for no reason. Every woman wants peace in her home."

"Men don't?"

She hissed. "Continue to deceive yourself."

I removed my glasses and put them back on the bedside table. My sisters thought I gave in too easily to her. She was a typical Lagos girl, they said. She always had to have her way and I should learn to put my foot down. They didn't know Moriam. All I had to do, if I really needed to get my way with her, was ignore her. She couldn't cope with that. As she carried on about Ismail, I deliberately said nothing.

Ismail's ex-wife, Sondra, was African American. Their marriage had lasted only two years. Ismail sent me their wedding photographs in Nigeria and I wasn't surprised that Sondra was light-skinned. The Rasaq-Karim brothers had always been attracted to light-skinned women, whether or not they were attractive, and whether or not they were naturally light-skinned. One or two of Ismail's brothers were married to women who bleached their skin. Moriam called them the Venus de Milo brigade.

We were not yet married when she saw the photo of Sondra and she was impressed that Ismail had found himself a black American. We didn't learn they were having difficulties until a year later when I called Ismail and he told me Sondra had stopped working once she'd had Hakeem. She put Hakeem in day care as soon as he was old enough and refused to have anymore children. After that, she sat in front of the television from morning till night, claiming she was selling Mary Kay makeup.

I wasn't interested in the details and even without meeting Sondra, Ismail's story had sounded one-sided. When we heard that Sondra had filed for divorce, I was a little curious about what had gone wrong between them. Moriam was convinced that Ismail must have beaten her or cheated on her. I told her Ismail wasn't the sort to hit a woman. I didn't say he was likely to cheat on one.

After his civics lesson on America, he had given me strict instructions. We were not to answer his phone if the caller ID had a 310 area code because Sondra sometimes called to harass him. I didn't ask why. It wasn't my business to. I assumed he had a new woman in his life, as Ismail always had to have a woman, or several at a time. I hoped Moriam would cook for him and not be difficult, meanwhile. If he wanted her to cook Nigerian food, he was probably with a woman who couldn't.

I needed her assurance more than anything else that night. The idea that we'd made the wrong decision by coming to America kept me up long after she fell asleep. Apart from our children adjusting to a new schooling system, I was worried about how they would adjust to the culture. Taslim was easily influenced and sometimes didn't consider the consequences of his actions. Bashira always did, but she believed the whole world was against her. There was a possibility that I might have to return to graduate school. Moriam would have to retake her nursing exams to get back into her profession. We had enough money to tide us over for the summer, but it was unsettling not knowing when and where I would find a job.

In the past, Moriam had accused me of being too introspective and keeping my opinions and emotions to myself. I would say my work required me to be contemplative. She always took that as an insult. She once said that while my mind was busy wandering, she was dealing with medical emergencies at the hospital. Mothers bled to death during C-sections. Babies suffocated from birth complications. Her work demanded that she respond immediately and if she didn't, her patients lost their lives. So, unlike me, she didn't have time to sit around and think.

I persuaded Moriam to get rid of her awful nightgown that week. She agreed to only if she could buy a couple of new ones. I suggested she change her underwear as well, while she was at it, and Taslim and Bashira fell on the floor laughing. They enjoyed moments like this, when I picked on their mother. It showed I was capable of giving as much trouble as I got. Moriam amused them further by chasing me around the house. Poor children. They'd grown up believing this was romance.

I didn't really care about their mother's old-mama underwear, but I was in the spirit for new beginnings. After she'd worn herself out trying to hit me, she asked me to come to the mall to help her choose her underwear, since I was so critical. I told her she could do that on her own. I was neither a sophisticated nor a perverted man.

"They may have books there," she said.

"All right," I said, after a moment's consideration.

I disliked shopping, but books were my weakness and Ismail had more business magazines: *Forbes*, *Fortune*, *Money*. I doubt he'd read any of them cover to cover. The few books he had were about self-improvement: how to achieve such and such a goal; how to master this or that skill; and how to confront and conquer fears. They were not unlike religious texts.

That morning, he'd left for work having eaten most of the sardine omelet Moriam had made for breakfast. The mall was a twenty-minute drive from the development he lived in. The development itself was on an avenue that had a bus route to the mall. Across the road from the mall was a park 'n' ride, where Ismail caught a bus to the 42nd Street terminal in New York. That was the main reason he'd bought the house, he'd said. "Location, location, location."

I told Taslim and Bashira to come with us to the mall to get them away from the television. Moriam was more worried about leaving them unattended. In Nigeria, we'd had her cousin, Kudi, whom we'd paid to watch them during the day. When Kudi was around, we had less fear. If armed robbers raided our flat, Kudi would do her best to protect our children. She was only in her early twenties and often threatened to beat them, yet they worshipped her.

They were reluctant to go shopping with their mother. They knew as well as I did that she could take hours to decide what to buy. Taslim said he was old enough to be left alone. Bashira promised to hide in the basement should anyone knock on the door. They complained and complained until we got to the mall, then they walked through the sliding doors as if they were entering paradise.

Taslim went straight for the sports shops. Bashira browsed the girls' accessories shops. Moriam marched ahead of me, carrying a list that included items like phone cards and key tags. In retrospect, we looked like a family of "Just Comes." I was wearing an anorak. Moriam was in jeans that had bleached patches. Bashira's torso had not yet caught up with her legs and Taslim's arms almost reached his knees.

Moriam found two nightgowns fit for a grandmother, in pastel pink and blue. I asked her to choose sexy styles. She said sexy styles did not wash well and paid for the nightgowns in cash. Afterward, we went to the bookstore, where I discovered I'd left my glasses at Ismail's house. Taslim read out the descriptions of the books on display. They were not books I would buy. He and Bashira asked if they could explore the department store on their own. Now, Moriam was scared they would get lost and thought she ought to accompany them. I told her to let them go on their own and set a time limit for them to meet us at the mall entrance.

"Stay together," Moriam called after them.

We went to the fine-jewelry section first. She said she was just looking. We got there, she saw the gold jewelry displayed in the glass showcase and pointed items out so fast the assistant said, "I'm sorry, I can only show one at a time."

I stood by as she tried on a bracelet that cost $395.

"It's a bit expensive," she murmured.

"A bit?" I asked.

"You can always charge it," the shop assistant said, ignoring me.

Her hairstyle made no sense. One part deliberately covered her eye, yet she kept shaking her head so she could see.

"We don't have a credit card," Moriam said.

"Would you like to open an account with us?" the assistant asked.

"How can I do that?"

"Just fill out the form. You'll get fifteen percent off."

Moriam took the application form and began to review the terms. I observed other shoppers, mostly women, wandering around as if they were in trances. One man hurried along as if he were ashamed to be seen. Another hovered by a table of ties.

"How does one qualify for a store card?" I heard Moriam ask the assistant.

"Pardon?" the assistant said.

Moriam repeated her question.

"Oh, just fill out the form and we'll find out if you qualify."

"On what basis is one rejected, please?"

"Pardon?"

I came to Moriam's rescue. "Why do people get turned down?"

"Credit history..." the assistant said, about to recite a list. Then she abandoned it as if she couldn't think of another reason.

"We're new in the United States," Moriam said. "We have no history."

I laughed. "I don't know about that! I've got a very long one!"

The assistant put her hand up, as if to stop me from exposing myself. "I'm sorry, I can't help you."

Moriam unclasped the bracelet and returned it. I knew I was in trouble, but she'd said what she had to, to get me to come to the mall, and I'd said what I needed to, to get out.

"What is wrong with you?" she asked, at a safe distance.

"I have a history," I said. "I may not have a credit one."

"I could have paid in cash!"

"You were the one who said we don't have money to waste. I was only trying to help. You think she could understand what you were saying?"

Moriam lifted her shopping bag. "She couldn't speak English and she was standing there saying 'Pardon?' to me. I wasn't going to let her get away with it, until you gave her license to. Honestly, I don't know how you could do that. No, seriously, you let me down, acting like a bushman."

"Good. Let's go home, then."

She was the one acting like a bushwoman, running all over the place as if this were her first and last chance to consume products.

"No. I'm not going anywhere until I find out how to get a store card."

"We don't have to get a store card here."

"I will get a store card anywhere I want."

She got her stubbornness from her mother, who haggled with suppliers as if she hated them. Why she was upset with the assistant, I didn't know. I pointed out the woman had to stand behind a counter all day, answering the same questions over and over from customers like her who confused shopping with class warfare.

She said the assistant had insulted her and she wasn't going to allow anyone to get away with that. She was a customer and entitled to respect. She then headed for another assistant in the men's department who stood by a summer sale rack in the suit section.

"I'll ask him," she said. "He looks as if he can speak English."

The man was Indian. He had a comb-over that reminded me of a physics teacher I once had and was just as patient. Moriam asked him about the process of applying for a store card and he spent the next ten minutes explaining it to her.

"You see?" she said, returning to me. "Someone with sense in his head. He said to get a credit history we need to get a store card. Simple and straightforward."

"But we can't get a store card without a credit history," I said.

"He said we can get someone with a credit history to cosign our application."

"Someone like who?"

Ismail, she said.

"What are our other options?" I asked.

A secured credit card, she said. But the interest rate would be high and we couldn't pay off all our debts for at least six months.

"Ismail is not reliable," I said.

"We have no choice. You have to ask him."

I was reluctant to ask Ismail for a financial favor, after the business of the money he'd borrowed and never repaid. I could very easily develop resentment for him if he turned me down, and I wouldn't be able to hide it while living in his house.

As we met up with Taslim and Bashira, Moriam shared what else she had found out. We would need a credit history even if we paid with checks drawn on a current account. We had to present our driver's licenses in order to pay with checks. To open a current account, we had to have Social Security numbers.

"So I'll have to wait a while for new sneakers," Taslim said.

"Unfortunately," Moriam said.

"This is worse than Nigeria," he said.

"Nowhere," Bashira said, "is worse than Nigeria."

I was surprised that she would denigrate Nigeria after a single trip to a mall. There wasn't an item there she hadn't seen before, imported from somewhere in Asia: T-shirts, jeans and sneakers. They were in every bend-down boutique on Lagos streets. For a moment, I considered explaining why there was some advantage to having a cash economy in a country like Nigeria, but that would have been heavy-handed.

"This credit business is complex," Moriam said. "Show this, show that."

"I'm just glad they didn't ask you to show your underwear," I said.

She swung her shopping bag, narrowly missing my shoulder, and our children were elated.

We had jollof rice and chicken for dinner that night. Moriam made it with some dry cayenne pepper she found in the kitchen cupboard. She thought the chicken was too plump and soft. I asked her not to say that in Ismail's presence, since we needed a favor from him. She had already disparaged American grain. I didn't need her casting aspersions on American poultry as well.

He returned from work and seemed suitably pleased that she had cooked. There was an African food store on 42nd Street, he said, and he rarely stopped there, but now that Moriam was around, he would make an effort.

"What would you like me to buy?" he asked.

"Fresh pepper," Moriam said.

Taslim and Bashira were setting the dining table and I was keeping an eye on them. Bashira, in particular, could easily end up breaking something. They seemed to be doing well, so I turned my attention back to Moriam and Ismail's conversation.

"They call them *habaneros* here," he said.

"Palm oil," she said. "I need that and some *efo*."

"You can't find fresh *efo* here," he said. "You can use spinach, though."

"Spinach? Are you sure?"

"I hear it works."

"Stockfish," she said, raising her finger.

"Soak it before you boil it, though," he said.

"What for?"

"It stinks. Actually, I wouldn't cook with stockfish while you are here. My neighbors won't appreciate that."

"Why?"

He widened his arms. "Do you know how many Nigerians in America have had the police come to their doors to say their neighbors could smell a dead body?"

I'd heard the "stockfish mistaken for a rotten corpse" story in London. Nigerians who repeated it swore they knew some-one it had happened to. I thought it was an urban myth that came from the fear of dying alone overseas.

"Okay, forget about the stockfish," Moriam said. "But buy *garri*, so I can make *eba*. And yam powder, so I can make *iyan*, for variety."

He whistled. "*Iyan*! It's been a while! But it's not the same when it is made from powder. I hear they mix it with instant mashed potato here. I'll get you real yams to make yam pottage."

She seemed to be winning him over and he admitted he usually ordered Chinese takeout, which he ate while watching television in his basement. He had not used his dining table in months. As we sat down to eat there, he told us about Sondra's kitchen skills.

"Man, that woman could cook," he said. "I'll give her that. She could throw down when she wanted to. Smothered chicken, candied yams, macaroni and cheese, and all that. She could cook Italian as well. Her pasta primavera was something."

Moriam said she would learn how to make pasta primavera for him. I was just relieved she had forgiven him. I would much rather eat than talk about food and our children seemed equally bored by the conversation. They were fussy about trying foreign meals. Indomie instant noodles were as far as they would go, and that was only because they'd grown up believing Indomie noodles were Nigerian.

After they'd finished eating, Moriam excused them from the dining table and I brought up what had happened at the mall, with the intention of soliciting Ismail's help. If he took pity on us, he might be more obliging.

"I don't think she was looking down on you," he said. "She works on commission and has to size customers up. If a customer doesn't look as though they're likely to spend money, then it's a question of 'Why waste my time?'"

"She must get an hourly rate," I said.

"Not enough to motivate her," he said.

"She was rude to us, Brother Ismail," Moriam said.

"That has nothing to do with being black," he said. "Green is all that matters in this country."

Moriam turned to me for an explanation.

"Money," I said.

"Where I work," Ismail said, "no one cares what color you are, so long as you can make some."

"But we had money on us," Moriam said.

He shrugged. "She might not have been able to tell. How were you dressed? How did you comport yourself?"

"Who was she to judge us?" Moriam asked.

"People make judgments based on appearance," Ismail said. "I'm just saying. Maybe you misinterpreted her intentions. I don't see why every time someone says something unpleasant to a black person in this country, they have to be labeled a racist. I'm sorry, but I've had enough of black people crying racism at every turn."

"I wasn't crying racism," Moriam said.

She really wasn't. She was crying out that she was a snob. The idea of the assistant being racist would never occur to her. Her only experience overseas was as a tourist and left to her, there was no such thing as racism, only plain stupidity.

"Look," he said. "You've learned your first lesson in America. Next time you'll know how to behave."

"Brother Ismail," Moriam said, "this is not my first time overseas. I know how to behave in a shop."

"It's not what you know that matters," Ismail said. "It's what you're about to find out."

Moriam kept her mouth shut from then on. Later, in the privacy of our bedroom, she said, "Your cousin's head is not correct. Who is he to talk to me in that way? Is he cursed or something?"

"Don't say anything when he talks," I said.

"Why didn't you say something?"

"Silence is the best answer for a fool."

"You should have said something. You should have, Lukmon. Seriously. I'm not playing."

"Just ignore him."

I was reluctant to bad-mouth Ismail in his own house and couldn't take her side, especially if we needed him to cosign our application. To cheer her up, I said he reminded me of Nigerian students I'd encountered in London, who wouldn't recognize racism if a right-wing skinhead tried to throttle them, but she again said she wasn't crying racism.

That set the pattern. Ismail would say something to annoy Moriam during dinner and she would wait to abuse him until we went to bed. I would tell her to be patient, as he was letting us stay in his house and four guests were a lot to handle. She would say yes, but we cooked, cleaned his bathrooms, vacuumed his carpet, polished his furniture, did the laundry and took out the trash.

Moriam cooked and our children cleaned. I did the laundry and took out the trash. I hadn't done laundry in years, and for the first time learned that it was necessary to separate clothes into whites, colors and blacks.

Instead of asking Ismail to cosign our store-card application, we decided to take the secured credit card route and opened a savings account at a bank with a dubious name. Then we applied for Social Security numbers and made inquiries about driver's licenses. Moriam was terrified of driving in New Jersey. She had only ever driven cars with manual transmissions. I tried to convince her that an automatic car would be easier to handle, and driving in America would be easier than driving in Nigeria. She said there were no rules in Nigeria. She could drive the wrong way up a one-way street if she pleased. In America, there were too many rules and far too many traffic lights. Route 4 put such fear into her, she decided to wait a while before she applied for a driver's license.

We were not completely unprepared. Before we left Nigeria, I'd gone to the United States Educational Advising Center in Lagos to find out about our transcript evaluations and credential reviews. I'd also sent my transcripts to the Educational Testing Service and Moriam's credentials to the Commission on Graduates of Foreign Nursing Schools. She'd taken the Test of English as a Foreign Language for non-native speakers. I was exempt because I had an undergraduate degree in English. That was when I found out I would probably need to get at least a master's degree from an American university to teach at college level. In case I had to apply for such a degree, I'd taken the Graduate Record Examination.

Moriam and I had passed the TOEFL and GRE, but the tests, evaluations and reviews had cost us hundreds of dollars. She had a couple of former colleagues in America she could reach out to for career advice. There was Stella, who lived in Maryland, but they were yet to get in touch, and there was Bisi, who lived in Philadelphia. They had all trained together at the University of Ibadan. Bisi told Moriam about the CGFNS exams and other matters, but whenever she called, Moriam put her on speakerphone because she ended up gossiping about other Nigerians in America. I referred to her as Bisi the Gossip, to distinguish her from another Bisi we knew.

My former colleague, Osaro, the only one I could trust in academia, lived in Brooklyn, but he was on a book tour in Germany. When he left Nigeria, Osaro didn't tell anyone he was leaving, for fear of being sabotaged. He took off during a summer holiday and never returned. Our senior colleagues in the English department branded him a deserter. He sent requests for his records and they ignored them. He called and begged me to get his records for him. I arranged for them to be sent to him in America. I didn't think he owed me anything in return, but he'd promised to give me advice about finding academic jobs.

The year Osaro left Nigeria, I thought our economy was at its worst. Ismail left a few years later, by which time our economy was so bad I was nostalgic about the previous regime. We had a Structural Adjustment Program that devalued the naira lower than it had ever been. Food was ridiculously expensive in Lagos. If you ate rice regularly before, you ate *garri* more. If you were keen on meat, beans began to look attractive. Government employees went on strike after strike. Ismail, who had a diploma in banking and finance, couldn't find a job in the banking industry.

I was lucky to find one. That was when Ismail borrowed the money from me and swore he would pay it back once he got a job. He eventually left Lagos and returned to Abeokuta to work in his father's business, which was beginning to struggle. His eldest brother, Mashood, was managing the business at the time and they got into terrible arguments. At one point, Ismail accused Mashood of fraud. Mashood retaliated with his own accusation that Ismail had embezzled money. They were half-brothers and Ismail had grown up wearing Mashood's hand-me-downs. Now that he answered to Mashood, his grudges came out. He said Mashood had mistreated him as a child by repeatedly conking his head in an attempt to damage his brain. Mashood asked, "What brain?" The rest of the details were too petty to rehash, but that was the first time I witnessed real division in the Rasaq-Karim family.

In my family, my sisters, Fausat, Latifat and Sherifat, were working as teachers in Abeokuta and not earning much. When Sherifat got married, we had to contribute money for her *nikah*. My father, proud man that he was, agreed to that only because he was retired. He was disappointed by the fighting in the Rasaq-Karim family. "Disappointed" was as far as my father ever went to voice his objection. My sisters saw the Rasaq-Karims' conflicts as victory for us Ahmed-Karims. Even my mother suggested the same, in her own way, by quoting the last line of a song we'd learned in my father's school that went, "Learning is better than silver and gold."

Ismail caused a scandal when he somehow found money to buy a plane ticket to America. Mashood said it was proof that he was indeed an embezzler and the rest of the Rasaq-Karim brothers, perhaps out of envy, chose to believe him. I didn't know who to believe, as Mashood himself had recently bought a secondhand car. My Uncle Rasaq expected complete obedience from his children and so long as you always agreed with him, you had morals. Mashood happened to be his most moral son. Ismail visited me in Lagos and spent the whole time lamenting about how Mashood had turned his father and brothers against him. I couldn't very well bring up the money he owed me. He left for America soon after that and, according to his brothers, refused to answer their phone calls from then on.

I could understand why Ismail wasn't in favor of Nigeria. His reasons were more personal than Moriam realized. I thought she would be more sympathetic if I reminded her of this. But one day she asked Ismail if it would be all right for Bisi the Gossip to visit her and he said he didn't encourage Nigerian guests at his house. Nigerians were never happy for other people's success and they were freeloaders, after which Moriam didn't want to hear any excuses I made for him.

Ismail was out most of the day, anyway. He spent his weekends with a woman he referred to as "Long Island." She was his boss and, like him, had risen up the corporate ladder despite the odds. He was a vice president and she was the head of his group. He'd broken through the color barrier and she had broken the glass ceiling by using her brains, he said. I took that to mean she was not attractive. He certainly wasn't getting meals from her because he came home every weekday expecting to be fed by Moriam.

Moriam was furious with him. She called him a glutton. I actually felt sorry for him. He didn't have the stability we had. We frustrated the hell out of each other, she and I, but we were still together. There was comfort in that—and history. She was there when my mother died, consoling me. She was there when my father died. I was the one consoling her on that occasion because she was particularly fond of my father. He always called her by her full name, Moriamo. He, too, apparently had a soft spot for troublesome women, though he was wise enough not to marry one. Despite her attempts to behave in his presence, my sisters had done their best to malign her character behind her back. Whenever we visited Abeokuta, she would greet my father properly, getting down on both knees, and he would shake his head as if he wasn't fooled by her show of humility.

My Uncle Rasaq was still very much alive, although these days he used a walking stick and was hard of hearing. He was no longer the rich man he was in his heyday, but he was, as he would say, satisfied with life and grateful to Allah for his blessings. He had one wife left, the middle one. He divorced his youngest wife and Ismail's mother passed away shortly after Ismail came to America. Before she died, she was too sick to get involved with the quarrel between him and his brothers. Had she survived, she would definitely have brought them all together. She was the senior wife in the family and Ismail, like me, was the youngest child. He worshipped his mother. He had a lot of respect, rather than affection, for his father, whom he called RK. About his father he would say, "RK taught me everything I know about business." About his mother, whom he called Iya, he would say there was no other woman in the world like her.

Having fallen out with his brothers, Ismail may have expected me to step in as a surrogate. One day, he sat me down in his living room and told me what he had been through in America when he first arrived.

He'd washed plates in restaurants and driven a taxicab in New York. He'd sold real estate for a while in New Jersey, which was how he was able to pay for his undergraduate business degree and part-time MBA before he went into financial planning. He was a fan of Donald Trump's and would sometimes take a bus back to New York to stand outside Trump Tower and look at it for inspiration.

"When I got my present job," he said, "I had to take elocution lessons to improve my client presentations. Everyone at work said I was articulate, but I knew I needed to lose my accent to get ahead. If you notice, I speak with an American accent now."

I'd only noticed that he spoke as if he were afraid of his own voice. His accent wasn't bad, but I wondered why he put pressure on himself by forcing one.

"I put Sondra on a pedestal," he said. "I gave that woman everything she wanted because her father had done the same."

Sondra's father owned a car dealership. He wasn't keen on having Ismail as his son-in-law. He didn't trust Africans or Muslims.

"He was always telling Sondra she deserved better. I was decent to that woman and let me tell you, decent black men are hard to find. Ask any black woman. Sondra knew. All I did was work. She was the one who got lazy on me. I'm not saying it's easy to look after a child all day, but at least cook and clean if you're going to stay at home. I tried to talk to her about it, but she said she wasn't going to be submissive like some African woman."

These days, Sondra worked as an insurance claims adjuster in Los Angeles. I was surprised she thought African women were submissive. She ought to meet Moriam. Perhaps I was oblivious, but all I'd ever witnessed in Nigeria was female resistance—in

Moriam's bossy ways, Alhaja's loud manner and the unbreakable bond between the Rasaq-Karim wives. They quarreled with each other but always came together to stand up to my uncle. They made financial decisions without his knowledge, after which they would get on their knees to ask his forgiveness. Basically, they wore the poor man out, and his youngest wife, if the rumors were true, had boyfriends on the side, which was why he later divorced her.

Growing up in Abeokuta, I had probably only one example of a mild-tempered woman: my mother. My sisters were awful. Fausat was seven years my senior and often entrusted with my care. She would threaten to abandon me in the nearest bush. Latifat would send me to ask favors of our father, knowing I was liable to get a conk. Sherifat would get angry with me because I wasn't expected to cook. I was only expected to clean. She was two years my senior and hated cooking. Whenever our mother called her to the kitchen, she would drag her feet and whine. She once asked Fausat, "How come he knows how to eat, but he doesn't know how to cook?" I was standing right there, so she was really asking me the question. Fausat, who didn't mind cooking, explained that boys didn't have to learn how to cook because they would one day get married and their wives would cook for them. "Look at him," Sherifat said. "Big head, skinny body."

The Rasaq-Karim boys called my sisters beasts of no gender for a reason. As the only son in my family, I was aware that my mother had fulfilled her duty to my father by having me, but I often overheard her saying she was glad she didn't have a house full of boys as the Rasaq-Karim wives had. This was usually after the Rasaq-Karim boys had been up to no good, like kicking a football through a windowpane or playing Donna Summer's "Love to Love You Baby" on their father's stereo, so loud the entire neighborhood heard. I was at their house a lot. I went there to get away from my sisters. But in their house, boys had to cook and clean, so I would often find Ismail and his brothers frying plantains or yams in the kitchen. It made me feel like a real man until I went back home to face the consequences of being one.

The only time I ever had to defend the women in my family was when Sherifat left her husband. The man was a moron. He couldn't hold on to a job and was always going on about his rich family. Sherifat decided she'd had enough of him one day and called him a lazy bugger. She was pregnant, yet he dragged her by the arm, out of their house, and locked the door. She came home by taxi and told my father she was never going back. She didn't even want their child to bear his last name, she said, because his family must have been cursed to raise a son like him. My father said fine. He'd never liked the man and was not impressed by his family. He asked me to go to Sherifat's house to collect her belongings. I got there and Sherifat's husband already had her suitcase on the veranda. He stood there ranting and raving. "Who is she calling a lazy bugger? You'd better warn your sister. You'd better find out where she learned to use such foul language. In fact, she is the lazy bugger! She never wants to cook! Your mother must have failed to—"

I punched him in the mouth before he could finish his sentence, and the idiot staggered and fell to the ground.

Ismail and Sondra were actually separated when his affair with the Long Island woman began. The woman was Italian American and they had to keep their relationship secret at work and outside of work because her family would disapprove of her dating a black man.

"They're not prejudiced," he said. "They're just old-fashioned."

I, too, was old-fashioned in that way. It was just as well I never looked at white women. I didn't even notice them and, to be honest, could barely tell white people apart.

In London, I'd gotten myself into embarrassing situations calling my English classmates by the wrong names. I took to calling them "mate" after a while. One was called Lucy. She had an interest in all things African, including me. In fact, she was obsessed. She insisted I was beautiful, even though I assured her I wasn't. She would invite me over for dinner. I was in my early twenties, hungry, on a budget and in another country. I would have slept with any woman who would offer to cook for me, but I noticed their tits and legs before I considered their culinary abilities.

Lucy always wore tight jeans and her legs were—put it this way—more pronounced from her knees down. I'd just come from Nigeria, where I'd never seen a woman with calves bigger than her thighs. I was used to the opposite. Still, I wasn't mature and a woman was a woman.

She sexually harassed me. She sexually harassed me into having dinner with her at her flat. I got there and "Is You Is or Is You Ain't My Baby" was playing. She offered me white wine to drink. I didn't drink wine. It gave me headaches. I was a beer drinker, but she had no beer, so she drank the wine on her own. She had made rice and *domoda* for dinner. I asked her what *domoda* was, even though I could guess from the aroma. She called it peanut-butter stew. Nigerians called it groundnut stew. Her ex-boyfriend from Gambia had taught her how to make it.

I almost vomited on my first bite. The peanut butter was so badly burnt it tasted bitter. Lucy began to cry. I asked why she was crying. She said the dinner was a disaster. She should have asked if I drank wine. She should never have made *domoda*. Hers never turned out right. I was only trying to comfort the woman when I put my arm around her. But she tried to kiss me, with her *domoda* mouth. Of course I turned away and she cried even more. Why wasn't I attracted to her? she asked. Was it because she was fat? I said she was fine, but I saw her as a friend. "I don't believe this," she said. "You're supposed to like fat women. It's part of your culture." I took offense on behalf of African women and left.

After Lucy, if someone had brought a stark-naked Englishwoman to me and said, "She's Miss World and all yours," I would have chosen a Nigerian woman with mosquito-bitten legs instead. I went for black women alone, so long as they would have me. In those days, a white woman would have to have at least four tits to hold my attention. Now, she would have to cook ten times better than Moriam before I would put up with being considered inferior to her and suffer the indignity of hiding from her family.

Sondra apparently lost her mind when she found out Ismail was having an affair with the Long Island woman. She stopped his immigration application and got full custody of Hakeem. Ismail couldn't defend himself because he was back to being illegal in America and had the fear of deportation hanging over him. As if that wasn't bad enough, Sondra then accused him of physically abusing Hakeem while they were together and threatened to have him locked up.

"I spanked my son a few times," he said. "So what? She's telling me that spanking is a legacy of slavery, when every bloody Nigerian I know back home beats their child. I can't forgive her for that and I'm not speaking to Hakeem until he behaves himself. All the money I spent sending him to private school and he's running around LA nightclubs and calling himself an MC. Sondra says he doesn't want to go to college anymore. He didn't just wake up one morning and decide that. When he was busy writing lyrics and listening to Tupac Shakur, she said I should let him express himself. Now look where he is. You should have seen him when I went for his high school graduation. His head was shaved like a thug's. This was the same boy who couldn't relate to black kids in his school when he first got to LA. He would only mix with the Jewish kids. A Jewish kid smiles at him and he makes a beeline for them. His mother called him a black Jew."

Hakeem was eighteen. Sondra wanted Ismail to talk him into going to college, but Ismail refused to until Hakeem stopped MCing. I thought Sondra had a valid point.

"He got into UCLA," Ismail yelled. "Now, he's telling his mother that getting a degree will interfere with his music career? Is that a serious person?"

"He's young," I said.

"Young? He's taller than you! He's even taller than me!"

"I'm talking about his level of maturity."

"He's sleeping with girls already! He's mature enough for that! Look, I'm not telling you this so you can change my mind. I made my decision as soon as I got back here. I just want you to know why I'm not in touch with him or his mother. And I don't care if anyone accuses me of putting a sister down. Sondra is the most stuck-up person I know. She looks down on Africans. She even looks down her nose on other African Americans and calls them ghetto. Yet I'm the Uncle Tom because I'm articulate and behave appropriately. Listen, let them not fool you with their 'black this, black that' business. They're just as divided as we are. Ours is by tribe and class. Theirs is by class and skin shade."

He was pissed off. He had to be to come up with "'black this, black that' business." I wasn't sure what he was referring to, black pride, unity or consciousness, but his latest umbrage with Sondra was that she had allowed Hakeem to move in with her cousin, Jerome.

"That one has been drugged up for most of his life, in and out of jail, and is tattooed all over his body. Now, he's rehabilitated and calls himself a drug counselor, and she's telling me to give him a chance because drug addiction is a disease. To be fair, Jerome is a nice guy and I'm not judging him. He was the only one in her family who supported her when she married me, but he's not the sort of man you want taking your son under his wing. That's all I'm saying. But, oh no, Sondra won't listen, as usual. She says Hakeem needs a male role model and if I'm not there, who else can she rely on. You see? That is the trouble with marrying these people. Even when they're upwardly mobile, they're one relative away from a bad situation."

I remembered Habib. Habib was our second cousin. He started smoking hemp at the age of twelve and smoked so much of it in his teens, he ended up in Aro, a neuropsychiatric hospital in Abeokuta. Habib, too, was a nice guy, until he started lacing his hemp with heroin, after which he began to steal money from his parents. My parents used Habib as an example of what could happen to me if I fell in with bad company. The day Habib was admitted into Aro, everyone in his family stopped talking about him. He was presumed missing. If outsiders asked about him, his family would say he was somewhere in Lagos. Habib came out of Aro looking like a vegetable. His family immediately found a village girl to marry him. He was a father now, but what he went through in his drug years never stopped me from trying hemp in my first year at university. What stopped me from ever smoking it again was the effect it had on me. I was so high I couldn't even recall my name. The experience spooked me. The Rasaq-Karim brothers would never have experimented with hemp. They were too careful for that. They chased girls from strict Muslim homes and defiled them for sport. That was as far as they went.

"The fact is," Ismail said, "Sondra was the one who wanted full custody of Hakeem. She was the one who moved to LA with him. She was the one who kept him away from me and she was the one who stopped me from interfering in his upbringing. Forget what she did to me. Put all that aside. I had sleepless nights because of that boy. I cried over him. Now he's giving her trouble and she wants me to be a father. She's not going to have her way this time. That's all I'm saying, but this is between me and you. You understand?"

"I understand," I said.

I honestly did. I couldn't imagine being excluded from my children's lives or not being there for them in times of trouble. From the day they were born, Moriam and I raised them together and nursed them through tonsillitis, chicken pox and God knows what else. Half the diseases they brought home, I had no clue about. Moriam would be the one to diagnose. I was more the rescue mission. Taslim broke his leg while dribbling a football; I drove him to the hospital. Bashira nearly knocked herself out on a cement surface while swinging. I ran over and carried her. I was so scared she'd suffered a concussion. My intelligent daughter. Who made her Bournvita every night? Who taught Taslim the Lord's Prayer began, "Our Father, which art in heaven," when he got punished in school for writing, "Our farter, witchcraft in heaven," because he thought that was what his Christian classmates said? I talked to him about sex from an early age, hoping that he would not make the mistake I had. He sat there looking confused. The next morning, his mother was yelling that I'd corrupted her son.

She wanted more children; I told her I'd had enough and our options for family planning moving forward were celibacy or the coil. She thought I was joking. "What about the pill?" she asked. I said I didn't trust her to take it.

I'd seen why, in Ismail's simple way, his problems with his family in Nigeria had turned him against Nigerians. His family had rejected him, therefore he had rejected his people. So I could see why his problems with Sondra would turn him against African Americans. He was rejecting Sondra's people. What I still didn't understand was why the difficulties he had faced in America had the effect of turning him in favor of America. I would have liked to discuss all of this with Moriam, but she might use it for blackmail and, frankly, what Ismail had revealed was far too personal and shameful to repeat.

We had been in America for just over two weeks when Taslim developed an American accent. He now said "wanna" instead of "want to" and "gonna" instead of "going to." Every word he uttered developed an R, and he reduced his Ts to Ds. He was hilarious. I would look at his mother, as if to ask, "What is wrong with him?" and she would shrug, as if to say, "I don't know."

One evening, she made yam pottage for dinner. The yam was from the African store on 42nd Street, but she didn't think it was the best quality. Ismail enjoyed it enough to have a third helping though, after which he started talking about pension plans. He believed Americans should have private portfolios and not rely on the government in their retirement years. He was also against any form of government taxation and assistance. He'd had enough of moochers who lived on welfare and did nothing but complain about the system, he said. Why couldn't they stand on their own two feet like normal adults? Why did they always expect to be babied? Why did they keep having babies? Hardworking taxpayers like him had to foot the bill. As for phony race-baiters like Jesse Jackson and Al Sharpton, their time was up. People like him had shown the American dream was possible for black men.

"Even their intellectuals will tell you that race is bogus," he said. "So why do they keep talking about it? Because it is a standard excuse for their failures. It's true! Let's face the facts here! They're not the only ones who have suffered in America. I mean, look at the Jews. Look where they are today, despite all they went through. They're successful people."

I could have said the Holocaust didn't happen in America, or last for centuries, just to begin with, but Ismail was more like his father than he realized. If you didn't agree with him, you were morally bankrupt.

"Black people are lazy by nature," he said. "It's in their DNA. It's time we just admitted it and stopped being politically correct about it. If I had a business, I wouldn't employ a black person to work for me. I would find an Asian to fill my minority quota. Watch the Asians. Study their ways. Hard work and economic power is what gets them ahead. Blacks? They'll end up ruining your business."

I didn't argue. I would win too easily. I needn't even point out the fact that he was black. All I needed to say were three words: You. Are. Illegal. There was nothing he could tell me after that.

Taslim asked Bashira, "Can you please pass the warder?"

"It's 'water,'" Bashira said.

"Pass your brother the water, please," Moriam said.

Bashira threw her hands in the air. "He keeps saying 'wanna' and 'gonna'!"

"Just pass him the water," Moriam said.

They were getting on my nerves as well. My next goal was to find a library they could go to during the day, instead of sitting in front of the television and arguing.

Bashira passed Taslim the water and he refilled his glass.

"Keep it up," Ismail said to him. "You won't have any problems adjusting in school when you start. If you speak with a Nigerian accent, no one will be able to understand you. You can also forget about speaking Yoruba from now on because it will only ruin your English."

I smiled at Bashira to assure her. She was a better student than Taslim.

"So what's going on with your school situation?" Ismail asked, turning to me.

"I haven't decided," I said.

"Summer school is almost over. You have to make up your mind soon."

"I will."

I was yet to hear from Osaro, who was still on his book tour in Germany. Going back to school would be my last option. I hoped my green card would work in my favor when I applied for academic jobs. My chances of getting a banking job were next to nothing with a Nigerian background. The Yahoos and their email scam letters had seen to that.

"So you and your kids might be registering for school in the fall," Ismail said.

"We might," I said.

He shook his head. "I don't know why you want to put yourself through that. As far as I'm concerned, you've got enough education. You're more educated than the average American. You're probably even more educated than your lecturers will be. If I were you, I would forget about going back to graduate school and face the future with a new career in mind."

"A new career like what?" I asked.

He shrugged. "The aim of getting an education is to make money, right? So make money by whatever means—cleaning, cabbing, anything—until you can move on to a better job and bring home the bacon. That's my advice to you. I certainly wouldn't go back to school for two years. What for? So you can eventually teach in some college? How much do college professors make, anyway? Peanuts!"

Food-related idioms aside, that Ismail would dare to speak to me like that in front of my family was no surprise to me, and perhaps I should have immediately put him in his place, knowing what I did about him, but I found some consolation in knowing my future in America looked exceedingly bright if a dullard like him had made it.

Moriam later suggested I should have told him that, as she stood before the mirror in our bedroom applying cream to her face.

"He's a very stupid man," she said. "If that were me, what I would have said to him, he would never forget. He would run under the table and hide there."

"We're not staying here forever."

"So? Does that mean he should abuse us every night? Can you imagine he's against speaking Yoruba?"

Ismail was an asshole. That was the perfect American word to describe him. I could now hazard a guess as to why he was loyal to America. America worked out well for him in the end. He became a success, eventually. What he didn't realize was this: Had he got a banking job in Nigeria when I did, he could have been more successful in Nigeria. The new banks there were highly Americanized. In my bank, employees went by their first names. Last names didn't matter. None of the old elitism did. You were hired for your potential, not because you came from the right family, or went to the right schools in Lagos, or had a British education. With the kind of drive and business savvy Ismail had, he would have ended up as a managing director or chief executive officer of a bank. He would own properties in Nigeria and England. America would be his third choice.

Moriam turned around, her face shiny. "What about asking you how much college professors make? What about talking to you like that? And he's done the same to me, so you can't say he misspoke. You can't say he didn't know what he was doing, and I just want to know how long it will be before you stand up for yourself."

I was not passive. She knew. I may not have been the sort to get into physical or verbal altercations, but I'd had a reputation for defending myself aggressively when I was a lecturer. I would respond to my colleagues' criticisms, point by point, and throw in a few underhanded insults.

"He's right," I said. "I need to find work as soon as possible."

"As a cleaner?"

"If I have to."

She snapped her fingers. "God forbid. I will go back to Naija before that happens."

She gave me a headache carrying on as if my working as a cleaner would reflect badly on her. I assured her that it was the fastest way to get out of Ismail's house. Whatever work I did would be temporary until I could get back into academia, anyway.

I still had some familiarity with the African canon: Achebe's works, Soyinka's works and others. Ayi Kwei Armah's *The Beautyful Ones Are Not Yet Born* and Ousmane Sembène's *God's Bits of Wood* were literary texts I could return to because their political and cultural perspectives were still applicable. Not that I was opposed to African women writers, but their domestic preoccupations put me to sleep. I would never say that publicly in America, knowing the hazard of gender politics, but there it was.

In Nigeria, I could get by as a lecturer with a certain degree of mediocrity—not teaching enough, not reading enough and not researching or writing enough. After the first generation of writers, to which Achebe and Soyinka belonged, and owing to the damage done to intellectualism and freedom of expression by the very governments they had championed, African literature was not exactly bountiful. You didn't need much effort to keep up. The issues that writers like them raised remained conveniently unresolved: the lack of sovereignty, the quest for equality and the need to reclaim language and culture. Every academic I knew wrote books on the same topics. Women's rights were usually left to female lecturers. Before I left the university, I was about to publish a book of my own, on J. P. Clark's works, but between my incompetent editor and even more incompetent publisher, my publication date kept getting postponed and I eventually abandoned my manuscript when I got the banking job.

I was no Ngugi-ist, so it didn't matter what Ismail had said about Yoruba. I'd taught in English and spoke and wrote English, happily. I wasn't one to champion the use of a universal African language like Kiswahili either, because chances were that Swahili people would find a way to show other Africans their Kiswahili was superior. Despite the damage done by colonialism, I didn't agree with language advocates of any kind. If my children had to drop U from their spellings, substitute S with Z and call Z "Zee" in America, then so be it. Wanna, gonna, warder, wardever. British English was never their language to protect, or defend, to begin with. The Yoruba they spoke was Lagos Yoruba, which wasn't the same Yoruba I'd spoken in Abeokuta. Language, to my mind, was its own best advocate and subject to necessity alone. Any attempt to own it, control it, or impose it on others, would only end in its mutation.

Ismail's lack of confidence surprised me, meanwhile. How could he believe my children couldn't handle more than one language at a time? Why was he concerned that speaking Yoruba would be detrimental to their English and not the other way around? Would he feel the same way about Spanish or Italian?

Yoruba was his first language, the language of his father's house. He'd learned the Yoruba alphabet at my father's school: A, *aja*, B, *bata*, D, *doje*, and so on. We'd read our first Yoruba folk stories and poems in J. F. Odunjo's textbook, *Alawiye*. The lyricism and economy of Yoruba fascinated me. One word could have several meanings. A change of intonation could alter its sense. We heard sounds and smells in Yoruba. We didn't have headaches; our heads broke us.

English wasn't that flexible, inventive, or poetic. English had damn too many synonyms, which, I'd often said, must have been useful in conning countries like Nigeria into becoming part of the British Empire. I could write English with grammatical perfection, which was more than I could say for some of my English classmates in London. But I spoke English with Yoruba in mind, which didn't always translate well. My fluency in Yoruba taught me how to break grammar rules in English. I stuttered in English once in a while. Never in Yoruba.

Ismail united my family for a short while. Taslim and Bashira could sense the tension in his house and perhaps blamed themselves for it, as children might. They stopped arguing and their mother became more patient. Perhaps she was being protective or perhaps she was trying to make Ismail look like the only crazy person in the house, but our children soon began to argue again and she slipped back into her bossy ways.

Every morning, she shouted—howled, more like it—at them from the top of the basement stairs to get up, get ready and make their beds. In the afternoons, she shouted at them to stop watching television and help her in the kitchen. They would ask why she shouted so much and I would say that was how she was raised. She would shout even louder, "Are you abusing my mother?"

Moriam shouted by force of habit. She really wasn't that harsh, but if you abused her mother and meant to, it didn't matter who you were. Run.

I got a job working Monday to Friday as a security guard in Manhattan. The store I worked in was part of a new chain of upscale cosmetic stores that sold makeup, makeup tools, fragrances and skincare products for women. To get the job, I'd had to show my new driver's license and pass a background check and drug test. I attended a one-day training course so I would know what to do in case of an emergency. I worked eight-hour shifts and wore a black jacket, white shirt and tie. Thankfully, I was not required to carry arms.

On my first day, the store manager, Jill, briefed me about signs to look for in identifying theft suspects, such as their over-sized bags and jackets. It was clear to me that there would be no point detaining a single thief during my job tenure. I wasn't earning as much as Jill was, and would never put myself at risk for a corporation that was not—as I would say in Nigeria—my father's business.

Where I was coming from, to be successful in retail, you had to run your own shop. If you hired someone to manage it for you, they couldn't care less if you made a profit or a loss, so long as they got paid. In America, retail managers like Jill truly believed it was their duty to make profits for the corporations they worked for by protecting their goods and motivating shop assistants at the point of sale. The Jills of America were the basis on which the retail industry depended and the laws also kept them in check, because if they had as much freedom to trade as people had in Nigeria, where rules and regulations were blatantly disregarded, they would quit their jobs and set up shop across the street from where they worked.

Jill was so proud of belonging to her corporation, she would tell her assistants about how it began with one woman's desire for a more individualized service while shopping for cosmetics, and how the lighting was specifically designed to make women look their best in mirrors. She would keep them updated about new branches, saying, "We've opened up in San Francisco," or

"We're in LA now." Always "we." She roused her shop assistants into frenetic states every morning, then had them behaving like robots all day. Customers would walk in and her assistants would immediately waylay them, saying, "Welcome," and "How are you today?" Most customers would mumble that they were fine and make a detour; a few wouldn't answer, as if they expected more sincerity. One or two responded with equal cheer, confusing the assistants, who would recover quickly enough to say, "How can I help you?" to which they would then get a muted, "I'm just looking."

It was a ritual, no less than the ritual of bargaining for meat in a Nigerian market. Whenever customers asked for assistance, they rarely got it because, below Jill, there was no loyalty to the corporation. In fact, there was such a high turnover of staff that new assistants had a hard time differentiating one product from another. The semblance of choice was a fantasy. The cosmetics were virtually alike. They were probably the same as cosmetics I'd seen in CVS. Their packaging just gave an impression of opulence.

Watching the customers, most of whom were middle-aged white women, it occurred to me that I could actually tell them apart if I made an effort. I could even tell if they were attractive. Only a handful were. The rest had been tricked into thinking they could walk into the store and buy products to improve their looks.

While I was at work, Moriam studied for her nursing exams. She also continued to cook and make sure Taslim and Bashira carried out their daily chores. She appeared to be taking my advice about not responding to Ismail's opinions. One evening, he said Africa might as well be called planet of the apes. Another, he said the idea of universal healthcare sickened him. The next, he said the New York Police Department officers weren't at fault for killing Amadou Diallo. Diallo should never have reached for his ID in his pocket. Ismail couldn't understand why so much fuss was made about the case, while no one bothered to address black-on-black crime. Some other evening, he launched into a theory about why black people should consider themselves lucky that white people were the majority in America. At least white people had guilt, he said. Hispanics would soon be the majority and when that time came, black people would miss the days that white people predominated because Hispanics would show them no mercy. I didn't ask if black Hispanics were included in his theory. If he didn't know Hispanics were of different races, I couldn't help him.

His political views were not all he espoused. In private, he talked to me about his preferences for women, as if we were still boys. He praised every race of woman but black. He liked white women. He said they didn't give trouble. He liked Hispanic women, whom he called *Ay Papi*. They took care of themselves and their men, he said. He liked Asian women as well. There was one in his office, meticulous from head to toe, apparently. She wore black pantsuits and red lipstick, which gave her a mysterious air. As for the black women in his office, this was all he had to say about them: "Too much junk in the trunk."

I only smiled. That was his own loss, and any woman who was flattered by his praise had to be brainless. Plus, I'd seen all manner of women walk through the door of the store I guarded, and the black women I saw rarely needed anti-ageing products.

It didn't bother me that Ismail's views were conservative. Most Nigerians I knew were, especially when it came to religion. Ismail wasn't remotely religious, but coming to America had perhaps forced him into a liberal position that didn't suit him. Suddenly he was a minority and his homegrown conservatism wouldn't work for him. So, instead of coming to terms with that, he rejected the imposition of being a minority. He arrived in America a Yoruba man, never mind that he was

Nigerian and African. Back home, he would be Yoruba, of Egba ancestry. Now, he was just black, so he rejected that label as well and the negative connotations that came with it. I didn't even mind that he abused Nigeria. So did I, now and then. That was the Nigerian way. We routinely called our country useless. What annoyed me was that despite the compliments he got at work for being articulate, he was no good at expressing his views. Or perhaps he couldn't express them without making racist statements, and the more I kept silent in the face of that, the more vicious he got.

"Would you hire someone with dreadlocks to run your business?" he once asked about a Caribbean interviewee he'd turned down. "No, I'm just asking. Can a CEO with dreadlocks command your respect?"

I saw that as a rejection of an image that threatened the one he had adopted in the corporate world.

"They're always going on about slavery," he said another time, about African Americans. "Everything comes back to slavery with them, and you dare not say anything because you're African, so you have no right to talk."

I saw that as a rejection as well—this time of guilt. He then asserted the old apologist argument that Africans held captive during intertribal wars were technically prisoners, and only when Europeans exported them overseas did they become slaves.

It occurred to me, that day, that it wouldn't matter if I argued with Ismail or not. He quite rightly took my silence to mean I disagreed with him, but that didn't stop him from trying to get me to debate him. At a certain point, he must have realized he would never succeed because he soon went back to provoking Moriam.

One evening, she brought up President Clinton's impeachment trial, and not even from a political angle. She thought his family ought to have been spared the embarrassment. Her position was that the media was at fault for turning the President's infidelity into a public spectacle.

"If this were President Obasanjo," she said, "he would tell everyone to clear out of his sight and refuse to answer any of their silly questions."

Ismail said the impeachment trial had nothing to do with infidelity and President Obasanjo wouldn't know the difference because he wasn't required to obey the Nigerian Constitution.

Moriam faked a laugh. "Brother Ismail, don't you have anything good to say about Nigeria?"

"Why would I have anything good to say about Nigeria?" he said. "No, tell me. Why would I have one good thing to say about that country?"

"I asked you the question first," she said, attempting to sound polite.

"All right," he said, sitting up. "Tell me one product that Nigeria manufactures today. No, tell me a product that is made in Nigeria, now, at the end of the twentieth century. If you can name one, I would be happy to hear of it, and don't bring up petroleum products, because the last I heard, our oil refineries don't work."

"Hah?" Moriam said, turning to me.

I didn't know what she was looking at me for. How many times did I have to tell her to ignore him? He was now blinking rapidly, and instead of taking a hint from that and ending their discussion, she said, "But that doesn't mean there's nothing good to say about Nigeria."

"Okay," Ismail said. "So why are you here, then? Why are you not there? No, answer me. If a lottery for...for Nigerian immigration opened today, who would enter it? Exactly, no one. Yet Nigerians are so quick to open their mouths everywhere they go: 'Oh, we're so great. Oh, we're so wonderful.'

They're always the loudest people in the room. For what, I don't know because I'll tell you what Nigeria is good at producing. Corruption. Plenty of it. Heaps of it. In fact, it is in the genetic makeup of a Nigerian to be corrupt. Nigerians invented corruption. They export it internationally and now they're all over the Internet with it. Those Yahoos can't even spell, yet they've figured out a way to con grandmothers in Idaho out of money. Only a corrupt mind can think up a scam like that. Only a Nigerian's." He tapped his temple.

Moriam had the good sense to ignore him after that. We were getting ready for bed when she asked me, "Are you telling me your cousin isn't annoying you as much as he is annoying me?"

I was annoyed that she'd argued with him.

"He is," I said, in Yoruba.

"What is wrong with him, for God's sake?"

I was angry with Ismail as well, and with myself, for letting him get to me.

"He has no pride, and he thinks that agreeing with his girlfriend's politics will help him advance his career," I said.

She pointed at me. "Finally. You know he's been using me as his cook since we came?"

"I know."

"You also know I have my exams ahead?"

"Yes."

"Do you want me to pass or fail?"

"I want you to pass."

"Why does he dislike Nigeria so much?"

I decided to tell her about Ismail's experiences in America, hoping she might make sense of his behavior. Instead, she turned on me.

"How come you didn't tell me this before?"

"He told me not to tell anyone."

"But 'anyone' doesn't include your wife. Everyone knows that."

"Listen, I'm telling you now."

She hissed. "Foolish man. So how soon can we move out of his place?"

"I don't know," I said. "We'll have to wait for our credit card."

"Can't we just leave after the credit card arrives?"

"Our money is tied up."

"You see? I knew your decision would backfire on us."

"We came to the decision together."

She pointed again. "Don't blame me for this. I asked you to get your cousin to cosign our store-card application long before our relationship with him deteriorated."

"I'm not arguing with you," I said, in English.

Yoruba was the language we disagreed in and there was an insult lost in translation. I hoped she'd finally learned her lesson. As for Ismail, if he wanted examples of what Nigeria had made, all he needed to do was look around his table. My family was an example, with our undue respect for him and extreme capacity for tolerance. We were products of our country, designed by tradition, packaged by hardship and stamped by military rule. You couldn't put a price on us. An American family would have told him where to go—in his own house.

It took me a while to get used to being invisible at work. Not that I wanted to be noticed, but I looked like any old uniformed security guard to customers. Only thieves paid attention to security guards, and everyone else seemed to be under the impression that we lacked intelligence.

One morning, a woman walked into the store. She was older than the usual customer and appeared affluent, as opposed to merely rich. She wore a pink skirt suit and dark sunshades. She was in a hurry and asked for directions. I couldn't help her, so she got impatient and was about to leave when Jill, who was nearby and had been watching us, approached her.

Jill did that a lot—butted in. She was omnipresent in the store, and because I was invisible, I'd overheard the shop assistants complaining about her managerial style during her lunch break. "She's like all over you," one of them said. "She doesn't, like, let you breathe for a second. Let me breathe for a second, Jill!"

She gave directions, and after the woman left, said to me, "We get a lot of them. They're either tourists or from out of town."

"Sorry I couldn't help," I said. "I'm new to New York."

"Oh," she said, adjusting perfumes on a shelf. "Where are you from originally?"

"New…Nigeria," I said.

She smiled. "I thought you were about to say New Jersey."

"I was, actually. I live there."

"Sorry to hear that."

"New Jersey's all right," I said.

I wasn't sure why New Yorkers disparaged the place. I'd heard assistants calling it "Joysie" and making fun of the pollution there.

"You're very well-spoken," Jill said, tilting her head.

"Am I?"

"Yes. Very articulate. You can always tell when you meet someone from Africa."

"Nigeria."

"Yes. You can always tell they must have been important there."

Another complaint I'd heard about Jill was that she sucked up, especially after she butted in. I almost told her we hadn't had enough conversations for her to come to that conclusion, but decided against it. I also didn't want to encourage her, in case I had another obsessed white woman on my hands.

I really wasn't articulate, outside my professional life, unless I made an effort. Most times, when people talked to me, my mind was elsewhere and I could barely be bothered to respond.

That day was a Friday, and after work, on my way to the 42nd Street bus terminal, I returned a few chin lifts to other black men who were trying to make a living by selling CDs. The chin lift was new to me. My natural instinct was to nod. Some of the black people I saw on my way were African and Caribbean. The white people were of European descent. A few Arabs and Hispanics looked biracial to me and I couldn't always differentiate between Asians and Hispanics, Hispanics and Arabs, Arabs and Jews, or Jews and white people.

I was relieved, rather than proud, to be black. Who wanted to be on the side with a history of destruction? What did black pride mean to me, anyway? If it meant that I would choose to be on the side of courage, regardless of the consequences, then maybe I was proud as well.

In England, I wasn't quite prepared for being black and I initially assumed racism was due to envy. Envy of my Nigerian heritage. It didn't matter that racism often involved white people, as Indians and West Indians sometimes behaved in similar ways to them. This was in 1979, 1980, when there weren't many African students in London, so I decided that racism was due to misconceptions about Africa, and for a while went around explaining that I hadn't lived in a hut in Nigeria; I'd lived in a house. I'd spoken English there. A lot of Nigerians did. Then I realized there was no point. I could explain until the day I died and someone would still assume I'd lived in a hut in Nigeria and couldn't speak English. It was a question of intelligence. Before I went to England, I'd been told that English people bathed only once a week and I was smart enough to know that couldn't apply to all of them. In England, I was often told that the English were covertly racist, as opposed to Americans, who were openly racist, and I didn't believe that either.

I had to figure out the whole rationale of racism on my own and was quite surprised that it wasn't necessarily related to intelligence, after which, any attempt to make me feel inferior amused me. Truly. For a start, if you ate food like toad in the hole and black pudding, you couldn't be that superior. Besides, everyone shat; every single one of us. So, unless you didn't, you had no business looking down on anyone else.

Overall, I found racism ridiculous, the most absurd incident occurring when an old man, who may well have been a flasher, sat on a bench next to me and asked if I had a tail. I was a student on a scholarship, so I could afford to laugh at him. Now, I had a family to protect and provide for, so I had to take racism seriously, even when it seemed inadvertent.

Whenever Ismail went away for weekends, Moriam called her elder brother Gani in Lagos to give him updates on our progress in America. Gani worked for a local government and was doing fairly well, but not well enough to be called a big man. Still, Gani was the big man in his family and Moriam and I had stayed in his house for a few weeks before we left.

The first time Moriam had called Gani, he told her we didn't know how lucky we were to be in America. Moriam, expecting more sympathy from him because of what she was going through in Ismail's house, decided not to call him for a while. She would rather call her mother, who would at least pray for her, but Alhaja never charged her phone until she was ready to use it. Even then, Alhaja was so lazy, she would have one of her shopgirls charge it and dial numbers for her.

Moriam was not able to get through to Alhaja that weekend. She was worried that Gani was too busy to take care of their mother in her absence. I told her Alhaja didn't need Gani. She had a whole bunch of serfs working for her.

The only person in my family I could reach by phone was my sister Fausat, who had moved to Ibadan after she got married. I called her using a phone card. Moriam was expecting a call from Bisi the Gossip at the same time, so before leaving the living room she asked me not to be long. The truth was she would rather not speak to Fausat, from whom she had maintained a polite distance for years.

"Hellohellohello," Fausat said, when I got through.

"Sister," I said.

"Hellohellohellohello!"

"Stop all this hello-ing. It's me."

"Lukmon? Is that you?"

"Who else? How are you?"

"We're queuing! We're queuing for petrol here!"

Fausat was in the normal Nigerian mode: panic-stricken. There was a national petrol shortage. She had sent her driver, Cosmos, out to get petrol with her only car and he had been queuing for two days.

"I haven't been able to leave my house!"

"How is Wura?" I asked.

Wura, her daughter, had recently sat her entrance exams into secondary school.

"She's out with her friends! They came for her!"

"Did she pass?"

"She passed! She made it!"

Wura was her youngest. She had been accepted into an American Jesuit secondary school in the capital. I was happy to hear that. Our father had admired Jesuits because of their respect for education. He couldn't care less about religious denominations. Fausat was married to an Anglican and my middle sister, Latifat, became a born-again Christian when she had trouble conceiving. In her first trimester, she went from saying "*Alhamdulillah*" to saying "God is good."

While I was a student at Mayflower School, I took to the idea of secular humanism and began to question how Islam was practiced in Nigeria. I couldn't, for instance, understand why Muslims were given status simply because they had been on *Hajj* to Mecca. They returned with titles: Alhaji, for men, and Alhaja, for women. I wondered why it was necessary for Nigerian Muslims to pray in Arabic and have variants of Arabic names. I felt the same way about Christianity, questioning why Nigerian Anglicans were content to belong to the Church of England, and why Nigerian Catholics were not incensed about the remote prospects of an African pope. I never voiced my opinions at home because my parents would have found them blasphemous.

No one in my family suspected I was agnostic. That was between me and God. I didn't even tell Moriam when I met her because she would only get upset. I simply went through the motions during our *nikah*, with such a pious expression that anyone would believe I was religious.

After my phone call to Fausat, Moriam returned downstairs and I told her what Fausat and I had talked about, only because she asked, yet she rolled her eyes as she did whenever I mentioned any of my sisters. Perhaps I was distracting her because when the phone rang, she answered it without checking the caller ID, assuming it was Bisi the Gossip, and pressed the speakerphone button.

"Hello, is Ismail there, please?"

I immediately guessed who was speaking.

"He's not home," Moriam said. "May I ask who is calling?"

"It's Sondra."

"I'm in trouble," Moriam mouthed.

"Who is this?" Sondra asked.

Moriam hesitated. "His cousin."

"Oh," Sondra said. "I've been trying to reach him. He gave me the impression that he'd put his house up for sale and moved to Long Island."

Moriam bit her knuckle.

"Hello?" Sondra said. "Are you there? Can you hear me? That's okay. I knew he wasn't being upfront with me. So what side of the family are you from, then? The royal side?"

Moriam didn't confirm. Ismail and I came from a line of traders, though. The closest we got to nobility was our grandfather, who was an unofficial advisor to the Alake of Abeokuta on Islamic issues.

"You know what?" Sondra said. "This isn't easy for me either, but I have to do it for the sake of my son. If you're a parent, you'll understand. Hakeem needs to hear from his father. Please tell Ismail that. I don't know why he's avoiding my phone calls. It's very disappointing. I would at least have thought his son would be important to him. Mind you, I thought he married me for the right reasons and look how that turned out. Are you there? Are you listening? I'm sorry. I just had to let that out. I don't know what he's told you about me, but I don't want any money from him. All I want is for him to contact our son. I'd really appreciate that. Thanks."

After Sondra hung up, Moriam and I faced each other.

"You distracted me," she whispered.

"You should have checked the caller ID," I said.

"I always do, but you kept talking about Fausat. Now look."

The way she glared at me, one would imagine that mentioning my sister's name had jinxed her.

I shrugged. "Ismail will just have to get over it."

"Please don't tell him. Let him find out after we've left his house."

"What if he finds out before?"

"I beg you, don't tell him."

"Ah, well."

The matter was out of my hands. We were better off keeping the phone call to ourselves. If I told Ismail about it, I would forever be the one who jeopardized our family's future in America.

Before Ismail came back from Long Island that weekend, Moriam ordered Chinese takeout for dinner. She didn't feel like cooking. She was nervous and tired—nervous about the phone call, and tired from studying and shouting at our children. Between lunch and dinner, one of them had left a trail of crumbs from the kitchen to the basement and neither of them would own up. Taslim said it was Bashira. She was the one who had eaten cookies. Bashira said the crumbs had come from a muffin and she didn't eat muffins.

"*Oya*," Moriam said. "Both of you, get on your knees and start licking, and don't stop until you finish every crumb."

I was in the basement, considering a crossword puzzle I'd given up on earlier. I was trying to figure out if the twelve-letter word I was looking for was "incidentally" or "accidentally."

"Keep the noise down," I said.

"Keep your mouth closed if you're not prepared to supervise," Moriam said.

I heard the children's footsteps on the stairs. Taslim appeared, picking at each stair with his fingers. Bashira followed him, dusting with her palm.

"What are you doing?" Moriam yelled. "Will you get a dustpan and brush?"

Bashira scrambled up the stairs as Moriam warned that she wasn't joking. She had to study for her exams and they were wasting her time.

"You're trying to kill me," she said. "All of you in this house."

"What if we succeed?" I asked.

"Are you very foolish?" Moriam said.

"Very foolish" was a new variation. "Foolish" was her attempt to be less harsh. She would never call me stupid in front of our children.

"Leave my children alone, please," I said.

That would rile her. I heard the front door open and assumed she was going outside. Then I heard rapid footsteps and thought she was hurrying downstairs to attack me. Instead, I saw Ismail, taking two stairs at a time. The staircase shuddered under his weight and he almost tripped over Taslim, who backed up against the wall in time to avoid a collision.

"What did you say to S-Sondra?" he asked. "What did you say to th-that woman?"

He took deep breaths and waited for an answer.

"Good evening, Uncle," Taslim said, prostrating himself slightly.

"Please," Ismail said to him, "go upstairs. I want to speak to your father alone."

I immediately thought of Bashira, who must have retreated somewhere. Taslim did as he was told as Moriam walked down the stairs.

"Brother Ismail," she said. "What happened?"

"He spoke to Sondra," Ismail said. "I s-specifically told him no one was to speak to her. Now, I'm driving back home and I get a message from her saying she spoke to my c-cousin."

As I approached them, I saw Bashira at the top of the stairs, carrying a brush and dustpan. The sight of her made me want to grab Ismail by his lapels and slam him against the wall.

"That's true," I said in Yoruba. "Sondra did call, but no one would have answered the phone had we realized it was her. She left a message for you. She wanted you to contact Hakeem."

I was covering up for Moriam and hoped that mentioning his son would calm him down. Instead, he waved his hands around.

"Why did you tell her I was not royalty? How did your conversation with her get that far? Even if you answered the phone without realizing it was her, why didn't you just ask her to call me back?"

We were facing each other now, and Moriam stood by my side.

"Brother Ismail," she said. "*Ni suuru.*"

"No," he said. "None of that nonsense. This is a man-to-man discussion. I want him to explain himself."

Moriam reached down. I honestly thought she would take off her slipper and use it to slap his face. Instead, she knelt on the floor.

"I'm sorry," she said.

"What for?" Ismail said.

"Don't send us out of here," she said.

"What are you doing?" he asked.

Moriam didn't budge. "I beg you in the name of God. We did not mean to offend you."

Yoruba was also our language of reconciliation because it was overly polite. As I expected, Ismail began to beg her back.

"Come on. This is unnecessary. Get up. I'm not angry with you. I said I'm not angry with you. What is this? There is nothing to forgive. Get up, go upstairs and see to the children. Please."

Moriam finally stood up and left Ismail trying to justify his behavior to me.

"I didn't mean to lose my temper," he said. "What pained me was when Sondra said I wasn't royalty. I mean, why would you discuss that with her? I'm just saying your conversation should never have gotten that far. That is all I'm saying. I'm finished with that woman. I will not let her use my son as a pawn..."

I let him talk without interrupting. When he was through, he paused as if he expected an apology from me.

"Anyway," he said, "the matter is over."

We both went upstairs and I followed him leaving every excuse I'd made for him behind: his brothers; the difficulties he faced in America; Sondra.

He went to the kitchen and I headed for the living room to check on my children.

"It was nothing," I said to them. "Go back to the basement."

They didn't return my smile. Taslim was fiddling with what looked like a paper clip and Bashira was pretending to read a book. I left them to recover and went upstairs. Moriam was in our bedroom.

"We're getting out of here," I said.

She seemed genuinely surprised. "Why?"

"I won't tolerate anyone treating our family badly."

"Don't mind your cousin. He is just childish."

"He's a bloody buffoon and I'm finished with him."

It was easy to say Moriam was manipulative. She could almost make me believe I was in control, but then I wasn't subjected to the same rules of conduct that she was as a wife. The way she'd handled Ismail showed how easily she could rise to a level of grace I was incapable of, even for the sake of our family.

She didn't argue. She knew I'd made up my mind. I lay on the bed as she went downstairs to warm the Chinese takeout for him. I would later hear her laughing and talking to him in the living room, as if nothing had happened.

FRIENDS

We moved into a block of apartments off Route 4, which was convenient for commuting to New York by bus. Our block had one-bedroom apartments. They were all we could afford. We were in Apartment C on the second floor, or first floor, as we called it. Apartment A, below us on the ground floor, was unoccupied. A woman called Cathy lived in Apartment B, also on the ground floor, and a man called Howard lived in Apartment D across the landing from us.

Howard was a smoker and he had a white cat. I could smell cigarettes whenever I passed his door and he sometimes let his cat out on the landing. On the day we moved in, he was talking to Cathy there. Cathy had a ladybug-shaped brooch pinned to her pocket and he wore a faded denim shirt. He had a disgruntled look about him, and Cathy, a gentle manner that reminded me of my mother's. I assumed they were both retired, so it was awkward to address them by their first names. Howard couldn't hide his surprise when I told him my family was moving into Apartment C.

"What, four of you in there?" he asked.

"No pets," I said.

For all I knew, we could be violating a housing regulation. Apart from the one bedroom, our apartment had a living room, kitchen and bathroom. My plan was for Taslim and Bashira to share the folding bed in the living room. During the day, it doubled as a sofa. Moriam thought it was better for her and Bashira to sleep in the bedroom, and Taslim and me to sleep in the living room. I told her the arrangement wouldn't work and she asked why not. I thought she would know the answer to that, having turned me into a eunuch in Ismail's house.

We were trying to be more polite to each other. So were our children, who said "please" and "thank you" more, and drew up a rota for cleaning the bathroom and washing dishes, which they observed.

For the first few days, we navigated around unpacked boxes and suitcases. The air conditioner in the living room was nailed to the window frame. The front door had so many locks I questioned the safety of our neighborhood. The paint on the walls appeared to be swelling in some corners and the carpet looked as if it had urine stains. We hadn't expected to live in an apartment like that in America, but we were grateful because we could switch on lights at any time of the day and have electricity, without having to buy our own backup generator, and we could turn a tap on and have water—water we could actually drink. The smell of each other, we were used to. We were also used to the occasional sight of someone else's urine or blood in the toilet.

Ismail had cosigned our lease, probably with the intention of getting us out of his house as soon as possible. The town we were moving to was all right, he said, but it had one of the worst high schools in Bergen County. He rated neighborhoods according to the percentage of white inhabitants and average income. I wasn't sure if that was the result of his politics or his stint as a real-estate agent, but a neighborhood was all right if it was predominantly white and if its inhabitants were in the median income bracket. I asked how students in the school district performed in their SATs, which was my main concern, and he said he wouldn't know because he'd given his son a private education. For me, that was a perfect opportunity to advise him to stop taking his frustrations with Sondra out on Hakeem, after which I got his answering machine whenever I called him. I didn't leave messages and eventually stopped calling. Obviously, I'd joined the league of relatives he begrudged.

We registered Bashira and Taslim at the middle school and high school in our district. Bashira would be in the eighth grade and Taslim would be in the eleventh grade, having turned seventeen. I finally got to speak to Osaro, who was back from his book tour in Germany. He said a green card would be useful in applying for teaching positions, but I was at a disadvantage because I didn't have a degree from an American university. He suggested I get a master's or doctorate in English and comparative literature. I told him I couldn't afford to go back to college, nor did I have the inclination. At any rate, finding a job couldn't take as long as getting another MA or PhD.

I bought a computer to help in my job search, meanwhile. A few of the African Studies departments were online and I spent time browsing them. Some were combined with African American Studies departments. They were multi- and interdisciplinary. I sent several query letters and got standard replies. None of them had vacancies. I checked the Modern Language Association job list and job ads in the *Chronicle of Higher Education*. Same situation.

Moriam continued to study for her CGFNS exams. During the day, she locked herself up in our bedroom. She was determined to pass the exams at her first sitting. She initially didn't know how to use the computer. Whenever she tried to, I got out of her way because I had no patience for the yelps she let out when she hit the wrong keys. Taslim and Bashira sometimes came to her rescue. They were quick to learn how to play games on the computer and surf the Internet. They were adapting faster than we were to American life in general and it showed in their language. Bashira misused the word "like," and Taslim overused the idiom "kind of." So, for instance, they might say their mother was kind of relieved when the school year began because she, like, found it hard to follow her review course notes while they were watching television in the living room. Even when she shut the bedroom door the noise distracted her.

We'd both expected Bashira to have a harder time than Taslim adjusting to her new school. In Nigeria, she had not only performed better academically, she had behaved better. Taslim was always in trouble, mostly for not paying attention in class, but he found it easier to make friends. I couldn't tell if he approved of his new school, though. Whenever I asked how his day went, he would answer, "Cool." He sounded more American now. Bashira, on the other hand, sounded the same and she gave a long list of complaints about her school, beginning with the lunch menu. "It looks like vomit," she said. "I feel sick just thinking about it." I asked if she'd made any school friends. "They're rough," she said. "You should see the way they abuse each other. One girl told another girl her mother was a—I can't even say the word. They started slapping each other and our teacher sent them to the principal's office. Me, I don't talk to anyone."

Every day she had another story like that and I didn't know if her school really was that bad or if she was just trying to get my sympathy. She and Taslim rode school buses. Moriam visited their schools during classes to see what sort of students they were mixing with. She spotted a few unruly students at Taslim's school and a group of girls at Bashira's who wore so much makeup they looked like high school seniors. We were now more concerned about how both our children would fit in socially. The facilities in their new schools may not have been the best in the state, but compared to the schools they'd attended in Nigeria, which had overcrowded classrooms and toilets so filthy that students would rather squat behind shrubs than use them, their new schools were an improvement.

One evening after work, while our children were doing their homework and Moriam was studying, I decided to do the laundry. I took a basketful of clothes to the laundry room, which was a five-minute walk behind the block. Howard was on the bench by the dryers, sitting cross-legged. He was smoking, and tenants were not allowed to do that in the laundry room.

"Good evening," I said.

"Hullo," he said.

He got up, went outside with his cigarette and came back empty-handed. As I loaded the washing machine, he cleared his throat so loudly I was sure he was trying to get my attention.

"How are you today?" I asked.

"Fine, fine," he said. "I can't complain."

He looked pale and had shadows under his eyes.

"Hey, do you have change for a dollar?" he asked.

"I have enough for a wash and dry," I said.

He waved. "Never mind."

I felt guilty about turning him down.

"Actually, I could give you two quarters and get more later."

"No, no," he said. "You use them. I'm sure you need them."

Again, he cleared his throat as I put my quarters in the slot.

"Are you all right?" I asked, looking back at him.

He was rotating his shoulder. "I have a slight ache in my shoulder. It's been like this all week, but I'll be fine. Why, are you a doctor or something?"

"My wife is a nurse."

"Really? Where does she work?"

"She hasn't started work yet."

He shook his head. "We have a lot of foreign doctors and nurses around here. I had a nurse from Jamaica once. I couldn't understand a word she was saying."

He mumbled, yet he had an air of authority, as if I ought to listen closely to what he said.

"How's your apartment working out for you?" he asked. "I hope it's not too small or anything."

"We manage."

"You're Luke, aren't you?"

"Lukmon."

"Luke-man?"

"Yes."

He was close enough and it could take me hours to correct him.

"Your wife's name is Maryanne, isn't it?"

"Moriam."

"What?"

"Moriam."

"Oh. I could have sworn Cathy said her name was Maryanne. I don't mean to be rude or anything, but sometimes you meet Afro-Americans and they have names like Muhammad. You know, like Muhammad Ali. Then you meet real Africans and they're just Maryanne and Luke. Cathy said you might be from South Africa."

"We're from Nigeria."

"Where is that, north, south, east...?"

"West."

"I was in North Africa once."

"Really?"

He nodded. "In the seventies, after the war. I worked on

air conditioning in an embassy there. Cathy's son, Peter, visited South Africa. He used to live in the apartment she lives in now. That was his place. He traveled all around the world, Peter. Hiking, mountain climbing. She lost him just after she lost her husband. White-water rafting accident."

I didn't know what white-water rafting was, but imagined it was an activity that white people participated in. Howard was still rotating his shoulder.

"Classy lady, Cathy," he said. "Real classy. Been through a lot, but she's good people."

"You should see a doctor about that," I said.

He huffed. "Doctors. They don't make you feel any better."

"Are you sure you don't want my spare quarters?"

"I'll get some from my apartment. I need the exercise."

He didn't budge, and as I started the washing machine, he pointed at the dryers.

"Those machines don't work, by the way. I told Bes to look into it, but he's done nothing about it. I tell you, it makes me so mad. Shouldn't a super know how to fix things? Where are the people who know how to fix things these days? I page Bes and he won't answer. Always one excuse or another, and now his wife's having a baby."

"He has a wife?"

"Yes. She's on bed rest."

"Why?"

"Oh, something. There's always something with them."

Our super, Bes, was Albanian. Whenever I saw him, he was watching his footsteps and jiggling his keys. His demeanor suggested he wanted to be left alone.

"Which dryer works better?" I asked.

"This one right behind me is the best. I wouldn't use those two if I were you."

"I'll remember that."

He shook his head. "I tell you, Luke, no one fixes things anymore. Take a look at the dumpster outside and you won't believe what you'll find. I don't know what Africa is like these days, but nothing got thrown away while I was there. Those people used anything, whether or not it was broke. Here, we throw everything away. We live in a throwaway society here."

The dryer stopped and he stood up shakily. I couldn't imagine my father doing his own laundry. He'd always had a relative on standby to attend to him.

"How's your cat?" I asked.

"She's in a funny mood today," he said.

"Why?"

He waved his hand. "Oh, she'll be all right. She just needs attention."

He could have been talking about his wife. I watched as he unloaded the dryer, extracting his worn-out socks and briefs.

"I'll be out of your way soon," he said.

Moriam found Howard amusing. She said he smoked in the laundry room all the time. She didn't mind if he called her Maryanne. She called him *Alakori*, a ne'er-do-well, because he always appeared hung-over. I thought that was disrespectful. He was a war veteran, after all, and to be honest, reminded me of her father, sitting in the corner on family occasions and making one tribalistic comment after another.

On Saturday, her old friend and colleague Bisi the Gossip came to see her, wearing a wig and jeans that were far too tight.

"What happened to you?" Moriam asked.

"I'm fat, aren't I?" Bisi said, smiling.

"Very," Moriam said. "You're enjoying this country too much."

Bisi fluttered her fake eyelashes. "I'm on a diet."

"You call this dieting?" Moriam asked, stepping back to examine her. "You have to reduce a bit more."

Bisi had driven from Philadelphia. We had not seen her in years. She was Moriam's roommate in nursing school and had a reputation back then. Before she left Nigeria, she was rumored to be sleeping with a professor of gynecology. Now, she was married to a Yoruba man who had been in America for over twenty years. He was much older than she was and had grown-up children from his first marriage. Bisi said he was stable. Other Nigerian nurses she knew in America were either divorced or in bad marriages. Their husbands were, as she put it, threatened by their earnings potential.

Her husband worked five days a week at his barbershop and took Sundays and Mondays off. She showed us her new Mercedes from the kitchen window. My first thought was, How could they afford such a car?

"You bought it yourself?" Moriam asked.

"Me?" Bisi said. "For where? My husband bought it for me."

She was probably giving her husband more credit than was due, but Moriam was impressed enough to slap hands with her.

"Don't oppress us! We've only just arrived!"

"Don't worry! Your own is coming!"

I left them in the kitchen and went to the bedroom. If indeed Bisi's husband had bought the Mercedes, and Bisi were half as promiscuous as she used to be, he was probably getting more action than I was.

I was reading Edward Said's *Out of Place* and tried to get back to it, but it was hard to concentrate because I could hear their voices clearly, especially after they drifted to the living room.

"Why didn't you bring your children?" Moriam asked.

"Feely is too far," Bisi said.

"Feely" was Philly.

"How far?" Moriam asked.

"Almost three hours, and I can't take all that 'Are we there yet?'"

"What is that?" Moriam asked.

Bisi laughed. "You'll find out when your children have been here long enough. American kids, they don't know how to keep shut. They're not satisfied until they've killed you with questions. You know me, nobody can kill me. I deposited them with their father."

Deposited. Bisi was lazy. When she worked as a nurse in Nigeria, Moriam said she would make patients wait for hours before attending to them. She could get away with that there because nurses weren't expected to be nice. In fact, they were notoriously wicked. At the hospital where Moriam worked, they ignored, shouted at and even laughed at patients. If they ended up killing a patient, no one would be surprised, unless they killed the patient intentionally.

"Your wig suits you," Moriam said.

"I'm completely white underneath," Bisi said.

"Why?"

"It's stress, my sister."

"Ah-ah?" Moriam said. "From what?"

"Work," Bisi said. "Work and kids. Where are your kids, even?"

"Their father sent them to the library."

"You see? That's the trouble with academics. Study, study, study."

I had sent Taslim and Bashira to the library before it closed. Not to study, but to get them out of my way. The library was at a safe walking distance on the high street. Earlier in the week, I'd been there to borrow books. Bashira was likely to come back with a new one. Taslim would probably come back with computer games.

When our children returned, Moriam and Bisi got so loud I gave up reading. I could now see why Moriam found it hard to study in our bedroom.

"Look at you two," Bisi said. "You have your mom's eyes and you have your dad's nose. You know your mom's nose is sharp like a beak? Yes! That is why she was always poking it into matters that didn't concern her!"

Bashira laughed nervously and Taslim's laugh sounded forced.

"How do Americans manage their names?" Bisi asked.

"Tell Auntie what your classmates call you," Moriam said.

"I'm Bash," Bashira said.

"I'm Slim," Taslim said.

"My children are Zoë and Matt," Bisi said.

"How come?" Moriam said.

"We're Catholic," Bisi said.

"So? They must have Yoruba names, too."

"They do, but who can pronounce Ereoluwatide and Ifeolawatide?"

Moriam laughed. "Who gave them?"

"Their grandfather."

"You can shorten them to Ere and Ife."

"You don't know Americans. They can't even pronounce simple 'Bisi.'"

"How do they pronounce it?"

"'Busy.'"

"Correct them!"

"Who has time for that? When I got tired of hearing 'Busy,' I switched to my middle name—Florence. Finish."

Someone turned on the television and their voices were less clear as Moriam asked after Stella, the other nurse they'd trained with, who now lived in Maryland.

"That one," Bisi said, her voice taking a turn.

"What happened?" Moriam asked.

"She married this typical Igbo man who refuses to mix."

"Here?"

"Right here in America," Bisi said. "Stella used to live in Feely. Oh, yes, she lived in Feely for a while. We attended the same church. She, too, is Catholic. Our children were baptized there and we took communion there. Nowadays, she will cross fifty states to attend Igbo functions, but she won't come to yours. You know me, I'm for unity. Nigeria is going downhill and that is why we're here, so we should forget about this 'You're from this tribe and I'm from that tribe' mentality."

"How come we Southerners are the only ones here?" Moriam asked.

"Because," Bisi said, "half the Northerners are so poor and brainwashed they think they have no choice but to go around begging on the streets. The other half have stolen enough government money to take care of their families for the rest of their lives. Hausas, you know what they're like."

It didn't surprise me that Bisi, in the course of denouncing tribalism, would reveal her own prejudices.

Moriam was born in a barracks up north. She grew up with Hausa children. Her father was ambivalent about Hausas. On the one hand, he had Islam in common with them; on the other, he was Yoruba, so he basically tolerated them. In private, he grumbled that Northern leaders in general were responsible for ruining Nigeria. He hated Igbos outright and blamed them for the Civil War. He often said Igbos were materialistic, Hausas were sly and Yorubas were quarrelsome. If ever I tried to get into a serious discussion about how and why each group came to be identified by those characteristics—bringing up the initial partitioning of Nigeria into North, South and West, the fractures between Yoruba political parties and the tenuous alliance between the Yoruba and Hausa during the Civil War, which intensified Igbo enterprise—he would say, "I fought in that war. I know what I'm talking about."

His attitude was dangerously common, and having had lengthy discussions in academia and seen the same attitude disguised as intellectualism, I never belabored my point. Perhaps I was too much a product of Mayflower School but tribalism, to me, was the most objectionable form of parochialism.

What frustrated me most about the general elections in Nigeria, apart from the widespread rigging that made me question whether political parties deserved to have the word "Democratic" in their names, was that it showed how much Nigerians still mistrusted one another three decades after the Civil War, and how we disregarded minorities, until we needed them politically. Yet, the reality was, within the three main ethnic groups—Hausa, Yoruba and Igbo—there was no unity.

When President Obasanjo won the election, Moriam actually got angry with me because I suggested that having a Southerner as president was a step forward, only because Nigeria hadn't had a Southern president in years. "Why?" she asked. "Because Obasanjo is from your state?" I couldn't understand her question. I'd not voted for Obasanjo. We'd both voted for the opposition candidate, who was from another state. He had a master's degree in economics from Yale, which I believed would be useful in reforming our economy.

She was just annoyed our candidate had lost, but Nigerians could be that simpleminded and, out of sheer opportunism, could support a presidential candidate from their state, regardless of his mandate or reputation. We always had reasons to justify ethnic partisanship. We were too diverse a nation to be united, even on matters of policy. Political parties were not defined along clear liberal and conservative lines, so the only rational thing to do was to vote, as we had, for the candidate less likely to do further damage.

"So Naijas in America are tribalistic," Moriam said.

"Extremely," Bisi said. "Worse than Naijas at home."

"It's backwardness," Moriam said. "Assorted Naijas are not like that."

"Assorted Naijas," short for Assorted Biscuit Nigerians, were the Nigerian elite.

"Those ones?" Bisi said. "They're just as backward, with their colonial mentality."

"It's true," Moriam said. "What am I talking about? They don't care so long as they can travel first-class to London. I should be calling them No Variety, because they're all the same."

Bisi clapped. "No Variety! I like that! How I miss that Naija sense of humor!"

Perhaps nostalgia contributed to the level of ethnic distrust among Nigerians in America. Bisi was homesick but reluctant to travel to Nigeria because on her previous trip, her relatives had inundated her with requests for gifts and money. She was about to leave for the airport when her uncle tried to grab her Louis Vuitton handbag.

She apparently couldn't get away with being lazy in America. She worked more than forty hours a week as an RN at a hospital. American hospitals looked like Nigerian hotels, she said, and Moriam would make good money, but every cent would be earned.

"Nurses are needed here, that's for sure, but they will work you like a dog."

"I don't care," Moriam said. "I just want to make enough to buy a house one day."

"By God's grace you will," Bisi said.

"You think England would have been better for us?" Moriam asked.

"England? Why?"

"Lukmon's master's degree is from there."

"My sister," Bisi said, "forget about England. Eastern Europeans have infiltrated the place. Their NHS is saturated. All you'll be hearing from them is 'I'm afraid we can't' and 'I'm afraid we don't.' England is the country of no. There are so many of us there they won't give your child a passport anymore, even if you give birth there. America says yes to you. Irish nurses come here, Caribbean and Filipino nurses. By the way, Vermont is one of the best states in the Northeast to be registered in. Yes, try and get registered in Vermont."

After giving advice, her usual gossip took a gory turn. She gave a history of Nigerians in America who were involved in random acts of violence. Oddly enough, they were all employed in healthcare. A man crushed his wife's hand in a garbage disposal unit. His wife was a nurse. Another man beat his wife to death with a baseball bat. He was a pharmacist. Some other man shot his wife to death. She was a doctor and so was he.

"Since when did Naijas start all this craziness?" Moriam asked.

"It's stress, my sister," Bisi said. "The stress in this country is too much. If you're not careful, it can make your head turn."

Osaro was less forthcoming when he visited me the following Sunday. He came by bus from New York, after he'd taken the subway from Brooklyn to Manhattan. When he arrived, I told Taslim and Bashira they couldn't watch television, so they left us in the living room and went to the bedroom to play computer games as Moriam studied there.

Osaro, with his slight stoop and hands behind his back, looked as if he'd come to commiserate. As soon as he walked in, his eyes darted around our living room. I could tell he disapproved of our apartment, which made me wonder how much he earned. He didn't appear to be wanting for money. He took off his suede jacket and carefully laid it on the sofa. I remembered how vain he had been in Nigeria, showing up for lectures in a shirt and tie, no matter how hot it was. He'd gotten a lot of attention from female students and his involvements with some of them were undoubtedly personal. In fact, he was so buddy-buddy with the student body that they were more shocked than the English faculty when they found out he'd left Nigeria for good.

"I should seriously start thinking about moving to New Jersey," he said. "I guess I could get used to the malls in Paramus and discount houses in Secaucus."

I assumed that was a New York joke, but I still didn't have a preference for either state. So far, New York was the store where I worked and New Jersey was the apartment where we lived. As far as sightseeing went, the most I'd done in New York was walk to the main building of the public library on Fifth Avenue.

In our part of New Jersey there was nothing much to see. All we had were plazas and malls, and shops like Toys "R" Us and IKEA. There was Chuck E. Cheese's, which Taslim and Bashira were too old for. There were also a few car dealerships worth visiting, but I would need a car to get to them. The town in which we lived was full of rental condos. Our main street had small independent stores and diners. Moriam did our grocery shopping at our local Pathmark.

Osaro asked about our former colleagues who had either left Nigeria or remained there. Some had no intention of leaving because they were genuinely content with their lives; others pretended to be because they had no means of getting out.

"What about that lady?" he asked, snapping his fingers. "Olu something?"

"Oluwole," I said. "She took a position in South Africa."

"Wow."

"It's the place to be, postapartheid."

"What about the professor who drove that battered old Volvo?"

"Essien?" I said. "He's in Germany now."

"Where in Germany?"

"I don't know."

"Sharp fellow. And Fashola?"

"Fashola is still there. You know Fashola. He will never leave Nigeria."

Osaro seemed guarded. He wasn't the Osaro I remembered, who openly made fun of our senior colleagues. We would have heated debates about writers like Achebe, Soyinka, J. P. Clark and Okigbo. I thought he allowed their biographies to interfere with his interpretations of their works. He deconstructed their biographies as if they were novels. I wasn't surprised he had written a memoir, but he was uncharacteristically modest when I asked what it was about.

"I'm tired of talking about that book," he said.

"You should have brought me a copy," I said.

"My brother, it was the last thing on my mind."

"Describe it in a few words."

He laughed. "There's nothing much to say! It's a typical coming-of-age story!"

His memoir, *Last Word*, was published by an independent press. I was sure I would eventually get to read it.

I myself had had literary aspirations in my PhD years.

I'd wanted to be a newspaper columnist. I was inspired by the revival of journalism when privately owned periodicals like *The Guardian* and, later, *Newswatch* came on the scene. Then Dele Giwa of *Newswatch* was killed by a letter bomb and that was the end of journalism for me. Before Dele Giwa, journalists risked being locked up. After Dele Giwa, they feared for their lives. Now, to survive as a journalist in Nigeria, you would have to be the kind that worked for government-owned newspapers —lackeys and praise singers, basically.

In my banking years, I'd toyed with the idea of writing fiction, partly because of the hoopla surrounding Ben Okri when *The Famished Road* won the Booker Prize. My first attempt was a novel, which was a throwback to novels I'd read in school, such as Fagunwa's *The Forest of a Thousand Daemons* and Amos Tutuola's *My Life in the Bush of Ghosts*. Okri had a road, Fagunwa and Tutuola had forests and bushes, so I decided on a rock as a symbol of my protagonist's journey. I chose Olumo Rock, which had given Abeokuta its name, "Under the rock." Olumo was a lookout and shelter for Egba warriors during ancient intertribal wars and Egba people were known as children of Olumo. I'd learned our anthem, "Rejoice, rejoice on Olumo," as a young boy, and had no clue what I was rejoicing about. Olumo, to me, was more a tourist spot and I'd walked to the top a few times.

I didn't have much success with the novel, because my cynicism got the better of me. It began with a story my great-uncle had told me when I was a boy. He saw a ghost on his way up Olumo and walked right through it. As I grew older, I found his story harder to believe. Actually, the more I thought about his story, the more I suspected he was nuts, but my narrative eventually failed because the idea of walking up Olumo Rock as a metaphor for life seemed contrived. I decided that perhaps what I really wanted was to return to academia.

I asked about teaching in America and Osaro had this to say: "You just have to know how to position yourself, you know, and carve a niche for yourself. But first you have to find your way into the job market. It's a question of showing your strongest skills and being flexible. I mean, you could start off doing adjunct work, though adjunct work doesn't pay well or necessarily lead to permanent posts. So if I were you, I would go back to school and study English and comparative literature. With that, you can teach American literature anywhere. I mean, you're just limiting yourself by teaching African literature. Also, African Studies departments hire professors who are not African, which is another story. But we're minorities here, and that can give you a certain amount of leverage. I mean, affirmative action is constantly under attack, but for what it's worth, colleges have to take that into consideration when they hire. It's a game, that's all. You just have to know how to play it."

He wasn't making sense, and his insistence that I should go back to college irritated me. I could barely afford to provide for my family with what I earned as a security guard. I'd come from Nigeria hoping to teach African literature in an American university. What other game was I expected to play?

He asked what it was like to teach in Nigeria after he left.

"State Security monitored us," I said. "Even students got involved in spying."

"Students?"

"So we heard, and the conditions for them were terrible, so it wouldn't have been hard to find recruits."

"What were the conditions like?"

"The usual. No light, no water, crowded hostels, lack of books. Students had to photocopy entire volumes."

"They were still doing that?"

"It got worse. One book, and twenty students would photocopy it."

"We've never followed copyright laws in that country."

"We just wanted students to follow the course."

"It must have been like living under a fascist regime."

"Fascism is an ideology. What we went through was utter chaos."

The worst damage caused by military regimes, I said, was how they undermined what was left of stewardship in academia. There was a collapse in standards, academic, moral and otherwise. We had always had lecturers who didn't grade their students' papers, lecturers who deliberately misplaced their students' scores and failed them, and students who cheated in exams. We had always had male lecturers who sexually harassed female students and female students who propositioned male lecturers. Some female students were renowned for going out with sugar daddies. They were called sugary girls. They flew to the capital on weekends to party with government officials. At one point, a group of male students got so resentful of them, they began to vandalize their sugar daddies' cars.

Whenever the male students acted out, they got involved in some form of violence. They assaulted female students and attacked rival cults. From one regime to the next, all that type of behavior became commonplace on campus.

I again asked Osaro about teaching in America, to get back on course.

"Students here can be very demanding," he said. "And they're not always grateful or polite. In fact, they can be very rude, some of them, and you have to be careful how you treat them. One misinterpreted move and you'll be in serious trouble. I once had a student accuse me of being inappropriate."

"In what way?"

He shrugged. "Who knows? I can't tell you what was going on in her mind."

I wondered if he had behaved inappropriately. He could get away with that in Nigeria. At the university where we'd taught, a student once asked a lecturer to stop sexually harassing her and he turned around and accused her of tempting him with revealing outfits.

"Over here," Osaro said, "you can't even raise your voice to a student without repercussions, and now, there's this new website where students can rate your teaching skills anonymously, for anyone to see."

"Aren't you allowed to respond?"

"No, but you could always hide your identity and defend yourself."

"America," I said, shaking my head.

"The land of the free," he said.

Osaro seemed miserable. He, too, complained about stress, though he didn't appear to be suffering from it. He couldn't stay long, but he invited Moriam and me to his apartment for dinner the next weekend. Moriam came out of the bedroom to say goodbye to him and she was all smiles. The moment he left, she was ready to comment on our conversation.

"He's not practical," she said.

"In what way?" I asked.

"What was all that nonsense about—'carve a niche' and 'position yourself'? Is that what we're going to eat?"

"It was useful to me."

"Continue to deceive yourself."

I couldn't always be honest with her. She rubbished any discussion that sounded vaguely academic. She was the same way with me when I worked as a lecturer. Whatever I'd had to say wasn't what we were going to eat.

Living in America, it was easy to get cut off from news about Nigeria and Africa as a whole. Based on the few news reports on Africa I saw, I could forgive Americans for thinking the continent was—not even a country, but an island divided into three landscapes: a drought-ravaged, disease-infested village on one side, a war-torn bush in the middle, and a safari park on the other side. The only African leaders the news programs were interested in following were the likes of Mugabe. Nelson Mandela was their sole example of a good one. Newspapers were only marginally better in their coverage, so I was forced to rely on the BBC World Service.

Taslim and Bashira still watched a lot of television. During the weekends, they sometimes left it on all day, and Moriam didn't mind so long as they kept the volume low and recorded programs she missed while she was studying. I once watched five minutes of a pre-recorded morning talk show with her, during which the host interviewed a celebrity who had adopted a baby from an orphanage in Africa. No country was mentioned and the host congratulated her for bringing the baby to a film set. This woman admitted she had a nanny. She'd probably pulled strings to adopt the baby. She might even have bought the baby on the black market. I thought about African mothers who routinely carried their babies on their backs to work.

I was actually quite put off by the way African children in general were portrayed on American television. They couldn't be healthy or happy. They had to be malnourished and sick and tearful, with flies on their faces. The charity ads were the most offensive in that regard, with their somber music and self-righteous voiceovers. If I were American, they would annoy me outright. No one was suggesting that donations to Africa did not help. Only thoughtless people and bourgeois Africans did that, but come on. I've just come back from work, I'm eating, and I'm watching footage so disturbing I can't even digest my food.

My children, meanwhile, appeared to be taken in by Hollywood movies set in Africa. Bashira made Moriam and me sit through one set in an imaginary African kingdom, in which gazelles and zebras ran wild. The usual hakuna-matata nonsense. Everyone was beautiful. The king and queen were stupendously rich. They sent their son to a university in America, where he pretended to be poor to fit in with ordinary Americans. At least the film was a comedy. Taslim persuaded me to watch another film that was meant to be a serious drama. It was set in an unnamed African country during a civil war. An American reporter who was covering the war met an English revolutionary in the bush. This revolutionary was fighting for the African people, yet he still found time to have an affair with the reporter. The first time she appeared on screen, violins were playing. The first African woman that appeared—drums. By the middle of the film, Africans were being slaughtered all over the place and the revolutionary and reporter were busy kissing.

Now that I worked in New York, Moriam would ask me to stop at the African food store on 42nd Street to buy whatever provisions she needed: yam powder, *garri*, palm oil, *egusi*, and the rest. One Friday, she asked for stockfish and I bought a bagful for $4.37. She boiled it on Saturday morning and opened the kitchen window to let out the fumes.

Our doorbell rang while she was in the kitchen. Taslim and Bashira were in the bedroom, so I went to the door, looked through the peephole and saw a black woman in a light-blue tracksuit.

"It's your new neighbor from downstairs," she said.

I opened the door. She was pretty and possibly in her thirties.

"Hey," she said. "I was just wondering if you're having problems with your plumbing."

"Not that I'm aware of," I said.

Moriam came out of the kitchen wiping her hands on a tea towel. I excused myself and returned to the sofa, where I'd been reading newspapers.

Her name was Nia. She'd moved into Apartment A. She said there was a strange smell in her apartment.

The smell was obviously coming from the stockfish Moriam was boiling.

"Cathy says she can smell it, too. You know Cathy in Apartment B?"

"Yes," Moriam said.

"I wonder where it's coming from," Nia said. "I guess we'll soon find out. I knocked on Apartment D's door, but there was no answer. Cathy says he's out. She's gone to get the super. She told me you're from South Africa?"

"West," Moriam said.

"Which country?"

"Nigeria."

Nia smiled. "I've met a few Nigerians before. She says your name is Marian."

"Moriam."

"Is that Nigerian?"

Moriam said yes, but it wasn't. She was used to people getting her name wrong. Back home, people had sometimes called her Miriam or Mariam.

"I only asked because my name is a Swahili name," Nia said. "It means 'purpose.' Your braids are nice. Where did you get them done?"

"I did them myself," Moriam said.

She called them Fulani braids. She braided Bashira's hair the same way.

"Do you do other people's?" Nia asked.

"I can do yours," Moriam said.

Nia smiled. "That would be great. I'm trying to grow out my relaxer, and it's at that phase. I don't know what to do with it. I usually go to a salon in East Orange. There's a group of Togolese women there. I work in New York and I really don't have time to think about my hair. Your braids look tidy. Do they last long?"

"About a month," Moriam said.

"That's perfect," Nia said. "I'm glad I stopped by, then. I should go and see if Cathy was able to get ahold of the super."

I'd been trying to think of a word to describe Nia. "Chirpy" came to mind.

As soon as she left, Moriam opened the windows in case Bes was coming to inspect our apartment. Then she went to the bathroom to get a lemon air freshener and sprayed the living room and kitchen. There was no point. The ammoniac smell remained.

Apart from having an unpleasant odor, stockfish was hard to chew. I was trying to figure out why it was so delicious when our doorbell rang again. This time it was Cathy, and Moriam opened the door.

"I'm so sorry," Cathy said. "Has Nia been here?"

She wore an apple-shaped brooch and her gray hair was in a single braid.

"She's just left," Moriam said. "She said she was on her way to see you."

"My, I must have missed her. I rang her doorbell, but she's not answering. I was with Bes. Bes, our super? I paged him, but I never heard from him so I went to his apartment. Nia thinks we might have plumbing problems in our block."

"She told me," Moriam said.

"Gosh, we've never had trouble with plumbing in this block before."

Moriam finally confessed. "It's my cooking."

"Oh!" Cathy exclaimed. "I wouldn't worry about that! I wouldn't worry if it's just your cooking!"

"I'm sorry," Moriam said. "I should have told her."

Cathy smiled. "Don't give it a thought. You should smell my boiled cabbage. Nia did say it might be your cooking, but she wasn't sure."

"It's Nigerian food," Moriam said.

Why was she blaming Nigeria? Stockfish was from Norway.

"Howard said you were from South Africa," Cathy said. "My son, Peter, went there. He took photographs of Ndebele people. I have them on my wall. You should come and see them sometime."

"I will," Moriam said.

"Now, you're Marian, aren't you?" Cathy asked.

"Moriam."

"Marion?"

"Moriam."

Cathy smiled. "I'll have to get used to that. It's a little more complicated than Luke."

"Lukmon," I said.

Her eyes widened. "Oh! I thought Howard said you were Luke!"

I could have smiled to put her at ease, but I had no inclination.

"Well," she said, walking backward, "I'd better let Bes know he's not needed. We can hardly find him when we do need him."

She left apologizing for troubling us.

"So," Moriam said, after she shut the door. "The story is true."

I swore I would never buy stockfish for her again. Not if it meant our neighbors would come to our apartment acting as if someone had died.

The next Sunday, Moriam and I went to dinner at Osaro's apartment. We left ahead of time and got to Brooklyn too early. Osaro was cooking when we arrived. His apartment smelled of groundnut stew and was full of masks and drums. They were hanging on walls and pushed into corners. His sofas were covered with Fulani cloth and his curtains were made of *adire*. I'd never seen a place decorated in such a deliberately Nigerian fashion.

"Did our bus take us back home or what?" I asked.

At first, Osaro didn't understand until I pointed at a drum that served as a side table.

"You're in Brooklyn, my brother," he said. "That's why I live here. I couldn't survive a day in Jersey. Brooklyn is the real deal."

He lived off Flatbush Avenue. We'd taken a bus from Manhattan so we could see more of New York, and were surprised to find Brooklyn divided into Asian, Hispanic, Jewish, Arab and black neighborhoods. On Osaro's street, we passed barbershops, hair braiders and beauty supplies stores. Around the corner from his block was a Caribbean deli and an African food market, but Brooklyn was at best a substitute for home.

Osaro wore a *dashiki* with a *kente*-print trim that was more Afrocentric than African. I was in a shirt and chinos, the concept of wearing clothes to show off my African identity making as much sense to me as walking around in a loincloth. Moriam offered to help him in the kitchen and I remained in the living room, where a Fela CD was playing.

"What jam is this?" I asked.

"'Dog Eat Dog,'" Osaro said.

I looked through his collection of Fela CDs, visualizing a Lagos street at night with fluorescent lights and traffic at a standstill. Fela's music was more available since his death. All I'd ever seen in Lagos were bootleg copies of his records.

Osaro's other guests showed up on time. First to arrive were Sharifa, an Egyptian playwright, and her husband, Ed, who was from Colorado. Ed was a redhead. He wore a faded gray T-shirt and open-toe sandals. Sharifa wore a Mexican poncho. I told her my sister was her namesake and she hugged me and said, "That is wonderful," her accent sounding French.

Carole, Claire and Lily arrived next. Carole was from Brooklyn. She was a professor at Osaro's college. So was Claire, who was from England. She was a graduate of the University of Birmingham in England, which she called "Birminkam Uni." Lily was Carole's adopted daughter. She was nine years old, with so much hair she looked like a dwarf tree. She ran around Osaro's apartment thumping drums and singing to Fela's music.

"What on earth?" Claire said, covering her ears.

"She's musical," Carole said.

"Cool," Lily said, pointing at a mask.

"Way cool," Carole said.

Lily called Carole "Mom" and Claire by her first name.

"What's your name?" she asked Moriam, wriggling as she waited for an answer.

"Mrs. Karim," Moriam said.

"Your real name, I mean," Lily said, glancing at Carole.

"Moriam," Carole said.

"Mrs. Karim to you," Moriam said.

Lily was off to her next drum. She needed home training. She was all over the apartment, and Carole never once stopped her. Occasionally Claire said, "Careful," but Lily only ignored her. I wondered how Osaro could tolerate her. At first, he acted as if he didn't notice; then he handed her a glass of 7Up, which was like fuel. She drank it and began to simulate a sword fight. I was trying to decide if her behavior was normal for an American child when I caught Sharifa eyeing her.

Sharifa was an actress as well as a playwright and had recently toured the States with her solo show. She had two daughters who were in their twenties. She swore a lot, sounding sophisticated regardless, because of her accent.

"After a performance," she said, "someone is guaranteed to ask me about the burka. They want me to tell them all about the burka, even though I've never had to wear one offstage. What pisses me off is that they don't want to consider how they are so controlled by fashion here. When I try to discuss that with them, they ask more questions about the burka."

I'd never heard the word "burka" pronounced so sexily. Ed was talking to Claire about camping and Sharifa interrupted him.

"I hate the outdoors," she said.

"I know you hate the outdoors," Ed said.

"I can't stand camping, hiking or backpacking," she said. "You won't catch me up a mountain. The outdoors is not for me."

She even made the word "outdoors" sound sexy. I couldn't get enough of her voice, even as the other guests' voices drowned out hers.

Pascal was the final guest to arrive. He was a Congolese writer and professor who specialized in francophone African literature. He wore a black beret and sported a gray beard. Sharifa kissed him three times and they spoke French until Osaro stopped them.

"No *Français* here," he said, before introducing Pascal to Moriam and me.

"Madame," Pascal said, bowing slightly.

"I don't speak French," Moriam said.

"As a rule," he said, "neither do I, but Sharifa here is a terrible influence."

"Oh, you're so full of it," Sharifa said.

They were all competitive. Whatever the topic, someone had to contribute an angle or get a laugh. They were quick in a way that academics back home were not. The academics I knew back home were more long-winded, taking their time to make points and sometimes sounding as if they'd memorized thesauruses.

Pascal and Sharifa soon went back to speaking French and Pascal dropped names like Césaire and Senghor, so I assumed he was pompous. The rest talked about an African Studies Association conference in November that they were attending. I knew what I ought to do, join in the conversation and network, but I didn't befriend people because they could do favors for me.

I could almost agree with Moriam about academics. Working as a security guard, I had to be silent on the job. Academics were insecure about keeping quiet for extended periods of time in case they ended up looking ignorant. Consequently, they sometimes had pointless conversations.

As I drank beer, I randomly listened to them.

"They're bastards," Osaro said to Claire. "They murdered that guy. They knew he wasn't reaching for a gun. How can forty-one shots be reasonable? The judge should never have granted them bail after their indictments. That was unconscionable."

"I had to learn," Sharifa said to Moriam. "I email my daughters every day now."

"How do they pronounce it?" Pascal asked Ed.

"'Missou-rah,'" Ed said, "which is odd, considering the way it is spelt."

"I wish people wouldn't say 'European' when they mean 'English,'" Claire said. "It really annoys me, that."

"She did," Lily said. "She called me a fuzzball and I'm not playing with her anymore."

"That's fine," Carole said. "You don't have to."

"Naipaul," Osaro said. "His prose is precise, but his politics is way off."

We ate in his living room, sitting on his chairs and sofa. It was nice to be out without Taslim and Bashira, even though they were on my mind. So were serial killers. One had been apprehended for murders in Yosemite National Park that summer. Moriam thought my job as a security guard was beginning to affect my sense of safety. Perhaps it was, but I'd warned Taslim and Bashira to keep the front door bolted until we returned.

After dinner, Osaro stood up and tapped his wine glass to make an announcement.

"I have one rule at my parties," he said.

"Ooh, ooh, what are the rules?" Lily asked, and accidentally kicked a plate.

"Careful," Claire said, and moved it.

Osaro smiled at Lily. "A guest must honor us with a poem."

"Ooh, ooh, I know a poem," Lily said, raising her hand.

"We can hear yours afterward," Osaro said.

"Yay," Lily cheered.

I'd forgotten how demanding academics could be.

Osaro looked through the books on his shelf.

"*Labyrinths*," he said, picking up a book. "Pascal, will you do us the honors?"

"Why not?" Pascal said.

"Which one?" Osaro asked. "*Heavensgate*? *Limits*? *Silences*? *Distances*? *Path of Thunder*?"

"*Silences* would be great," Pascal said.

Moriam was smiling away, though she had no clue what they were talking about.

"'Lament of the Drums,'" Osaro said.

"Okay," Pascal said.

"All right, folks," Osaro said. "This poem is by Christopher Okigbo."

He handed the book to Pascal. "Lament of the Drums" was a poem I had taught. It was purposefully rhythmic, like a funeral dirge. Pascal read it and we clapped when he finished. I was still recovering from the pretentiousness of the moment when Lily decided it was her turn to recite a poem. Then she decided she was no longer ready to.

"I can't," she said, doubling over.

"Go on," Carole urged her.

"Come on," Claire said.

"I'm shy," Lily said.

"I was shy," Pascal said.

"No," Lily said, folding her arms. "You can't make me."

Again I caught Sharifa eyeing her as Ed said, "You can do it."

Lily unfolded her arms. "Okay, okay, here goes."

"Good for you," Ed said.

"You know this one," Carole said. "Take it slowly."

Lily stretched out her arms and with an intense expression recited Dr. Seuss's "Green Eggs and Ham."

The girl should have been in bed. When she finished, she curtsied right into the plate she'd kicked and ran over to Carole, leaving footprints of groundnut stew on the floor. Osaro insisted he would clean up the mess, but Carole grabbed his mop from him. Claire held Lily on her lap to prevent further mishaps. Sharifa, who had stopped talking from the moment Lily stepped on the plate, decided it was time for her and Ed to leave.

"Pleasure to meet you," she said.

"You too," I said.

"Say hello to my namesake, Sharifa."

I fancied the pants off her voice. Pascal, too, said he had to leave and she again kissed him three times before she realized they were heading in the same direction. Moriam and I were left with Carole, Claire and Lily.

Osaro was returning Okigbo's *Labyrinths* to his bookshelf when I saw copies of *Last Word*.

"Is that your book?" I asked.

"Yes," he said.

"Let me have a copy," I said.

He seemed nervous handing one to me, so I put it aside and took the opportunity to ask him about the African Studies Association conference, but he started rambling again.

"Well, ASA conferences can be impersonal. They're for African Studies scholars in general, not specifically for African literature scholars. They can get quite busy. I wouldn't go to one to network. I would wait for the African Literature Association conference."

"When is that?" I asked.

"Next year."

"I can't wait that long."

"It's in April."

"Will you be there?"

He shook his head. "Too many Nigerians."

Carole had finished mopping the floor and was ready to leave. We all got caught up in saying goodbyes and gravitated to his door.

"I liked 'Green Eggs and Ham,'" Osaro said to Lily.

"Well, I didn't," she said, rubbing her eyes.

"She gets cranky right about this time," Carole said, stroking Lily's hair.

"Who does her hair?" Moriam asked.

Even I could tell that Lily's hair was a mess, not that I cared, but Carole and Claire exchanged glances as if they had no idea what Moriam was talking about.

"No one," Claire said. "We just leave it."

"How come?" Moriam asked.

"It hurts her," Carole said.

"You should oil it and plait it," Moriam said. "It will make it softer."

Carole reached for Lily's shoulder. "We don't see why we have to hurt her to make her hair softer."

She ushered Lily out. After they'd left, Osaro shut the door and leaned against it. I thought he was about to tell us Lily was a handful.

"Man," he whispered. "You can't ask questions like that here."

He was looking at me, not Moriam.

"Like what?" I asked.

"'Who does her hair?'"

"Why not?" Moriam asked.

"You might be seen as a homophobe."

Moriam turned to me for clarification.

"Against homosexuals," I explained.

"I was only trying to tell them how to take care of her hair," she said.

"No problem," Osaro said. "Carole is overprotective and the girl is a brat anyway."

We took the subway back to 42nd Street. A group of black teenagers got into our car at the next stop. They were laughing and roughhousing. They got off at the following station and another teenager, who may have been Hispanic, got in and started making farting sounds.

Our bus to New Jersey was practically empty. Moriam and I were in the third row from the front and she was still upset about Lily.

"They couldn't even comb the girl's hair," she said. "They just let it grow wild."

"That is their business," I said.

"Seriously. I don't understand. What happens when both parents are women? Who does what the husband is supposed to do, and who does what the wife is supposed to do?"

"I don't think it works that way."

"How does it work?"

"You'd have to ask them."

She may have been intrusive to ask the question, but she was no homophobe. She was homo-ignorant, more like it, and so was I. I wasn't even sure why her question was offensive.

Back home, Osaro and I had had a few female students who dressed like men. One called herself Firefly. I didn't know if she was gay or not, but her head was shaved and she wrote gender-unspecific poetry. She was so popular with the English faculty that we sided with her when a group of born-again Christian students called her an abomination. They demanded that she grow her hair and wear dresses. She refused to and all Osaro had to say about her was that she needed a man to straighten her out.

Moriam herself had encountered *yan daudu* growing up in the North. She and her brother Gani would imitate their feminine walks. Gani was a polio survivor and had a slight limp. He was teased in school about that. His classmates called him an isosceles triangle. One day, he and Moriam came across a *dan daudu* and began to strut like him. The *dan daudu* then limped like Gani and called him a worthless thief bastard. From then on, they left *yan daudu* alone.

"I hope we've done the right thing by leaving Nigeria," Moriam said.

"Why?"

"What will become of our children here? Look at how those children on the subway were behaving."

"They were just having fun."

"What about that crazy girl who was making funny noises?"

"She was probably high."

"What about Lily, running around all over the place? I've never seen anything like it before."

"Come on. There are many like her at home."

"Where? Which Nigerian child would get away with that? Which Nigerian mother would tolerate that kind of behavior? I don't know. Over here, you have to be careful. You have to watch your children well and discipline them. Otherwise, before you know it, they will be slapping your face."

I laughed. "No child of mine will slap my face."

"What would you do?"

"Don't worry. They will find out."

"Do you know the police can arrest you for beating your children here?"

"I will send them back home before that ever happens."

"Home where?"

"Home to Naija. The sun will first of all straighten them out, before the mosquitoes get to them. By the time they've received a few whacks here and there from relatives, their heads will be correct."

I'd had too much beer. Moriam wasn't amused.

"It's not right. Those women are confusing the girl."

"She's all right," I said. "At least she has parents."

"They're neglecting her."

"How?"

"Look at the state of her hair! They should take her to a black salon if they don't know what to do with it!"

Lily was black? I had no idea. I was still in two minds about the girl on the subway, who may have been Arab.

"How were you able to pinpoint her race?" I asked.

"The girl is black," Moriam said. "I'm sure she is."

She fell silent and looked out of the window.

As we approached George Washington Bridge, I switched on the light and read the back description of *Last Word*. It didn't take me a second to find out why Osaro was reluctant to give me the book. This man, who had hung around female students, and probably slept with half of them, claimed he was "actively involved" in the students' union and left Nigeria "to escape persecution."

He was in America on political asylum. Perhaps that was his only way of staying. Not everyone was lucky enough to win a green card. He couldn't, after all, walk into an immigration office in America and say he was fed up with living in Nigeria and needed a change of scenery. He would have to tell a story, a story of persecution. Americans enjoyed a good story of persecution.

"What is the book about?" Moriam asked.

"I won't know until I read it," I said.

She didn't read for pleasure and I didn't discuss literature with her.

"As for that Osaro," she said, "I don't understand your friendship with him. He doesn't seem to want to help you find a job."

"We're colleagues, not friends."

That could mean he saw me as a rival, though I couldn't understand why. He had tenure.

"What about Pascal?" Moriam asked.

"What about him?" I asked.

"Isn't he a writer?"

"I haven't read anything he's written."

"Why not?"

"His works are not translated into English."

"How come you didn't ask him about a job?"

"I'd only just met him."

I was still preoccupied with Osaro. No wonder I was the only Nigerian academic he had invited to his dinner. No wonder he was avoiding other Nigerian academics. He was no better than Ismail, whose way of making progress in the business world was to shrug off his minority status. In Osaro's world, being a minority could give him status. The more disadvantaged he could claim he was, the better. The worst part was that his Nigerian colleagues might not expose him. They might say his so-called political exile was his own business. Perhaps a few of them might be driven, out of rivalry, to accuse him of lying, but they would eventually give up. Nigerians were used to corrupt conduct. In fact, we admired corrupt conduct if it went unpunished.

"You should grow a beard," Moriam said.

"Why?"

"It would suit you."

I had no idea why she would say that until I recalled that Pascal had a beard. We were both sexually frustrated. She was studying. Our bedroom wall was too thin. Our children might hear us. Two people spoke French to each other, and for us, it was like watching porn.

Last Word was a work of fiction. The back cover might as well have described it as such. Osaro wrote that he was born in a bush. His father was a palm-wine tapper. His mother sold fish in a market and his entire village raised money for him to go to school in the nearest city. He stayed with his uncle, a mechanic, who starved him and beat him so badly he couldn't attend classes. He escaped his uncle's house and returned to his village, where there was an outbreak of illness caused by oil-polluted water. His father fell sick and died. His sister left their village to work as a prostitute in Lagos. He went in search of her and ended up as a houseboy. An expatriate couple hired him, and because of them, he was finally able to complete his education.

I couldn't call him after I'd read the book. How could we talk about it? Who would believe his story? Anyone who did believe it deserved to be deceived. Perhaps his publishers were even party to his deception. He had all the right elements to be marketed as an African writer in America: good looks, intelligence, charm and a last name that, even for me, was unpronounceable. His American readers would love that. Trying to get his name right would help them to feel they were making a real effort to acquaint themselves with a foreign culture. Editors would feel virtuous for getting his story out.

A review of *Last Word* by a literary magazine said it was "an important story," and another by a newspaper said it was "a powerful story of a young man's quest for education in contemporary Nigeria." The book was what I would call highly competent, but one look at Osaro and any Nigerian could tell he would never put himself in a situation in which he was likely to suffer, let alone endure political persecution.

What I knew about him was this: His father was a senior civil servant in Benin City. The man made the mistake of having more children than he could afford. He still managed to send Osaro to university but couldn't finance his postgraduate education. Osaro ingratiated himself with a rich uncle in Lagos who supported him through graduate school.

I told Moriam what he'd done and she said, "I knew there was something wrong with him."

Bashira wanted to read the book. At first, I said she couldn't because she was too willing to suspend her disbelief.

"Aw, man," she said.

"'Aw, man,' what?" I said.

Her accent was beginning to change and hers was actually better than her brother's.

"Why can't I read it?"

"Because it's too adult for you."

"But it's about a boy."

"It's still too grown-up for you."

"I still wanna read it. Please, Dad..."

I gave in. Bashira loved reading, so much that I would often find bookmarks in the sofa that she'd left overnight. She was discovering American writers now, Louisa May Alcott and others. She said all that her teachers knew about African literature was *Things Fall Apart*. I told her *Things Fall Apart* was probably all they wanted to know.

Every day she gave a new list of complaints about what had happened in school. How so-and-so said she spoke funny and so-and-so said she acted white. She would make me stand in different positions to reenact whatever had happened. She did the same to Moriam and went into great detail describing the school meals she hated, such as beef and bean burritos and sausage on a stick.

She had taught her classmates how to pronounce her full name correctly, which gave us some assurance that she was becoming more assertive.

"Bashira is easy," she said. "We have a Qarverious and a Zanquana. Miss V's name is Villanueva and Mr. P's is Papadakis."

I would ask if she needed help with her homework and she would sometimes say yes, unlike her brother, who was still keeping quiet about his school. He now called Moriam and me

"Mom" and "Dad." Like his mother, he didn't read for pleasure, so whether or not he wanted me to, I often checked his English homework.

As Taslim prepared for his PSATs, Moriam registered for the CGFNS exams and sat them. She said they were so-so. She couldn't say for sure if she would pass or fail, but she'd always lacked confidence about exams, only to end up performing well. I hoped that would be the case. She asked Bisi the Gossip to pray to Saint Jude for her and took offense when I said there was no difference between saying novenas and juju chants. Bisi told her about a website for Nigerian nurses where she could get information about state registration and job applications, after which I couldn't get her off the Internet. From then on, she followed postings on the website's message boards regularly and started using email.

At the exam venue, she'd met up with a few nurses she had known in Nigeria. They had come from Queens, the Bronx, Paramus, Paterson and Edison. Some had left their children in Nigeria; others had expired visitors' visas. They planned to regularize their papers as soon as they got jobs. She'd noticed how Yoruba and Igbo nurses kept to separate groups to discuss the exams. She had always talked about her colleagues and friends, but following her exams, she became intense. This one said this. That one did that. Verbatim. Sometimes I listened and other times I pretended to. On occasions like this, between her accounts and Bashira's reenactments, I was thankful for Taslim's silence.

Women were too damn communicative for their own good. Whenever Bisi the Gossip called Moriam, Bisi spent most of her time talking about Titi, another Yoruba nurse in Philadelphia. Ever since Bisi bought her Mercedes, Titi had apparently been trying to put her down. Titi said the Mercedes was an ostentatious car and she didn't know why every Nigerian aspired to own one, including Nigerians who didn't have two cents to rub together.

After this, Bisi flew her cousin over from Nigeria to look after her children so she could work extra shifts to make more money. She and her husband were planning to buy a bigger house. Titi said it was typical of Nigerians to buy houses that were too big, leaving them overmortgaged. Bisi thought Titi was envious, yet she invited Titi and her family for Thanksgiving dinner.

To me, Titi and Bisi sounded crazy, and Moriam seemed to have a lot of time on her hands to listen to gossip, now that she wasn't studying. She was also watching television more and going to the mall practically every day, coming home with lists of what she would buy when she started work. Through Bisi, she got the phone number of an elderly nurse known as Auntie. Auntie was a sort of godmother of Yoruba nurses in New Jersey. Moriam telephoned her to ask for job tips, and Auntie, in the course of giving Moriam advice, said that white Americans preferred Africans to African Americans because Africans were better educated and worked harder.

We were in the living room when Moriam told me this, and she was tidying up. Behind Auntie's back, she called her "Iya Insurance," a nickname given to Nigerian women of a certain age, who, heaven help you if you made the mistake of running them over.

"She said that?" I asked. "What did you tell her?"

"What was I supposed to tell her?" Moriam said.

She could have told Auntie the United States didn't grant visas to illiterate Nigerians, for a start.

"She'd better not expect anyone to march for her if she ever gets in trouble here," I said.

"Oh, don't start talking about race," Moriam said. "I heard enough about race in your cousin's house."

It occurred to me that talking about race made Moriam feel as if she was being pushed into a defeatist position she was not willing to accept, but I was questioning her allegiance, not her ability to stand up for herself. We had not argued in a long while and I wasn't looking for a fight. In fact, I was hoping for some peace and quiet because Taslim and Bashira had gone to the movies. I knew she had said nothing out of respect for Auntie, but I got angrier thinking about what Auntie had said. I actually wished the woman would get into trouble in America, not life-threatening trouble, but enough to put her on television and scare her into publicly renouncing what she had said.

Stupid old woman, I thought. What she'd exposed was tribalism on a diasporic level. I'd heard Nigerians say the same about West Indians in England, where Nigerians by the dozen applied for unemployment benefits as soon as they could, and where white people, who were so inclined, might express a preference for African Americans over Africans. I was aware that some West Indians in England considered Africans unsophisticated. In other words, our cultures were not as suitable as theirs were for Western consumption. I was sure there were African Americans who would agree with that idea. I'd always been skeptical of African American artists who claimed they found freedom in a city like Paris. They must have chosen to ignore the history of France in Africa. Perhaps they chose not to care about it. After all, what had Mother Africa ever done for them? Perhaps all they were looking for was respite because they had to know there was no freedom, privilege, dignity, nothing whatsoever in being the favored black.

During my master's degree, I read about African leaders like Lumumba, Sankara and Nkrumah. I also read essays on the works of black intellectuals, such as Booker T. Washington, W. E. B. Du Bois and Marcus Garvey. I didn't have time to read their actual works, but the ideological disagreements between Du Bois and Washington didn't surprise me, nor did the bitterness between Du Bois and Garvey. Expecting pan-Africanism to lead to black unity was as unrealistic as expecting federalism to unite Nigerians. Back then, I took the position that black people had no right to talk about racism until we stopped disparaging each other. Now, I was more inclined to imagine how much further ahead we would be if we respected each other and stopped perpetuating stereotypes. Stereotypes we didn't even start.

If there was anywhere in the world that pan-Africanism stood a chance, it would be America, I believed. America was the birthplace of the movement and the African diaspora was well represented. But would we actually come together and work for the benefit of one another? I doubted it. Tribalism and nationalism would get in the way. Money, too, as it always did. Add ego to the mix and we would end up fighting each other.

Moriam's stance on race gave me anxiety, meanwhile. She had to have an opinion on what Auntie had said. She couldn't keep dismissing discussions about race. She often accused me of deceiving myself, but she was the one who deluded herself in that regard, and she could get herself in trouble if she continued to. She wasn't quite the clueless Nigerian who wouldn't know better until a right-wing skinhead throttled her, but she might approach one to ask for directions and assume he was merely being rude if he told her to get the hell out of his sight.

"Why wouldn't white Americans prefer her when she's so eager to be preferred?" I asked.

"You're still talking about this woman?" Moriam said.

"Keep on strutting around like the new wife in the house. When the head of the house gives you the beating of your life, then you'll know who is who."

There was no such proverb. The real one went, "The new wife should be aware the treatment of the old wife awaits her." My analogy may have been off, but African immigrants hadn't had a long history with America. We had not been tested generation after generation. White Americans did not see us as a threat, yet.

Moriam laughed. "What are you talking about?"

"I'm talking about us Africans," I said. "We sold ourselves to every corner of the globe. Now, we're coming here a hundred years later with our tails between our legs, and instead of watching and listening, we behave as if we have it all figured out."

"Lukmon, what are you saying?"

"I'm saying that African Americans understand the system. Make no mistake. So, you'd better pay attention to what they have to say."

"Why are you telling me this?"

"I'm telling you where we stand before anyone confuses you. Divide and rule. That's how Africa was conquered. Remember that. As for Auntie, who is so happy to be preferred, she will see when her grandchildren begin to call themselves African Americans."

It was an insult to be preferred by white Americans. What was their assumption? That we were too stupid to know what was going on, or too cowardly to fight it? Either way, African Americans had to be given credit for accepting us. We were in their country and were sometimes exempt from being black, for whatever reason. If the tables were turned, I would loathe them on sight. The least we could do as Nigerian immigrants was to stand by them. We would probably not even be able to stage a protest in America without their help. Some of us were divided along ethnic lines. Most of us believed that getting ahead was all about making money. We would betray our own for a few more crumbs from the *oyinbo* man's table. How would we begin to organize politically?

"Who told you they need Africans on their side?" Moriam asked. "All the centuries they've been here, who defended them? Us?"

"Forget that. We're here now and this is about black unity."

Moriam walked off. "Please. If we follow your way of thinking, we might as well pack up and go home instead of coming here to take their jobs. You're just being negative. Negative and unfriendly."

"Negative" was a new word she had picked up. What she meant was "analytical." She knew where we stood as Nigerians in America. She was just being difficult as usual.

I didn't come to America to make friends. Fall was too cold to socialize anyway, but through Moriam's regular contact with Bisi the Gossip, I continued to hear news about other Nigerians in healthcare, sometimes encouraging. A pediatric surgeon was part of a team that separated Siamese twins. A nurse was given a national community-health leader award for her work as a breast-cancer screening advocate. The most I could hope for was that my family would belong to that group of Nigerians, not the group that was involved in random acts of violence.

Moriam, in the meantime, had befriended everyone in our block. She saw Howard in the laundry room once in a while and talked to him, even though she still called him *Alakori* behind his back. She was convinced he was an alcoholic. He told her about his shoulder and she, too, advised him to see a doctor, but he complained about an Indian doctor he'd once seen who didn't know what he was doing.

She and Bashira went to Cathy's apartment to see the photographs Cathy's son, Peter, had taken of Ndebele women.

Ndebele women apparently painted the walls of their huts with bright geometric patterns. Cathy was a retired art teacher. She made the clay brooches she wore. She called them pins and sold them at craft markets. Moriam allowed her to recruit Bashira as her assistant. Cathy took to Bashira from the day they went to her apartment. She said Bashira was polite and asked intelligent questions about her pins. I warned Moriam that if the woman harmed our daughter in any way, I would hold her responsible.

She was in and out of Nia's apartment as well. She started braiding Nia's hair because she needed extra money to buy whatever she wanted at the mall. She could have taken a job at the mall, for all the time she spent there. She was still not comfortable with the idea of leaving Taslim and Bashira unattended in our apartment, so she would go to the mall during their school hours. Every month, while I was home, she went to Nia's apartment to braid her hair and sometimes came back to tell me what they'd talked about. Nia was a social worker and gave her tips on what to look out for as parents of teenagers. Drug addiction and pregnancy were foremost on our minds, which didn't mean we didn't trust our children. We were worried about how their new friends would influence them. Nia suggested we should snoop on them if necessary. She seemed to have encountered just about every family problem there was in America: drug and alcohol abuse; physical and sexual abuse; children who were abandoned by their parents and left to the foster-care system because no one would adopt them.

I couldn't believe how much personal information she shared with Moriam in the course of having her hair braided. Her mother owned a beauty shop. Her late father, a musician, had been a long-term patient in a psychiatric hospital. She was still paying off her student loan, which was why she was renting. She had a twin sister called Zuri, meaning "beautiful" in Swahili.

When she was a girl, people had told her she looked African, not as a compliment. She once dated a man who was into African food. She'd eaten jollof rice before. The Togolese braiders she used to go to in East Orange braided her hair too tight. She was tender-headed.

I referred to her as "tender-headed Nia" from then on. She described America as a big old domino waiting to fall over. Moriam asked what she meant by that and she said Americans were not ready to be honest about racism. They argued about that. Moriam said racism was a sign of stupidity. Nia said racism was a sign of moral depravity. Moriam said the only way to handle racism was to disregard it, to which Nia replied that it would behoove Moriam to educate herself about civil rights history. This was another reason why I'd tried to warn her earlier. She'd barely arrived on American soil, and instead of listening to what Nia had to say, she was telling Nia how to live. I knew their friendship was in trouble when Moriam repeated the word "behoove" to me. I didn't know how they managed to remain friends after that, but perhaps they preferred to be direct with each other. They even came clean about the stockfish incident. Moriam confessed she was cooking and Nia admitted she knew as soon as she walked into our apartment. She said the smell reminded her of her grandmother's ham hocks.

Nia was from Atlanta. She planned to go there during the holidays to spend time with her twin sister. She was the elder twin and Moriam, in her usual presumptuous manner, gave her the Yoruba name for the firstborn of twins—Taiwo. Nia's last name was Reed, Howard's was Ostrowski and Cathy's was McFadden. I admired Moriam's ability to get along with all of them, but had no interest in getting to know them myself. I didn't even want them coming to our apartment. Whenever she talked about them, I would say, "Whatever you do, keep them out of here."

One evening Osaro called, long after I'd stopped feeling guilty about not calling him. I wasn't ready to speak to him, but I was glad to hear from him. We might as well put the matter of his book to rest.

"My brother," he said.

I wished he wouldn't call me that, especially as he'd done nothing to help me find a job.

"I read your book," I said.

"What did you think of it?"

"It's different."

I wasn't trying to retaliate; I would have been better prepared to lie had I called him.

He laughed. "That's a different take!"

"Why?" I asked. "What have other people said?"

"If you mean Nigerian academics, they haven't said anything so far, but you know what we're like. We have that crabs-in-the-barrel mentality. I know they'll never support me. I really don't need them to review the book anyway. It's doing fine without their help."

That was the Osaro I knew—hubristic. Now, I wondered if he had sociopathic tendencies. His charade of being in political exile showed he would say anything to get ahead.

"Did you really go through that?" I asked.

"Yes," he said. "If anyone doubts me, they can. The trouble with Nigerians is that we don't want to air our dirty linen. The moment someone opens their mouth, the next step is to shut them up. I won't be silenced. That is what *Last Word* is about. We have to start telling our truths."

I could have taken him on but decided to end his phone call on a good note.

"Well," I said. "Best of luck with your writing."

After that, Moriam would prompt me to call him, to see if he knew of any job openings, and I would tell her, "Forget Osaro." The door had been opened for him and he'd shut it behind him. No other Nigerian would be allowed access. Moriam eventually asked why I was refusing to follow up with him.

"He's too busy hustling," I said.

"Don't you have other friends here?" she asked.

I didn't need friends, I said. Friends were for weak people.

I had plenty of them in our block, owing to her. I occasionally bumped into Nia downstairs and she would talk to me as if we were familiar, which made me wonder what Moriam told her about me. Nia was chirpy all right, and I would describe Cathy as quirky. Howard reminded me of myself, reveling in my displeasure. Whenever we saw each other, which was rarely, we greeted one another and moved on. I respected him for that. At least I knew where I stood with him. Sometimes I found him talking to Cathy on our landing and it was obvious that he was in love with her.

I continued to monitor Bashira's arrangement with Cathy. The only reason I allowed her to go to Cathy's apartment on Sunday afternoons to help with her pins was that Bashira had no friends, and Taslim did. Taslim would go out to meet his friends on the weekends, leaving Bashira at home. I didn't want her to feel left out. She seemed to like Cathy, whom she called Mrs. McFadden. She would come home waving the five dollar notes the woman gave her for her help. The whole arrangement made me uneasy. Why would a woman of that age have time for a teenager? Couldn't she hire a real assistant? I would ask Bashira pointed questions about Cathy's apartment. Were there padlocks on her front door? Did she leave her windows open? Bashira would look at me as if I were losing my mind. I was only trying to determine if there was a risk of her being locked up in Cathy's apartment with no chance of escape.

One day I finally came out with it. "Watch out for Mrs.

McFadden. She might be a child molester."

"What!" Bashira said.

"Ah, Lukmon," Moriam said. "Your mind is warped. You stayed in London too long."

The holiday season was soon upon us and I was reluctant to get involved. Not because I was an agnostic, but because no matter what I believed, crime was on the rise.

What I missed most about Nigeria at that time of the year was the spectacle of drunken people dancing in bars. Even if you didn't participate in the merrymaking, you couldn't help but get caught up. It was the same in America. There was a festive spirit I couldn't ignore. In New York, the bars got fuller and louder; in New Jersey, women wore pumpkin and reindeer sweaters. I didn't know how people survived the holidays with all the advertising that went on, though. There were so many signs along Route 4, reminding people that they had financial obligations, with shiny and glittery decorations that were enough to make a person of meager means panic. My job as a security guard may have biased me, but I decided the holidays were a season for making sacrifices in commercial shrines and shopping was an act of barbarism.

At work, Jill was on the lookout for thieves. She hired a store detective for the holiday period, a middle-aged white woman, who targeted one type of customer—young, black women. This stupid detective would page me after she had surveilled suspects and I would then have to escort them to Jill's office. What pained me most was that the suspects were always guilty. They hid lipsticks, foundations, whatever they could in their handbags and pockets.

Jill must have noticed the detective's pattern of singling out young, black women, but I once overheard her say she didn't see color. She had an evasive way of describing minority customers in general: "That little lady with the lovely eyes" (Asian); "That beautiful woman with the great big smile" (African American); "She was very va-va-voom" (Hispanic).

Her shop assistants would torture her by pretending they didn't know who she was referring to.

Jill was the sort of American who would fall apart if you accused her of racism. To her, being labeled a racist was tantamount to being tarred and feathered. She was always pleasant to me, as she was to everyone else at work, but so long as her store detective continued to profile young, black women, I could trust her no further than the thieves I escorted to her office.

I was learning about the peculiarities of racism in America, and this was what I'd found out by following public discourse:

One. Racism went in one direction only, white to black, which meant I could say anything I wanted about white people and it wouldn't count as racism.

Two. It was very American, quintessentially so, to deny an accusation of racism. If Jill were English, she would simply blink at her accuser and say, "Don't be silly."

Three. By definition, other minorities could be racist, but their racism was downgraded to prejudice because they had no power.

In fact, from what I'd observed, minorities barely tolerated each other. Though, any animosity they had toward one another was nothing compared to the animosity they had toward white people, which made me pity white people for a moment. It wasn't fair that minorities were given a pass. I didn't know what names—from mildly offensive terms to outright slurs—other minorities had for each other, but for Nigerians, African Americans were *Akata*, Hispanics were *Cocoye*, West Indians in England were *Jamo*. In America, they were Caribbean. Asians, for some reason, went unnamed in either country, though I'd once heard a Nigerian in London call Chinese people *Panya* and Indians *Birdie num num*. White people were *Oyinbo*, the Yoruba word for stranger. A cruel trick of language, but the Yoruba word for black was *dudu*, so black people worldwide were *Dudu*, which didn't translate well in America.

I called white Americans "*oyinbo* Americans" and African Americans "*dudu* Americans." I didn't use the word *Akata*. Most Nigerians who did weren't even aware that it meant jackal in Yoruba. Whether it referred to the animal or a person who did menial tasks, it was insulting.

Finally, Americans discussed racism nonstop, most especially the use of the N-word: whether it was used as a slur or a term of endearment; whether it should be used at all; and whether other races could use it.

My question to non-African Americans who wanted to use the word was this: Why did they want to use it so badly? Or as Nigerians would ask, why was the word sweeting their mouths? Couldn't they use some other word that African Americans habitually used? "Crazy" would be a good word. "Crazy" was a word that black people worldwide often used to describe people they couldn't understand.

The palaver about the N-word was distracting. I didn't have to wait for a white person to slur me to determine if they were racist or not. It was easy to tell. Jill? Yes, despite her pleasantness. Howard? Absolutely, even though he was sad and lonely. Cathy? I was keeping an eye on her. Any attempt to patronize my daughter and she would qualify.

I was so prepared for being black in America that I could separate the racist from the person and deal with the unracist part of them. In fact, racism was a given now. Yes, because it was safer for me to assume white people were racist until proven otherwise. It was also reasonable to, because if I were white, it would take a lot of effort not to be racist in America. You passed someone sleeping on a street, what color was he or she likely to be? You watched breaking news about an innocent suspect shot to death by the police, well, you could easily misconstrue that black people were inferior.

As for black-on-black crime, or whatever it was called, I wasn't worried about that. I was coming from a country where practically every crime committed was black on black.

One day at work, the store detective saw an African American man pocketing what she thought was a powder compact. Why the stupid woman imagined a man of his means would steal a powder compact, I didn't know, but she paged me so I had to approach him.

"Yes?" he said, as if he were expecting me.

He wore a tailored suit and tortoiseshell glasses. He was possibly in his forties and his confidence was unnerving. I told him the store detective had seen him take an object from the shelf and slip it in his pocket; therefore I would have to escort him to the manager's office. He did as I told him without protesting. We got to the office and the alleged compact turned out to be his black patent-leather cardholder.

"Good," he said. "Now listen."

He was an attorney and because we had detained him and searched his personal belongings with no just cause, he was going to sue everybody from the CEO down. They would be hearing from him in due course.

"Goddamned African," he said to me, before he left. "You're lucky you didn't mess with me."

"There's no need to speak to him like that, sir!" Jill said, after he'd safely slammed her door. "He was only doing his job!"

She apologized for what he'd said. I wasn't sure what

humiliated me more, his dressing me down in front of her, or her coming to my defense on the assumption that I was there to do her dirty work. She concluded he must have planned the whole incident and his lawsuit wouldn't stand a chance if he had a pattern of filing frivolous legal actions.

That evening, I didn't return a single chin lift on my way to the 42nd Street bus terminal. I didn't even notice them. I came home, threw my jacket off in the bedroom and sat on the bed. Moriam was there. Taslim and Bashira were in the living room. I pressed my hands together as if in prayer. It took me a moment to tell Moriam what had happened.

"How dare he talk to you like that?" she asked.

"He might as well have spat in my face."

"You were not the one who accused him."

"We're not wanted here. We should just go back to Nigeria."

"Come on," Moriam said, turning on me. "After one bad experience?"

"Listen," I said. "I interact with Americans every day. I observe them for a living. There is too much racism here and we don't belong on either side."

"There's tribalism in Nigeria!" Moriam said. "We've even brought it here!"

"It's not the same."

"What is the difference?"

I wasn't in the mood to explain.

"We're not ready for racism," I said. "That is one difference."

Moriam sat next to me on the bed. "Oh, come on. America is not that bad."

"Yes, it is. Yes, it is. If we're not prepared, how can we bring up our children here?"

"They will cope."

"In what way? How?"

"The man was angry. They'd just accused him of stealing. If that had happened to me in Nigeria, I would have destroyed the place."

I clapped. "Are you hearing me? This is bigger than what happened today. How often do you leave this apartment to face the world outside?"

She shook her head. "Your job is affecting you. You can't see any good in people working as a security guard. Find another job."

"Teaching is what I want to do. Any other job would be mindless work."

"So take your mind off what happened. You have to be able to block out incidents like this, you hear me? This country won't change if we leave. We will cope. Every single one of us in this family."

She wasn't listening. My hands were tied in Jill's room. I was prepared for what racist white people could do, not for what black people could do because of what racist white people had done to them. The implications were out of my control. No white person ever called me a Goddamned African. My own cousin was the first person in America to compare Africans to apes. Separate reasons—the first saw me as a traitor, and the second as a painful reminder of his origins. I was yet to experience the frustrations that would give rise to that kind of reaction, but I knew where their need to lash out at the person closest to them came from.

I tried to explain myself to Moriam without sounding analytical. Forget where we were coming from, I said. We were black in America. Black people were supposed to be on our side. What if an African American professor took one look at my CV and thought, African? End of application. What if a Caribbean teacher decided that he or she would not let our children get ahead in school?

I would come home from work and Bashira would tell me her black classmates believed that all Africans were poor. I would tell Bashira the media was at fault. The media was racist. She would tell me they called her a nerd because she studied hard. I would say the educational system was to blame. The educational system was racist. Moriam would ask, "So every institution in America is racist and no one is responsible for their behavior?" The way I saw it, our daughter had to be, and so long as she was aware that racism was the root cause of her problems in school, she wouldn't take her classmates' views to heart. What if she now turned around and said I had no reason to feel humiliated because the retail industry was racist?

"You're too negative," Moriam said. "Stop being negative. This job of yours is allowing your mind to focus on negative things. Once I start working, you won't have to work there anymore."

"What do you mean?"

"You can stay home."

"For what?"

"To look for a job."

"What kind of man does that?"

"They're called stay-at-home dads."

"What would I do when I'm not looking for a job?"

"Well, you keep on asking the children about what they learn in school. You want them to be on par with American students and get into good colleges, don't you?"

"Yes."

"So tutor them while you're at home looking for a job."

"That is out of the question."

She might as well have asked me to get a vasectomy. It would never occur to me to rely on Moriam to be the wage-earner of our family.

"Just bear it in mind," she said. "You don't have to give me an answer right now."

Sometimes ignorance was necessary. "What you don't know," and all that. The more I found out about racism in America, the more anxious I became. Moriam, on the other hand, remained optimistic. She found it overwhelming to define where we stood as Africans in America to prepare for obstacles ahead. Her approach was to focus on our family and deal with the ways in which living in America affected us as they occurred.

I began to give more consideration to what Moriam had said about staying at home to tutor our children when Taslim got his PSAT results. His mathematics scores were fine, but his reading and writing scores were below average.

At work, I'd had enough of Jill and her detective. I'd also had enough of watching customers. I had no health insurance and couldn't afford to fall sick. The only bug that concerned me as the new millennium approached was influenza. I'd heard it could make malaria seem like a mere cold, and the chillier the weather got, the more customers came in sniffing and blowing their noses. Some of them seemed to cough and sneeze around me deliberately, and I came to the conclusion that they derived a sense of community from spreading their germs.

Two weeks before Christmas we had snow flurries in New Jersey and I could have sworn that they were blizzards, the way the winds cut through my coat. Taslim and Bashira's schools closed for the holiday, after which we had our first heavy overnight snowfall. I volunteered to work on Christmas Eve and Christmas Day. Moriam was upset because she wanted me at home. In her family, they celebrated Christmas for the sake of their Christian relatives and she insisted on continuing the tradition. I told her Christmas was just another excuse to eat and she said I was being negative as usual.

We were in the middle of Ramadan. I asked why she would make Christmas lunch when she ought to be fasting. She said because Jesus was recognized as a prophet in the Koran. I said at least Santa Claus appeared every year bearing gifts. Jesus was still nowhere to be found. She said I'd ruined every Christmas for her from the day she met me.

"You don't even know what you're celebrating," I said.

"Thank you," she said. "You don't know how to celebrate, but you know how to eat."

I was in the mood to wind her up again, but there wasn't enough room in our apartment for her to chase me around, so we stood at opposite ends of the sofa, talking over Taslim and Bashira.

"Anyway," I said, "you're in the right country to celebrate Christian holidays."

"Why?" she asked.

She had a lot of latitude to interpret them how she wanted. Christmas could be about Santa Claus, elves and presents, and Easter about a giant bunny or eggs, or chocolate.

"Americans will worship anything," I said. "Including a rat."

"What rat?"

"Mickey."

"You're not serious. Americans don't worship Mickey Mouse."

"They do at Christmas."

She walked away. "Honestly, you behave like a child. The moment someone mentions religion, you must say something."

Our bedroom situation hadn't improved, so perhaps I was back to taking out my sexual frustrations on her.

Before Taslim was born, I finally told Moriam I was agnostic and she cried for days. She said we were both going to hell. I allowed her a week of melodrama. When she realized that nothing would shift me, she said, "All right, I accept you as you are, but never tell my children."

She was a lousy Muslim. A poor example for them to follow. She cherry-picked which Islamic pillars to observe. She prayed every night, in bed, with her eyes shut, like a Christian. Every morning, she said her only *surah* of the day, *Al-Fajr*, the dawn prayer. She never performed ablution. After her shower, she covered her head with a scarf and faced Mecca, if she bothered to get the direction right.

For Thanksgiving, she'd made a roast turkey, though the significance of that holiday was lost on her as well. She had no idea who the Pilgrims were. I didn't know much about them either, but I at least knew they'd existed. I told her she was celebrating genocide. She ordered me to leave the apartment. I worked that day, and when I came home, she was watching the Macy's parade. Mickey Mouse wasn't part of the procession, but the sight of that rodent was beginning to bug me. Thanksgiving itself was subject to interpretation. Was it secular or religious? I still didn't know.

That Thanksgiving, Moriam had given me an update on the rivalry between Bisi the Gossip and Titi. Titi had arrived at Bisi's house for Thanksgiving lunch in a new Range Rover and passed a comment about Range Rovers showing understated elegance, so Bisi vowed to retaliate by buying a Lexus for Christmas.

On Christmas Day, they had me thinking about why I never made friends easily. Throughout secondary school and university I'd had acquaintances, rather than friends. During my PhD, they became fewer and fewer. After I got married, I could count them on one hand. Moriam didn't approve of them. One drank too much and another chased women. I wasn't sure about her gripe with the third. I still saw them regardless, until I got the banking job and gradually stopped hearing from them.

With friends, you had to maintain a balance. You couldn't do better than them and expect to keep your relationships going. In my banking years, I made new acquaintances that Moriam called fair-weather friends because they took it for granted that I would pay for their drinks. I told her fair-weather friends were not the ones to watch out for. The only ones to be wary of were friends who showed up to gloat when times were bad.

Perhaps I was childish, and warped, but I was fascinated by Bisi's and Titi's attempts to upstage each other. I was actually looking forward to hearing the latest news about them when I returned from work on Christmas Day. What was Titi likely to do when she saw Bisi's new Lexus? Break down and start crying over the hood of her Range Rover?

I'd barely opened the front door when Taslim, who was watching television with Bashira, said, "Dad, you'll never guess what happened today."

"What?" I asked, already nervous.

I was expecting to hear our block had been burglarized, as Nia was in Atlanta for the holidays and her apartment was empty.

"Mr. Ostrowski had a heart attack."

"Mom saved him," Bashira said. "She gave him the kiss of life."

"She had no choice," Taslim said. "His heart stopped beating."

Moriam was in the bedroom. She came out and confirmed it was true. Cathy had come to our door to say Howard had collapsed and wasn't breathing. She had already called 911. They hurried to Cathy's apartment, where Howard's cat was meowing. Howard was slumped on a sofa. His eyes were closed. Moriam rested his head on the arm of the sofa. She lifted his chin and put her hand over his nostrils. He may not have survived if she hadn't started CPR on him. He regained consciousness before the ambulance arrived and Cathy went to the hospital with him.

"That man," Moriam said. "I'm sure he drinks heavily. His breath smelled of alcohol. God saved him today."

She truly believed that God had saved Howard. I believed science had. Sometimes, when she was asleep, I watched how the hairs on her skin stood up, or how she breathed. Observing how the human body worked gave me enough evidence to believe in science, but the very thought that Moriam had saved Howard humbled me to her.

I took a shower and changed out of my work clothes. Cathy rang our bell about an hour later. Taslim and Bashira were on the Internet and Moriam answered the door.

"He's fine, he's fine," Cathy said before Moriam could ask.

She wasn't as traumatized as I thought she would be and had a smile I'd seen on the faces of women who had endured a lot of grief. Today she wasn't wearing a pin. She sat on the sofa with Moriam.

"Poor Howie," she said. "Who would have thought he'd end up in a hospital on Christmas Day?"

"Are they taking good care of him?" Moriam asked.

"Oh, yes," Cathy said. "His daughter Lisa's there now. Thank you, Marion, for what you did."

"It's okay," Moriam said.

"Where do you work?"

"I haven't started work yet."

"Well, wherever you end up working, I hope they realize what a great nurse you are. I'm sorry I was such a mess earlier. I'm no good with these things. John was in and out of the hospital. He died in a hospital. So did Peter. Peter's was sudden, though."

I knew Peter was her son, so I assumed John was her late husband.

"Do you have family in New Jersey?" Moriam asked.

"No," Cathy said. "My sister Rosemary's in Florida. She wants me to come down. I will, once I've sold the house. I'm lucky. The apartment downstairs belonged to Peter so I don't have to worry about where to stay. My niece Dana thinks I should sell it and the house, but I'm not ready to. Her husband Brian keeps telling Rosemary and me that we should be smarter about money, but we come from a long line of gamblers and bankrupts. Without John, I would've probably been a bag lady."

She talked with some pride about her hapless Irish family, cousins, aunts and uncles included. Someone's bakery business folded. Someone else lost a ton of money in Las Vegas. Another got divorced three times and his alimony payments were hard on him. I didn't know how Moriam could keep up. I thought Nigerian family stories required some effort to follow. Cathy's were impossible.

She finally smiled at me. "I hope I'm not ruining your Christmas."

"I don't celebrate Christmas," I said.

"You don't?"

"No, but my family does."

"Do you celebrate Christmas in your country?"

"We celebrate anything we can," I said.

New Year's Day was the biggest celebration, funds permitting.

"It must be hard to move to another country," Cathy said to Moriam. "I couldn't do that. You hear about people trying to survive from day to day in other countries and here I am going on about a house I'm not ready to sell."

Moriam responded with a compassionate expression she reserved for her patients.

"You're not looking for a house or anything, are you?" Cathy asked.

"Not yet," Moriam said.

"When will you start looking?"

"When I start work."

"Would you be interested in renting a house until then?"

"Maybe," Moriam said.

"Would you be interested in renting mine?"

Moriam didn't hesitate. "Are the schools in the area good?"

"Oh, yes. I taught at the high school there. The schools are very good."

"Is your rent high?" Moriam asked.

"I haven't found anyone to rent it since I moved out. It's a three-bedroom house, but not in the best shape."

Moriam sat up. "I would like to see it, please."

"Maybe we can work something out between us," Cathy said. "My realtor has been of no use."

I had even more admiration for Moriam after that. Not only was she good at making friends, she was good at making friendships work for her. Watching her and Cathy talk was like coming to the ending of a film in which a magic Negro and a white savior were united.

Howard was not "Poor Howie" for long. Moriam and I saw him a few days later. Cathy drove us to the hospital. He had been discharged from the ICU and was on a ward for acute patients, hooked up to a heart monitor and IV drip. He lay in bed, in a hospital gown, and held Moriam's hand as if he were about to marry her.

"You and I are special friends now," he said, patting her knuckles.

Moriam smiled. She had experienced undue affection from patients before, usually after she had birthed them.

"We don't want to tire you," Cathy said. "Marion just wanted to check on you."

"I'll be fine," he said. "Thank you for the flowers."

They were carnations, and not even fresh. Moriam had bought them from Pathmark.

"Try and rest," she said to him.

"All I do is rest," he said. "I need to get up."

"No, you don't," Cathy said.

"Why is she here?" Howard asked Moriam.

"When's Lisa coming?" Cathy asked.

Howard turned to Moriam. "She wants me to stay with my daughter until I get better. My daughter hasn't spoken to me in years. Would you stay with her?"

"I would," Moriam said.

"Her boyfriend's no good. He wants her tubes tied. You're a nurse. You know what that means. She says to me that she wouldn't want to bring a child into this world after what I put her through, like I'm the bad guy. We're speaking now. I'm not bitter. I can let bygones be..." He ran out of breath.

"Okay, that's it," Cathy said. "We're leaving."

Moriam and I said goodbye to him and he managed to wave.

"I'll see you soon," he said. "Maybe sooner if Lisa decides she's had enough of me."

"Marion will be gone by then," Cathy said.

He frowned. "Are you going back to South Africa?"

"Marion's moving out of the apartment," Cathy said. "She is moving into my house. Remember I've been trying to rent it out? Well, Marion and her family are my new tenants."

Howard seemed agitated but too weak to do anything about it. He breathed steadily until his energy returned. I was expecting another retort from him.

"You keep calling her Marion," he said. "Her name is Maryanne."

DAUGHTERS

Howard was discharged from the hospital in the New Year. I hoped for his sake that he was receiving respite care from his daughter, instead of insults—*Alakori*. Someone saved his life and he still couldn't get her name or country of origin right.

Tender-headed Nia came back from Atlanta before the New Year and was shocked to hear we were leaving. She sat on the sofa in our living room and raised her hands heavenward.

"How can you go?" she asked. "Who will I talk to from now on?"

I suspected she was more upset about having to find her way back to the Togolese braiders in East Orange. Moriam asked for their address because Bashira wanted to get her hair braided with extensions.

Cathy's house was in Essex County, near the Oranges. It snowed heavily in that part of New Jersey on the morning we moved in. She kept apologizing for the state of the house, which was unexpectedly spacious and furnished. I wasn't surprised her realtor had had trouble finding tenants. Her house was too expensive to rent. She offered it to us for less than her realtor had advertised it. The house had a family room, living room, dining room and a kitchen with a breakfast table. It also had three bedrooms, two full bathrooms and a guest toilet. Moriam felt we were shortchanging Cathy, but I didn't feel guilty about that. Clearly, the woman was no good with money, but her late husband had made sure she was well taken care of. He was a tax accountant and it was easy to guess which room he had claimed. The living room had sofas in neutral colors and whitish walls. The rest of the house was painted in primary colors, the family room in bright green.

The houses in the neighborhood were sanctimoniously uniform. I'd seen grander houses in Nigeria, but never in a place as clean and quiet. The roads were lined with trees, now skeletal in the winter. The stop signs and speed bumps were covered in snow. There were no neighbors in sight. Driving down the street in the removals van we'd rented, I sensed they were watching us. We were the only black family around. In fact, I was the only black man that walked in the neighborhood until we bought ourselves a Toyota Corolla. The nearest bus stop was a fifteen-minute walk away. On my way there, whenever our neighbors drove past in their SUVs and minivans, they smiled and waved. Their children were honest enough to stare. One little boy in a red anorak slipped on the ice while staring at me. He was with his mother, who was picking up their dog's feces in the snow, as the dog trotted ahead. His mother rescued him and dusted him down, even though he didn't have that much snow on him. She may have been using the opportunity to find out what direction I was heading.

In that part of New Jersey, the homes ranged from two-garage houses to mansions. There was a park and mountain reserve. I found a bus route to a park 'n' ride where I could get a bus to 42nd Street and Moriam found the nearest malls. The less expensive one was in Livingston and the other was in Short Hills. The schools in the district were less crowded and had better facilities than those our children had attended. Bashira's new school had so many computers I wondered if there had been rampant fraud in her previous one. Perhaps the fraud was at the district level, because our local library was cleaner and warmer than the library in our former neighborhood. I went there every week to borrow books to read on my bus rides to New York. My commute was longer now, and any job I applied for would require some knowledge of literatures ethnic and postcolonial, so I had a lot of catching up to do.

I was beginning to see why being a stay-at-home dad was worthwhile. Looking for full-time employment was itself a job, and having perused more copies of the Modern Language Association job list and job ads in the *Chronicle of Higher Education*, I now realized how specialized the field of African literature was in America. Networking would be the best way to find a teaching position. There was an African Literature Association conference coming up in Illinois and I had enough money to travel there and back by Greyhound bus.

Moriam passed her CGFNS exams. The National Council Licensure Examination was next on her agenda. If she passed that, she would be able to work as a registered nurse in New Jersey. After the CGFNS, I was sure she would pass the NCLEX, but to find a job, she would need a driver's license, so I gave her lessons in the Corolla. She found driving in that part of New Jersey easier because there was less traffic. She wasn't quite ready for the turnpike, but she practiced by taking Taslim and Bashira to school and picking them up. As usual, we were concerned about how they were settling in. Taslim had been reluctant to change schools because he would miss his friends. In fact, he made new friends fairly quickly. He also began to play basketball, though not that well. Football, or "soccer" as it was called in America, was his favorite sport and he was looking forward to playing in the summer.

Bashira had been surprised to learn that American girls played soccer. She had never been interested in sport. Unlike

Taslim, she was eager to change schools, but as soon as she started the semester, she was back to complaining about school menus, this time the chicken cacciatore, sloppy joes and macho nachos.

"What about friends?" I asked.

"They have cliques," she said.

"What kind of cliques?"

"Cool-girl cliques."

"Are they like bubblers?"

"Daddy, please don't use slang."

Bubblers were the popular girls in her school back home. Some of them were quite nasty. I told her not to worry about the ones in her new school. They were not exactly tough. One loud "boo" and they would probably run off and hide in their parents' SUVs.

Not only was she lonely, she was embarrassed about being lonely. I was sympathetic but I had to play that down to encourage her to socialize. In the mornings, she was sluggish when it was time to get up for school. After school, she fell asleep in the family room. At night she had bursts of energy, when she would dance to her CDs. She was a Lauryn Hill fan and played *The Miseducation of Lauryn Hill* over and over. She had no in-between moods. Yet she was at that middle stage in her life, not quite a child or a young adult.

On the day we found out that Moriam passed the NCLEX, she asked, "Does this mean we can move out of here?"

"No," Moriam said. "No more moving for us."

"What, so we're staying here forever?"

"Until you get into high school."

"Or until Mrs. McFadden comes to her senses," I said.

I was relieved about Moriam's results and was going to get the car tires pumped that day. Taslim was waiting for me.

"You mean we're never ever moving again?" Bashira asked.

"You can't keep leaving one school after another," Moriam said.

"I've only left one!"

"One is enough, my dear."

Bashira threw herself on the sofa as Moriam pleaded with uncharacteristic patience.

"You have to go to school," she said. "That is your job. Your only job for now. Come on, now. Daddy will be at home with you."

"And you'd better do as I say," I said.

Bashira eyed me. I only hoped she had the audacity to face up to her classmates in the same way.

That month, February, was Black History Month, which seemed more like a meager concession in a grossly unfair divorce settlement. Later in the week Bashira and I worked on a project about Harriet Tubman. She'd wanted to do one on Madam Tinubu, whom she had learned was a great Nigerian patriot, until I pointed out that Madam Tinubu was a slave trader.

"I don't think that will go down well with your class," I said.

"Why is she called a great nationalist in Nigeria?" she asked.

"Because she resisted the British."

I'd learned that when I was a boy. I didn't find out her reason for doing so until secondary school. The British she'd resisted were abolitionists.

She frowned. "That's messed up. But if you think about it, at least my children will be able to say, 'My mother came to America by plane.'"

"And," I said, "of her free will."

Really, the poor girl had had no choice in the matter, but her mother and I were not refugees. We didn't have to flee Nigeria because of a war or political persecution. We came to

America to work. We were not descendants of Africans who were forced to come over and work. We'd never had to live with the consequences of that.

Without me, our children would probably know nothing about the history of the slave trade in Nigeria because they'd never learned about it in school. They had very little idea about the history of race or racism in America either, and their mother's indifference wasn't helping matters, so it was my duty to teach them about that as well. I told Bashira that being black didn't make us African American, anymore than it would make us Hausa, Kenyan or West Indian. We had to honor our separate histories and cultures.

The question of how she should identify herself in school came up. Her classmates sometimes called her African and she'd heard me correct that.

"Would you call yourself African in Nigeria?" I asked.

"No."

"So."

"But what am I here?"

"What passport do you have?"

"A Nigerian one."

"Therefore you're Nigerian until you get an American one."

"But there's no box for Nigerian here. There's no box for Nigerian American either."

That got me thinking. I'd seen combined boxes during my job search—African American or black; African American or African. She would have to choose the "African American" box in school. Alternatively, if there was an "Other" box, she could choose that instead. What box did Caribbean American students choose? I wondered. Their ancestors, too, originated from Africa, and if African Americans were so called because they didn't know which countries in Africa their ancestors came from, Nigeria itself wasn't a country until the British decided to make it one.

"Tick the 'Other' box," I said.

"They say 'check' here, not 'tick.'"

"Check the 'Other' box, then."

"Didn't you say all human beings come from Africa?"

"Homo sapiens do."

"So every American is originally from Africa."

"Well, technically, but don't say that in school if you want to make friends."

Moriam passed her driving test and got a job at a hospital about a mile from where we lived. She started an orientation program, during which she worked eight-hour shifts from Monday to Friday. I stopped working the week before her program started and took over most of her chores at home. Taslim and Bashira began to ride their school buses, but I shuttled them to and from their after-school activities, and on weekends dropped them at the movies and wherever else they wanted to go. I also drove Moriam to work and back. A second car would have been ideal, but we couldn't afford one yet. Our fixed deposit had gone toward the Corolla and we had real debts and a credit history now.

I was relieved that we would soon be eligible for health insurance. Moriam had tended Taslim and Bashira whenever they'd had minor ailments, a cold here, a stomachache there. She would buy the necessary medications and complain about their prices, yet she wouldn't consider store brands. If a commercial for a certain drug appeared on television, she would say, "You see what we're paying for?"

I just hoped no one in our family would fall seriously ill or have an emergency that would require hospitalization. Everywhere I looked in New Jersey there was a hospital, so I wondered why there wasn't a healthcare system that covered everyone in the state. Moriam said that going by what she'd heard from other nurses at the hospital, the majority of Americans would rather die than have one.

In some ways, I was better suited to staying at home. For a start, I didn't need to be in an overly tidy environment. When Moriam was at home, she shouted at Taslim and Bashira from morning till night about the state of the family room. She would order them to clean up and each time would finish the job herself. I would tell them to clean up once. That was it. I only helped them with their homework and extracurricular activities. I made sure Taslim did community service and joined school organizations to build up his college portfolio. I supervised Bashira's science project and coached her for a spelling bee. Moriam would have found that too demanding.

She continued to cook because she didn't trust me in the kitchen. We ate rice and stew almost every day now, with or without fried plantains. I went to the African food store on 42nd Street when she was in the mood to make more elaborate Nigerian meals. I even bought stockfish because, living in a house, she could cook it without fear of scaring our neighbors.

Oddly enough, Bashira began to lose weight that winter. At first we thought it was because she was wearing oversized sweaters; then, we noticed her jeans were hanging off her. I assumed she was not eating well in school. She still complained about the cafeteria meals. Moriam suggested she take snacks—sandwiches, potato chips, apples, anything to fill her up—but she wouldn't.

One Saturday, Moriam passed Bashira in the hallway and asked, "Are you on a diet?"

They'd just come back from East Orange, where the Togolese women had braided Bashira's hair with extensions.

"No," Bashira said.

Moriam hitched up one side of Bashira's jeans by a belt loop. "What is this, then?"

Bashira cried out, "Ow!"

"How did that hurt?" Moriam asked.

Bashira rubbed her lower back. "You like...scratched me."

The hallway that led to the bedrooms was the most intimate section of the house. In the family room, we had the television to distract us. In the kitchen, we often ate in silence, and all Taslim needed to do was swallow loudly to get on Bashira's nerves. We didn't use the dining room or living room. In the hallway, we actually had to look at each other face-to-face.

Bashira flipped her braids over her shoulder. She was picking up new habits from her classmates. She flung her extensions this way and that and tucked them behind her ears. Almost every word was prefaced with "like." She was like really tired or like really bored. She also said "wool" instead of "well," asking, "Wool, how was I supposed to know?" for instance.

Taslim hobbled out of his bedroom with his T-shirt inside out. Earlier that week, he'd sprained his ankle in school while playing basketball, so he was off practice for a while.

"Why is everyone yelling?" he asked.

"You and who is yelling?" Moriam said.

"We're always yelling in this house," he said.

"We're Nigerian," Moriam said. "We yell."

He raised his forefinger. "Yes, but do we communicate with each other?"

"Shut up over there," Moriam said.

"Hey, can I go watch a movie, Mom?" he asked.

"No."

"Why not?"

"I beg you, don't disturb me."

"Please," he said, pressing his palms together.

Moriam sighed. "Okay, what movie is it this time?"

"I don't know yet."

"Don't tell me. Another one about killing people and blowing up buildings."

"I said I don't know."

"Will you take your sister?"

Taslim glanced at Bashira. "Who, misery guts?"

Bashira was still rubbing her back where she claimed Moriam had scratched her.

"Who are you calling misery guts?" Moriam said.

"Dad, can I go watch a movie?" Taslim asked.

"Go *and* watch," I said.

Moriam pointed at him. "Don't you ever call my daughter misery guts again."

He limped on as Bashira continued to rub her back.

Moriam didn't comment on Bashira's weight for a while, and I wouldn't have, until the following Sunday when we were having dinner in the kitchen. Moriam had made a pot of chicken stew and we were eating it with rice. We had all served ourselves except Bashira, who said she wasn't hungry.

"Why not?" I asked.

"I had cookies," she said.

"Who is Cookies?" I asked in Yoruba.

She rolled her eyes. "Okay, Dad."

Apart from Bashira's occasional rudeness, Moriam and I were sometimes "Mom" and "Dad" to her.

"Cookies can't fill up a normal person," I said.

"But this is all we ever eat," she said, gesturing at her plate. "There's no variety in this house."

"I've suffered," Moriam said, shaking her head.

Now that Moriam worked, she made beef stew and chicken

stew every Sunday. That was it for variety. Once a month, she went to a farmers market in Paterson to buy the meat.

"But there's none," Bashira said. "Not anymore."

"You want variety?" Moriam said. "Go to the kitchen and make some."

"Or whip up something, as Americans do," I said.

Taslim laughed. "She can't cook!"

"Can you?" Bashira asked.

"Whip, whip!" he said.

"Enough," I said.

Bashira folded her arms. She was wearing a T-shirt, and for someone who didn't exercise, her arms appeared taut.

"Are you sure you're not on a diet?" I asked.

"She's on something," Taslim said.

"Stop it," Moriam said.

Bashira eyed him. "I. Am. Not. On a diet."

"Yes. You. Are," he said.

"Shut up," Bashira said.

"No 'Shut up' in this house," Moriam said. "We say, 'Please be quiet.'"

She'd made that rule and often broke it.

"Hey," Taslim said. "Why is it that Nigerian parents never say 'I love you'?"

"Why would we say that?" Moriam asked.

"American parents say 'I love you.'"

Moriam turned to me. "With all their 'I love you, I love you,' the minute their kids can't have their way, what do they get in return? 'I hate you.'"

I could have asked when she'd ever heard an American kid say that, but I knew the answer: on television.

"Are you a baby?" she asked Taslim. "Do you have to keep hearing 'I *yove* you, I *yove* you' over and over?"

He smiled. "Seriously, I've been thinking about it. It's one of life's major mysteries."

When no one else bothered to respond, he dabbed the corner of his lips daintily. If he didn't know by now, his mother and I were raised by typical Nigerian parents. We hailed one another to show affection, "my child," "my husband," "my wife," and underneath all the shouting there was love.

"Retard," Bashira whispered.

"Who is a retard?" Moriam asked.

Bashira pointed at Taslim. "Wool, he said I was on a diet!"

"Are you on a diet?" Moriam asked.

"Wool, he said I was!"

"Why is it bothering you if you're not on a diet?"

"You people," I said. "Okay, there is variety, you're not on a diet and you are not a retard. Now let us eat in peace."

Bashira dragged her chair back. "It wasn't such a big deal when he called me misery guts!"

"Is a misery guts in the same category as a retard?" Moriam asked.

"Whip, whip!" Taslim said.

Moriam raised her fork. "Shut—"

Bashira stood up. "It's no use."

"What is no use?" I asked.

"Wool, whatever I do she takes his side!"

"Who is 'she'?" Moriam asked. "You're calling your mother 'she'?"

Bashira tossed her braids back. She was about to cry, and if she did, I, too, would lose my temper. What was she crying for?

"I'm not on a diet!" she said. "I don't know why everyone keeps accusing me of being on one!"

She marched out of the kitchen as if we'd accused her of taking drugs.

"What is wrong with her?" I asked Moriam. "Should I go after her?"

"Leave her alone," Moriam said. "It's because she's in America she forgets whom she is talking to. It's all this 'Mom, Mom,' business. If she were calling me 'Mama' today, would she dare open her mouth to call me 'she'?"

"Disgraceful," Taslim said, shaking his head.

"And you," I said in Yoruba. "Stop calling me 'Dad.' No one should call me 'Dad' from now on, you hear me? I am 'Daddy' to you."

"Okay, Daddy."

"In fact, I'm 'Baba' to you. Yes, because back home that is what you would be calling me as you prostrate yourself before me."

Taslim bowed. "Yes, Baba."

"Can you imagine?" Moriam said. "Telling me there is no variety?"

"Calling you 'she,'" I said.

Moriam and I became Mama and Baba when we'd had enough of our children. Now that I was at home, I realized how much they imitated television characters. I'd assumed they imitated their classmates, but the programs they watched were changing their mannerisms as well. Commercials were the worst influence. Mothers danced while doing housework. Fathers were dumb. Children were clumsy. They spilled milk and orange juice everywhere. It was enough to question if there was a conspiracy in the advertising industry to misrepresent the American family. I'd considered limiting Taslim and Bashira's television time, but they were used to Moriam's rules, and Moriam enforced no rules when it came to television. In our house, she was the one who fell asleep with the remote in her hand. We now had cable television, which, I had to admit, was great for sports. I was an

Arsenal fan and would have liked to follow the English football leagues, but they were not covered regularly and we would have to pay extra to watch the channel they were on.

That evening, Bashira remained on my mind. Could I have been more patient with her? Had I been too quick to get irritated? Growing up with sisters who could be just as temperamental had not prepared me for raising a daughter. My sisters didn't challenge my father until their late teens, when they wanted to go to parties. My father didn't let them out of the house at night. I was allowed once in a while and the most my sisters would say to my father about it was, "That's unfair," and he would look at them as if he had no obligation to explain himself.

Later, in our bedroom, I asked Moriam, "Do you think we were too hard on her?"

"No," she said.

She wore a Victoria's Secret nightgown. Her taste was changing. She'd gained weight from eating at the hospital cafeteria, but had always been confident about her figure. Bashira was not as self-assured.

"Could she have anorexia?" I asked.

"Ano-what?"

"Rexia. You know, when people don't want to eat."

"Have you ever heard of a Nigerian with anorexia?"

"Can't there be one in the whole country?"

"Which anorexia patient did I ever talk about in all my years of working there?"

None, I had to admit. The women she'd talked about were pregnant women with high blood pressure. They could never understand why they were gaining too much weight. Yet whenever Moriam asked what they'd had for breakfast alone, they gave long lists: "*Akara, ogi, moin-moin, puff-puff...*"

"She's here," I said. "She's not there."

The television programs she watched seemed to show one skinny airhead after another, but she was never overweight. She was what I might call plump. Or, at least, she used to be.

"She's just being stubborn," Moriam said. "She thinks she can get away with it because we let her. She has to adjust to the food in school, whether she likes it or not."

"Her grades are slipping."

"Are they?"

"They're not as consistent as they used to be. She says she can't understand the math here and the spelling is different."

"She is an intelligent girl. She's not trying hard enough."

She really wasn't. I sometimes wondered if she was rebelling against having to stay in her school.

"What about Taslim?" Moriam asked.

"He's doing better, at least in math. He prefers the American way of teaching. Bashira wants to stick to the old way."

"She's like you," Moriam said. "Too rigid in her thinking."

I preferred the British way of teaching because students knew what to expect. The British weren't as big on projects as Americans were. Projects could give a student like Bashira anxiety.

"I wonder why she's losing weight," I said.

Moriam shrugged. "She's just being fussy. If we'd forced her to eat, she would have."

Bashira was meant to be a daddy's girl. My sisters often called her that, only to annoy Moriam. She was actually more of a mummy's girl.

When she was a baby, she had a habit of scratching her mother's neck for comfort. As soon as Moriam held her, she would reach out. She needed my approval more than she needed her mother's, though, even back then. If, for instance, she tried to poke her finger into an electrical socket and Moriam ordered, "Don't do that," she would stop for a moment and try again. All I needed to say was "No," and no matter how softly I spoke, Bashira would cry. Sometimes, after I tickled her, I would whisper the word "no" in her ear, just to get a reaction. Her switch from laughter to tears was hilarious.

When she was a toddler, I made her repeat words like "pivotal" and "tantamount" for my amusement. Yoruba words were funnier: *farabale*, *patapata*. Medical words were the best. "Say 'folliculitis,'" I would tell her. "Say 'encephalitis.'" She always got them right.

She came to me for laughs and went to Moriam whenever she needed attention. She loved the anthem Moriam made up for her, which didn't make sense in English or Yoruba: "Bashira, why are your cheeks so fat? Oh, why? Because when you grow up, you will be rich. Of course, you will be. You will be rich and then you will become Chief Justice of Nigeria. Chief Justice Bashira. I greet you."

Bashira would dance and clap to that.

Her clashes with her mother began when she turned thirteen. I believed they were hormonal, because they were otherwise inexplicable. There were days I wished I could disappear until she passed through puberty. Actually, I wished they would both disappear because they were both as crazy as each other.

The next evening, Moriam called Nia for advice. Perhaps she thought Nia wouldn't judge her as a Nigerian would. I just hoped Nia would have a more sensible solution than forcing Bashira to eat. We were in our bedroom and Nia was on speakerphone.

"It's been a while," Nia said.

"My sister," Moriam said. "You know how it is."

Nia told Moriam the new tenant in Apartment C played his music too loud, after which Moriam told her about Bashira.

"Do you think she might have an eating disorder?" Nia asked.

I was thankful. A Nigerian friend might have suggested Bashira had a tapeworm.

"She doesn't eat as much as she used to," Moriam said. "To me, that is not an eating disorder."

"I don't mean to be funny or anything," Nia said, "but have you thought about the fact that in less than a year, she's moved from an all-girls school in Nigeria to a co-ed school here, and now she's in a predominantly white school?"

"Of course," Moriam said, though I was sure she hadn't given it a serious thought.

"Don't you think that's kind of hard on her?" Nia asked.

"Adjusting to a new country is not the end of the world."

"Moriam."

"You just have to do it! I did!"

"Okay, okay, let's stick to the issue at hand. What about counseling?"

"She doesn't need counseling, Nia."

"Are you kidding me?"

"She's a normal child."

"Moriam, I'm not saying she's not normal. I'm not even saying she has an eating disorder, but come on, now."

Moriam glanced at me. "We don't do that in Nigeria."

"Well, you're here now," Nia said. "Listen, getting counseling is nothing to be ashamed of. The teenage years can be hard on a girl. When I was about Bashira's age, my sister and I used to take part in beauty pageants and she would always win. She was naturally skinny. I didn't starve myself, throw up, or any of that, but I would exercise my weight off. You know what I mean? I was good at track. I trained like mad and won medals. Winning sports medals was my thing. Then Zuri got on the cheerleading squad and it just ate me up. It's stupid now, but it was difficult for me, that's all I'm saying. I see it all the time. Teenage girls here have major image issues. It's all that pressure to conform to the blond and blue-eyed ideal—which, by the way, even white girls can't live up to."

That was a revelation. I'd heard that the female students I'd had in Nigeria, who wore long weaves and bleached their skin, were trying to look like African Americans.

"So you think counseling will help," Moriam said.

"Yes," Nia said. "If she's losing weight, that's no good. Something's got to be done."

"She might not want to go for counseling, though."

"Take her to a doctor for a regular checkup."

I nodded. That was a good idea.

"Okay," Moriam said.

"By the way, how did she get on with the hair braiders?" Nia asked.

"She likes her braids, but she says they talked about her."

"Does she speak their language?"

"No."

"So how would she know they were talking about her?"

"She could tell from their expressions."

Nia laughed. "I thought it was just me. I'm telling you, Moriam, those women work my nerves. They are so rude."

After their phone call, I looked up anorexia on the Internet and printed out a checklist of symptoms. Moriam said any normal teenager could have one or two of them and Bashira wasn't showing any of the clinical signs. In any case, we would have to wait until we were covered by health insurance to take her to a doctor.

She couldn't have been that sure of herself because the next morning after breakfast, she tried to manipulate Bashira into talking about weight loss.

"Do you think I'm fat?" she asked.

"Why would I think you're fat?" Bashira asked.

"I want to go on a diet," she said.

Bashira snorted. "What for?"

"To be thin, you know, like a model."

"Mom, when have you ever wanted to look like a model?"

"It's the trend."

Bashira snorted again. "'It's the trend.'"

"What? Don't your classmates count calories?"

Bashira shrugged. "I don't know."

"So should I go on a diet?"

"Mom, if you go on a diet, I will know the whole world has turned upside down."

Any idiot could have decoded Moriam, so I continued to monitor Bashira. She certainly wasn't exercising her weight off. After she finished her homework, she lay on the sofa and watched MTV. She wasn't just becoming thinner; she was also becoming ruder—not in obvious ways. She knew she couldn't get away with blatant rudeness, so she might turn away as I spoke to her or widen her eyes while answering a question. She was critical. Sometimes when she was at home on the weekends and watching television alone, I sat with her and made statements about characters like, "She looks as if she likes mashed potatoes," to make her laugh, or "I can see his epiglottis," so she wouldn't feel embarrassed about a kissing scene. She would tell me to stop acting weird.

She criticized Moriam as well. When Moriam said she wouldn't be able to attend her parent–teacher conference because she was working, Bashira asked, "So what's new?" Then came the day when she accused Moriam of controlling her because Moriam asked what she'd eaten for lunch. Moriam yelled at her that day, "Will you clear out of here?"

After Bashira had left the family room, Moriam turned to me and said, "What is wrong with that child? Who does she think she's talking to?"

I told her Bashira was just being a teenager and to ignore her.

"Is this how you allow her to talk to you?" she asked.

I said I wasn't involved. The matter was between them.

"Warn your daughter," she said, raising her forefinger. "Warn her well. Otherwise she will see a side of me she won't like."

I'd seen that side and wasn't enamored with it.

She got so fed up with Bashira's rudeness she actually went on her Nigerian nurses' website to find out if there were any threads on how to discipline Nigerian children in America. She found one in which the moderator had asked: "Does Beating Work?" And someone had anonymously posted: "It helps."

My reasoning was this: If Bashira could be that rude to her mother, knowing how angry her mother could get, whatever she was going through had to be bad.

Their arguments over hair were their most volatile. Like Moriam, Bashira had thick hair that apparently grew too slowly. Moriam had been grooming Bashira's since she was a toddler, yet it barely reached her shoulders. I didn't know how long Moriam had been growing hers, but it was about the same length.

When we were dating, I assumed her hair was long until she yanked off her fake ponytail. Now, I wouldn't know if Bashira's hair was braided with extensions or not, if Moriam didn't tell me. She said extensions could be made from real hair. I said it wasn't possible to have that much real hair available for sale. The demand from black women alone would leave the rest of the world bald. She said the hair came from India and Brazil, and Brazilian hair was more expensive. I wanted to know where used extensions ended up. There had to be mountains of them.

If I could find them and figure out a way to recycle them, we would be rich.

I couldn't believe how much time and money Moriam and Bashira spent on their hair. Moriam had gone back to relaxing hers after she got her job, so in her free time, she drove to the nearest black hair salon to get it washed and styled. She spent hours there, most of them waiting. She came home and complained about the lack of professionalism at the salon. The stylists had attitudes, she said. I assumed their attitudes were black on black.

Was I the only man who felt sorry for women because of their hair ordeals? I wondered. I was actually proud of my wife because of what she'd managed to accomplish despite the time she spent on hers. She had probably spent as much time as she would take to qualify as a cardiothoracic surgeon. If she and Bashira came home without a hair on their heads, I would be happy. There would be one less argument in the house.

The next week, Bashira lost a hair extension in school. The girl didn't even notice. Someone found it, picked it up and pinned it to the notice board. She was too embarrassed to claim it. She came home to tell me it was the Togolese braiders' fault. They didn't braid her hair well. She then told Moriam she wanted to have it braided all over again.

"What for?" Moriam asked.

"My extensions are falling out," Bashira said.

"Who asked you to get your hair braided with extensions?"

The shouting began.

"Mom, I told you real hair lasts longer!"

"Not if you keep touching and shaking your hair! Stop touching and shaking it! That's what happens when you go around doing that! Your extensions fall out!"

Bashira walked off in tears. "Wool, they wouldn't if I'd used real hair!"

"Look at this child," Moriam said to me. "I've just come home from work. I'm tired. I drove her all the way to those Togolese women to get her hair braided in my free time. Her hair cost fifty dollars. Fifty whole dollars and she wanted me to buy real hair extensions of...of almost twenty dollars. Hair that is meant to last two months, and she can't even wait a month to get it redone because her extensions are falling out."

I said I would take Bashira back to the Togolese women to have her hair redone.

"You're a man," she said. "This is not your concern."

I said if she wouldn't take Bashira to the Togolese braiders, I would, to have peace and quiet.

"Please," she said, raising her hand, "don't spoil my daughter. You're not going to marry her. If you can't stay home and raise her properly, then I will."

She capitulated. I never once raised the issue with her again, but the woman gave in and allowed Bashira to have her hair braided with real hair extensions. She even allowed her to have micro-braids, or whatever they were called, for over a hundred dollars. Perhaps she felt guilty about shouting at Bashira, who sulked for days after that.

I took Bashira to the Togolese braiders in East Orange on Saturday morning. Moriam was working and I'd dropped her off earlier. We got there and I could swear the building was begging for an immigration raid. There was a blue sign on the door saying, "Fatima Hair Braid." The "'s" was missing. I pushed the door. It creaked open—actually, it didn't creak. American doors did. This door cried out as if it were being dislocated from its hinges and gave up halfway. We walked in and the red carpet inside was so badly stained it was the color of mud.

How could a building in the United States of America resemble a hut somewhere in Africa because the tenants happened to be African? I wondered. I glanced at Bashira and she shrugged.

We were home. Three Togolese women sat side by side in the main room. One of them was eating fried chicken. It was nine o'clock in the morning. She didn't even look up. There was a mirror in front of her and she couldn't be bothered to raise her head. Of the other two women, one covered her head with a scarf. I guessed she was a devout Muslim. She was in the presence of a man who wasn't her husband, so she adjusted her scarf accordingly, for the sake of modesty. Never mind that I wasn't in the slightest bit attracted to her. The second woman stared at me, her skin so bleached she was turning green at the temples.

"Good morning," I said.

Not even a *bonjour*. Moriam had said they spoke their language, French and limited English. They could at least have learned how to say "Good morning" by now. I was standing there with my daughter, whom they ought to recognize, and two of them were looking at me as if they were in danger of being pillaged.

Nia was wrong. They were not rude. They were downright disrespectful.

I deposited—yes, deposited—Bashira with them and drove to my barber. I hadn't yet found a barber near our house. Mine was an African American man about my age. He wasn't trying to keep up with trends. He left my hairline unshaped, as I preferred it.

I drove back to East Orange with a Whopper Value Meal, no onions, no cheese, from Burger King. Bashira hadn't even requested one. She preferred Burger King to McDonald's. Taslim was the Big Mac eater and he ordered them without stipulations. I got to the hair braiders', expecting to find Bashira's hair almost done. Two of the women were attending to her, the devout one and the bleached one. They'd barely finished one tenth of her hair.

"What's going on?" I asked in alarm.

"They're micros, Dad," Bashira said.

"So?"

"Micros take a long time," the devout one answered in perfect English and smiled for the very first time.

I could just imagine her taking prayer breaks. I gave Bashira the Whopper meal and asked her to call me when her hair was done; then I drove home to eat lunch. Taslim was out with his friends. I was reading Richard Wright's *Native Son* now. Before I got back to it, I called Moriam at the hospital to tell her about my ordeal with the Togolese women.

"Micros can take all day," she said.

I'd been betrayed. She knew, Bashira knew and so did the women. Why hadn't anyone warned me beforehand?

I'd almost finished reading *Native Son* when Bashira called to say, "Hey, Dad, I'm done."

No manners. I drove back to East Orange to pick her up. I had to admit her hair looked okay. She'd had it pulled up in what I thought was a bond. "It's called a bun," she said. I was just grateful her hair was in one place and secure so she wouldn't shake it. I thanked the women and paid the devout one, who mumbled, "*Merci*."

We'd barely stepped out of that dungeon when Bashira asked, "Dad, please can we stop at Burger King for fries?"

"Yes, Bashira, we can stop at Burger King for fries," I said.

"And a Mello Yello?"

"And a Mello Yello, Bashira."

"What's wrong?"

"Nothing."

"Thank you, Dad. I'm so hungry."

I patted her shoulder. At least she was eating and her manners were back.

Simple manners my children had once had, they had lost: saying "Good morning"; stepping aside for their elders; apologizing, whether or not it was necessary; showing some humility. They barely managed to say "please" and "thank you" these days. Moriam and I were at an impasse on the subject of manners. She thought Nigerians were overly polite because they had enough time on their hands. In America, life moved at a faster pace, she said; therefore, Americans had less time to be polite. She took it a step further by suggesting Americans might mistake humility for lack of confidence. I actually thought it was the other way around, but I gave up arguing with her.

She was still worried about Bashira's weight, which was why she had given in to Bashira's excessive hair demands. I told her how our day had ended and she said she'd made an appointment for Bashira to see a doctor.

"You'd better tell her yourself," I said, "because I'm not going to."

Moriam smiled. "Now you see why I shout."

"I swear," I said, "if she ever mentions those Togolese women to me again..."

"Oh-ho. You're beginning to know your daughter."

We told Bashira about her doctor's appointment in the family room that evening, while Taslim was taking a shower after a basketball game.

"Why am I seeing a doctor?" she asked.

"For a general checkup," Moriam said.

"Is Taslim having one, too?"

Moriam hesitated. "He will have one after you."

Bashira seemed convinced and was about to leave the room, when she stopped.

"Is this because of my weight?"

"Why would it be because of your weight?" Moriam said.

"I'm just asking."

"Are you talking back?" Moriam asked.

"No."

"I hope not," Moriam said.

Bashira turned to me. "This is because of my weight, isn't it?"

"So what if it is because of your weight?" I asked.

"Then just say it is. Just be honest about it."

I shook my head. That was the problem with being too lenient with children.

"You're going to see the doctor," I said. "End of matter."

"Great," she said. "Now, I'll have someone touching me without my permission."

Moriam raised her voice. "Will you..." and stopped herself from saying "shut up."

"It's my body," Bashira yelled.

"Listen," Moriam said. "I don't want to hear *peem* from you. You hear me? This is the last time I'm warning you."

"But it is my body," Bashira said, lowering her voice. "You can't just tell me what to do with it. That's like...child abuse."

Moriam slapped her chest. "Me? *Emi*? Lukmon."

"Go to your room," I said.

Even Bashira looked surprised, but she did as I'd said.

"You see?" Moriam said. "This is why she is getting out of hand. 'Go to your room.' What will 'Go to your room' do? If she were in Nigeria, would you tell her to go to her room?"

I said Bashira didn't have a room of her own to go to in Nigeria and Moriam turned on me.

"I asked you to discipline our children," she said, "as a father should, and you wouldn't. I warned you that they would start misbehaving and you didn't listen. Now your daughter is insulting me and you're saying 'Go to your room.' Tell her to be careful. Tell her to be very careful. Otherwise, she will see what will happen to her in this house if she ever talks to me like that again."

She, too, left the room. That was another problem. We had too much space. When we didn't have enough space, no one could go anywhere to be on their own.

On the day Moriam's orientation program ended, I picked her up from work as usual. We were on our way home when she said our family was now covered by her health-insurance plan, but we couldn't bring up anorexia when we took Bashira to the doctor.

"Why not?" I asked.

"Because it will affect her premium when she applies for health insurance later in life."

"Um, should that concern us this very minute?"

Moriam was territorial about health-related issues, so I had to be careful. She said Bashira didn't have anorexia. She, too, had lost weight in her teens. I was the one who had brought up anorexia in the first place. Anorexia was more complex than an obsession with skinniness. Being an academic didn't make me a medical expert.

I let that pass, knowing her orientation program had been challenging.

"Why are we taking her to a doctor, then?" I asked.

"To rule out the possibility of any other medical conditions."

"What if it's anorexia?"

"Will you stop mentioning that word?"

"I'm just saying."

"No. I've warned you, Lukmon. You're not a doctor. If you go and bring up anorexia and it ends up in my daughter's health record, I will direct her straight to you when she can't get health insurance in the future."

I said fine.

A week later we took Bashira to the doctor. Before we left, this girl, who had been watching television, suddenly decided she had to finish her homework the moment I said it was time to go. I told her to get herself ready in five minutes and meet me in the car. She pouted so much, her mouth reached the car before she did.

We then picked her mother up from work. There were mounds of dirty snow in the hospital parking lot and it was still very cold. Moriam was in her scrubs and a winter coat. She asked why Bashira wasn't wearing one. Bashira said it was because I'd made her get dressed in five minutes. She was in a sweater and jeans. Moriam said she would catch a cold. Bashira said she was warm enough. They went back and forth in the car.

We got to the doctor's clinic and I stayed in the reception area and waited for them. The doctor examined Bashira, after which she called me into her consulting room to join them. Her last name was Decker. She had freckles and wore her reading glasses on the tip of her nose. I sat down and she pronounced Bashira a normal, healthy teenager, pending the result of a full blood count. Then she asked, "What country in West Africa are you from?"

Here we go, I thought. You went to work and someone would ask where you were from. You went to the laundry room and someone would ask where you were from. You were in your own bloody apartment and someone would knock on your door and ask where you were from. Even at the doctor's.

"Ouaga-damn-dougou, Burkina frigging Faso," I wanted to say.

"Nigeria," Moriam said.

"I was thinking maybe Kenya," Dr. Decker said.

"Kenya is in East Africa," Moriam said.

Dr. Decker smiled. "I was no good at geography. I hear there's a shortage of doctors and nurses in Africa. I've always wanted to go there."

She looked at me as if she expected me to congratulate her.

"You should," Moriam said.

"It's hard to find time," Dr. Decker said. "But in medical school, I had this dream to work with African children. I suppose you dreamed of coming here to work."

"Not when I was a student," Moriam said.

"Would you mind if I ask a question?"

"No," Moriam said.

"It's of a medical nature, and I don't know if it's appropriate in front of your family."

Moriam nodded. "They're used to me talking about medical matters."

"It's about female circumcision," Dr. Decker said.

I minded her question. I minded the fact that she was no longer talking about Bashira and blamed Moriam for not bringing up anorexia.

"We call it female genital mutilation over here," Dr. Decker said. "Do people practice it in your country?"

"Yes," Moriam said.

"Did you ever come across a case?" she asked.

Moriam said she'd seen several. That was the first I'd heard of that.

"Clitoridectomy?" Dr. Decker asked.

"A few."

"Infibulation?"

"No."

"Fistulas?"

"Not from infibulation, from obstructed labor."

I was Moriam in the midst of liberal arts academics, except I wasn't smiling.

"How widespread is the practice?" Dr. Decker persisted.

"It depends on where you are," Moriam said.

Dr. Decker shook her head. "Why do they do this to girls?"

"I don't know," Moriam said.

She minded Dr. Decker's questions, as well. I could tell. She'd once told me about a retired nurse in Nigeria who formed an NGO to eradicate female genital mutilation. The nurse contacted foreign organizations for funds. Soon, she was renting an expensive office and driving a new car. Other nurses got envious and started looking around for their own female medical causes to champion: breast cancer, ovarian cancer, anything that paid better than nursing.

On our way back home, Moriam went on and on about Dr. Decker.

"Why did she ask me about female genital mutilation? Why didn't she ask about high infant and maternal mortality rates?"

I was no longer interested in what the woman had said. I was thinking about Bashira. The moment she stopped being a patient and turned into a cultural study, the woman's curiosity became dangerous.

"Talking to me about female genital mutilation," Moriam continued. "My daughter is sitting there and she's opening her mouth to talk to *me* about female genital mutilation. How am I supposed to know why they practice it? Am I the one who mutilated anyone's genitals? Honestly, sometimes, I think these *oyinbos* are sick. It's as if they enjoy talking about African women's genitals."

"What is female genital mutilation?" Bashira asked.

She seemed relieved she was no longer the focus of attention.

Moriam ignored her. "Telling me there is a shortage of nurses in Africa. Does she come from New Jersey? Why is she not working in her hometown, wherever she is from?"

"You're an African woman," I said. "Therefore, you're honorable and oppressed."

"So because I'm honorable I shouldn't leave my country to find work? And who is oppressed? You should see them in the cafeteria. They can't even eat without abusing themselves. 'I'm so fat! I'm so disgusting! I'm such a pig!'"

She must have been referring to white women because I couldn't imagine black women saying that. Dr. Decker had looked underweight to me. Perhaps Moriam should have asked what she knew about eating disorders. Criticizing American women for verbally abusing themselves after eating wasn't helping our daughter, either.

We got home and I suggested that we take Bashira to another doctor if we weren't pleased with Dr. Decker.

"No," Moriam said. "No more doctors for my child, before someone starts asking more stupid questions."

We were in the family room, which had become a place of contention.

"Obviously, she wasn't the right doctor for us," I said. "And Bashira will have to see another doctor someday."

"It's enough!" Moriam said. "The girl is well! There is nothing wrong with her!"

"I didn't say there was!"

Why did she say that with Bashira standing there?

"Dad," Bashira said. "I don't want to see another doctor."

"Are you prepared to see Dr. Decker again?" I asked.

She waved her hands. "I didn't want to see her at all! I don't need to see anymore doctors! Why can't you just...let it go?"

"You see?" Moriam said. "Now look at what you've caused."

She walked out of the room and I vowed to myself that I would never again interfere if Bashira was rude to her.

"Go to your room," I said to Bashira.

I didn't know what else to say. She obeyed, but moments later I heard her bedroom door slam—in a house we didn't own. I went straight there and yanked that door open.

"You do not," I said, "under any circumstances, slam any door in this house."

Bashira's shoulders were hunched, as if she were scared I would hit her. My expression must have been that grim.

"Now," I said. "I don't know what is going on, but I will not leave this room until you tell me. You understand me? I will stand here and you're not allowed to move an inch until you tell me what is wrong with you."

She spoke through her teeth. "I. Don't. Want anyone. Touching me without my permission."

She was about to cry. I lowered my voice.

"No one will do that to you, but you must tell me why you're not eating well."

She wiped her tears with the back of her hand. "I hate the food in school!"

"You refused to eat snacks."

"I don't want to eat snacks!"

"You don't eat your mother's cooking, either."

"She cooks the same stews over and over!"

"She is busy."

"I don't have to eat if I don't want to!"

"You do," I said. "In fact, you must eat well to stay healthy. I will buy whatever you want, so Mummy can cook your favorite food, *eba* and *efo*..."

"Stop!"

She hated *eba* and *efo*.

"What else don't you like about school?" I asked. "And you had better give me more than 'They have cliques.'"

"They're gross."

"Who is gross?"

"The girls in my school. They do gross things at lunchtime."

"Like what?"

"They suck on bananas."

An image came to my mind. Bashira was obviously enjoying my discomfort.

"You see?" she said. "I told them it wasn't funny and they started calling me a loser."

"Who called you a loser?"

I would go to her school and sort them out, their parents included. What kind of children had they raised?

Bashira guessed what was going through my mind. "No! You can't do that! It will only make things worse! It's just a small group of them and everyone keeps away from them!"

"Are they white?"

"I don't care if they're white!"

They were white, the monkeys. I remembered being called Herbie. I remembered how Gani was called an isosceles triangle. One bully could ruin an entire childhood.

"You have to learn to ignore them."

"Taslim, too, said I should."

"He knows about this?" He was in trouble with me.

She sat on her bed. "He said they were the losers. Please, don't tell Mom. She'll only go and see the principal. It will be so embarrassing. The last time someone did that, they like brought a bullying expert to school and nothing changed. They still called the boy 'Big Boobs.' Then he had to go on Prozac and be home-schooled."

I sat next to her. "Would you like to be home-schooled?"

"I'll never have friends, then."

"Mrs. McFadden was—is your friend."

"She was old."

She shut her eyes and began to cry again. I could have cried myself. My daughter had inherited my inability to make friends.

"I'm sorry, but I have to speak to your principal, Bashira."

Her eyes opened. "Dad! You can't! If you do that, I'll never tell you anything again. I mean it."

"These are small girls we're talking about."

"I'm the one who has to go to school with them, not you."

"Okay. Okay."

I had not always given her the freedom I gave Taslim to fight for himself. I didn't even give her the dignity of suffering her own problems. If she was being bullied at school, then I was going to report the girls involved, whether or not she wanted me to.

All I said to Moriam that night was that we should work together to build up Bashira's confidence. She was too tired to argue and fell asleep shortly afterward. I couldn't for a while.

The next morning, after I dropped Moriam at work, I called Bashira's principal, Mr. Carey. I'd met him before and he called me "Mr. Cream" and Bashira "Bazra."

"Yes, of course, Mr. Cream," he said. "What can I do for you?"

I told him about Bashira, using the right words: "bullying," "safe environment," "long-term consequences" and "self-esteem."

"Mr. Cream," he said, "we take bullying very seriously, and if a student is being bullied, we do our best to make the environment safe enough to encourage him or her to speak up. I commend you for doing that despite Bazra's reluctance.

You're right that we wouldn't want it to affect her self-esteem. What I would recommend is one, meeting with you and her to ascertain what happened."

He'd said the words "bullied" and "bullying" with such a smug tone.

"She doesn't want a meeting."

"I understand. This will be a preliminary meeting only, nothing more, and we will hold whatever she tells us in the strictest confidence."

The man seemed to be reading a script.

"She didn't want her mother or me to know."

"I understand, Mr. Cream. Quite often this is the case, but as I have said, we have ways of assuring students in these situations that speaking up is for the best."

"What about supervising the students at lunchtime? If they are simulating sexual acts in the cafeteria, that isn't right."

I could tell he was nodding. "Yes, yes, we have to take things one step at a time. The first step is to speak to Bazra and establish exactly what happened. Then and only then, will we approach the students in question to hear their side of the story."

"I don't think that will help, Mr. Carey."

"I understand, and I know Bazra might feel the same way, but unless she is willing to speak up about the bullying, I'm afraid there is very little we can do."

During the week, I kept my promise to buy ingredients for Bashira's favorite Nigerian meal, pounded yam and okra stew. Moriam made the stew with stockfish. She'd seen a posting on the message board of her nursing website warning that stockfish was carcinogenic, but that didn't stop her. She also taught me how to make jollof rice, so Bashira could take some to school in Tupperware.

Like me, neither of our children knew how to cook because Moriam had always been in full control of that task in the kitchen. Taslim couldn't believe it when he found me preparing jollof rice there.

"Um," he said, "is everything okay?"

"Pass me the water," I said.

The less time Moriam spent in the kitchen when she was meant to be resting, the better. She was working over forty hours a week now.

I poured extra water from a mug into the pot, as she had instructed, and added salt and a bay leaf.

Jollof rice was actually easy to prepare. Bashira thought mine was sticky, but she ate it anyway. Taslim thought it was fine.

"At least you won't be hungry in school anymore," he said.

"What if they say it smells funny?" Bashira asked.

"Tell them they smell funny," he said.

I slapped hands with him. "My son!"

In Bashira's previous school, some of her black classmates believed that Africans had body odor because of the food we ate, and my take on the matter was that anyone who didn't use deodorant in a hot climate was bound to.

Taslim hadn't told me what was happening to Bashira in the new school because he would have handled the girls himself. I'd explained that she wasn't able to, so he had to let me know if she had anymore problems with them. I also asked him to try and go to the movies with her once in a while and he promised to.

On Friday, they went to see a movie together, but he fell asleep halfway through because it wasn't his usual action-packed blockbuster. The next day, I took Bashira shopping to buy clothes in her new size. I got anxious as we walked into the mall. What was it about malls that spooked me? I wondered.

Was it the mannequins in the store windows, or the instrumental music, or my reluctance to spend money?

Bashira was careful about checking price tags, but I told her not to worry. As she browsed, I realized there was very little a girl her age could wear without looking too grown-up.

"It's as if you're either a girl or a woman," I said in our final shop.

"Mom says I'm fussy," she said.

We were in a store for young women and, to my mind, the clothes were provocative. The assistants were ringing up purchases, showing customers to changing rooms and hanging clothes back on racks. Bashira took an interest in jeans that were torn at the knees. There was no point trying to give my opinion. A few mothers in the store looked as resigned as I was.

I soon noticed an assistant nearby was occasionally glancing at Bashira, who didn't realize she was being monitored. She took her time and tilted her head to one side. It just bothered me that she could be shopping on her own, without me to protect her, and someone would make an assumption about her and end up humiliating her.

"Excuse me," I finally said to the assistant.

"Yes?" she said.

"Why are you watching my daughter?" I asked.

She tucked her chin in. "I wasn't—"

"Stop watching her, please," I said. "She's not doing anything wrong."

Bashira walked over with the jeans. "Dad, can I have these?"

"No."

"Why not?"

"I don't like them."

The assistant turned to Bashira. "You could try—"

"She wasn't talking to you," I said.

The assistant's face turned red. "Um, I don't appreciate you speaking to me like that."

She actually sounded tearful. I expected Bashira to be embarrassed, but in an equally shaky voice, she rounded on the assistant, as if she alone was allowed to be rude to me.

"Hey," she said. "Don't speak to my father like that."

Now, I was embarrassed as everyone stared at us. I tapped Bashira's shoulder and she dropped the jeans as we walked out of the store.

Outside I asked her, "Are you okay?"

"Yes," she said. "Their clothes weren't nice anyway."

She brushed off the incident. She said it was no more annoying than encounters we'd had at McDonald's or Burger King. Sometimes employees assumed that because you were black and they were black, they could get away with being rude. I wasn't particularly worried about that.

She didn't think the shop assistant was racist. She said the woman had acted funny. I asked what she meant by that and she said, "Snobby."

I wasn't worried about that either because her mother was the snobbiest shopper I knew. Whenever Moriam was mistaken for a shop assistant, she abruptly answered, "I don't work here." One day, she made the same mistake, asking a white woman nearby, "Do you have this in size eight, please?" The woman apparently stared at her in shock. Bashira, who was there, said, "Mom, I don't think she works here." Moriam said in Yoruba, "She looks as if she does."

Bashira and I headed for the entrance we had come in through. I thought we were leaving the mall, but we passed Victoria's Secret and she wanted me to go in with her.

"I can't," I said.

"Please! I need to buy new underwear!"

"They'll think I'm a pervert."

"How will I pay?"

"Choose what you want, take it to the counter and call me when you're ready."

"Someone might think I'm stealing again! Please, Dad!"

She pulled my arm. I refused to budge.

"What are you buying there?"

"Bras."

"For God's sake."

She covered her nose. "Whoa."

"'Whoa' what?"

"You said 'God.' Do you believe in God?"

"Only when I'm shopping."

I almost prayed she would change her mind, but she didn't. We went to Victoria's Secret and I bought her the bras. I told the assistant at the checkout she was my daughter and that one looked at me as if to say, "Who cares?"

After that, I left shopping to Moriam. I continued to cook, though, and on my second attempt to make jollof rice, burned the rice and somehow managed to melt the plastic handle of the spoon. Bashira was in the kitchen with me that day and I was the dumb dad in commercials.

"What do you enjoy doing?" I asked her. "Talk to me."

"I don't know," she said.

She was capable of asserting herself against anyone in our family only when we opposed her. If we gave her free rein, she refused to accept it.

"You seem to enjoy listening to music and dancing," I said.

She snorted. "Yes, Dad, I enjoy 'listening to music and dancing.'"

She was too cynical. At her age, I would have been impressed if a girl had said that to me.

"You must enjoy doing something," I said. "What do you like doing most?"

Reading, she said. I hadn't expected that. These days she watched television more.

"You should read more, then," I said.

I was used to giving her comfort and advice, but listening to her opinions would take more practice. We had an interest in books in common, so I decided we should start a book club, since going to the movies or shopping with her was out of the question.

On my next visit to the library, I took her with me. I recommended we read Salinger's *The Catcher in the Rye* and Capote's *Breakfast at Tiffany's* because they were on display for young adult readers at the front of the library. But the librarian suggested she might also want to consider novels by women of color on another display. I let Bashira decide and she went for the women of color. I told the librarian we would come back for the novels by men of no color soon and that one took offense.

"Actually," she said, judgment stiffening her neck, "Salinger and Capote were quite colorful characters. You should read about them sometime."

I said I would, sure that she eyed me until I was out of sight.

Bashira talked about characters in the novels we borrowed as if they were her classmates: Celie, Lucy, Pecola Breedlove and Selina Boyce. This one was cool. That one got on her nerves. I read the novels after her. Alice Walker had my attention from page one, even though she protested about the evils of men until the final page. Toni Morrison pulled me in from her prologue. I'd read *Song of Solomon* and *Beloved*, so I was prepared for her water-spirit ways. Morrison lured you deeper by playing hard to get, but you had to give her your full attention. If you were not a mindful reader, she would swim on and leave you to drown.

Osaro invited me to his reading at an independent bookstore in New Jersey. I really wasn't interested in seeing him again, but Bashira wanted to go, even though she knew his memoir was made up. She had never been to a reading before.

We arrived there, and apart from Osaro, there wasn't a Nigerian in sight. The rest of the audience, about ten of them, looked as if they would show up for any author. There was a trio of young women in the front row and an elderly couple next to them. We sat behind a middle-aged woman with thinning hair and a skinny guy with a serious expression. He had a sci-fi novel in his hand. I guessed the woman was his mother, and a mystery-novel reader. She had a copy of Alexander McCall Smith's *The No. 1 Ladies' Detective Agency*.

They may not have been Osaro's intended audience, but he was ready for them with a smile. The bookstore owner followed him, carrying his bottled water. He beckoned at me to come over as she put the bottle down and arranged hardback copies of *Last Word* on a table. Ever the African writer, Osaro wore an *ankara* tunic and trousers, despite the cold weather. He was amused by my wool sweater and corduroys.

"I see you're well settled in suburbia," he said.

I could have reminded him that he was similarly dressed when he last visited me in New Jersey, without an American audience to impress.

"Who is this young lady?" he asked.

"Bashira," she said.

She curtsied as she shook hands with him. What was it about writers? You saw them in a bookstore and they had an air of importance. You saw them elsewhere and they looked like nerds.

"It's practically empty in here," Osaro said.

"It's cold outside," I said.

He smiled. "Only a reading would bring me to this neck of the woods at this time of the year."

He might never give up on mocking New Jersey, so I didn't encourage him. Bashira and I returned to our seats and she tiptoed as if she were humbled to have been singled out for recognition.

After much ceremony involving the bottled water, the bookstore owner introduced Osaro to the audience, citing his biography. I crossed my arms as she mentioned his political exile, noting how the mystery-novel woman sat up and her sci-fi son gaped as if any serious thought he'd previously held had just been trivialized.

Osaro thanked everyone for coming and began to read. He started with an excerpt from the section where he found out his village had raised enough money for him to attend school in the city. He then read an excerpt from the section where his uncle, the mechanic, gave him his first flogging, his voice catching at the end. I glanced at Bashira, who nudged me as if I ought to show sympathy. Osaro cleared his throat and appeared to pull himself together while the rest of the audience leaned forward to listen more closely. Finally, he read an excerpt from the section where the expatriate couple hired him as a houseboy and promised to educate him. The audience clapped. One of the trio in the front row blew her nose. Another raised her hand when the store manager invited questions.

"Do you miss your family back home?" she asked.

Osaro nodded. "Very much."

The mystery-novel woman raised her hand. "How the heck do you forgive someone like that?"

"You just do," Osaro said, with a benevolent expression.

"What would happen if you went back to Nigeria today?" a man with a wool cap asked. "Would the government come after you?"

Osaro shook his head. "No. We have a democratically elected government now. Decree 4, the decree under which enemies of the state could be arrested by State Security agents and detained indefinitely, can no longer be upheld in a court of law."

"How long ago did you come here?" the man asked.

"A few years now," Osaro said. "I was lucky to escape. But, you know, the fear of government never leaves you. When I first arrived, I was afraid I wouldn't be granted political asylum. It took me a while to get over that. Now, every time I get an official-looking document..."

He paused for effect and the audience laughed. I wondered about his immigration status. If he was in America on political asylum, shouldn't he be sent back to Nigeria now that we had a democracy?

"Me and my husband have the same reaction to official-looking documents," the mystery-novel woman said.

"Why?" Osaro asked.

"He's a small-business owner. It's tax season."

"Tax season can have that effect on you," Osaro said.

He was spectacular. He'd won them over with his story, which assured them their lives were better than his. The man in the wool cap regarded him as if he were a war hero. The elderly couple looked as if they were ready to adopt him. I wasn't sure if the mystery-novel woman wanted to mother him or sleep with him.

Would it ever occur to her that if Osaro were indeed a political exile, the last person he would want to discuss his immigration status with was a New Jersey housewife who thought tax season was comparable? I didn't know, but her son asked Osaro which African writers he would recommend and he reeled off a list of names: Achebe, of course, Soyinka, Ngugi and others. All men.

"What about Alexander McCall Smith?" the woman asked, raising *The No. 1 Ladies' Detective Agency*.

"Well," Osaro said, "I wouldn't call him an African writer."

She lowered the book. "Why not?"

"Let's put it this way. His work is not, uh, shaped by the concerns that African writers have, and his approach to writing about Africa is what I would describe as paternalistic. Mind you, he can't help that, being white, middle-class and male."

The trio in front laughed.

"But he writes from the point of view of an African woman," the woman said.

She sounded angry, as if Osaro had betrayed her. He must have noticed her change in tone because he started going on about how tricky it was to determine if a work of fiction was authentic when it was set in a foreign country.

"We just have to be careful, you know," he said. "We have to be careful about how we interpret what we read. Then there's the question of whether a writer like Alexander McCall Smith should be allowed to write from an African woman's point of view."

"I think he should be allowed to write whatever he wants," she said.

"Yes, but is he capable?" Osaro asked. "Even I would have a hard time writing from the point of view of an African woman."

He was truly spectacular. He never once criticized *The No. 1 Ladies' Detective Agency* but talked about how commercially successful it was and how difficult it was for African women writers to get published, though he had not mentioned any.

He held everyone's attention, including Bashira's. At the end of the question-and-answer session, she made me buy her a copy of *Last Word* so he could sign it. I bought her a copy of *The No. 1 Ladies' Detective Agency* as well, hoping he would notice, but she asked me to hold the offending book before joining the line to get her copy of *Last Word* autographed.

It took her a while to reach Osaro because the trio stayed to pester him with more questions about his terrible life in Nigeria. I asked the store manager if she could recommend other white, middle-class male writers besides Alexander McCall Smith. She suggested Raymond Carver, John Updike, Richard Ford, Rick Moody and David Foster Wallace.

I bought their short-story collections and later read them on my own because I felt they were too grown-up for Bashira. Living in the suburbs, I could understand their preoccupations with drug abuse, alcoholism, extramarital affairs and divorces, but no self-respecting African writer could get away with focusing on issues like that. They would at least have to address a dictatorship or a civil war, especially if they wanted attention from Americans. I actually enjoyed their stories. To me, they were strange and exotic. I didn't quite pity their protagonists, but they made me more grateful for my relatively ordinary suburban life.

She tricked me, Bashira. She took advantage of my absentmindedness. She knew I paid attention when we talked about books and not about hair.

Her micro-braids lasted three months. I drove her to the Togolese women early one Saturday morning to have her extensions taken out. She was there for almost five hours as two of the women worked on her. She called me when they were done. I went straight there and brought her back home with tangled hair. Moriam had already made an appointment for her to go to another salon. This one was more professional than the last, she'd said. They would not make Bashira wait long. All the arrangements were in place. I didn't have to worry. I didn't even have to think. The hairstylist would take care of Bashira's hair and I would never have to go back to the Togolese women again.

The final part was all that mattered to me. Those women were out of my life. I hoped Bashira had carried on listening to her mother, because I stopped paying attention after I heard that. I was in awe that she could keep up in school with all the instructions Moriam gave her over hair.

We were reading novels by men of no color now. The librarian and I had made peace. I'd learned something from Osaro about how to deal with white people. You didn't challenge them until you'd charmed them with a sob story. I told her the American canon was new to me and there were only a handful of public libraries in Lagos, which were not well stocked. It was true, and as far as I was willing to go, but she loved me after that. She asked if Nigerians studied the British canon. I said yes, but while I was a student in England, I'd read books by writers like Kundera and Marquez, whose works she described as existentialism and magical realism, and writers like Naipaul and Coetzee, whom she said fell under commonwealth literature. She suggested I read Hemingway and Fitzgerald, as well as Salinger and Capote. So, apart from *The Catcher in the Rye* and *Breakfast at Tiffany's*, I also borrowed *The Snows of Kilimanjaro and Other Stories* and, on a whim, chose *Lolita* instead of *The Great Gatsby*, which I'd read before. *Lolita* wasn't strictly part of the American canon, she said. It was written in America but first published in France, so technically it was world literature.

The woman couldn't help but classify books. I read *The Snows of Kilimanjaro and Other Stories* first and found Hemingway's tendency to under-write overrated, perhaps because, as an African in America, I constantly had to explain myself. I appreciated his sincerity, though. The man went to Africa to kill animals. He didn't care what the colonials were doing there and all he wanted to hear from Africans was "Yes Bwana."

I didn't give Bashira his book because I would have had to explain every story to her. I didn't let her read *Lolita* either because, as far as I was concerned, Humbert Humbert was a child molester. We read *The Catcher in the Rye* and *Breakfast at Tiffany's* and I told her Holden Caulfield was a juvenile delinquent and Holly Golightly was a loose woman. She accused me of controlling what books she read and how she interpreted them. I didn't deny that.

That Saturday, my plan was to drop her at the hair salon, return *Lolita* and the other books to the library and pick up another novel. We were in the kitchen and about to leave when she asked what novel we should read next.

"*The Great Gatsby*," I said.

"Why?"

"It's a Nigerian story."

"How?"

"Someone appears on the social scene with a lot of money and everyone in society sucks up to him, even though no one is sure where he is coming from, or if his money is legitimate."

She'd made an attempt to pull her hair back, but the effect was what I would describe as puffy.

"Are we ready to go?" I asked.

"Yeah," she said, casually. "But I want to try something different with my hair."

"How?"

"I don't know. I just want to try something different."

"What did your mother say about that?"

"She wants me to get a texturizer."

"What does that mean?"

"Dad, don't worry about it. Mom said I should get a texturizer and a press and curl afterward. Please don't ask what a press and curl is. I just want to try something different with my hair, that's all."

"Do whatever you want," I said. "All I need to know is when I should pick you up."

I dropped her at the salon and collected *The Great Gatsby* on my way home. She called about three hours later and I drove back to the salon to pick her up. I noticed her hair was no longer puffy but didn't comment.

Moriam came home from work while Bashira and I were in the family room. Bashira was lying on the sofa and watching television. Taslim was in his bedroom, surfing the Internet or whatever he did there. I was reading *The Great Gatsby* and considering Nick Carraway's assertion that reserving judgments was a matter of infinite hope.

"My wife," I said, as Moriam walked in.

She was in scrubs. Sometimes she was too tired to respond. Bashira sat up to greet her and Moriam stared at her.

"What happened?" she asked.

"To whom?" I asked.

"Bashira. Why did she get a haircut?"

Bashira sat there not saying a word.

"I left her there," I explained. "You said you'd made all the arrangements. She said she wanted to try something different."

"Dad said I could," Bashira said.

Traitor. I was expecting an attack, verbal or otherwise, but Moriam turned around and left the room. Bashira watched wide-eyed as I stood up and followed her.

Our bedroom door was shut. Moriam must have closed it softly. That was a terrible sign. I opened it and found her lying on our bed. She was looking at the ceiling.

"Moriam," I said.

"No," she said, in a voice so low it could have come from her navel. "Twelve years, I grew that hair. Twelve years. I leave her in your hands for one day. One day, and you allow someone to cut it."

"I wasn't there."

"Please."

"She was the one who allowed them to cut it."

"Please, Lukmon, just leave me alone."

I thought she would never recover. She behaved as if she were in mourning for the rest of the week, talking to herself and sighing. Bashira walked around the house furtively. One day I overheard Moriam talking to Bisi the Gossip on the phone.

"He didn't even notice," she said. "I'm telling you. He's like an *oyinbo* when it comes to hair. It's true. What do men know about women's hair anyway? If they'd shaved her whole head, he wouldn't have been able to tell. She had it cut. The whole back. A layered bob. I'm trying not to think about it. Yes, it will grow. It will grow eventually."

Another day, she and Bashira held a hair summit in the kitchen. They sat at opposite ends of the table as Taslim and I watched.

"I never gave you permission to cut your hair," Moriam said.

"Mom, it's *my* hair," Bashira said.

"Yes, but I never said you could cut it."

"Mom, I'm almost fifteen."

"So what?"

"You can't control me."

"No. No. Stop using the word 'control.' Wait, wait. I haven't finished—"

"Mom, it's only hair. It's not that serious."

"Yes, it is. Yes, it is. Because, you see, once you cut your hair, you become dependent on hair salons. Every other week, you have to go there to get your hair styled. The shorter your hair, the more dependent you are."

"Mom! You're making it sound like I'll be there every day!"

"Because it's my money you'll be spending. You'll be spending my hard-earned money and you will never be free from hair salons with a hairstyle like that."

"But I'm free," Bashira said, spreading her arms. "I really am."

"No, you're not. Not if you have to keep going to hair salons."

"I won't go often."

"You see? This is what I'm saying. You're naïve. You had virgin hair. I've been relaxing my hair for...for donkey's years now. I've been where you are before. I cut my hair into a style once in Nigeria and I paid for it. From then on, I couldn't free myself from hair salons."

"I still don't understand why you're making such a big deal of it."

"You're not white! Stop thinking you're white!"

Bashira laughed. "Mom, I think I know what color I am."

"Well, let me tell you this. That hairstyle you have on your head is a white hairstyle."

"Oh my God!"

"Yes. Yes, because you can't have layers without straightening your hair."

"Okay, so if I were white, would you say I can't wear braids?"

"I would discourage you from doing that on a regular basis because your hair structure—"

"Oh, wow, we're on hair structures now."

"Listen to me. I am a nurse. I know what I'm talking about. Your hair structure would not be strong enough to tolerate braids on a regular basis if you were white."

"All right. So I think I'm white, then. But you've just said you cut your hair into a style in Nigeria. Did you think you were white?"

I knew the answer to that. She thought she was African American.

"You're not listening," Moriam said. "Black women don't go around cutting their hair into white hairstyles unless they're prepared to go to a hair salon on a regular basis. They must be able to pay for their hairstyles, or someone else has to."

"I said I won't go there often."

"You're saying that now because it hasn't happened to you. Just wait until it rains and your hair reverts. I'm telling you, I didn't free myself from hair salons until my hair grew back. It took years. I wanted you to keep your hair the length it was, so you could pull it back into a bun whenever you wanted, instead of having to go to a hair salon."

"Mom, why don't you just call this what it is? Why don't you just say you're trying to control me?"

"Not control. Not control. You keep using that word. I'm trying to free you. I want you to be free from hair salons."

Crazy talk, I thought. Crazy, crazy talk over dead matter.

Taslim finally got tired of them and said, "Come on, Mom. She had a haircut. It's not as if she got hooked on crack."

The way I saw it, Moriam would have preferred that.

One evening about a month later, we were on our way to Pathmark. I was driving and it was raining. The rain came down like a heavy spray and I strained to see through the windshield. The weather was milder now and we were looking forward to spring. Trees were already turning green.

"See how she's changed," I said, about Bashira.

Moriam shrugged. "Let her not change."

Bashira and Taslim were at home. We'd stopped making them go grocery shopping with us.

"She's eating properly," I said.

"Let her not eat properly."

"Her grades are improving."

"Let them not improve."

Moriam was in Mama mode and no one had provoked her. She was actually more lenient now that she worked, because whatever our children said, she could always say, "Speak to your father."

"I'm just thankful it wasn't anorexia," I said.

"I told you it wasn't."

"The girl is too secretive."

"She takes after you."

I was still paying for "Hair-gate," but she was right. I never told her about the girls in Bashira's school and their banana tricks. She would have gone straight to the school to sort them and their principal out. They no longer bothered Bashira anyway, and she was still eating my jollof rice at lunchtime.

"You know," I said, "I'm not doing badly as a stay-at-home dad. I could do this for a while."

Moriam patted my thigh. "Don't get too comfortable."

Bashira made a friend! Alice! I hugged her when she told me. "My daughter!"

Alice was in her grade. They became friends because Alice, too, ate home-cooked meals at lunchtime. They had talked to each other before, but Bashira thought Alice was shy and Alice assumed the same about Bashira. Her parents were from Korea.

"Honestly, Dad," Bashira said, "her family is just like ours."

I asked how Alice's family was like ours, but she wouldn't elaborate.

Initially, I would pester Bashira about Alice when she came back from school. "So did you hang out with Alice today?" I would ask and she would say, "Dad, please stop trying to use slang."

She was flippant about their friendship, but she had a new air about her, walking confidently to her school bus in the mornings, as if to say, "I have people." After a while, I stopped asking about Alice. In fact, I began to take Alice for granted until the day Bashira came home from school and asked if she could spend the night at her house.

"Absolutely not," I said.

"Why?" she asked.

"Because your mother and I don't know her parents," I said.

"You'll meet them when I go over to stay."

"What if they're child molesters?"

"Come on, Dad. Everyone is a child molester to you."

"Speak to your mother," I said.

Later, I picked Moriam up from work, and as we drove home, I told her Bashira wanted to spend the night at Alice's house. She thought Bashira should have Alice over for the day and vice versa a few times beforehand.

"Would that be enough?" I asked.

"We'll find out more about her parents that way."

"What if they pretend in front of her?"

"There's nothing we can do about that."

I laughed. "What am I talking about? We'll pretend in front of them!"

"So everybody is pretending to everybody, then," Moriam said.

I was winding her up again and she was in no mood. To be honest, I was nervous about meeting Alice's parents. I hoped they were my kind of immigrants—bad ones, not the kind who aspired to be honorary whites.

"We'll wait and see," I said. "I hear Asian Americans and African Americans don't gel."

"Why are you bringing up race?"

"You've brought race up before."

"When? When have I ever brought up race?"

"Several times."

"Tell me one."

I couldn't remember any, apart from Hair-gate, and I wasn't about to mention that. But she herself had witnessed heated exchanges at a Korean-owned beauty supplies store where she bought hair products—the owners being curt with customers, and the customers asking if they spoke English.

She sighed. "I'm tired of this. We're from Nigeria and they're from Korea. If we can't get along in America, we can go our separate ways."

I didn't care what she had to say. I was not giving up on Alice. Alice, I realized, would be the first American-born kid to visit our house. Taslim always met up with his friends elsewhere. I wasn't sure if he was embarrassed about us or them, but so long as they kept out of my way, I was happy. Alice would be the test of whether an American-born kid could survive our family.

Bashira and I were now reading what my friend the librarian called immigrant literature. She'd recommended a few debut novels she thought Bashira would enjoy, all of which were by writers whose parents had immigrated to America. I'd never in my life encountered a more pathetic group of protagonists. They had no confidence whatsoever. They were ashamed of their cultures and their sole aim and focus was to assimilate. They were desperate to be accepted by white people but barely acknowledged the existence of black people. These were characters whose parents had come from countries older than America, with cultures Americans could learn from, yet they longed to be the boy or girl next door. It was propaganda. Truly.

The next Saturday, Bashira went to Alice's house for the day. Moriam dropped her off after breakfast. Bashira banned me from tagging along. She said I might say something weird. When Moriam returned, I asked what she thought of Alice's parents. She said they'd seemed all right, but she didn't spend enough time with them to be able to discern.

"Didn't you go into their house?" I asked.

"Only to the door."

"You abandoned our daughter at their door?"

"I was too tired to enter."

Of course I didn't believe that, nor did I believe that Alice's parents were child molesters, but I wanted some assurance that they would treat Bashira well.

In the evening, Moriam went back to their house to pick Bashira up. They came home and I questioned Bashira in the kitchen as Moriam wandered off somewhere. Taslim was in his bedroom surfing the Internet again. I'd given up on restricting television, so I didn't bother to try to restrict Internet time.

"So how's Alice?" I asked Bashira.

"Fine," she said.

"Anything to report?"

"Nope."

"What did you have for lunch?"

"Hamburger Helper."

"Don't they eat Korean food?"

"Dad, please."

"I'm just asking. We eat Nigerian food. So...do they speak English at home?"

Bashira gasped. "That is—"

I frowned. "What? Don't we speak Yoruba at home?"

"It's not the same," she said.

"Why not?"

"Wool, would you ask if they spoke English at home if they were Irish American?"

"Which Irish Americans do we know?"

"Mrs. McFadden."

"I guarantee Mrs. McFadden doesn't speak her language."

"That's not the point."

"I bet you Mrs. McFadden asked if you could speak yours."

"She doesn't speak her language because her parents didn't. She said I was lucky to know mine."

Bashira argued well, but I was not her mother.

"Exactly," I said. "You're lucky, and guess what? If you went to Miss Villanueva's house, I would ask if she spoke Spanish at home."

"What's the difference between Miss V and Mrs. McFadden?"

I hesitated. She was a better arguer than I thought.

"Mrs. McFadden was born in America," I said.

"How do you know?" she asked. "How do you know she wasn't born in Ireland? How do you know Miss V wasn't born in America? How do you know Alice's parents weren't?"

She was trying to entrap me. I would never say white Americans didn't speak their languages, even if I thought that.

"Alice takes Korean food to school," I said. "Anyone who gives their child home-cooked meals to take to school can't be American-born."

Bashira wrinkled her nose. "Oh, you know what I mean."

Moriam returned to the kitchen, looking distracted.

"Where were Alice's parents born?" I asked her.

She frowned. "What is my business where Alice's parents were born?"

"I'm trying to prove a point to your daughter. Did Alice's parents sound American-born to you?"

"What is my business how they sounded?"

"I'm just wondering."

"Are you bringing up race again?"

"He's always bringing up race," Bashira said.

Judas, I thought.

"Your mother brought up race with you," I said.

"That had to do with my hair."

"Yes, Lukmon," Moriam said. "That was to do with hair, not skin color."

"Both of you are confused Africans," I said.

They could imply whatever they wanted. My point was this: We had come from another country and so had Alice's parents. Why did we have to find common ground in Hamburger Helper? I would have preferred to eat Korean food if I were Bashira. I would expect Alice's family to speak their language at home. That was the trouble with immigrants. We were always trying to fit in with mainstream America when we ought to be changing it.

Two weeks later, Bashira invited Alice to our house. She asked Moriam to buy hot dogs and fries because Alice wouldn't want to eat Nigerian food. I threatened to make Alice eat stockfish and the protests began.

"Dad!" Bashira exclaimed. "Why?"

"It's very sweet," I said.

"I think you mean tasty," she said.

I shrugged. Tasty, delicious, savory, they all came down to one adjective in Yoruba: sweet. Taslim and Moriam were with us in the kitchen and I was prepared to take all of them on.

"I will make her eat *eba* and *efo*," I said. "With her hands."

"Ah, Lukmon," Moriam said. "You're such a bushman."

Bashira slapped her forehead. "Oh my God, he never stops."

"You're calling your father 'he'?" I said.

Taslim laughed. "Baba's back!"

"Dat's right!"

"You shouldn't force people to eat your national cuisine," Moriam said. "It's bad manners."

"Thank you," I said, "Mrs. Etiquette."

"She won't even know what she's eating," Bashira said.

"Does she know what's in a hot dog?" I asked.

"That's true," Taslim said. "What *is* in a hot dog?"

"Dat is the one-million-dollar question."

When Alice arrived, Moriam was out buying hot dogs and fries, and Taslim was wherever he was. Bashira opened the door and she and Alice walked into the family room. They didn't know what was in store for them.

"Hello Alice," I said. "Welcome to Wonderland."

"Thank you," Alice said, glancing at Bashira.

"Dad, can you come here a minute, please?" Bashira asked.

She marched ahead of me to the kitchen. When we got there, she pointed at me as her mother would.

"Behave yourself," she said. "I know you're proud to be Nigerian and all that, and so am I. But you're acting weird right now. Stop acting weird. You'll scare her."

"Okay, okay," I said.

I let it go, but what impressed me most about Alice was that she wasn't fazed. When Moriam came back with hot dogs and fries, she sat at our kitchen table with us, shaking her bangs from her eyes. When I spoke Yoruba, she was fine. When we ate pounded yam and okra stew, she ate her hot dog and fries. She didn't even blink when I deliberately ate a cow foot with my fingers and sucked on the bone. She was the perfect American friend.

WIVES

Moriam had always known her experience as a labor and delivery nurse in Nigeria wouldn't count in America. At the hospital where she worked, no one cared that she'd delivered babies before. All she was permitted to do was start IVs, draw blood and write notes in charts about fetal heart rates, frequency of contractions and centimeters of dilation. Childbirth in America was too clinical, she said; every procedure was by the book. If patients had the slightest pains, they asked for epidurals. Whenever their blood pressure went up a little, their doctors suggested C-sections. American ob–gyns gave any excuse to induce labor and there were no powerful midwives at her hospital.

She meant powerful enough to defy doctors. When she was a student nurse in Nigeria, she'd often talked about a matron whom newly qualified doctors called "Matron Medusa." Everyone was afraid of the woman and no one could confront her because she'd been at the teaching hospital for years.

The hospital Moriam now worked in wasn't a teaching hospital, but it had better facilities than the one she'd worked at in Nigeria. It was sanitary and well organized, with medical equipment that wasn't just sitting around accumulating dust. The Women's Care Center had framed prints of watercolor paintings on the walls, Braille numbers on the room doors and sliding doors with buttons for wheelchair users. Nurses had to be polite and professional at all times, as patients rated the hospital's services in surveys. But every service and item supplied had to be accounted for, down to the swabs. Nothing was too sacred for an insurance price tag, death included.

Moriam preferred scrubs to the white dresses she'd worn back home, but she complained that her colleagues didn't always take time to say a simple "Good morning." Her nursing manager, Nancy, was the worst offender. Nancy would see her first thing in the morning and start talking as if a whole night hadn't passed. On top of which she called Moriam "girl." "Girl, we have a busy morning ahead," she might say, or "Whatcha doing, girl?"

Apart from repeating conversations verbatim, Moriam enhanced them with accents. I was still driving her to and from work, and on our way home, she would imitate Nancy and grumble, "Who is her girl?" or "Who does she think she's girl-ing?" She was beginning to see why I brought up racism. Or perhaps I was beginning to understand why she didn't. She didn't have the language. The words failed her or bored her, so she gave up on them. It was up to me, therefore, to interpret what she meant.

Her inability to express herself well on issues of race was similar to Ismail's, but she wasn't angry about being black. She just wanted what the white nurses at work had—a steady income and all the goodness it brought, without ever having to deal with being black.

I once asked why she wasn't offended by racism and she said, "Because I don't rate racists." She was being sincere and the idea that she truly believed she had the power to determine whether they offended her or not fascinated me. "What if one attacks you?" I asked. That would be a criminal act, she said. "You mean a hate crime," I said, correcting her. Most crimes were, she said.

Her answers only increased my concerns for her. I was as determined as she was to win the argument, so I reminded her of the brief civil rights lesson Nia had given her. She said she wasn't talking about the olden days. I couldn't decide what annoyed me more, her dismissive attitude or her use of the word "olden." I asked how she would feel if Nancy were racist, and she replied, "If she is, that's her business. I don't have time to sit around wondering if she is or not."

Because Moriam set history aside and rejected labels, racism, to her, was somewhere on a continuum of bad behavior she refused to give her attention to, and there was nothing I could do to convince her otherwise. About Nancy calling her "girl," I said African American slang was often appropriated and used in the wrong contexts, and she said, "Please, Nancy doesn't do any of that," as if I were crediting the woman with too much intelligence.

Claudette, another nurse who worked at the Women's Care Center, had issues with Nancy, too, but she could articulate them better. Claudette was from Jamaica and gave Moriam a rundown on Nancy the first time they were alone in the nurses' station.

"That girl get on my nerves," Claudette said. "Last year she tol me she was traveling to the islands. She wanted to know about tourist attractions. So I ask her, 'Which *country* you going to?' She said, 'Trinidad and Tobago.' I tol her I ain never been to Trinidad before, let alone Tobago, and even if I did, I won't be going to no tourist attraction there."

Claudette was a divorcee in her fifties, with a mortgage and a son in college. Nancy was single with a fiancé.

"She racist," Claudette said. "The whole hospital is. They don't want to hire no black people. That's why they got two of us here, thinking we won't kick up a fuss because we foreign."

Moriam asked what Claudette thought of a friendly nurse called Kim, who had four holes in each ear and one in her nose, though at work she was ring-free.

"She crazy," Claudette said. "They all crazy."

Claudette only spoke to Moriam in that accent, apparently. When other nurses were around, she spoke as if she were related to the Queen of England, answering, "Yes, certainly, I will see what I can do," or "No, that will not be possible at the moment."

During orientation, Moriam met a Nigerian ER physician called Dr. Aderemi. He was a graduate of Lagos University Teaching Hospital and had worked in England before he came to America with his family. His daughter, Anjola, went to Taslim's high school and they were in the same grade. Moriam liked him; she said he was easygoing. She found some of the other doctors condescending, but she had been used to that in Nigeria. She also noticed that nurses flirted with doctors, but she had been used to that as well. There was some gossip about a doctor who recently had an affair with a nurse, but I wasn't paying attention when she relayed the details. I was thinking about our own sex life, meanwhile. She was working days and nights now and found it hard to adjust her sleep patterns. Her paycheck compensated for her hours. She earned more than I had as a security guard, which would have been all right, if we were having sex more often.

I could now debunk one lie that housewives told. When they said they were too tired to have sex, they just didn't want to have sex. When I was employed, I'd wanted to have sex every day. Now that I was at home, I still wanted to have sex every day. Sex I didn't have to work too hard at, but regular sex all the same. But whenever I reached for Moriam, which was usually early in the mornings, she elbowed me. Some days she said, "Make it quick," as if she'd ever had to tell me that. She was always too tired to have sex, but she was never too tired to go shopping.

Shopping woke Moriam up. It invigorated and excited her. It brought her to climaxes: "Ooh! I saw some gold earrings at

Nordstrom!" "Ooh! Ooh! There's a sale on at Bloomingdale's!" "Ooooh! I love Saks!" Not Sears, not JCPenney. One moment, she would be whining that her feet hurt; the next, she would be strutting up and down a mall. She would come home with only one shopping bag, as if I wasn't aware she had hidden the rest. One night she lay on our bed as if she were in a state of postcoital *tristesse*. I asked what the matter was and she said a leather jacket she'd been eyeing had just been reduced by fifty percent.

She started calling me a whore. I hadn't had enough sex in my life to be called one. I didn't have any until I got to university. I was seventeen and ready for action. My first girlfriend joined the Scripture Union before I had a chance to sleep with her. Suddenly, she was talking about remaining a virgin until she got married. If she hadn't broken up with me, I would have broken up with her. My next girlfriend was so loose, she ended up sleeping with three guys I knew. After her, I slept with a few unremarkable and remarkable women until Moriam came along.

I warned Moriam that I would send her back to Nigeria and get my sisters to fly over a village woman who would cook, clean and fulfill her wifely duties if she wouldn't. She found that funny. The trouble with me, she said, was that I always had sex on my mind. I wondered what she would say if she knew how truly whorish men were. How it didn't take much to trigger us: the smell of perfume, exposed cleavage, a certain kind of walk. I was so whorish, I denied it to myself. Was I just looking at that half-naked woman? Nope. Did I find women who looked twenty-something attractive? Of course not! I wasn't always proud of myself, but I controlled myself. Controlling myself was part of being a married man. Yes, I had moments when I imagined myself with other women. So what? I was always faithful to my wife.

She was too comfortable in America; that was the problem. In Nigeria, she would be afraid of the competition. She would have to perform her wifely duties on a nightly basis in case some other woman might. So, like every frustrated American husband, I started doing DIY jobs around the house. I bought myself a toolset and screwed in doorknobs, and fiddled with locks. I called Cathy to tell her when the heater in our bedroom started making strange noises. Moriam found the bedroom too cold, I found it too warm, and between us, we may have damaged the thermostat.

Moriam was usually the one to call Cathy. She sent our rent checks by mail because Cathy had a way of avoiding discussions about money. She thought talking about money was impolite. I thought that was an affectation, a dangerous one at that. She could have a tenant who would take advantage of her.

Cathy said the heater had always made strange noises and asked if we were happy in her house otherwise. I said we were.

"I'm so pleased for you and your family, Luke," she said. "You're good people. I know good people when I see them. I didn't always use to. I spent many years surrounded by people I thought were nice and it turned out they were not. I can tell you this, since you live there now. I didn't want to live there on my own. I used to go to craft fairs just to get away. Some of my neighbors got very upset with me. They said I was neglecting my house and it was bringing down the value of their houses. They even said I wasn't in my right senses because my lawn wasn't being mowed regularly. It got really nasty. I put the house up for rent, but no one would rent it, so I decided to move here until I was ready to sell it."

I could imagine that Cathy had felt isolated. I hadn't yet met any of our neighbors. She told me Howard was still living with his daughter and a couple from India had just moved into his apartment.

"Lovely people," she said. "Just lovely. He does computers and she does computers. They're working on a website for me, so I can sell my pins. Honestly, Luke, people who come to this country work so hard, and it hurts me how we take things for granted over here."

"Well..."

She didn't know I'd stopped working and anyone who said people "did" computers would have no clue what the Indian couple was doing with her website.

"You do," she insisted. "And it makes me so mad because we're not open to foreigners in this country. I'm sorry, but it has to be said."

I mumbled something about Americans being accommodating to immigrants before we said goodbye. As soon as I dropped the phone, I said to Moriam, "I hope this woman is not a serial killer."

"Why?" Moriam asked.

"Is this how she talks?"

"Cathy can talk," Moriam said.

"She doesn't seem to care what is going on here. She's calling me hardworking. What if we stop paying her rent and decide to squat here? What if we wreck the place?"

Moriam shook her head. "You have nothing better to do."

I'd assumed Cathy had rented her house to us out of kindness. All of us in that small apartment, she may have thought, Let me do my bit for humanity. Now, I was beginning to think she had rented her house to us to spite her neighbors. That would make more sense. Moriam had met a few of them. She thought they were all right, but was too busy to befriend them.

"Seriously," I said. "Maybe our neighbors suspect her of being a serial killer. Maybe she has bodies buried somewhere in the backyard."

"Leave the woman alone," Moriam said. "She lives on her own. She lost her husband and son."

"What if she killed...?"

"Lukmon."

"I'm only asking. I don't understand why she is renting her house to us. Would she have rented her house to us if we were African American?"

Moriam eyed me. "She definitely wouldn't say you are hardworking."

Moriam thought she was being funny. She thought I was trying to be funny, when all I was trying to do was protect our family. In fact, now that I was at home with, as she would say, "nothing better to do," she was convinced I was becoming worse.

The woman was funny, without trying to be. She picked up swearing from Kim, the nurse with the ear and nose piercings. "What the damn hell?" she would say.

Initially, I wouldn't correct her. It was like watching one of our children attempting to smoke a cigarette and exhaling instead of inhaling. She never swore in front of them, but "damn hell" was her favorite. I finally told her her swearing wasn't satisfying. The whole point of using bad language, I said, the only point, was that the words had to be satisfying to say.

"Oh, get the shit out of here," she said.

We still had no variety when it came to meals at home. In Nigeria, people joked that RSVP was an acronym for "rice and stew very plenty." In America, rice and stew could very quickly become repetitive. I'd gained confidence from cooking jollof rice and wanted to make other Nigerian meals, but Moriam wasn't having that.

"You will dirty my kitchen," she said. "I can't have you dirtying my kitchen."

We were in the kitchen, which I reminded her wasn't hers. I promised to clean up if she taught me how to cook.

"No," she said. "I want to rest in my free time, not teach anyone how to cook."

"Listen, just write the recipes for me, woman."

Nigerian food didn't need recipes, she said. You watched and you learned.

I'd seen her cook. Only Bashira was allowed to be around her and all Bashira was permitted to do was scoop her stews into Tupperware containers—or "plastics," as Moriam called them. She was big on freezing stews. She froze them for weeks and months. None of our meals tasted fresh anymore.

"Okay, okay," I said. "So, what if I cooked once a week for the family, on the weekend, when you're home?"

"Why would you do that?"

I was cooking for sex as well. The fewer opportunities she had to claim she was tired, the better. Plus, she didn't always enjoy cooking but felt duty-bound to do it, which made me more determined to relieve her now and then.

"You only cook Naija food," I said. "I can't cook Naija food better than you."

"At least you know."

"So, what if I did that?"

She sighed. "Don't dirty my kitchen, Lukmon. That's all I ask."

She suggested I make pasta. She'd eaten the best pasta on trips to Rome with her mother, she said, and her spaghetti had to be al dente. She went on about Rome itself, how she'd walked down streets and Italian men whistled at her and called out, "*Ciao Bella*." I could have brought up fetishization at that point, but instead told her that if the men knew what it took to get into her pants, they wouldn't be wolf-whistling her.

I agreed to make pasta dishes regardless, and looked up pasta primavera on the Internet in our bedroom one night, since she'd made that in Ismail's house. Pasta primavera wasn't even Italian. It was Italian American cuisine. So was shrimp *fra diavolo.* I looked up authentic Italian pasta recipes and found *spaghetti alla carbonara* and *bucatini all'amatriciana.* Both recipes contained pork, but Moriam was in two minds about pork, and not because she was Muslim. She wouldn't touch a pork rib with barbecue sauce because the sauce would be too sweet, but she ate bacon once in a while.

She walked into our bedroom and I told her the recipes recommended I use *guanciale.*

"What is that?" she asked.

"Salami made of pork cheek," I said.

"Use bacon. I don't know anything about any *guanciale.*"

"I thought you were the Italian food expert."

"Use bacon, please," she said. "Don't waste my money."

Pepperoni, I would later find out, was Italian American. I was getting used to American cuisine, the super-sized meals, cheese toppings and fillings, and the general beefing up of foods originally from somewhere else to satisfy their big appetites. I once had a croissant for breakfast. I would never normally look at one, but this was twice the regular size and stuffed with an omelet, ham, tomatoes and, of course, cheese. The damn thing was as heavy as pounded yam. It kept me full all day.

Now that I no longer worked, I'd stopped paying attention to bills, so whenever they arrived by post, I handed them over to Moriam. Our electricity bill was usually our highest. I'd given up reminding Taslim and Bashira to turn off their lights when they were not using them. Their mother's problem was overusing the washing machine. I could understand separating clothes into whites, colors and darks, but she also washed her nightgowns and underwear separately, on the delicate cycle, whereas in Nigeria, she would have handwashed them. She now had a full wardrobe of clothes, not to mention scrubs, yet she continued to shop for more, which only meant more laundry.

One night, she was asleep with the remote in her hand when I saw a credit card bill on her bedside table that made me cry out.

She woke up. "W-what happened?"

"What did you buy in Bloomingdale's?"

I showed her the bill as she found her bearings.

"Is that why you're shouting?"

"What did you buy there?"

"Um…a few sweaters."

"What are they made of? Gold?"

Cashmere, she said.

"Moriamo, we're not rich people."

"Don't start," she said, wagging her forefinger. "Get that penny-pinching mentality out of your head. We are rich and will always be, *insha'Allah*."

Her mother had raised her to believe that abundance came from God. She thought my family was frugal.

"We won't be rich if you keep spending money," I said.

"Isn't that why I'm working?"

"Spend less, work less."

She nodded. "Thank you. That is your philosophy. Mine is to enjoy what I'm working for."

"What about saving for a house?"

"God will provide."

"I thought you were the provider here."

"Give me that, my friend."

She grabbed the bill, returned it to her bedside table and went back to sleep.

Before she'd nodded off, she had been watching a recording of *The Oprah Winfrey Show*. She loved Oprah and her cohorts, Suze Orman, Iyanla Vanzant and Dr. Phil. They bugged the hell out of me. I'd seen each of them at work. Dr. Phil's message was always the same: "Whatever you're doing wrong, stop." Iyanla—her name meant "Big Mother" in Yoruba—reminded me of my aunt, a perpetual settler of family quarrels. My aunt pacified and comforted everyone, listened to their various gripes, quoted a few proverbs and sermons and got them to kneel and prostrate themselves before each other. The moment she left, everyone went back to misbehaving. As for Suze Orman, I warned Moriam that anyone who smiled that much while doling out financial advice was not to be trusted.

And Oprah. If Oprah recommended a brand of cashmere sweater, Moriam would buy it. If Oprah recommended a kitchen appliance, she would go in search of it. She stopped short of buying books. She actually cried while watching Oprah hand out gifts, as if Oprah were a saint. What she was witnessing, I told her, was the power of television. Oprah was the wealthiest salesperson in America and her most popular product was the American dream. She said I was envious of Oprah.

Maybe I was. I answered to Oprah in my house. One morning I found Moriam meditating. Why? I asked. Oprah, she said. Her capriciousness toward religion frustrated me. "You call yourself a Muslim," I said. "You celebrate Christmas holidays because of your Christian relatives and now you're dabbling in New Age religious practices?" She said she was a spiritual person.

Moriam bought into ideas without thinking. She still did the dawn prayer, *Al-Fajr*, but she was finding her purpose in life because of Oprah. She talked about being connected and getting what we put "out there in the universe." She thought Oprah would make a wonderful president and applauded hackneyed statements like, "Happy wife, happy life," and "Women run the world."

And men? According to the television programs she watched, usually on the Lifetime Movie Network, we were violent and depraved. We abused and subjugated women. We raped and killed them. We stifled them simply by being men.

It was enough to make an African man question himself. One day, she was watching a movie in our bedroom about a man who had tied up his wife in the basement of their house because she'd threatened to leave him. Prior to this, he had broken her ribs and given her a black eye. The woman managed to escape and find his gun. The man was returning home with a bag of groceries, and whistling.

"You would think that every husband in America is a maniac," I said.

"Sh," Moriam said. "She's about to kill him."

Being a househusband wasn't exactly challenging work, but I often felt worthless. I went shopping for groceries during the day and the only men I saw in the store looked like retirees. I attended PTA meetings at my children's schools on my own. Stay-at-home moms didn't even bother to show up. I was still trying to get used to my new role, when, of all the phone calls to get from Nigeria, Moriam's brother Gani rang to say her mother wanted to visit us.

As usual, Gani called at about three in the morning because he couldn't be bothered to calculate the time difference. Moriam answered the phone. At first I thought someone in their family had died. They spoke for about twenty minutes, by which time I was fully awake.

"When is Alhaja coming?" I asked Moriam afterward.

"When she gets a visa," she said.

"Has she applied?"

"Not yet. She needs a letter from us and other things."

She was still drowsy and went back to sleep. I couldn't. Whenever Alhaja had visited us in Nigeria, she'd made it clear she wasn't pleased with me or the little flat her daughter and grandchildren had to live in. She called me "Lukmon-ee," and her "ee" didn't come from affection. My name was dignified. She was trying to humiliate me. She encouraged Moriam to trade on the side to make extra money, even with my banking job. She was also in the habit of giving Taslim and Bashira money in my presence, which I felt was underhanded. Our children had no pride when it came to money. They would run to the door to greet her when she arrived and jump for joy when she gave them some.

Alhaja treated me as she had Moriam's father. The man wasn't doing badly in the military when she was married to him, but his drinking sometimes got in the way of making sensible decisions. He gambled and loaned money to questionable friends. Alhaja ridiculed him for being complacent. She would say his colleagues were doing whatever they needed to do to get government contracts while he was waiting for the contracts to land in his lap.

For Alhaja, there was no point in relying on men for anything, other than to produce children. She raised Moriam to believe the same. Moriam didn't respect her father. She said she did, because Alhaja had raised her to be respectful of him. She knelt to greet him and called him "sir," but whenever I brought him up in a conversation, she made a disapproving "hm" sound.

I dreaded the possibility of her mother visiting us in America. Alhaja would never understand why I wasn't working while Moriam was. She wouldn't appreciate the value of helping Taslim and Bashira adjust to the American system of education.

She definitely would not want to hear a word about my going back to academia, and would be shocked that I cooked, Italian food at that. Cooking was a woman's job. There would be nowhere for me to hide. The library was out of the question. My friend the librarian thought I was employed. I went there outside working hours. I would rather die—yes—than while away my time at the mall. Alhaja might even find me there. She was accustomed to traveling, so she might figure out a way to get around. I could just imagine the scene: me sitting at a table in the food court and Alhaja spotting me and calling out, "Lukmon-ee!"

The image kept me awake for practically the rest of the night. So did the fear that Alhaja might expect me to go shopping with her. The last time I was forced to go shopping with a woman other than Moriam, I was a student in London. My sister Fausat came to stay with me in her second trimester. I was in the final stages of my master's dissertation and she dragged me to Marks and Spencer and Mothercare almost every day. I broke out in hives after she left.

In the morning, Moriam and I were having breakfast with Taslim and Bashira at the kitchen table when I casually said to her, "So Alhaja is coming to America."

Actually, we were not having breakfast together. We never did that. I was waiting for Moriam to finish her tea. Bashira was scraping the bottom of a yogurt tub with a teaspoon and Taslim was walking around with toast in his mouth. He removed it on hearing what I'd said.

"Alhaja's coming?" he asked.

"Mom told us about ten minutes ago," Bashira said. "Weren't you listening?"

"That's weird," he said.

"What is weird about it?" Moriam asked.

"I can't see Alhaja here," he said.

He looked at me for support, which I had no intention of giving. I was about to take Moriam to work and didn't want to be harassed. We hadn't had a showdown with our children since Bashira's last tantrum. She was happy at school and doing well. Taslim, too, was making progress.

"Finish your food and get ready for school," Moriam said.

Taslim laughed. "Come on, Mom, all I said was—"

"Finish eating and get yourself ready," she said.

She was fiercely loyal to her mother. Not even our children could make fun of Alhaja.

It occurred to me that morning, as I drove Moriam to work, that I was not only panicking about Alhaja coming to stay. I was also panicking about how Moriam would change with Alhaja in our house. With Alhaja around, she might turn on me for not working, even though it was her idea in the first place. She had already warned me not to get comfortable with our current arrangement. She could give Alhaja the impression that I was content to stay at home.

In case she had forgotten, I reminded her that the African Literature Association conference was coming up in April and I intended to be there.

"You told me already," she said.

"I just want to be sure you heard," I said.

I had to get a job as soon as possible if Alhaja was coming to stay. I had no choice. At the same time, I hoped the US Embassy in Lagos would deny her visa application.

In April I attended the African Literature Association conference in Illinois. The conference was on African women's literature and the convener, Lateef Adeyeye, was a professor I had known in Nigeria. He was in his sixties, soft-spoken and had an air of detachment from the general commotion in the university union, now occupied by a few hundred African literature scholars. There was a concourse and food court on the first floor, conference rooms on the second floor and a banquet hall and union motel on the third floor. Even though the conference was on African literature, anglophone African writers dominated the panel discussions. A few sessions focused on francophone African writers whose works had been translated into English, but there were none on writers who wrote in African languages.

A number of Nigerian academics were present. The keynote speaker, Tanimo Imana, was a Nigerian playwright who had enjoyed a lot of popularity in her day. She, too, was in her sixties. She had a PhD in theater arts from the University of Ibadan and had taught at the University of Ilorin before she retired.

Professor Imana was born into a polygamous Yoruba family. Academics often described her plays as provocative. I personally found them painfully protracted. She had her characters reciting long soliloquies in the form of praise songs. I could see why Professor Adeyeye would invite her, being a Muslim from his part of the country, but I couldn't imagine Professor Imana getting involved in that kind of cronyism. She was against sharia law practices relating to marriage, polygamy in particular. Her stance was personal. She left her husband when she found out he'd married a second wife without her knowledge.

Outside the panels, Osaro may have been absent from the conference, but he was the main topic of discussion. *Last Word* had recently won a national prize for nonfiction, which was accompanied by a monetary award of $25,000. The general consensus among the attendees was that Osaro didn't deserve the prize. I found that out when I met up with Ranti Shonubi, a fellow student from my PhD years at the University of Ibadan. She was the first person I recognized in the concourse, which was like a marketplace when I walked in. I'd just picked up a conference brochure when I saw her. Ranti was one of the most beautiful women I knew. She wore a tight *ankara* outfit so low in front her breasts looked liable to pop out. Her hair was shorter than mine. I wasn't usually attracted to bald women, but I'd never seen a more perfectly shaped head and found it refreshing that she didn't seem to care about hair.

She was as contrary as I remembered. We'd barely greeted each other when she launched into an attack on Osaro.

"He is a liar," she said. "Plain and simple. As for these *oyinbos*, any far-fetched story any African tells them, they believe. Can you imagine? He said he fled Nigeria to escape political persecution and they couldn't even verify that information before giving him a major literary prize. The book wasn't even that good! The runner-up's was much better! But oh, no, she was African American and all she was writing about was depression. Don't mind these *oyinbos*. That is how they are. They're always trying to cause confusion with their random acts of tokenism. That was all this year's prize was about, and Osaro's book was published at the right time. I'm sure PEN America will be calling him soon."

When we were doctoral students, Ranti was one of the women I listened to in silence. I thought it was wise to. She could lash out unexpectedly. She was a feminist back then, yet she was always in one revealing outfit or another. She walked as if she were daring someone to call her a slut and made every woman around her look boyish.

She, too, had had literary aspirations. She'd written short stories, which were probably still unpublished. She and Osaro had left Nigeria in the same year, so they must have encountered each other in the small circle of African literature academics in America. I couldn't rule out the possibility of professional envy.

"Everyone is talking about him," she said. "Of course some people are defending him—you know how Nigerians are. Someone wants a favor, so they keep quiet and hope he might do something for them. Then you have those who might support him for tribal reasons. I wouldn't talk to him if I saw him today! He is a disgrace! What is it? He's calling himself an academic and he's behaving unethically, lying all over the place, and giving the rest of us a bad name. Honestly, *oyinbos* are ridiculous. It is unbelievable to me that they buy his story."

She stopped for a moment as an *oyinbo* academic walked by. He wore a *dashiki* and a string of wooden beads around his neck.

"You see what I have to deal with?" she said in Yoruba. "That one calls himself a specialist on African women's literature. The only African woman writer he recognizes is Nadine Gordimer."

Ranti was in the women's caucus and I imagined that caucusing, for her, meant getting into academic disputes. She was of the impression that Professor Imana was ignoring her because she'd criticized her negative stance on polygamy. She felt the professor's stance was rooted in Western thought. I could easily have challenged that. First, an African academic who lived in America had no right to criticize an African writer who lived in Africa about being influenced by Western thought. Second, I knew plenty of Nigerian women who weren't in favor of polygamy and their exposure to Western culture was at best limited. But they accepted polygamy because they were raised to or because they had to. My mother, quiet as she was, would never have put up with competition in our house. If my father had had other wives, she might not have quarreled with them, but she would have found a way to make life difficult for them.

Ranti was no longer a feminist. Or, as she explained, she was now in favor of African-centered womanist ideology that was less hostile to men. I was just relieved.

"You remember how I was in Ibadan?" she asked. "Ra-di-cal. Remember? I used to go to feminist conferences when I first came to America. Now, you won't catch me at a feminist conference in this country. These *oyinbos* don't want to know what African women have to say. They don't even want to hear that you might have a different point of view. All they want you to do is patronize African women with simplistic messages of empowerment and demonize African men."

I could have told her Lifetime Movie Network wasn't doing badly demonizing American men. But I once dared to suggest that African women had no business getting involved in foreign gender wars that didn't concern them, and she almost bit my head off.

The more she talked, the more challenging it was to concentrate on what she was saying anyway. Why did women do that? Expose their breasts and expect men to listen to them? If my chest were exposed, hairs and all, wouldn't she look?

"They think feminism begins and ends in the West," Ranti was saying. "Once I realized that, my eyes opened. Look at the most powerful women in this country. How many female CEOs of major corporations do they have? How many female managing directors? Let us not bring up the fact that America hasn't yet produced a female president. Hillary Clinton is not even allowed to talk. All she is allowed to do is smile and wave. If she does more than that, they vilify her. In Hollywood, they make more money than any women in the world, but they're retired by the age of forty. So what do they do? They mutilate their faces and bodies. America is a sexist country. In fact, I would go as far as to say it's misogynistic. Yes! But they're always ready to point fingers at Africa!"

Now, she sounded like a proponent of cultural relativism. I remembered Sharifa talking about the burka and Moriam going on about her colleagues who called themselves pigs after eating.

She paused for a moment as Professor Imana approached us. I had not seen Professor Imana since I left the University of Ibadan and had forgotten how tall and regal she was. She wore a *boubou* and head tie. She walked straight past us without acknowledging Ranti.

"This is serious," I said.

"Don't mind her," Ranti said. "She thinks I hate her. Why would I hate her? I'm just doing my job. She is a prime example of what I'm talking about. Feminists here love her. I'm going to her panel today, whether she wants me there or not. When I've finished with her, she won't be able to ignore me anymore."

I'd never understood academics who took pleasure in hounding writers, but Ranti was soon off on another tangent, this one about how she was denied tenure. Someone delayed her application. Someone else discredited her work. Things got so bad for her that an *oyinbo* academic accused her of reverse racism.

"The politics in this place is too much," she said. "I can't stand half the faculty in my department. I don't talk to them unless I have to."

She couldn't stand her students either.

"They call me 'Rotting,'" she said. "Can you imagine? I tell them, 'Call me Professor Shonubi if you can't pronounce Ranti, and if you can't pronounce Shonubi, just call me Professor.' Common courtesy they don't have, and you can forget any knowledge about Africa. You have to start from the very basics with them, providing them with geographical maps and social statistics before you begin to discuss African literature with them."

I wondered if she was married. She wasn't wearing a ring. Making allowance for age, she was still in good shape.

"How are you coping in America?" she asked, as if noticing me for the first time.

"So-so," I said.

"Do you like it here?"

"It's not too bad."

She sighed. "I'm telling you, I would go back to Nigeria today if I could. It's just that it's hard to make the move once you get stuck in academia."

The concourse was filling up and it was harder to hear her above the noise. I could barely maintain eye contact, given the number of people walking past. I leaned over and spoke in her ear.

"Forgive me for saying this, but I'm here to look for a job. After I get one, I might be more willing to talk about the disadvantages of having one."

She laughed. "Look at you! You haven't changed! Still sarcastic! Sorry. It's all the *wahala* I have to deal with here and I don't have anyone else to talk to. Don't worry. We will talk more about that when you're settled. We should have lunch together later. Are you coming to the Imana panel?"

"I'll try and make it," I said.

Her perfume smelled great, and for a bitter woman, she had a lovely smile.

She left and I leafed through abstracts in the conference brochure, craving the banality of business words like "profits" and "revenues" as I skimmed over words like "womanhood," "gender" and "sexuality." Then, just as soon, the image of Alhaja sent me in search of my next contact.

Pascal, Osaro's Congolese friend, was presenting a paper on Assia Djebar's *Vaste est la prison*. I headed for the conference room where he was scheduled to be, but it took me a while to get there because I stopped to greet several academics I knew. Some couldn't remember my name and vice versa. One of them stood on a stair above me and barred my way.

"Don't I know you from somewhere?" he asked.

He was a scruffy-looking man with freckles.

"I'm not sure," I said.

"Your face is familiar," he said. "Yes. I know you."

It turned out we did know each other. We'd met as students in London. I took his card and said I would email him.

He was Urhobo. Most of the Nigerian academics were Yoruba or Igbo. I'd never attended an ALA conference before, but politics in American academia was nothing compared to politics in Nigerian academia, which at its worst had been known to degenerate into juju curses and physical altercations. In the department I'd worked in, relations between faculty members had very quickly become strained whenever a trip overseas was at stake, but I left before I was senior enough to be considered for one.

I found Pascal in the first-floor lobby with his colleagues from the francophone caucus. He wore a black turtleneck and beret. He remembered me from Osaro's dinner. I told him I was looking for a job and it turned out we were staying at the same hotel, so we arranged to meet later.

"Have you heard about Osaro's prize?" he asked.

"Yes," I said.

"He's the talk of the town," he said.

"So I hear. I should email him tonight to congratulate him."

I was curious to find out what he thought about Osaro's prize but not enough to ask. He introduced me to Helen Darko, Steve Gilbert and Chinedu Obiora, who were presenting papers on anglophone African writers. Steve was the *oyinbo* academic in the *dashiki*. He had just returned from South Africa. Helen was

Ghanaian. Her personality was as colorful as her appearance. She laughed so hard at something Pascal said to her in French, her *kente* stole fell off her shoulder. Chinedu looked out of place in a suit. He seemed friendly enough until Pascal mentioned I was job-hunting, to which he responded, "Things are tough."

There were noticeable circles at the conference. Igbo, Yoruba and Ghanaian academics stuck to their groups. African academics were the majority and *oyinbos* were the minority. My perception may have been wrong, but the *oyinbos* seemed to gravitate toward non-Africans. Everyone was united on how disorganized the conference was, though. The panels ran late and into each other. Some of them were canceled at the last minute, so conference rooms were empty when the attendees arrived. Meanwhile, our convener, Professor Adeyeye, walked around seemingly calm in his blue *agbada* and matching cap.

I was late for the Imana panel. She was at the center of the table, flanked by a presenter and a moderator, three of them, angry-looking African women.

"Okay," the moderator said. "This session is beginning to get out of hand and there's no need for that. We can exchange ideas without getting heated up. So, can we move on to the next question, please, and not waste anymore time on this topic?"

I wondered if the topic had involved Ranti, who was in the front row with a notepad and pen poised. I sat in the back row as a man raised his hand.

He cleared his throat and looked downward. I could already tell he was a time waster.

"Um, your plays," he said.

"Yes?" Professor Imana said.

"They are...rather dramatic."

"I should hope my plays are dramatic."

"Sorry, I meant to say..."

"What is the question?" the moderator asked, after a moment.

"Her plays are way over the top," the man said.

"And?" Professor Imana said.

"Why?" the man asked.

"Why what?" Professor Imana asked.

"Why are your plays so...intense?"

Professor Imana couldn't disguise her irritation.

"Have you read any of them?"

"I've seen one or two," the man said.

"Yes, but have you read any?"

"They're not available in the United States."

"Read my plays, please," Professor Imana said. "Then we can discuss them."

The man folded his arms. I doubted he was an academic. He may not have even seen any of her plays.

"Next question, please," the moderator said, checking her watch. "Actually, this has to be our final question because we're running out of time."

Ranti raised her hand and the audience laughed, which told me I may have been right in thinking that she had caused trouble earlier.

"I'm just wondering what you have to say about my, uh, assertion that you and other playwrights of your generation have failed to, uh, capture the attention of a new generation of Nigerian theater enthusiasts. You never quite addressed that."

"I've certainly captured your attention," Professor Imana said. "You've done nothing but bombard me with questions from the beginning of this panel."

Ranti nodded. "Yes, you could also say I've done a lot to draw attention to your works. But since you refuse to, uh, speak to the issue, my question to you is this: What would you like your legacy to be?"

"What is your name again?"

"Ranti Shonubi, associate professor of African literature. You might be familiar with my most recent essays on your works, 'Feminizing Our Fathers' and 'Politicizing Polygamy.'"

"No," Professor Imana said.

"You're not familiar with either essay?" Ranti asked.

"I'm not familiar with anything you've done," Professor Imana said.

"I could summarize—"

"That won't be necessary," Professor Imana said. Then she addressed the audience. "You know, in my forty years of writing, most of which I've spent examining the inequalities that Nigerian women face, it never ceases to amaze me that my toughest critics are educated Nigerian women. I understand their concerns. They don't want to be regarded as victims. But in being protective of ourselves, we cannot ignore women whose voices are not heard—"

"Heard by whom?" Ranti asked.

"They don't have the platforms we have," Professor Imana said. "You cannot deny that."

"They have their own platforms," Ranti said, "which may not be visible in the West, where every African platform becomes a spectacle."

Professor Imana turned her face to the moderator like a child refusing to take more medicine. I was sure Ranti had more to say, but she took her cue and kept quiet.

Women were their own worst enemies, I thought. That was no cliché. If only they would come together, they might end up running the world. I agreed with Professor Imana. Whenever I talked about Nigerian women, I was referring to women I knew.

Ranti, too, was right. Disadvantaged Nigerian women did have voices and it was presumptuous to speak for them. So why were they confronting each other? They ought to be confronting men.

"Well," the moderator said, rubbing her hands together. "That was a highly spirited and enlightening session. If Professor Imana would be kind enough to end it with a few closing remarks...?"

"Listen," Professor Imana said, facing the audience. "I've never been much use in forums like this and maybe I should have stayed away. To be honest, I don't think about what we've discussed today, or my legacy. If anything, I think about whether my work is worthy enough to belong to the tradition of African literature. The professor here said the future of African literature is in the hands of academics and I disagreed with her. I didn't mean to offend anyone, but the dependency is the other way around. It's just a fact. None of you would be here but for African literature. It is true that African literature has been restricted to classrooms and lecture rooms, but it will find its way out. It's a matter of time, and you'd better be ready when that happens, or else it will be out of your hands. So if indeed you are the guardians of African literature, remember the standard that was set at the conference at Makerere University in 1962. I wasn't privileged to be there, but it was attended by the best African writers and literature scholars of my generation. Now, here we are today in 2000, holding an African literature conference in Illinois. Ask yourself why. Give that your time and consideration."

The moderator thanked her and the audience for coming. The audience clapped. A few people approached the table as Ranti sat where she was, scribbling notes.

Ranti and I had lunch at the food court. She wasn't impressed by the array of fast foods on offer and shared the general view of Professor Adeyeye's mismanagement of the conference.

"Ade *yeye*," she said, diminishing the meaning of his last name from "the crown befits its titles" to "a joke of a crown," with a change of tone. "The man doesn't know what he is doing. The whole place could be exploding and he would be walking around like this."

She imitated Professor Adeyeye's calm expression.

I worried about Ranti's sanity. She had always been trouble, but not to this extent.

"It's not exactly Makerere University in 1962," I said.

She hissed. "Don't mind the woman. She was just trying to insult me. The point I was making was that African writers need African scholars. What is wrong with saying that? Who else but us can analyze African literature with any depth of understanding? Who else but us can be the guardians of African literature? Even if African literature does find its way out of classrooms and lecture rooms, it will only be because of writers like Osaro who write under the Western gaze and they will be nothing more than exotic appendages to the literary landscape. What is she talking about? What did half her generation of African writers and scholars end up doing when they came abroad? Sleeping with *oyinbos*. Before they knew it, they'd forgotten all their revolutionary ideas. I'm telling you, facing West has never benefited Africans."

Ranti wasn't interested in hearing about my job search; she just wanted to vent. I could have told her the dependency between African scholars and writers was mutual, but perhaps because of the racket in the food hall, the fluorescent lights and the sight of Africans queuing up to buy dubious pizzas and tacos, and greasy burgers and fries, I wasn't inclined to respond.

I nodded now and then, hoping *I* wouldn't become preoccupied with the dangers of Western thought while teaching in America. If I'd come all the way from Nigeria to do that, I was better off packing up and going back. Western thought wasn't responsible for the disorganized conference. The conference itself reminded me of the Nigeria I'd left. We had contentious panels, attendees gossiping about Osaro's literary fraud and a convener walking around as if he were unaware of the chaos surrounding him.

One aspect of academia I didn't miss was listening to colleagues who took a certain position, knowing it wasn't absolute, and defended it to the end. So what if African writers wrote under the Western gaze? They couldn't help that. Osaro had written purely for Western consumption, which was unusual, but he would only end up alienating African readers. If they bought his book, they wouldn't finish it. If they finished it, they would be as pissed off as Ranti. Her staunch Afrocentric stance was perhaps due to her displacement overseas. Academics in Nigeria were not that consciously Afrocentric. It was no longer fashionable or useful to be. A cosmopolitan approach to literary criticism was more practical. They were teaching students who were born at least two decades after independence, students who looked up to hip-hop celebrities and didn't know or care about Diop and other African scholars whose works we had studied. Yes, their schooling was Eurocentric, but they might argue that Afrocentric culture was dominant nonetheless because the African diaspora influenced culture worldwide.

Again I wondered if Ranti was married. We'd had a longstanding flirtation in university. She would walk up to me and hug me. I called her "talker thief woman" back then. "Talker thief" was what my aunt, the perpetual settler of family quarrels, would say when she meant to say "talkative."

My mind was all over the place. I put down my burger. Ranti had already given up on hers. She picked up a french fry and ate it.

"Do you like Oprah?" I asked.

She tucked her chin in. "Winfrey?"

"Are there others?"

She rubbed her forefinger and thumb together. "Why are you asking me about her?"

The realization that I'd been lonely at home.

"My wife likes her."

Ranti pulled a face. "Really?"

"Are you married?" I asked.

"No," she said, looking askance.

"How come?"

She lifted her chin. "My choices aren't that great."

"Any children?"

She nodded. "Only one."

Her daughter, Morayo, was a freshman in college. She'd never married Morayo's father. She didn't want to. Nigerian men were mad, she said.

"Not all of us."

"I thought you were one of the nice ones. Why are you asking me about Oprah? Are you having problems at home?"

I shook my head. Ranti was too much trouble.

"Can't a man complain about being misunderstood?"

"Not to a woman like me."

"Why do women here worship Oprah?" I asked.

She pointed. "Hey! Respect your wife and stop stressing me out! Asking me questions about my private life stresses me out! Look at you. I was hoping for some intellectual stimulation and all you can come up with is, 'Do you like Oprah?' Since you ask, I'm not an Oprah Winfrey fan. Would you like to know why?"

There was a time when I would have taken her answer to mean she was interested in me.

"I hear too much about Oprah at home," I said. "Tell me about jobs."

She was helpful. She suggested I apply for fellowships and promised to tell me about any opportunities she heard of. She was planning to sleep in, the following morning, but would stay until the end of the conference. She had films to watch and the final dinner to attend. I told her I had to head back home first thing in the morning.

She gave me her card and we went our separate ways. Our next panels were concurrent. I attended a session on Nawal El Saadawi, followed by one on Tsitsi Dangarembga and Yvonne Vera, after which I went to a conference room that had been set up for book publishers and sellers. There were books by francophone African women writers like Mariama Bâ, Calixthe Beyala and Véronique Tadjo, and anglophone African women writers like Ama Ata Aidoo and Buchi Emecheta. Bessie Head was duly remembered and Nadine Gordimer wasn't left out. Gordimer, like Coetzee, was sometimes absent from the category of African literature because her works escaped into world literature. I'd read her books in England, so I bought works by other African women writers, pledging to get past my indifference to them. Then I treated myself to novels by Zakes Mda and Nuruddin Farah. As I paid for their books, it occurred to me that I would never describe them as African men writers. There would be no need.

In the evening, I returned to my hotel. The hotel restaurant was only marginally better than the food court, but I had dinner with Pascal there. We ordered steaks and baked potatoes. He thought I should apply for a visiting position while looking for a permanent one.

Pascal was a political exile. The real deal. Laurent Kabila had wanted him killed. He told me only because I brought up Osaro's prize, about which I was ambivalent. On the one hand, I thought Osaro's colleagues could do more than talk about the matter. On the other, if Osaro had written about his authentic Nigerian experience, no one would publish his book, let alone give him a prize.

"You must have heard the rumors," I said.

Pascal nodded. "Oh, yes."

"What do you think?" I asked.

"It is unfortunate," he said. "Osaro is merely a victim of his own imagination."

He didn't say more about the book, but instead revealed more about himself. He'd fled to France. He had been in the United States for two years. He was married to a Frenchwoman who stayed in France with their son because she didn't want to live in America.

"You prefer to live here?" I asked.

He wiped his mouth with his napkin. "For now? Yes."

I was wrong about Pascal. One on one, he was the kind of academic I found easy to be around. He was intellectual without being pompous. The truth was that I was insecure about returning to academia because I'd peaked too early in my career and my banking detour had left me rusty.

We had almost finished eating when Helen Darko joined us.

"Ah, madame," he said. "*Ça va*?"

I stood up with him and they kissed each other twice. They were obviously more than colleagues. She asked for a menu and Pascal ordered a bottle of wine. I decided it was time to excuse myself.

I loved my wife. She didn't always understand me and I didn't always understand her. We had no interests in common, but I loved her all the same and respected her. She also scared me a little because she was crazy. That was why I remained faithful to her. My encounter with Ranti reminded me. Ranti was someone I could talk to, yet I was reluctant. Not because she initially overwhelmed me. I had colleagues who were just as opinionated—Osaro, for one. Had Ranti been Osaro, I would have said, "Look, man, give me a minute. I'm here to look for a job." Later, I would have said, "I disagree with you and this is why." The truth was that I didn't engage with Ranti because, despite her erratic personality, I was attracted to her.

I left her card at the hotel. Obviously, I needed to have sex with Moriam more often, so I was on a mission when I returned home, but the woman was still busy going on shopping expeditions. The day after I arrived, she went to the mall—on a weekday, in her free time, and after lunch, while our children were in school, when she was supposedly predisposed to having sex. This was the same woman who had been too tired to have sex the night before. She'd been too tired to say she was too tired. She'd given me a hind kick. She spent over three hours at the mall and came back with one shopping bag.

"Where are the rest?" I asked.

"What rest?" she asked.

We were in our bedroom and I was genuinely perplexed. She always came home with one shopping bag, yet the contents of our wardrobe kept increasing. New jackets, sweaters, trousers and shoes manifested themselves with no evidence as to how they got there. She occupied my side of the wardrobe now, and my clothes were squeezed into the corner. The three pairs of shoes I possessed had been cast out on the floor.

"The rest of your shopping bags," I said.

"What shopping bags?"

"Come on. You must have hidden them somewhere."

"I don't know what you're talking about."

I was on the Internet when she walked in and had just emailed my CV to Pascal and a congratulatory message to Osaro. I logged off as she dropped the shopping bag on our bed. She slipped out of her half-price leather jacket and on a whim I got up, walked over and began to frisk her.

"What are you doing?" she said, blocking me with her free arm. "Will you stop?"

I raised my hands in surrender and went back to where I was sitting. She hung up her jacket in the wardrobe, unzipped her jeans and pulled them down without ceremony. For me, this was a striptease act.

"When was the last time we had sex in this house?" I asked.

She looked up. "Sex? Again?"

"You can't remember, can you?"

"How can I remember when I'm busy? You think I'm a... light bulb you can just turn on and off when you like?"

"Of course. I'm a fantastic lover."

"I cook, clean and go to work—"

"You don't have to cook. I told you already. You don't have to clean, either. This house is clean enough."

She cleaned because she wanted to clean. She cleaned as if she were undergoing penance and she was critical of my efforts to cook. I'd made *spaghetti alla carbonara* for the family a week before I went to the African Literature Association conference. I used *pancetta* instead of bacon. She said I should have used bacon instead, because *pancetta* tasted off.

"Sex, sex, sex all the time," she now said. "You're like an Eveready battery. I'm tired of this."

"You're not too tired to go shopping."

"I go shopping to relax."

"You go shopping to have sex with clothes."

"Keep joking, Lukmon. You sit here reading books all the time. You go to the library to borrow books. You go to a conference to talk about books. Your whole life is books. You don't know what is going on outside of books. At least I take care of myself. At least I make an effort to look good."

She did. Every other week, she came back from the salon looking waxed and polished, her hair shiny and smelling of coconut. That was why I continued to put up with her bad behavior.

I laughed. "What is wrong with my appearance?"

"Look at your stomach," she said, pointing. "How can you have a stomach that big when you're skinny? Go to the gym and work out."

I patted my stomach. What was she talking about? I was a handsome man, with a perfect physique, except for a small pouch.

"Keep laughing," she said.

"Stop spending money," I said.

She eyed me. "It's my money. You went on a trip and came back with a suitcase full of books. Did I talk?"

Her guilty conscience was pricking her. She went to our wardrobe and retrieved a pair of gray sweatpants. Instead of sitting on the bed like a sensible person to put them on, she hopped around trying to until she fell.

"Piss," she said.

"Swear properly," I said.

She couldn't help but smile. She put on her sweatpants sitting on the floor and stood up.

"You see?" she said. "Now you've made me feel like shopping again."

"Yes," I said. "Go and shop, and when you're finished, come back here and make up for your bride price."

"Whore," she said, and headed for the door.

My wish came true! The US Embassy in Nigeria denied Alhaja's visa application! They stamped her passport—*Bam*!

The visa officer said there was no guarantee she would return to Nigeria if she visited the United States. Gani, who acted as her interpreter, tried to explain the stamp would prejudice her future visa applications. The officer ordered him to step back and remain silent until he was spoken to. Alhaja began to curse the man, in Yoruba. The man immediately called a security guard, who escorted her and Gani off the premises.

"That's a shame," I said, when Moriam gave me the news.

We were in the family room. Taslim was in his bedroom and Bashira was at Alice's house. I had some sympathy. I really did. Alhaja could be a nuisance, but she was no international security threat.

"No wonder everyone hates them in that embassy," Moriam said. "Honestly, I want to give them back their green card. Let them take it. What has it done for me? It's not exactly as if I came here and found the land of milk and honey. All I do is work, work, work from morning till night. How dare they deny my mother a visa?"

The US Embassy in Nigeria had denied visa applications from honest dissidents who had tried to escape the last military regime. They denied applications from sick Nigerians who were seeking medical treatment. As far as they were concerned, every single Nigerian wanted to be American.

"They're very stupid," Moriam said. "They forget their country was founded by immigrants. Now, my mother can't come here because some...foolish man decides that if she comes, she might not want to leave?"

I was surprised she attempted to contextualize what had

happened. Usually, she brought every issue down to a personal level, which was why she continued to abuse the man.

"No wonder he was posted to Nigeria," she said. "If he were any good at his job, would he have been sent there? He is lucky the embassy is considered US territory. Alhaja would have slapped his face if she saw him outside that building. He doesn't know how lucky he was."

Alhaja was the lucky one. If she'd dared to slap him, the Nigerian government would have extradited her to the United States to face assault charges. What diplomatic clout did they have? What did they care about protecting Nigerian citizens, let alone an old woman who couldn't listen to a simple instruction in a foreign embassy?

"She can always reapply," I said.

"She doesn't want to," Moriam said. "She swore she would never set foot in this country after what happened to her at the embassy."

God bless America, I thought.

Alhaja spoke English. She didn't need Gani to translate. She was up to her usual tricks, pretending to be a confused old woman. She had tried that in Italy numerous times. Moriam herself had told me. On Alhaja's return trips to Lagos, she would show up at Rome Fiumicino Airport with more luggage than she was allowed to travel with, and suddenly, she could no longer speak English. She could only speak Yoruba and needed a translator. A woman who was an expert on haggling in several languages, asking "*Quanto costa*?" at every turn.

How dare she try that at a US Embassy? I thought. How dare she curse a consular officer of *my* United States of America? She was lucky he was obliged to follow the law. A Nigerian consular officer would have confiscated her passport right there and then. And banned her from traveling. For life!

America was still all right for making and spending money. Despite what Moriam had said about being overworked, she didn't cut down on her work hours or her trips to the mall. Whenever I suggested we should save money, she brought up Bisi the Gossip, who had a Lexus and a Mercedes, or Dr. Aderemi, the Nigerian ER physician at her hospital, who apparently drove a Porsche. If Bisi and her husband were a benchmark for what we could accomplish in America, Dr. Aderemi and his wife were reminders of a lifestyle we could never attain, no matter how hard we worked.

Dr. Aderemi worked the graveyard shift. His wife, a lawyer, worked for a nonprofit organization in New York that handled immigration cases. She had an undergraduate and a master's degree from London University. In Nigeria, they would never have spoken to us, let alone have befriended us. Her father was a former government minister and legal counsel to an international oil company. His was a retired professor of pediatrics who owned a children's hospital. It was typical that Dr. Aderemi had given Moriam all this information. The Nigerian elite overseas were like displaced royalty, so full of themselves, yet insecure. The few I'd met in London were always going on about their backgrounds, as if anyone cared.

The Aderemis invited us to their house. I refused to go with Moriam and the children the moment she told me they lived in a gated community. She was hoping Dr. Aderemi might encourage Taslim to study medicine. Taslim had shown no interest in studying medicine. She had no idea how hard he would have to work to get into a medical program. I told her the likelihood of him gaining admission to one was slim. He could get into a pre-med program, but applying to the medical schools afterward would be far more competitive. She again said I was being negative.

They all went to the Aderemis' without me and predictably, when they returned, Taslim was impressed. He said the houses in the gated community were huge. There was a swimming pool, clubhouse and tennis courts. There were sidewalks on which people could jog.

I was glad when his friend called him on his cell phone and interrupted him. He went to his bedroom to continue their conversation in private. I was dropping him off at the movies later. Bashira had no plans to go out that day. She remained in the family room as Moriam told me more about the Aderemis'. They had four bedrooms, four bathrooms, a computer room, a study, an attic, a basement bigger than the apartment we had lived in, with a movie theater, and a three-car garage. Dr. Aderemi drove the Porsche and his wife, Desola, drove a Jaguar. They of course had their obligatory Mercedes, an SUV, presumably for their rocky trips to the mall.

To be fair, Moriam did talk more about Desola's concerns for their daughter, Anjola. Anjola was at an age when she ought to be dating and Desola was worried about not knowing her prospective boyfriends. She'd grown up in Lagos, where she would be well acquainted with Nigerians of her sort. She wasn't insisting that Anjola date a Nigerian in America, but she thought it would help.

"Meanwhile," Moriam said, "Anjola told her the Nigerian boys she meets here are only interested in dating white girls."

"They're foolish," I said.

"Maybe they don't have much choice."

"They have inferiority complexes."

"At least we don't have to worry about Bashira yet," Moriam said.

"What!" Bashira said. "I'm almost fifteen! Girls date as young as thirteen!"

"Not in Nigeria," Moriam said.

"Yes, they do!"

"It's not common there."

"Yes, it is!"

"Not in my time."

"Huh? You told me you knew plenty of girls who dated that young."

They were still at it, but their arguments didn't last, and I had to be careful about interfering because they could turn on me.

"Anyway," Bashira continued, "what do I care if some Nigerian boys only want to date white girls? If they don't want to date me, guess what? I don't want to date them!"

"Be quiet over there," Moriam said. "I'm talking to your father."

I didn't even want to think about Bashira dating, let alone talk about it. As for Taslim, I couldn't imagine a serious girl agreeing to go out with him, with the hip-hop songs he listened to that referred to women as bitches. I certainly wouldn't expect him to find a nice Nigerian girl in New Jersey to date, or settle down with.

Bashira and I had finished reading the immigrant novels my librarian friend had recommended, and she'd particularly enjoyed how their protagonists exposed their parents' bigotry when it came to dating and marriage. I told her they behaved as if they had no agency. They complained about being constrained by their parents' cultures and religions, and about being barred from American social and class structures. They were heartbroken over American xenophobia and racism, and unforgiving of their parents' prejudices. America happened to them. They didn't happen to America.

I suppose I was challenging her to have more sympathy for their parents, and to recognize that she had influence in America.

Even I had some influence, on my librarian friend, for one. I'd told her that much of what she classified as classic American literature was immigrant literature. "Gosh," she'd said, "I never thought about it that way. I guess the immigrant literature I'm referring to is...multicultural."

We were all multicultural, I said. I didn't tell her, because she might take offense, that I wasn't a fan of that classification either. I'd seen her array of multicultural writers. They were educated in America and proficient in English. Some of them set their stories in their countries of origin. It didn't matter what lofty platforms they stood on—human rights, civil rights, women's rights—they had one culture in common, self-centered middle-class culture, whether they cared to admit it or not.

Moriam was still talking about the Aderemis. She said they traveled to Lagos every Christmas. In the summer, they spent time in London. Sometimes their friends from Lagos and London came over to stay with them. To me, they were all one big gated community of Assorted Nigerians.

In my marriage, I was beginning to feel like the protagonist in *The Beautyful Ones Are Not Yet Born*. Ayi Kwei Armah referred to him as "the man." The man's wife, Oyo, was pushy and her mother was even pushier. Oyo constantly mocked him and put pressure on him to make more money. I empathized with the man, but perhaps because Bashira and I were now reading novels by African women writers, and I recognized my place as a househusband was not that different from theirs, I began to make fun of the Aderemis' lifestyle.

"Why do they need four bedrooms if they have only one child?" I asked.

"If you'd come with us, you would have been able to ask," Moriam said.

"What do they need to live in a gated community for anyway?" I asked. "Who are they gating out? Don't they want to mix with the rest of us? Why are we Nigerians so willing to buy into any concept without thinking? A gated community, one child, a four-bedroom house and three cars?"

"Anjola's getting a new car," Bashira said.

I hoped she wasn't envious. All I could think of were the bills Dr. Aderemi had to pay.

"My dear," Moriam explained to her, "her parents think the cars they have are too big for her to drive. Her father works in the ER. He sees teenagers who are brought in after crashes and he doesn't want her to get rides from her friends."

Bashira turned to me. "Taslim says he wants to drive."

"I'll teach him in the summer," I said.

In our Corolla. He couldn't wait. What hadn't he said about being the only seventeen-year-old in his school who was still being dropped off and picked up? Not that I paid him any mind.

"But if he takes the car, I can't go anywhere," Bashira said.

"We'll get two cars, then," Moriam said.

"We don't need two cars," I said.

"Yes, we do," Bashira said.

"We can't afford them," I said.

"*I* can," Moriam said.

"Taslim wants to be a doctor," Bashira said.

"Because he doesn't use his brains," I said. "He sees the Aderemis' flashy lifestyle and thinks that is what being a doctor is about."

"Actually, he and Dr. Aderemi talked for quite a while about studying medicine," Moriam said.

"They were probably talking about his daughter's new car," I said.

"Were you there?" she asked.

I didn't have to be. Dr. Aderemi was just another acquisitive Nigerian and I wasn't impressed.

I shrugged. "I'm sure he's under pressure to keep up with his neighbors. But I suppose buying your seventeen-year-old a car makes more sense than having a movie theater in your basement. Either way, he shouldn't blame his materialism on what he sees at work. What happens in the ER is about life and death, not about whether he buys his daughter a car."

Even to my own ears I sounded like a woman.

Moriam put her hand on her hip. "Do you know what he goes through on a daily basis?"

"Didn't you say he was an ER physician?" I asked.

"Yes," she said. "But do you know what he deals with in the ER? The heart attacks, the broken bones and bleeding. Would you be able to handle any of that?"

Bashira interrupted. "He said he had a good night yesterday. The worst thing he had to do was pull a cucumber out of a patient's..."

"Rectum, my dear," Moriam said.

I frowned. "Why would a patient have...?"

An image came to my mind, as it had when Bashira told me about the banana girls. Why did Americans sexually assault fruits and vegetables?

"Don't worry about it," Moriam said, "since you can't figure it out. But that was a good night for him and you're looking down on him because he wants to buy his daughter a nice car."

"If I were a patient in the ER," I said, "I know which doctor I would prefer and it wouldn't be the one with a Porsche."

"If," Moriam said, "you are lucky enough to be conscious when you are brought into the ER, I can assure you that the last question you would be asking your doctor is what car he drives."

Bashira nodded. "Yeah, Dad, especially if you have a cucumber stuck up your..."

"Rectum, my dear," Moriam said. "Rectum."

I told Bashira "especially" was pronounced *es*pecially not *ex*pecially. She must have picked that up in school. She and her mother. They knew what they were doing.

Nigerians and Americans were similar in one sense. We were forever chasing success, however we defined it—the latest model of Mercedes or a house in the suburbs. In America, you could fall short if you were disadvantaged in some way—by your race, gender or background, for instance. You could develop a sense of failure if success was unattainable. In Nigeria, failure was part of the chase because the country didn't work. The country was always there as an excuse.

I had to get a job as soon as possible. I needed to for my own self-respect. Success to me was teaching African literature in an African Studies department. I couldn't very well blame racism for my poor job prospects. Well, maybe I could make a case, but any Nigerian hearing me would tell me to find my way back home. I finished reading the books I'd bought at the ALA conference and continued my job search. If someone had told me about a position in Alaska, I would have applied for it.

One Friday afternoon, Pascal called to tell me about a visiting professorship in Mississippi—Middlesex, Mississippi. The city was about one and a half hours' drive from Jackson. The college was a private liberal arts one, and the chair of the English department, Professor Wes Holmes, had taught at the University of Ibadan as a Fulbright Fellow in the 1970s. He was looking for someone to start in the spring semester. I was interested in applying for the position, though it meant leaving my family in New Jersey. Moriam had no intention of moving houses until we were able to buy one. Taslim had his SATs and college applications ahead and I couldn't imagine Bashira wanting to change schools now that she had a friend. It was only reasonable to wait until I found a full-time job before we started looking for a house. But I didn't anticipate Moriam's reaction when I told her about the position.

"Mississippi?" she yelled.

"What's wrong with that?" I asked.

We were all in the family room and she looked as if she could smell something unpleasant. Bashira mouthed the word "Mississippi" to herself and Taslim watched Moriam with a worried expression.

"Not New Jersey?" Moriam said. "Not New York or anywhere in the tri-state area?"

"Well," I said.

"Over my dead body," she said, snapping her fingers. "Why would you go there?"

"To work."

"Can't you find a job elsewhere?"

"This is the first chance I've had to get a teaching job."

"Good. That should encourage you to keep looking."

"No," I said. "I'm through with that. You need work experience to get a job."

"I would rather live in a village in Nigeria."

"Middlesex is a city. I've looked it up on the Internet. Forty thousand people live there. It has a university. There are schools and hospitals."

"No," Moriam kept saying and shaking her head.

"I'm not asking you to come with me," I said, even though I was.

"You'd better not," she said.

"What would you miss about New Jersey anyway?" I asked. "The malls?"

"I am licensed to practice in New Jersey," she said, "in case you've forgotten."

Her reaction amused me, but she had to understand how dicey my job prospects were.

"Look," I said. "This might be my only opportunity to get some experience teaching African literature. What would you rather have? A husband with a job in Mississippi or a husband with no job?"

She crossed her arms. We all watched her expectantly.

"All right," she finally said in Yoruba. "Let it not be said that I stood in your way. Let it not even be mentioned in this house that I prevented you from making progress."

"So," I said. "The matter is settled."

As I left the family room, she talked to herself. "How can I tell anyone my husband is working in Mississippi? What kind of...curse is that?"

"I think you should stay, Mom," Taslim said. "You've worked hard to get where you are."

Sycophant. All he cared about was leaving his friends. They were planning to apply to Rutgers, Fairleigh Dickinson and other in-state universities, and so was he. I just hoped he would work on his listening and comprehension skills first.

Later, I checked on Bashira in her bedroom, in case she, too, was of the impression I expected her to leave New Jersey.

"Local champion," I said.

"Hey, Dada," she said.

I was sometimes reduced to "Dada," while Moriam was elevated to "Mother" or "Madre."

"What is this?" I asked.

She sat in front of her dresser mirror putting on eye makeup. Her bedroom was tidier than her brother's and smelled of tropical-fruit lotions like mango and papaya.

"I'm trying out a new look for the summer."

"What, the clown look?"

"Very funny. Alice and I are going shopping this weekend and I wanna see if this will work with what I'm gonna buy."

She spoke in a nasal California voice. Bashira had about ten different accents. I could barely remember her real one anymore.

"Are you still allowed into her house?" I asked.

"*Mais oui*! Her mother adores me!"

"Who is taking you shopping?"

"They'll come for me, innit?"

"Who? Her father?"

"H'why certainly!"

The Southern accent was new, perhaps because I was applying for a job in Mississippi. I hoped Alice's parents didn't dislike her. Alice was just as bad with the accents.

"So what do you think about this new job?" I asked.

"I hope you get it," she said.

"Yes?"

"Mm..."

"You don't think I should wait to find something nearer home?"

"What if you don't?"

"That's what I was trying to tell your mother."

She shrugged. "You know what she's like."

"Will you be okay when I'm gone?"

"Yup."

"It will be just you and your brother at home most of the day. Your mother will be away at work."

"We'll be fine."

"You'd better behave yourselves."

"We will, Dad."

I patted her shoulder. "Thank you, my daughter. You're the only one in this family who has wished me luck."

She rolled her eyes. "Oh, stop feeling sorry for yourself."

She was right. I was wallowing in self-pity. I actually put myself off. I was grateful for her support, though, and hoped she would cope well in my absence. Her makeup phase was new. Her fifteenth birthday was around the corner, but she didn't want a birthday party. She wanted braces instead. Moriam said her teeth were perfectly fine, yet she still wanted braces.

That night, they all went out and I watched the news on my own. A cab driver from Cameroon had won the New York lottery. For the first time in a long while, I was able to watch someone on television who had money. I wasn't quite ready for Oprah, but I could stomach this man. New York was his home, he said, and he had no plans to go back to Cameroon. He was single and had no children. He stood there smiling and raised his fist at the camera.

Poor guy, I thought. I would never have shown my face on national television. I would have chosen to remain anonymous.

I got the job. I emailed my CV to Wes Holmes and he offered me the position within a matter of days. He hired me to teach a class in African literature and two English composition classes in the spring semester. I called Pascal to thank him. He'd done what no Nigerian had done for me.

Taslim and Bashira came back from school and they seemed bored by the latest development. I waited to break the news to Moriam, thinking an opportune time would be in the car, as I drove her back from work.

"I can't believe this," she said. "With all the degrees you have, it's in Mississippi you get a job?"

"Can't you just say congratulations?"

"Mississippi is the most racist state in America! Claudette said they haven't officially abolished slavery there!"

"I thought I was the one who brought up racism."

"Maybe that's why God decided to send you there, so you can talk about it all you want."

"Thank you," I said.

She shook her head. "You see why it's necessary to be religious?"

"Oh, they're very religious there," I said. "In fact, Mississippi is probably the most religious state in America, but that doesn't stop people there from being racist."

"Just be careful," she said. "You'd better not let them capture you, the KKK or whatever they're called."

It was refreshing to see her get riled up about racism for a change. The rest of the drive, she muttered "Mississippi" to herself and shook her head at intervals. I was already thinking about my syllabus.

We got home and I went to Bashira's bedroom to ask whether I should teach novels by African men, since I'd done that before, or by African women, since we had been reading them together. She was in front of her dresser mirror, putting on makeup again.

"Black beauty," I said.

"Don't call me that," she said, pulling a face.

I looked at her reflection. Her eyelids were gold.

"Is that mascara?"

"It's called eye shadow."

I called all makeup mascara.

"You're always beautifying yourself these days."

She rolled her eyes, as usual. "I'm trying out new looks for the summer."

She was like this once in a while. I ignored her. Moriam would have cautioned her.

"There's nothing wrong with looking attractive."

"I'm not trying to look attractive."

"What is the point of putting on makeup, then?"

"I'm putting it on because I want to."

No matter how many books we read and discussed together, and no matter how much I used them to guide and instruct Bashira, I could never fully understand what was going on in her head. Did she or did she not think she was attractive? To me, she was perfect, but fathers with ugly daughters would say the same. She looked like Moriam, which was a plus, but Moriam was the color of Goody Goody, a toffee we had both eaten when we were kids. I'd actually called her Goody Goody when we were dating. Bashira was as dark as me, and if some of the novels by women of color we'd read were to be believed, her complexion was not attractive in America. Back home, dark-skinned women were the norm, so light-skinned women stood out and got more attention. They could even get away with being ugly.

"It's better for a woman to be smart than attractive," I said.

Bashira looked up. "Who said?"

"In my humble opinion."

"Maybe. But if you're smart, you can always figure out how to look attractive."

I tapped her shoulder. "Listen, I came here to ask your opinion on books."

"Yes, Papa," she said, sitting up.

Now she was a Jane Austen character. I told her I didn't have in my possession any of the novels I'd taught and some could take a while to order on the Internet. I wanted to start working on my syllabus immediately.

"So who should I teach?" I asked. "The men or women?"

"Teach the women," she said.

I was surprised. She'd found some of the novels by African women too African. I'd asked what she meant by that, afraid that America had succeeded in turning her against herself. She'd explained that they were not modern enough for her. I assumed she didn't feel the same way about novels set in America because America was still new to her.

It took Moriam a while to get used to the idea of me working in Mississippi. I knew she had recovered once she was back to telling me what had happened at work.

That week, she had a Nigerian patient who was admitted to the ER. The woman was in labor with no health insurance or history of prenatal care in America. Dr. Aderemi wasn't available, so Moriam was called to translate. The woman was in pain and crying. She claimed she spoke only Yoruba and that she was in the United States on vacation. She gave an address that couldn't be verified and said she'd forgotten the zip code. Moriam suspected she spoke English and had deliberately traveled to the United States to deliver her baby. The woman gave birth to twin boys and named them Taiwo and Kehinde. As she recovered in the Women's Care Center, Moriam confronted her about risking her sons' lives to avoid paying her medical bills.

"You all could have died," she said in Yoruba.

"By the grace of God we didn't," the woman said.

"What you're doing is fraud," Moriam said.

"I'm not fraudulent," the woman said.

"Just admit it," Moriam said. "I won't report you."

"Report me if you like," the woman said.

Moriam got impatient and began to treat her as she would a patient in Nigeria.

"Are you trying to tell me you didn't know you were having twins?"

"I'm here on vacation. How was I supposed to know I would go into labor?"

"You must have known your due date."

"Who can predict?"

"Where is your husband?"

"In Nigeria."

"Please tell the truth," Moriam said.

"In the name of God," the woman said, raising her hand.

She went into a lengthy explanation about how she'd woken up, eaten fried eggs for breakfast, and before she knew it, she was in labor. She immediately called a cab to take her to the hospital.

"Do you realize what a bad reputation Nigerians have here?" Moriam asked.

"So what?" the woman said. "So what if we have a bad reputation? Is that my fault? Anyway, what is wrong with Nigerians coming here to have babies? You should know it's only because of the hardship we face at home."

"You could afford a plane ticket," Moriam said.

The woman eyed her. "That's the trouble with people like you. Just because you're enjoying America, you don't want the rest of us to."

"It's because of people like you that England changed their laws," Moriam said.

"Listen," the woman said. "You're upsetting me. Be very careful. Otherwise, I will report you to your manager."

Now, Moriam suspected the woman had done this before.

"Is it worth risking your children's lives for an American passport?" Moriam asked.

"Ask my sons when they're older," the woman said. "All I know is that I'm going back to where I came from. Look at you. I'm still bleeding and you're harassing me. I should have known. Only a Nigerian-trained nurse. It's a wonder you got a job here.

Let me tell you, the *oyinbo* nurses have been nothing but nice to me, and you're not their immigration services, so please take my blood pressure and leave me alone."

The woman's blood pressure was high. She had no visitors. The nurses had to buy her balloons. Moriam misjudged her. She wasn't intimidated. America protected her. In Nigeria, without a deposit, she would have had to deliver her twins herself. In the parking lot.

Moriam decided to have a barbecue to celebrate our first July Fourth. The weather was warm and I'd mown the front and back yards two days before. She invited her friends, tender-headed Nia and Bisi the Gossip. Nia could make it; Bisi couldn't because her cousin, whom she'd brought from Nigeria to look after her children, was now slacking. The girl apparently lazed around all day watching BET videos and Bisi was ready to send her back to Nigeria.

I didn't know why Moriam bothered to invite Bisi. She was tired of her unpleasant news. When she told Bisi I was going to Mississippi, Bisi told her about a Nigerian professor in Jackson who was jailed for rubbing hot sauce in his son's eyes. She invited Dr. Aderemi and his family as well. They were going to another barbecue, but he said they would stop by afterward. I suspected she was homesick—she was yet to recover from her mother's ban from the United States. I knew she had to be when she asked me to invite not only Pascal but Osaro and Ismail.

I invited Pascal, whom I would have had over anyway. Then I called Osaro, who said he'd been on the lecture circuit since winning the prize. I was sure he'd received my email congratulating him, though he claimed he hadn't.

One way to look at the matter of *Last Word*, now, was that Osaro was only guilty of calling his book nonfiction. Fiction, after all, was often nonfiction disguised. There was no crime in that. Had I cared to write about my experiences in America, I could write whatever I wanted and no one would accuse me of lying, so long as I called it fiction. I would give my honest opinions; otherwise, there would be no point. But I would have a field day making Osaro sound slimier and Moriam sound harsher. Our children, I would be fair to. Teenagers were weird anyway. There would be no need to embellish. As for someone like Ismail, it would give me the greatest pleasure to depict him as dumber than he was, if that were at all possible.

I rang Ismail after Osaro and was surprised that he answered my call. He, too, must have been lonely, but his arrogance got the better of him. He said he was busy but would try to make it. He and Osaro had predictable reactions when I told them about my job in Mississippi. He said Mississippi wasn't part of the United States and Osaro advised me to join the Mississippi NAACP.

On July Fourth, Osaro and Pascal arrived together. Osaro brought Fela CDs and Pascal was back to charming Moriam.

"Something," he said, "is different about you."

She smiled. "It's my hair."

"Ah," he said. "It suits you."

He was pushing it. Getting me a job didn't give him license to flirt with my wife. I could have been jealous if Moriam didn't have such a puritanical streak in her. Her hair was dyed a color she called cinnamon. I'd told her the color made her look like a loose woman and it was a shame she wasn't.

She got Pascal and Osaro beers as I put Fela's *Overtake Don Overtake Overtake* in the CD player and lit the barbecue coals. Bashira came out of the house to greet them, then pretended to choke on the smoke fumes before returning indoors. Taslim was asleep. They were both worn out from assisting their mother. She'd bought steaks, chicken drumsticks, lamb cutlets, a whole salmon and jumbo shrimps the day before. She was not having hot dogs or hamburgers, no matter what anyone said. She had marinated the chicken drumsticks with lemon juice and thyme, the lamb cutlets with balsamic vinegar and rosemary, and the salmon with soy sauce, orange juice and dill. She'd skewered the shrimps and kept them aside with the steaks.

Left to me, I would have used every spice in the kitchen, but Moriam was particular about not overpowering the flavor of seafood and meat. I warned her not to attempt to take over the grill and she finally agreed that barbecuing was a man's job.

It was all I had to do. The grill was on the patio in the backyard. That morning, Taslim and Bashira had cleaned and set up a table next to the grill. They'd also cleaned the garden dining set at the other end of the patio. In the afternoon, Moriam made jollof rice, plantains and coleslaw and prepared some corn on the cob. Taslim and Bashira raised and opened the umbrella of the dining set. Then they laid a red-white-and-blue tablecloth and matching tableware on the table by the grill. They planned to eat in the kitchen during the barbecue because Moriam and I were old people, our friends were old people, and they didn't want to be around us.

I put the steaks on the grill as Moriam and Osaro talked about President Clinton's impeachment trial. Now that we were in an election year, the details of the trial kept coming up in the news. Moriam only followed the news on television. Whenever she did, and the trial details were rehashed, she changed channels.

"Americans have too much time for silliness," she said. "Look at us in Nigeria. We heard our former president overdosed and died with women in his bed. Did we care?"

Sex, I realized, was silly to Moriam, and the rumor about

our former president was that he'd overdosed on Viagra and died with Indian prostitutes in his bed.

"The issue of the women should have been taken more seriously," Osaro said.

"Why?" she asked.

"We don't pay enough attention to women's rights in Nigeria," Osaro said. "Why were the women there? Who flew them in from India? All that should have been investigated and exposed."

"It was a private matter," Moriam said.

"But that's the trouble with us," Osaro said. "Everything gets swept under the rug, whether it's the nature of our president's death or who he was with at the time of his death. You'd think we would take more interest in a country where women are being trafficked overseas. You should hear what is going on in my hometown. All these young women are being conned into becoming sex workers in Europe."

Moriam shook her head. "Not all of them."

"I don't...understand," Osaro said.

"Not all of them are," she said. "Some of them know what they're traveling overseas for. It's when they get into trouble overseas that they claim they were conned."

"How can you say that?"

"Because I'm a woman and nobody can traffic me."

Only my wife would reason like that. She'd once told me about a teacher who'd preyed on girls when she was in secondary school. Specifically, he pinched their breasts. How that gave him pleasure I didn't know, but I asked if he ever did that to her and she said, "If he'd tried that with me, he would think twice before he tried it again."

"These are undereducated women we're talking about," Osaro said.

"Being undereducated doesn't make you a fool," Moriam said.

"It can make you impressionable," he said. "If you come from a small town in Nigeria, you would have no idea what living overseas is like."

Osaro didn't know who he was dealing with. Moriam was on the wrong side of his politics. Most Nigerians were. In a country where being a victim could lead to a sudden loss of life, finances, business contacts, and the nearest and dearest of associations, Nigerians couldn't afford to be victims unless they had something to gain.

"Do you think every woman wants to study as I did when I came here?" Moriam asked. "Do you think every woman wants to do what I do as a nurse?"

"I'm not sure where you're going with this," Osaro said. "Are you comparing your nursing career to the sex trade?"

"I'm saying that just because a woman says she doesn't know what she's doing, doesn't mean she doesn't. I had a patient a few weeks ago. Nigerian woman. She came here to deliver twins. She said she didn't know she was having twins. She even said she couldn't speak English. All lies."

Only my wife would be that insistent. But the most powerful woman she knew, Alhaja, pretended she couldn't speak English whenever necessary. To Moriam, women were always in control. They stooped to conquer.

Osaro and Pascal looked alarmed. The period of grace she had given them was over. This was the real Moriam, not the one who pretended to be demure in company and made small talk. I was at a vantage point, standing at the grill, and was able to ascertain what each person was saying. Why Nigerians couldn't talk to each other without getting polemical, I didn't know.

I tuned out until Dr. Aderemi arrived with his family. Moriam shepherded them in my direction. Dr. Aderemi was a quiet guy and a bit on the pudgy side. His wife, Desola, called him Flabby. I wasn't sure if it was a short form of his first name, Afolabi, or a dig at his weight, but she was skinny and spoke in the fastest voice I'd ever heard.

"Really nice to meet you," she said. "Such a lovely garden."

"We hardly use it," Moriam said.

"Why? So gorgeous. Be out here all the time."

More accurately, she often rushed the beginning of her sentences and I couldn't quite catch them. Her English accent was handy. Americans would consider her cultured.

Their daughter, Anjola, was polite. She greeted everyone with smiles and without initiating handshakes. She even curtsied. Obviously, someone had worked on her. Taslim and Bashira came outside to talk to her and they sat at the table near me as she told them about her escapades in her new car. Bashira yelled, "Omigosh," at intervals and Taslim threw peanuts into his mouth. I couldn't tell their accents apart. They all sounded American. I could understand teenagers wanting to fit in, but I couldn't imagine American teenagers adopting a pitch-perfect Nigerian accent within a year.

The argument between the old people resumed after the young people retired to the house. This time, Osaro and Dr. Aderemi were on one side and Desola was on the other. Desola's voice was the most strident. In fact, she sounded as if she were facing a tribunal.

"Don't agree with you, Flabby," she said. "Don't. Nigerian women here are more conservative than Nigerian women at home. Much more. Meet them all the time. Come to my office to regularize their papers. Become more conservative when they immigrate to America. Women at home are not that conservative. More progressive back home. Because of the lack of adequate childcare facilities in America, that's why. Can only advance so far in your career here. Won't get very far if you don't have someone to take care of your children. Would be further ahead in my career if I'd stayed in Nigeria. Didn't say it was a sacrifice, Flabby. Didn't say it was."

Dr. Aderemi was even quieter after that, and for someone who cared so much about women's rights, Osaro didn't seem receptive to her from then on.

Desola was a demon. Moriam enjoyed a heated debate as much as the next Nigerian, but she would never have gone that far in public with me. I missed being around Nigerian women who knew their place. I'd never encountered as many badly behaved Nigerian women as I had in America. There seemed to be a high concentration of them. Or perhaps back home, there would be enough moderate women to dilute the whole lot of them.

Ismail showed up while I was barbecuing chicken drumsticks. Moriam answered the door and he handed her an apple pie as if it were a peace offering. He walked toward me with a smile on his face and we went through the usual ritual of hailing each other.

"Lukmon, Lukmon!" he said.

"Ismail, Ismail," I said.

"Lukmon, Lukmon!"

"Ismail..."

I ran out of steam. He probably hadn't forgiven me anyway. His smile didn't reach his eyes. Moriam got him a beer and introduced him to the others. He then asked for a tour of the house and must have inspected everything from the flowers by the front porch to the mulch in the backyard because it took them a while.

"I wouldn't go as far as to call this an upper-middle-class neighborhood," he said to Moriam, as they returned, "but it's a better neighborhood than you were in before."

He pointed at me to show his approval and I pointed my barbecue tongs at him.

I was trying to make sure the drumsticks were well done before replacing them with cutlets. Moriam had predicted that I would undercook the chicken and overcook the lamb, and I was determined to prove her wrong.

The cutlets were done when Desola brought up my supposed favorite topic.

"Strange thing is," she said. "Was in England for years. Never heard this much talk about race relations there. Went to school and university there. Never heard this much talk about race."

Dr. Aderemi kept out of the discussion this time. So did Moriam, who was probably relieved to be in the company of another badly behaved woman. Osaro was still going strong.

"Well," he said, "there's good reason to talk about race relations in America."

"Too much," Desola said. "Too much talk about race relations in this country."

"I would agree with that," Ismail said.

"Drives me potty," Desola said. "Changes nothing. Might even make things worse."

"I concur," Ismail said.

He was clearly impressed—with Desola's accent.

"Don't talk about race relations this much in England," she said. "Would be pilloried for doing that there."

The Nigerian elite could go either way. They could be very English, as Desola was, or they could be borderline English, as Dr. Aderemi was. For Nigerians like them, England—London, in particular—was where they escaped to find some semblance of order. Despite their fascination with America, it was still uncharted, barbarian territory.

The Aderemis sampled my steaks, lamb and chicken. They were ready to leave when I started grilling the salmon. Moriam accompanied them and they stopped to say goodbye.

"I have to apologize for my wife," Dr. Aderemi said in Yoruba. "She hasn't been to court in years, so everywhere she goes, she gets into arguments."

"What!" Desola said.

She slapped his shoulder. I was surprised she understood Yoruba; it made me question the authenticity of her English accent.

"I'm used to that," I said. "I warned my own wife the other day that I would send her back home if she didn't learn how to behave herself."

"Oh, don't be so silly," Desola said.

She and Moriam were enjoying the attention. Dr. Aderemi and I deliberately ignored them.

"If we were home," he said, "they would be serving us food on their knees."

Desola howled in delight. "Could wish!"

"Leave them alone," Moriam said, patting her shoulder. "Let them continue to deceive themselves."

"Probably weren't listening to a word I said about how America sets us back," Desola said, as they went indoors to get Anjola.

"I hear you're going to Mississippi," Dr. Aderemi said.

"I am," I said.

"I know a few Nigerian doctors there."

"Really?"

"They say it's not so bad."

"That's good to hear."

"I even considered going there myself, but I was already in trouble for bringing my wife to America. If I'd asked her to go to Mississippi, that would have been the end of my marriage."

Poor guy, I thought.

"Take care, my man," I said.

"You, too," he said.

I doubted I would see him or his family again. We were about the same age and probably had a lot in common, but I was a small-town boy at heart. I snubbed rich Nigerians. I had some advantage, coming to America with a higher education and money, but their kind didn't need to leave Nigeria. They took over their parents' businesses and continued their longstanding tradition of elevating themselves above others.

Ismail hurried over as Moriam saw the Aderemis out.

"That woman is something," he said.

"She is," I said.

"Is that their Mercedes outside?"

"Yes."

Knowing him, he was intimidated, but with a wife like Desola, Dr. Aderemi deserved a Mercedes and a Porsche.

"How's Hakeem?" I asked.

"He's all right."

"What's he doing now?"

Ismail frowned. "Still deejaying."

"He's sticking to music, then?"

"I'm not asking questions anymore. I advised him to give it up when he came to see me."

"He visited you?"

"Briefly, this summer. His mother sent him over."

Ismail was still an asshole, but I genuinely wished him and Hakeem well and hoped he would sort out his immigration problem. Perhaps Hakeem could put in a green card application for him, so he could be part of the American dream he believed in.

Nia was last to arrive and she was the only bona fide American at the barbecue. The rest of us were resident aliens. Ismail was markedly cold when I introduced her, though she didn't seem to notice. He shook her hand and immediately left us to join Pascal and Osaro.

Nia didn't eat meat, so Moriam took over the grill temporarily and put some shrimp skewers on, concerned that I might burn them. I was too hot to resist. I sat on a chair by the barbecue table and used a napkin to wipe sweat from my face. Bashira came out to greet Nia and predictably, they were all soon talking about hair.

"She wants to get a relaxer," Moriam said. "I told her she can't."

"Don't do it, Bashira," Nia said.

Bashira raised her hand. "That's it. I'm out of here."

She returned to the house. She was walking a fine line. If she carried on that way in my absence, Moriam might kick her out.

"How's she doing?" Nia asked.

"She's fine," Moriam said.

"Is she still eating well?"

"Yes."

The shrimps were ready. Moriam put them on a plate as Nia peered at our barbecue spread.

"This is some gourmet barbecue," she said. "Y'all don't have ribs?"

"My wife is a food connoisseur," I said. "She doesn't approve of ribs."

"You've gotta have ribs if you're having a barbecue," Nia said. "It's how we do it down South."

"Maybe he'll learn when he goes there," Moriam said.

Nia turned to me. "Where?"

"Mississippi," Moriam said. "He got a job."

Nia gasped. "Oh, no!"

"Oh, yes," I said, with a smile.

She turned to Moriam. "Are you going with him?"

"No way," Moriam said.

"Oh, good," Nia said. "I know it's not ideal, but people do have interstate marriages these days."

She was another troublesome one, I thought. Why didn't she have a man in her life? It had to be her fault.

Nia was thinking of traveling to Ghana. She said she was looking for an Ashanti brother. I just hoped she wouldn't find one who was looking for a green card. She and Moriam went to sit with the others, and I joined them after I'd finished grilling the shrimps and corn. As we ate and drank, we gave her advice on other African countries to visit.

"Try Senegal," Pascal said. "Or Côte d'Ivoire."

"Too French," Osaro said.

"What do you mean, 'too French'?" Pascal said.

"Go to Ghana," Osaro said. "Ghana gives you a real taste of Africa without the stress."

Moriam got up to check that the food on the table by the grill wasn't attracting flies. She'd done that a few times already.

"You could also try Lagos," I said.

"You want to kill her?" Ismail asked.

"Lagos can't be worse than Mississippi," Nia said.

"Trust me," Ismail said, abandoning his reserve. "Lagos will disabuse you of any romantic notions about going to Africa."

"I will go with an open mind," Nia said.

"Go with your eyes wide open instead," Ismail said.

She laughed off his attempt to scare her with stories of armed robberies and other disasters she would encounter in Lagos. I couldn't decide if he was trying to stop her from visiting Nigeria or to justify why he was in America.

Moriam had once said Nia took offense whenever she criticized Nigeria. Americans, I believed, had an innate sense of national pride, even when they criticized their country. With Nigerians, our sense of national pride kicked in only when foreigners criticized us.

After Moriam returned, I myself went to the table by the grill to get more chicken. I was full, but she'd marinated them to perfection. I came back and the topic of conversation had turned to spanking. How, I didn't know.

"Are you hearing?" Ismail said. "This lady here says she's against spanking."

"Nia," she said.

"Sorry," he said. "I didn't mean to offend you."

"I'm not offended," she said, shrugging.

"Okay," he said. "Nia here says she's against spanking."

"How did we get to that subject?" I asked.

I moved my can of beer out of the way. There was a time I would readily admit I'd spanked Taslim. Not anymore.

"Beats me," Osaro said with a laugh. "Where's the bathroom?"

Reluctant to get up again, I pointed at the house. "Um, go to the kitchen and—"

"Don't worry," Moriam said. "I'll show him."

Osaro smiled at her. "Madam. I hope I'm not troubling you."

His "Madam" was to imply she was trouble, but she smiled back and stood up.

"I should wash my hands," Pascal said.

He had finished eating. So had everyone else. Their plates were loaded with crumpled napkins, corncobs, bones and remnants of rice, plantains and coleslaw. He and Osaro got up and followed Moriam to the house, leaving me with Ismail and Nia.

Ismail sat back in his chair. "My ex-wife was against spanking," he said to her. "Or should I say she was against me spanking our son. She's African American."

"Yes?" Nia said.

"Yes," he said. "She thinks spanking is a legacy of slavery."

I immediately raised my hand to stop him. I was also partly warning him not to go further, for his sake, but Nia spoke to him as if she were calming a child.

"Well, I'm a social worker, and from my experience, I've seen no evidence that spanking or any methods of corporal punishment are effective ways to discipline children."

"Yes, but do you think spanking is a legacy of slavery?" Ismail asked.

I now expected a barrage of insults, but Nia took her time.

"I'm not sure what one has to do with the other," she said, "but if you're suggesting that because I'm African American, I share the same view as your wife—"

"Ex-wife," Ismail said.

Nia waved. "Don't get us confused. I'm not her. We just happen to share the same view. But if I may finish what I was saying, I was spanked as a kid. I didn't like the experience. I didn't think there was anything strange about it. I just happen to believe, because of my experience as a social worker, that spanking doesn't work."

She sounded too measured. I suspected that was the voice she used to dispel accusations of being angry. She should have heard Moriam and Desola. But African women were not in danger of being labeled angry in America, even when they were.

Nia was angry—with Ismail. She stood up and walked around the garden until Moriam and the others returned. Perhaps she felt outnumbered.

Osaro soon brought up Juneteenth, probably to gain her approval, but she didn't seem interested in joining the discussion. I'd never heard of Juneteenth before, and it made me wonder if I had any business celebrating July Fourth. I still had no faith in American ideals—the dream, equality for all, or freedom as a God-given right. If I accepted the dream, I would have to accept that Mickey Mouse was real. As for equality, I had more expectation that Jesus Christ would return. I didn't believe that freedom was God-given, either. I was raised to believe that freedom came after death and only through observing God's laws. I struggled with that concept as well, but my father's opinion that the pursuit of freedom in the temporal world was childish and irresponsible stuck with me. He often said that just because food was available, on display and inviting, didn't mean I could eat it all. His words usually kept me in check at American buffets. To be honest, I didn't even accept the idea that the will of the people should prevail. People, en masse, had made terrible blunders throughout history. They'd shown appalling lack of judgment. They had been deliberately and unapologetically cruel. Why the hell would I trust their will? I barely trusted the will of people who shared my views.

Nia left soon afterward and so did Pascal. Osaro and Ismail stayed until sunset, drinking beer and arguing. Their opinions were all over the place and hard to follow. Moriam started to pick up bottles, to drop a hint, as Fela's "Lady" played. They were talking about Internet scam letters now.

"I received one at the office," Ismail said. "'Dear Sir, we have been trying to get your contract fund transferred into your account, and Nigerian bureaucracy *have* made it impossible for the funds to be released.'"

He went on: Yahoos were an embarrassment; their grammar was terrible; he'd had to deny he was Nigerian at work to save face.

"No," Osaro said. "No. You don't deny your country. Let me land. Let me land. The fact that one Nigerian does something doesn't mean we're all culpable. One in six Africans is a Nigerian, so we have a higher percentage of crooks."

I wasn't sure when Nigeria switched from a country he had been protected from to a country he had to defend. But he positioned himself left of every issue, and could end up contradicting himself. They had both had a lot to drink, but Ismail was in worse shape.

"You've been away too long, my friend," he said. "You've forgotten your people. Nigerians are criminal by nature. Any corner of the globe, they find and ruin."

Ismail, too, contradicted himself. Was Nigeria a country that instilled discipline or a country that encouraged social misconduct?

"Excuse me," Moriam said, picking up a beer bottle by Osaro's chair. Her hands were full and there were more empty bottles of beer on the table. I got up to help her. They were wearing me out. They weren't even trying to argue anymore. They were just pontificating.

As I picked up a beer bottle, Osaro said, "Lukmon, you're shaming the rest of us."

Ismail smirked. "Maybe he's preparing for his single life in Mississippi."

It always surprised me how easily Nigerians went from arguing to sharing jokes. I could easily have pointed out that they both lived alone and did their own housework, but I allowed them to have their fun.

"Seriously, though, my brother," Osaro said to Ismail. "No matter what anyone has to say about Nigeria, one thing our country has given us is pride. Nigerians always walk with pride, wherever we are. Why is that?"

Ismail gave this a moment's consideration.

"Because they're idiots," he said.

After I'd cleared the bottles with Moriam and she'd gone indoors, I had an opportunity to retaliate for the joke they'd had at my expense. I returned to find they'd discovered common ground in bashing the Nigerian government.

"My thing is this," Osaro said. "Don't pretend you're running an economy. You're not fooling anyone. When you start talking about privatizing industries you've run down, industries that you and your cabal intend to buy up, even I, with a basic knowledge of economics, have to call BS on that."

"They're all useless," Ismail said. "From the crooks that call themselves state governors to the overpaid morons sitting in the House of Reps and Senate. Let's face it. Nigeria is not ready for democracy. We need a dictator to run that country."

"The good news is that political exiles are now free to return home," I said.

That shut Osaro up. Ismail, still in the middle of his anti-Nigerian-government tirade, was unaware of the July Fourth fireworks heading in his direction.

"Who wants to return to that useless country?" he asked.

"Everyone wants to go home now and then," I said. "Except illegal immigrants who won't be allowed back into the United States."

I had no qualms. They left shortly after that.

That night, I walked into our bedroom wearing a towel, after taking a shower, and Moriam said, "You look pregnant."

She was in a see-through nightgown. She got up from the dresser stool and I caught sight of my reflection in the mirror. I had to admit; I was developing a potbelly.

"You're lucky I bother to shower," I said.

I was at home most of the day. It wasn't necessary to pay attention to my appearance. She was more interested in buying sexy nightgowns than in having sex anyway. Sex had to be negotiated and renegotiated with her. The temperature of our bedroom had to be right. Her mood had to be right. Flowers were a waste of time. Taking her out to dinner could come across as a plot and she might end up criticizing the menu. I had a chance if I helped her clean up, as I'd done.

We heard fireworks going off. A neighbor had left a notice in our mailbox about a fireworks display in the park, but I'd thrown it in the garbage.

She yawned. "Today was nice."

"Where are my pajamas?" I asked.

"There."

They were hanging on a chair. I walked over and put them on as she staggered to bed.

"Did Osaro take his Fela CDs back?" she asked, getting under the sheets.

"Yes."

"That man annoys me."

"Why?"

"He's always pretending he cares. He doesn't care, and I wasn't going to let him get away with it this time. Look at him talking about Nigerian women in the sex trade. What has he ever done for them?"

I would never have guessed she was attacking Osaro's hypocrisy at the barbecue, and was now impressed that she'd summarized him so succinctly. He really didn't care about anyone but himself. I could well imagine him on the lecture circuit, championing social justice causes, yet acting inappropriately with women on the sly. For the right speaking fee, he could easily transform himself into a liberal mouthpiece. He had something to gain. So did the people who would pay him. Wasn't that how things worked in literary circles? A few select writers going on about what was wrong with the world, collaborating with institutions that perpetuated the same problems they tackled.

Still, his CDs were useful. Ismail's apple pie was past its expiry date.

"Ismail annoyed Nia today," I said.

Moriam nodded. "She told me. She said she's not surprised his wife left him. I said I was surprised the woman married him in the first place."

"I was surprised she answered him so calmly."

"She's used to dealing with dysfunctional people."

I lay down on the bed with my head on her stomach. "Am I heavy?"

"No."

We hadn't been this close in a long while. I shut my eyes as we listened to the fireworks. America, to her, was a giant workplace and mall. What was my America? Dialogue—as we'd had earlier, as I'd heard since I arrived. It wasn't always interesting to me. I didn't always join in or listen, but the right to free speech was defended. That was the America I respected, the America I wanted to contribute to, and the America to which I was now formally invited.

"What did you think of Dr. Aderemi?" Moriam asked.

"He's okay."

"What about Desola?"

"Mrs. Lawyer?"

"I like her."

"If you ever invite that woman to this house again, you'll be in trouble with me."

"Didn't you hear what she's been through?"

"Nope."

"Weren't you listening?"

"Her English was too much."

I didn't care what Desola had been through. We all had problems. I had to work in Mississippi and I was grateful. Her husband pulled a cucumber out of his patient's rectum on a good day. America had us by our balls, so I didn't want to hear a damn word Desola and her skinny, highly strung, uptight self had to say about being a wife or mother.

She had a silver-spoon upbringing, by any standard, and despite evidence to the contrary, America affirmed my own belief that everyone should be treated with due respect. I no longer had tolerance for the Nigerian way of looking up to people simply because they were rich. Back home, you were tainted by your poor background, even after you progressed from it. Even if you were elected president, Nigerians would mock you for not wearing shoes when you were a child.

Moriam told me what the woman had been through, anyway. She had been a partner in her father's law firm in Nigeria. She'd planned to take the New York bar exam when she arrived in America but found out she would have to go back to college to do that. She gave up her share of her father's partnership before she became an American citizen because America would tax her income in Nigeria. She didn't get paid for the immigration work she did in New York. She volunteered.

Her *noblesse oblige* aside, I had to acknowledge my own propensity for inverted snobbery and inherent male chauvinism. Perhaps I'd gotten the wrong impression of Desola. Perhaps she was even right that I called outspoken women troublesome. America constantly challenged my perceptions and opinions, even when I lapsed into old ways of thinking.

"She came here because of her husband's career," Moriam said. "Now, her career is over. America is not worth it for everybody. Look at us. If you were not at home, I wouldn't be able to put in the hours that I do."

I shut my eyes again. "Hm."

"You're a good husband."

"I'm a better wife than you."

She bent over and hugged me, her skin smelling of soap. Women were wonderful. Women were fantastic. Women would be amazing if they'd only be quiet occasionally, and have sex more often.

"You worked hard today," Moriam said.

"I hope you enjoyed it because this is our last July Fourth."

"What are you saying?"

"No more July Fourth for me."

She sat up. "What! This is just the beginning!"

"Then you barbecue from now on because I'm not doing it."

"Men are supposed to barbecue on July Fourth!"

"Who said?"

She laughed. "It's in the Constitution."

I nodded. "The Constitution. What do you know about it?"

She might have told me, but I was apparently snoring a second later. I found out the next morning when she told me off for falling asleep on her.

SONS

Summer vacation ended and the new school year began. Bashira was now at Taslim's high school and she no longer wanted braces. She was too old for them, she said. She was fifteen. Taslim was eighteen, a senior, and preparing for SATs. Or as Bashira would say, SATs were in the air. If she played her music too loud, he would ask, "Can you turn your music down, please? I'm studying for my SATs." Whenever she called him, it didn't matter what for, he would answer, "I can't talk right now. I'm studying for my SATs."

He wouldn't even clean up after himself because of the SATs. I let him get away with that until Moriam discovered he hadn't changed his bed sheets in weeks. "Have you seen your son's room?" she asked. "What kind of dirtiness are you allowing in this house?"

I went to Taslim's bedroom to check. Normally, I spent only a few seconds in there because the place was a mess and had an odor of sweaty trainers. His bed sheets, originally light blue, had turned tan in part. Of course I found masturbation stains, which his mother may not have recognized, so I asked him to change his sheets weekly from then on.

I no longer talked to him about sex. Moriam had filled that slot. To be more precise, she warned him about sexually transmitted diseases. In fact, she warned him about them so often that even I was tired of hearing about them. Morning, noon and night: sexually transmitted diseases, sexually transmitted diseases. Every weekend: condoms protect, condoms protect. One day we were eating at the kitchen table and she said condoms couldn't fully protect him against herpes simplex virus type 2.

"Dad," he said. "Can you please tell Mom I don't want to hear about herpes while I'm eating okra stew?"

"Or any stew," Bashira said.

She had period pains and looked as if she was about to throw up. I didn't want to hear about any STDs while I was eating, full stop, but Moriam was paranoid about them. After lunch, she emailed Taslim photos of herpes and links to online information.

One of us had to give the boy a break. I was helping him with college applications, which was challenging enough, especially when it came to his essays. If I hadn't insisted he start working on them early, Taslim would have left them to the last moment and submitted his first drafts.

"They want to know the real you," he said. "They don't want no fake essay. They tell you that, and they say parents shouldn't get involved."

I wanted to tell him that no one gave a hoot about him. All they cared about was a story that fit the American narrative: hard work, drive, overcoming odds, community service, confidence, independence, and the rest of it. To avoid an argument, I said his essays would give the wrong impression if they were badly written. He wrote a couple of generic ones about himself and thought they were good enough. I read the first out loud in the family room; he'd claimed that he had come from "nothing" and America had given him "everything." The worst part was where he'd stated that coming to America was "a whole nother" experience for him. I asked where he'd learned that "nother" was a word.

"In America," he said.

"So Nigeria is nothing to you now?" I asked.

He smiled. Taslim was in the habit of doing that when he was under pressure. He didn't get angry easily. It took him a minute to catch on when I was joking. He took me seriously most of the time, but was also indifferent to what I said. He was the same way with his mother.

He now wanted to study business administration. He didn't know why. I thought he envisaged himself living in a certain type of house and driving a certain type of car.

"You have to begin by thinking about why you want to study business administration," I said. "Then think about what you're interested in doing within the field."

Business knowledge was necessary in every field, he said. He was right, but I worried about his lack of depth and focus. Bashira had already decided on her career. She wanted to be an English literature professor and I'd told her she was too young to be sure.

Personally, I would have preferred that Bashira study law and Taslim study engineering, but it wasn't worth getting agitated about their careers. We weren't in Nigeria, where becoming a lecturer was the beginning of a life of penury, or where doing business often came down to hustling for government contracts. Whatever they chose to do was in their hands, so long as they didn't ask me for money later in life. Still, Taslim had to get through his SATs and college applications, and my job was to read every draft of his essays and suggest revisions until he got them right.

The next day he came back to the family room with a whole nother essay. I read it and immediately recognized the writer.

"Who wrote this?" I asked.

"Huh?"

"I said who wrote this essay for you?"

He shifted from one foot to the other.

"Your sister wrote it, didn't she?"

"Uh..."

I pointed at him. "You're getting your little sister, who is in her first year of high school, to write your college essay for you?"

"She didn't mind."

I handed him the essay. "Go and rewrite it, please."

"Dad—"

"You'd better go back and rewrite that essay."

He turned around at the door. "How did you know Bashira wrote it?"

"I just know," I said.

What guy would write, "I learned to put my inhibitions aside and embraced my new life in America"?

"So girls write different?" he asked.

"Different*ly*," I said.

I wasn't becoming a purist. I spoke and wrote American English now. I couldn't pinpoint when holidays became vacations, flats became apartments and shops became stores, but I didn't want my children to speak or write it badly.

I'd tried to encourage Taslim to read for pleasure, but he couldn't be bothered. He was always on the go with his friends: at the movies, at a sports game, at parties, in and out of the house. I gave the boy *Native Son* to read after I read it and he said he hated literature. "How can anyone hate literature?" I asked. He said what he meant was that he didn't read literature books unless they were assigned by his teacher.

He'd barely left the family room when his sister came charging in, essay in hand.

"Dad!"

"What is it, Bashira?"

"Did you say girls write differently from boys?"

"Shouldn't you be apologizing for helping your brother cheat?"

She rolled her eyes. "I just want to know if it's true you said that."

"Yes, I did. So what?"

"But that is so...Okay, okay. I'm going to get some books now. Right now. And I'm not going to tell you who wrote them. I'll read from them and you tell me if they were written by a man or by a woman."

"I'm not going to do that," I said.

"Why not?"

"Because I have no time."

We no longer read books together, and now, all she did with her open mind was confront her mother and me.

"Okay, fine," she said. "But for the record, I want you to know that what you said was sexist."

"So I'm sexist," I said. "But you shouldn't use clichés in essays. Haven't we talked about that?"

"You said they were all right sometimes."

"If used sparingly."

She walked out muttering to herself.

I needed to have more patience with both of them. During the summer vacation, I was their driver. I took them to the mall, the movies and restaurants. I dropped Bashira off at Alice's house on Fridays and picked her up on Sundays. I dropped Taslim off at parties and picked him up late at night and in the early hours of the morning.

His friends were turning eighteen and getting new cars. I'd taught him how to drive in the Corolla and he'd learned pretty quickly. He practiced by driving to his SAT preparation course and back. He seemed keen to prove to his mother and me that we could trust him to drive on his own. On his eighteenth birthday, we bought a Toyota Camry and handed him the keys to the Corolla. He was so happy to have a car at his disposal he didn't complain about not having a birthday party. He'd wanted one, but all we did was give him money to go out to dinner with his friends, and he was satisfied with that—or so it seemed to me. With him, it was always hard to tell.

Now that I no longer shuttled Taslim to his soccer practices and games, I didn't attend his matches as often as I used to. The next Saturday, he came home from a game his team had won. He'd scored three of their five goals. I wasn't there to witness and neither was Moriam. We were in the kitchen, which smelled of *habaneros*. She was cooking chicken stew again. She replaced the lid on the pot and lowered the heat on the cooker.

"Guess what?" Taslim said.

Moriam wiped her hands with a tea towel and flung it over her shoulder. "What?"

"Coach says I am good enough to get a soccer scholarship," he said.

"Hey!" Moriam said, throwing her arms in the air. "My son has arrived! My son has arrived in America!"

I thought she was making a fuss because she hadn't gone to his game. She never did, and I was only too happy to remind her now and then that American mothers took their sons' games more seriously.

"What is 'hey'?" I asked.

"Didn't you hear? He can get a sports scholarship."

"Do you know how many boys are going for sports scholarships? They're being groomed from the moment they can walk. You think every one of them will be Michael Jordan?"

"We're not talking about basketball here," she said. "We're talking about soccer. Soccer is what my son plays, Super Eagles-style."

She demonstrated a dribble. I'd watched the last FIFA World Cup with Taslim. The Nigerian Super Eagles didn't even qualify for the quarterfinals.

"Half of Puerto Rico can play soccer better than them," I said.

She waved. "We can beat Puerto Rico any day. They learned the game from us."

"You don't know jack about the game and neither do Americans. They can't play. They see an average striker and they make a fuss."

"Who are you calling average?" she asked. "Taslim is not average."

"He was at home."

"What are you talking about? He was never average in Nigeria."

"Actually, Mom," Taslim said, reaching for the refrigerator door, "I was."

She rounded on him. "You were the best!"

He laughed. "You never saw me play."

"I don't care! Your coach says you are good enough to get a scholarship!"

"Calm down," I said.

"What's wrong with that?" she asked, turning to me. "What is wrong with going for a sports scholarship? Wouldn't you want him to get one?"

I shrugged. "As far as I'm concerned, he doesn't need a sports scholarship. He has enough brains to go for an academic one. I'm not having anyone put my son in that category."

"So what if they put him in that category?" she asked.

"If he gets a scholarship, would you care whether it is for soccer or math?"

Taslim was pouring himself a glass of water. I spoke to him instead. He might be more rational.

"Please tell your mother how it works, since she thinks any college that gives you a sports scholarship would care about your education."

"Taslim will care," she said, gently. "Won't you, my dear? Yes, you will, because it is possible. I've seen those basketball players. They play basketball and they graduate summer come louder."

Taslim spat out water. "Mom."

"It is up to you as an individual," she said. "Go for your sports scholarship. Just make sure you graduate, so you can become a sports star and buy your mama a house."

"I don't need my son to do anything but face his studies," I said. "Anyone with common sense knows that not everyone can be a sports star."

"How do you know he can't be one?"

"Is that what you're pinning your hopes and dreams on?"

"Who is pinning my hopes and dreams on anything?"

"I personally don't see my children as a meal ticket or retirement plan."

"Who is seeing my children as a meal ticket or retirement plan?"

"You guys," Taslim said, putting his empty glass on the table. "It was just a suggestion. I haven't even considered it yet."

"You must, my dear," Moriam said, softening her voice again.

Throughout the year, no one had singled Taslim out for any sort of academic scholarship, and a year was not enough for him to catch up with classmates who had had private tutors and college prep courses.

"Why can't he just study harder for the SATs?" I asked.

"Why didn't any of his teachers or counselors at school tell him he could get top scores on the SATs and get into an Ivy League college?"

"He already knows that," Moriam said.

"Because I told him, and that's why we should continue to remind him that he can do better on the SATs, not become a soccer star and buy his mama a house."

"Come on, you guys," Taslim said. "I'm just trying to play soccer here. I'm not trying to buy anyone a house."

"All right," Moriam said, folding her arms. "I don't want a house anymore."

"Mom."

"What? After all I've done for you, you can't give me a house? Who gave birth to you? Who carried you on her back? Who fed you? Who suffered for you? You wouldn't even be kicking a soccer ball today if I hadn't nursed your leg. Now you're saying you're just trying to play soccer."

"Your mother has lost her head," I said. "Which reminds me, tell her how one injury can end a sports career."

"I beg you," Moriam said. "That is my domain. You don't know anything about injuries."

Taslim shook his head. "Man, I'm not sure I want to play soccer anymore, if this is how you two are going to carry on."

He left the kitchen and Moriam accused me of putting him down. I always talked to him as if he had no sense, she said. Why did I make him feel guilty about becoming a soccer star?

Perhaps Bashira was right that Moriam favored him. She wouldn't have defended Bashira that way. I said we were Nigerians and we didn't play with education.

She lifted her elbows. "Yeah, yeah, yeah. 'We are Nigerians and we don't play with education.' How can you teach American kids when you hate their country?"

I looked at her as if she had indeed lost her mind. What was she talking about? I criticized Nigeria. I criticized England as well. Did I hate them all?

"I don't hate America," I said.

"Yes, you do," she said.

I remembered how she'd reacted when Alhaja's visa application was denied. I loved America then.

"Did you hate America after what happened to Alhaja at the US Embassy?"

"No," she said. "I was angry."

"It took you a while to get over it."

"I'm still angry, but I don't hate America. You hate America. The American way of life."

"There are many ways of life here."

"The main one."

She was right, but that didn't mean I hated America in its entirety. Besides, what was mainstream America? An illusion. I was allowed to hate an illusion.

"So I hate one aspect of American life. Anyway, I don't intend to teach my personal views to students."

"But you can't hide them, and it's their Constitution that will protect you if you talk."

"I'm not the one who goes around championing freedom of speech."

"What? Americans do?"

"Yes, so they should understand it's my civic duty to criticize the country. In fact, I take pride in doing that. It's the American way."

She eyed me. "You think you know too much. That is your problem."

Moriam and I didn't have different views on education, but she knew my family would have preferred me to marry a university graduate. She had also heard some of my academic colleagues in Nigeria insinuate that nurses were no more than glorified orderlies. Having listened to numerous accounts of her experiences at work, I knew better, but perhaps that was what her reaction was about.

One afternoon, just before Taslim sat the SATs, he came to my bedroom. I was preparing my course notes, bearing in mind my students might need geographical, historical and other information about African countries to study African literature.

Taslim fell backward on my bed. "Dad, you have to help me out here."

I was immune to his SAT theatrics.

"What is it?"

"I can't take this anymore. You've got to pay someone to write my essays."

"No."

"Why?"

"Because it's cheating," I said.

He sat up. "It's not considered cheating. There are people who do this for a living. Professional organizations. Go online and look. You tell them what you want and they write it for you."

"It's cheating, Taslim."

"No, it's not. It's like taking SAT prep courses."

"Cheating."

"Dad, it's torture for me to write essays."

"How will you manage in college, then?"

"I mean personal essays. Seriously. I just want to concentrate on my SATs right now. I don't have time to write about my life or my goals."

"SATs are not enough to get into college."

"Dad, I need to stay focused on my SATs."

"You have to do both."

"The essays are not that serious."

"You'd better take them seriously if you want to get into college. Otherwise, get a job at McDonald's and stop giving everyone stress."

"I'm the one taking SATs here!"

"We're all taking SATs in this house."

I was concerned about his SAT scores, but he was doing well on his practice tests and his college essays had to be written.

He got up from the bed. "Mom agrees with me. She thinks I should concentrate on my SATs."

"I agree with her. Concentrate on your SATs and then on your essays."

"But she doesn't see why I should spend so much time on them at all."

"Your mother doesn't read them," I said.

"That's just it. She doesn't read anything she doesn't need to and look where she is today."

I took that personally. For all my education, Moriam was more accomplished than I was. But she didn't know what his college applications entailed. I still had some hope that Taslim would get into a good college. I wasn't quite the pushy Nigerian father who expected his child to get into Harvard. He wasn't exactly the overachieving Nigerian American kid who would get into every Ivy League college he applied to, either. All I wanted was for him to gain admission to a college that would make our move to America worthwhile. Princeton, for instance, and preferably to study engineering. Was that too much to ask?

"Write your essays yourself, Taslim."

"I don't have time, Dad. I really don't, and I don't see why you won't just let Mom pay someone to write them for me."

I looked him in the eye. "Did you ask your mother to pay someone to write your essays?"

"Um...yes?"

"What did she say?"

"She kind of said you'd be against the idea."

"So why are you asking my permission?"

"Because."

"Don't waste my time, Taslim."

He raised his hand. "Okay, okay, but don't blame me when I don't do as well as I can on the SATs. That's all I'm saying."

"Listen, for once. I said concentrate on your SATs now, and then write your essays."

He left the room with his back hunched.

I didn't worry about Taslim the way I did about Bashira. He didn't need my approval or his mother's attention. I hugged him often and told him "well done" after his games. I even said, "I love you." I was doing that now, but I didn't worry about his emotional state.

He was hardy. If I told him off, he forgot within a few minutes. If Moriam yelled at him, he laughed or ignored her. When he was a toddler, he would actually get lost in our little flat. We would find him behind chairs and under beds. He disassembled gadgets and stuck objects in his ears. He once slipped out of the door and ended up outside in an old oil drum that had tipped over. He hadn't been out of our sight for more than ten minutes and he wasn't even crying when we found him.

A couple of days after his essay meltdown, I asked him to load his plate in the dishwasher. He'd left it in the sink, presumably because of the SATs. I was leaving the kitchen and on my way to the bathroom with a copy of *The New York Times*.

"Make me," he whispered.

I turned around. "What did you say?"

He smiled. "Nothing."

His timing was perfect. If he'd answered a second later, I would have threatened him. He was physically stronger and taller than me and could probably beat me up if we fought, so now that he was older, I kept him in check by intimidation.

Taslim wasn't rude. His sister was. He just didn't listen. The only thing he listened to at home was hip-hop music. He was a Jay-Z fan. I would call Jay-Z "Ja-Z," and he would correct me. There was Ja Rule, Ja-something-else and there was Jay-Z. I'd listened to his hip-hop CDs before and couldn't understand a word of what was being said. I didn't know how he could. My sister Fausat said it was the same with her children in Nigeria. They understood what hip-hop MCs said. She couldn't, and hip-hop gave her indigestion.

To me, hip-hop was okay. I just wished MCs would speak more slowly. Apart from Bashira's treasured Lauryn Hill album, she had an array of CDs that she and Moriam sang along to in the car, by singers I could comprehend: Mary J. Blige, Erykah Badu, India.Arie and Jill Scott. I was from the old-school era so I appreciated their music. When I was a teenager, Earth, Wind & Fire was my favorite group. I had bell-bottom jeans and platform shoes. At the University of Ife, I watched reruns of *Soul Train* on the local television station. I was never an aficionado of music, popular or otherwise. I would much rather read than listen to music, and I couldn't read while listening to music. I was the guy at parties who asked DJs if I could read their album covers to find out who wrote and produced the songs.

Taslim actually stopped playing his hip-hop CDs because of the SATs, and I was impressed. During summer vacation, he'd said they helped him study. Immediately after he sat his SATs, he went back to playing them again and I thought I should make another attempt to understand why he was such a hip-hop fan.

Perhaps I could even get him to talk to me. We'd hardly talked over the summer because he was out with his friends. Once he started studying for the SATs, we didn't have time, and I'd probably alienated him by monitoring his essays. Moriam must have alienated him further by harassing him about sexually transmitted diseases. I could understand her anxiety. We had no idea if he was having sex or drinking or taking drugs. With Bashira, we knew what she was capable of. She had Alice and a small group of girls who thought they were different because they read books. They got back at popular girls in school by calling them dumb. That was the extent to which they went. Taslim had his soccer friends, his basketball friends and other friends. There was no limit to how he could be influenced and he would have ways of hiding what he got up to. I thought I might have a clue if I could get him to talk.

One evening, when his mother was at work and his sister was in her bedroom, I went to his bedroom. He was playing Jay-Z's "Big Pimpin'." He sat in front of his computer, bobbing his head. I recognized his postexamination euphoria and the beat of the music was slow enough for me to understand some of what was being said, but the gist was lost on me.

Taslim said I didn't have to get the gist to enjoy the lyrics. I'd pretty much said the same to Bashira about poetry, so I couldn't argue with him.

We were alike in one way. We needed a reason to talk. Bashira and Moriam talked for no apparent reason and were inclined to go on about their feelings. Talking to them had forced us to be more forthcoming.

I told him I was a fan of Earth, Wind & Fire and he said their lyrics were wack.

"What are you talking about?"

"Soul, funk and disco music have wack lyrics."

"You kids these days don't know anything."

He turned up the volume of his music as if that would help me understand the lyrics better. Hip-hop artists rhymed, he said. They had flow. I said I didn't consider them songwriters.

"Okay," he said. "So who would you consider a songwriter, then?"

I said Stevie Wonder; he said fine. I said Bob Marley; he said okay. I said Lionel Richie. He said he'd heard of him but didn't know any of his songs. I said Smokey Robinson and he asked, "Who?"

"God," I said. "What have I raised?"

He laughed. "You don't believe in God!"

"Who said?"

"Bashira. She said you believe in God only when you shop."

I'd slipped up with her. Before that, I'd kept my promise to Moriam to hide my agnostic ways, but they'd never seen me pray and rarely heard me mention the word "God."

"I believe in God whenever I can't believe what is happening to me," I said. "Add Rod Temperton to that list."

"Who?"

"Rod Temperton."

"Never heard of him."

"You've heard of Michael Jackson, haven't you?"

"Yes."

"So look up Rod Temperton."

"Is he black?"

"Of course," I said.

Taslim logged on to the Internet, did a search and told me Rod Temperton was English, and white.

"He can't be," I said.

"He is."

"Stop lying, my friend."

"I'm not. He's from a place called...Cleethorpes?"

"He wrote 'Rock with You' and 'Off the Wall.' Is he the same person?"

Taslim checked again. "It's him. Look."

I did, and my mouth fell open. Rod Temperton, who wrote "Boogie Nights" and "Give Me the Night," and co-wrote "Yah Mo B There," was white.

"What the hell is going on?" I asked.

"Face it, Dad. You're racist."

"The music industry is."

"Don't tell me. They rip off black artists."

"Everyone knows that."

"Give me the facts, and you'd better come up with something more than Elvis."

"Okay, since we're talking about Michael Jackson, look at what he had to do before they gave him recognition."

"What, bleach his skin?"

"*Thriller.*"

"*Thriller* was a hit!"

"Yes, but you couldn't groove to it."

"I'm not even going to ask what that means. What else?"

"Chris Blackwell broke up the Wailers."

"Who is Chris Blackwell?"

"The person who introduced Bob Marley to the world."

"How did he break up the Wailers?"

"Ask Peter Tosh."

"Never heard of him."

"Exactly. Marley was a rebel, a revolutionary, like Peter Tosh, until Blackwell got hold of him. Then he started singing about love and peace."

He laughed. "White people do love their Bob Marley."

"Because he sang about love and peace," I said. "They love

all black people who advocate love and peace. But listen to his early songs. He didn't like them."

"Face it, Dad. You just don't like them."

I didn't know where he'd gotten that impression. In fact, I didn't think about white people much. They remained on the periphery of my vision until they represented a clear and present danger. Whiteness was what I disliked.

"They got Marley singing about love and peace!" I said. "Like a bloody Beatle!"

"What if he just evolved as an artist?"

"Why should you evolve if the world doesn't?"

"Just admit it, Dad. You're racist."

I reached out to slap his head and he dodged. He was a good-looking boy. I had to admit. He was already sprouting a mustache and had that annoying popular but personable smile. Girls liked him. Everyone liked Taslim. He was everything I wasn't at his age, but I just wished he would use his brains more.

He got his SAT results by phone. His math score was the same, his critical reading score was slightly higher than before, but his writing score had let him down again.

He had no chance of getting into an Ivy League college now. I just had to accept it. He was still ahead of most American high school seniors anyway. He'd kept in touch with friends from his previous school, a few of whom would be satisfied with a high school diploma. One of them had already decided that high school was not worth finishing and was waiting tables in a diner.

Yes, we were Nigerians and we took education seriously, but there was no need to make Taslim feel like a failure. He could have done better on his SATs had he read more. He might even have gotten into an Ivy League college with higher SAT scores, but we would struggle to pay his tuition fees without financial aid. We could barely afford to send him to the in-state colleges he was applying to.

Moriam and I had had the best educations in Nigeria for minimal fees. The educational system there later deteriorated because the government was incompetent, and corrupt. Any sector that depended on income from the treasury was hopelessly underfunded. So again, as I had with healthcare, I asked myself: Why couldn't a country as developed as the United States provide affordable education on all levels and across the board? I just wanted to know. I wasn't expecting a handout. Moriam apparently earned too much for Taslim to qualify for financial aid. We discussed this in private so as not to worry him. She suggested he should get a student loan. I told her I didn't want him to be saddled with one, or to choose colleges based on their fees. She promised to stop shopping—and actually did. She started putting money aside for his college tuition. Only for her son would she do that. I continued to guide him through his college applications in the meantime. They were due in the winter, but I wanted to make sure he completed them before I left for Mississippi. He was applying for business degrees but wasn't sure about his major. I thought he should major in accounting. With an accounting major, he could join a firm and take the CPA exams. As a CPA, he could eventually set up his own firm or work for a corporation.

He was more willing to take advice from his three friends who lived nearby: Riz, Ben and Dre. They called him Taz. They were like delegates to the UN, united by hip-hop. They consulted each other about their college applications as if the world was in the middle of a nuclear crisis. Dre was African American, Ben was Jewish and Riz's parents were from Pakistan. I had to be very careful about how I described them because Taslim might accuse me of racism. I couldn't tell them apart on the phone, and listening to him converse with them, I could believe—with imaginary trumpets blowing in my ears—that given the equal educational opportunities, it was possible to break down the boundaries of race and raise a generation of Americans who could get along despite their different backgrounds.

Almost possible. The verdict of the Diallo case in February had shown me that I couldn't be unduly optimistic. Not just because the officers were acquitted. A subtext of the trial that troubled me was that Amadou Diallo may not have been schooled on how to behave when the police approached him, because he was African. Coming from Nigeria, where the police were often drunk as well as armed and could get away with shooting innocent citizens, I thought that was nonsense. I'd often talked to Taslim about being careful where he went and cooperating with the police, but it would never be enough.

I decided to speak to him again before I left for Mississippi. I had to make sure our discussion wasn't about race, though. He would not listen and neither would his mother. Earlier that month, her colleagues, Claudette and Kim, had had an argument over who deserved a public holiday more, Martin Luther King, Jr. or Mother Teresa. Kim thought Mother Teresa was more deserving. Claudette said that was racist of Kim and Kim burst into tears. "You can call me anything," she said. "But don't call me a racist."

I found that so ridiculous. What if Claudette had called her a child molester? If I were white, I would rather be called a racist than a child molester.

Moriam made Claudette apologize to Kim, regardless. Claudette at first refused to, then she reluctantly did, adding, "I did not call you a racist. I said that was 'racist of you,' meaning your opinion was racist. Not you."

Moriam felt Claudette took the "race thing" too far. She was still not inclined to talk about racism herself, but she was protective of her son, so I told her we both needed to talk to him about staying safe and cooperating with the police. He had to hear it from her as well, since she would be parenting on her own while I was gone.

She agreed with me and we cornered Taslim in the family room one Saturday night when he was on his way out to meet his friends at a restaurant. We told him why, directly.

"Yeah, yeah," he said.

"What is 'yeah, yeah'?" Moriam asked. "We're telling you to be careful of the police and you're telling us 'yeah, yeah'?"

"I know how to handle them," Taslim said. "You've told me before and I watch the news."

"You raise your hands slowly," she said, demonstrating. "And say in a calm voice, 'I am innocent.'"

"They'll definitely shoot me if I do that," Taslim said.

"Please," I said. "Don't get our son killed. This is serious. Now, listen. All we're asking is that you use your intelligence. Don't go anywhere that isn't safe. I don't care if you're with your friends. We know the four of you are buddy-buddy and all that, but when you're out there, you're not the same."

"Who is not the same?" Taslim asked. "Dre?"

"Dre is African American," I said.

"You mean black," he said.

"I didn't invent the term African American."

"Dre wouldn't call himself one. So who do you mean, then? Riz?"

"Riz is a foreigner like you," Moriam said.

"Riz has never even been to Pakistan!"

"Tell that to Americans," I said.

"He *is* American. So who are you talking about, then?

Ben? Because if you're saying Ben is white, he doesn't consider himself white."

Moriam shrugged. "If Ben says he's not white, who are we to say he is?"

I didn't know what had led Ben to dissociate from white people. All I knew was that he could be accepted as white if he made an effort.

"Ben is as white as snow," I said.

"Is that fair?" Taslim asked. "To totally ignore the fact that he's Jewish and label him white?"

"Ask his fellow Americans."

"And how would you like it if his dad said, 'Be careful hanging around that black boy,' hm?"

I turned to Moriam. "We're talking about the police killing young, black men. Instead of listening, he's talking semantics."

"So let's talk about the racism in this house, then," Taslim said. "Didn't you say the other day that Rod Temperton couldn't be white because of the songs he wrote?"

He was no good at arguing. I gave up on the idea of keeping race out of our discussion.

"You're black!" I said. "You hear me? *Dudu*! That is all that matters. And Ben is white! *Oyinbo*! No *oyinbo* was ever brought from Africa in the history of America! So just watch where you're going with him! I don't care if you're all hip-hopping around together! When the police appear, you're just another N-word to them! What? Why are you looking at me like that?"

"'Another N-word'?"

"I didn't invent that term either."

"Dad, only the media uses it."

"Yes, blame the media for everything. I'm trying to give you advice that will save your life and you're blaming the media."

"Mom, he's gone Baba on me again. I can't deal with this."

My leg was shaking. Moriam patted it still and intervened.

"Taslim," she said. "All we're saying is...Okay, take Amadou Diallo, for example."

"Oh, here we go. So, now, every time I go out, it will be 'Amadou Diallo.'"

"Didn't you hear about the verdict?" I asked.

"Yes, I heard about the verdict," he said. "But I'm not going to be afraid every time I leave home."

"Please listen," Moriam said. "This is important. The police said they made a mistake when they killed him. We don't want you going somewhere where the police can say they mistook you for a criminal."

"Amadou Diallo wasn't in a white neighborhood when the police killed him, though!"

"This boy," Moriam said. "He never listens."

"He wasn't!"

"So what?" I asked.

"So the police killed him anyway, and he could just as easily have been killed by someone who lived there. But you've never once told me, 'Oh, don't go to a black neighborhood because someone might kill you there.'"

"Why would I warn you about black neighborhoods? Are we in one?"

"We're in a white neighborhood and the police have never stopped me here."

"Do you have to get killed before you realize you're black?" I asked. "We're giving you the reality about living in America and you're giving us hypothetical situations. You're black. That's all there is to it. We're living in a white neighborhood, so watch where you go because when hip comes to hop, your friend Ben doesn't have to worry."

Taslim laughed. "Calm down. I get it. But you guys are just as much a part of the problem. Don't you see? Dad, I went to that...pizza restaurant this summer and you said I should watch out for the mafia."

"It was a joke."

"It was racist."

"It was culturally insensitive. Italians are not a race."

"What if that was a Jewish restaurant?"

"Judaism is not a race."

"Yes, but what would you say if it were a Jewish restaurant?"

"I would not say a word."

Everyone knew you could survive cultural insensitivity and even racism in America, if you apologized, but you would never be forgiven for anti-Semitism.

"And you, Mom," Taslim said.

"Me?" Moriam said.

"Yes, you. You're just as bad, saying, '*Oyinbos* kiss dogs on their mouths.'"

"I was just playing!"

"So what if she said that?" I asked.

Everyone knew *oyinbos* kissed dogs on their mouths. That was standard practice for them.

"It's offensive to use the word *oyinbo*," Taslim said.

"Oh, they can handle it," I said.

"By the way, I wouldn't go around calling black people here *dudu*, if I were you."

"It's a Yoruba adjective and we've been called worse."

"What about what Mom said about white people?" he asked. "What if Ben's mom said that about us?"

"You would never go to their house again," Moriam said.

"You see?" Taslim said. "That proves my point. You guys are racist."

"Who is racist?" Moriam asked.

"You are," he said. "Just admit it."

"I'm not a racist," Moriam said. "Who has time for that?"

"Dad. He's the opposite of racism."

"It's called reverse racism," I said. "The opposite of racism would be none at all."

"Reverse racism is racism."

I shrugged. "So I'm racist, then."

I was already sexist, according to his sister. For a moment, I was fed up with American political correctness. I missed being around Nigerians who would say, "Yes, I hate Yoruba people. And-so-therefore?"

Taslim lifted his chin self-righteously. "All I'm saying is, if you're going to bring up racism, let us begin by admitting to what happens in this house. That's all I'm saying."

He left the family room limping. For him, that was an air of dignity.

He was like his mother: afraid of being afraid. The only fear Moriam gave in to was the fear of being a mother.

"What's wrong with him?" she asked.

"He's not serious," I said. "He can't even defend his thesis. We're warning him about the police and he's talking about kissing dogs."

"Who is Rod Temperton?" she asked. "Did the police kill him?"

Taslim was right in one sense. I was yet to experience blatant racism in America. In fact, the only time I heard the—yes—N-word, was when he played his hip-hop CDs at home. Since he listened to them intently, I hoped they might remind him that the police were not his best friends.

Despite Taslim's revived social life, fall was calmer than summer for us at home and I finally felt assured enough to hand over the responsibility of driving Bashira around to him. He even took her to the hair salon. He dropped her off there and picked her up. He complained once in a while that he wasn't able to leave home on time because of her, but I had no sympathy. He just had to get used to doing my daily rounds.

He and Bashira were rarely at home once the holiday season began. On Halloween, they went to separate parties and Moriam and I stayed at home. In our neighborhood, leaves had turned yellow and orange. She put a plastic jack-o'-lantern on our porch and gave out sweets, or candy, as we now called them, to trick-or-treaters. They came from our neighborhood and others, accompanied by their parents. They had such confident stares, as if they knew their homes had equity and their national borders were secure. A boy of about six, dressed in a skeleton costume, grabbed a handful of candy from Moriam before running off to his mother's minivan. Moriam smiled and waved at his mother. She said he was cute. Had we been in Nigeria, she would have said he had no home training and jack-o'-lanterns were juju.

She was completely sold on American holidays now. For Thanksgiving, she hung a wreath on our door. We had turkey for lunch even though we were in the middle of Ramadan. She watched the Macy's parade and that old rodent Mickey showed up again. I would have liked to watch football, the real one, but we were still refusing to pay extra for our cable service. On Black Friday, she went to the mall in the early hours of the morning—just to see what was happening, since she was no longer shopping. I warned her she was liable to get trampled on or mugged. She didn't listen. She came back without a shopping bag, and I didn't ask questions. For Christmas, she decorated our door with lights and for *Eid al-Fitr* she gave in to her Lagos Muslim impulses and roasted goat meat. On New Year's Day, which was the biggest day in Nigeria, she went to work, like a true American.

January 2, I flew into Middlesex. It was a Tuesday and as I expected, winter was much milder there. When I left New Jersey it was snowing. In Middlesex? Not a snowflake in sight, but I was surprised to find a city that was similar to a few I'd driven through in New Jersey. I took a cab from the regional airport and passed a billboard that said, "Yes, we can read. A few of us can even write," with photos of authors like William Faulkner, Tennessee Williams and Richard Wright.

Mississippi ought to have more confidence, I thought. In fact, Middlesex with its strip malls, schools and subdivisions had more character than comparable cities in New Jersey due to its high frequency of churches and bail-bonding companies. Downtown, there was a crumbling graveyard that dated back to a yellow-fever epidemic in 1878 and a recently restored theater, which was built in the 1920s in Moorish Revival style. I was able to read the information on their plaques because my cab driver, an elderly African American man, drove that slowly. Near the college, the landscape was more generic with the usual fast-food chains, diners, Asian restaurants and a Super-Walmart.

Every conversation I had required my full concentration, from the one with my cab driver to the one I had with the blond college administrator who showed me to my lodgings on campus. I couldn't understand their accents and they couldn't understand mine. If my English sounded heavy to them, theirs encompassed just about every vowel sound.

"We have a lot of geeusts from out-of-teeaown," the administrator said, referring to academics who visited Middlesex College, a few of whom were foreigners.

"I was just fixin' to tiell you theeat," the cab driver later said, when I told him I might need a car to get around.

The only cab company in Middlesex was the one he worked for. There were hardly any pedestrians, even downtown, where numbered streets and avenues crossed, but I spotted several car rental companies and dealerships on the highways. Pickup trucks and SUVs were popular on the roads, and Hummers seemed to be the latest fad.

I decided to stick to walking within the college area rather than buy myself a car. I needed the exercise and the weather was mild enough. I had a tendency to take beautiful surroundings for granted, but Middlesex College campus was highly impressive, with red brick buildings and towers. The grounds were well kept and spotted with magnolia, ginkgo and dogwood trees, but I had no clue what kind of trees they were until the administrator told me.

I settled into my one-bedroom apartment and got used to the idea of sleeping alone and cooking for myself. I went shopping for food in Walmart and found everything I needed there, including plantains and okra.

Moriam had persuaded me to bring two bags of *garri*. She teased me about not being able to look after myself, as if I were her spoilt son she'd sent off to boot camp. She said it wouldn't make financial sense for her to come over with the children. It was obvious she had no intention of visiting Middlesex. She actually mocked me for living there, as if I were somehow rendered uncivilized because I was able to. Whenever we spoke, she called me "Mississippi Burning," after the movie based on the murders of civil rights activists James Earl Chaney, Andrew Goodman and Michael Schwerner. Taslim and Bashira would tell me to watch out for burning crosses. I soon began to understand the sentiment behind the billboards I'd seen near the airport.

The people of Middlesex, meanwhile, seemed to think Africans were backward. Every time I spoke to someone, they would say, "You're not from around here, are you?" Or, "You have an accent," to which I would reply, "So do you." They would then tell me they loved my accent and I would tell them I loved theirs, after which they would ask where my accent was from. I would say "Africa," assuming they hadn't heard of Nigeria, and they would be amazed by my ability to speak English.

My conversations with them were a cross between mutual curiosity and condescension, and despite my proclivity, I ignored the history of slavery, the Civil War, Jim Crow laws and the civil rights movement because if I didn't, every thought I had would involve racism.

Middlesex College was founded in 1889 and it had just over a thousand students, ninety percent of whom were undergraduates. The latest student demographics said that sixty-five percent of the students were white, thirty percent were black and five percent fell under "other." There was on-campus housing, but most students drove. I met my boss Wes that week, after he returned from his vacation. He was a tall, gray-haired man with a beard. He introduced me to administrative staff whose names I couldn't remember, except the bookstore manager, Mrs. Turner, and the computer manager, Odell. Wes was the only full professor in the English department. The rest of the faculty were associate professors, assistant professors or instructors. He explained that they were in and out of their offices and I would meet them when classes began.

Classes were scheduled to start the following Monday. Registration day was Friday, and he invited me to have dinner at his house that evening with his wife, Anne, and two of my colleagues I was yet to meet, Tim Justice and Laura Broussard. Tim specialized in postcolonial literature and Laura in American literature. They were both associate professors.

Wes lived outside Middlesex, so he gave me a lift in his car, a navy Volvo station wagon that smelled of cigar smoke and dogs. Along the way, we passed parts of the city I hadn't seen on a highway that ran parallel to a train track: a trailer park, a rundown motel called Morocco, creeks with Native American names, farms and barns. We turned off at a four-way junction and passed a lumber plant and an Amish old country store. I was beginning to wonder if we would ever get to his house when we passed a cotton field. Then we arrived at a lake and took a graveled driveway, which led to a bungalow, hidden by pines.

Wes's house was how I imagined a dog- and book-lover's would be. He had wall-to-wall bookshelves and dog toys all over the floor. His dogs barked in another room until he went in there to, as he said, hush them.

Anne showed me a view of the lake from a veranda that extended from their living room. She had a ruddy complexion and shoulder-length gray hair. She was an ob–gyn and unnervingly clinical about death. After Wes returned, she told me about their neighbors who had recently lost their teenaged son in a car crash. He'd played high school football and was something of a local hero. She then told me about the Nigerian doctors that Bisi the Gossip had mentioned. The man shot his wife to death in nearby Pearl, where a high school shooting had occurred in 1997, and the court deemed the shooting accidental.

Anne was from Illinois and was put off by what she called the gun culture in Mississippi.

"The South's not that different from the Midwest in that regard," Wes said.

"Have you been to the Midwest?" Anne asked me.

"Only to Illinois," I said.

"How did you find it?"

"Similar to Mississippi."

"Mississippi and Illinois are very different," she said. "It may not be obvious to you."

"You may be right," I said. "I passed through Chicago and parts of it looked like New York to me."

She laughed until she coughed. I imagined that she and Wes had had South versus Midwest arguments before.

They were Democrats and still smarting about the elections. Middlesex was a Republican city, Wes said, and would always remain one. The voting process was biased against Democrats: registration was harder, lines were longer and voting machines fewer.

"A lot of things happened here during elections," he said. "They needn't have. Democrats didn't show up to vote, anyway. If we had, this would be a Democratic city. We might even have a blue state if people came out to vote."

I was sure he meant black people.

"That would be the day," Anne said, adjusting herself into a more upright position. "Over here, people have enough sense to know they shouldn't use racial slurs in public, but it's perfectly okay to trash a Democrat."

"They call us Demo-craps," Wes said.

I remembered Moriam comparing tribalism to racism. Politics in America was tribal in nature; racism really wasn't. Tribalism began with rivalries, the histories of which were distorted over time. Racism began with falsehoods, invented from the outset. That was the difference.

The 2000 presidential elections had taught me to be less scornful of elections in Nigeria. Before the Florida recount, the hanging chads and the Supreme Court's decision, I'd truly believed that voting was problematic only in countries like Nigeria; now, I realized that even under the watchful eye of CNN and other news programs, the voting system in America was equally prone to ineptitude, manipulation and hysteria.

"These people are insane," I would say to Moriam, whenever we saw delegates on television wearing red-white-and-blue pins and bows, and waving flags. They amused me, unlike the swing voters, who pissed me off with their self-satisfied expressions.

"What is wrong with them?" I would ask Moriam and she would say they ought to be sent to Nigeria to live for a while. Maybe then they would decide who to vote for.

"I hear your wife's a labor and delivery nurse," Anne said.

"She is," I said.

"New Jersey's a more progressive state to work in," she said. "What gets me about people here is their hypocrisy. I see them all the time. They come to me, young women with unwanted pregnancies. They do what they have to, yet they all vote Republican."

"It's duplicitous," Wes said.

"I know you're not supposed to let politics get in the way of medicine," Anne said, "but the evidence is there. Then they tell you it's about the Constitution. It's all about following the Constitution. That's conservative reasoning for you."

"They're not true conservatives," Wes said. "They couldn't tell you anything about conservative principles."

"It doesn't matter what their principles are," Anne said. "All I have to go by is how they vote."

"My father was a true conservative," Wes said to me. "We didn't always see eye to eye, but he was a true conservative."

"This country is not as divided as you might think," Anne said. "If you want to find out what people in these parts really think about the right to choose, ask an ob–gyn."

Wes had a laid-back manner. I knew I could work with him. Anne, I felt, was doing what wives did when they were forced to live in their husband's territory.

She was the first female ob–gyn to open a practice in Middlesex and it took her a while to build her reputation because the male ob–gyns in town didn't give her a chance.

"Cox had the biggest practice in those days," she said. "His father and grandfather were doctors, so he was dealing with families he'd known long before I came along. Davis, too, had a fairly popular practice, but he doesn't have a good bedside manner. He's a bit too reserved. Cox is the country-club type. Davis is more low-key. He lives on a farm. He's actually a better ob–gyn. Cox is too quick to suggest hysterectomies. Every time one of his daughters gets married, he's working overtime. I guess someone has to pay for those wedding receptions. That's why all the African American women in town started coming to me. I would tell them they didn't need to have hysterectomies. Before I arrived, Cox was just whipping out their wombs. Now, we have Abernathy, who pretty much does the same, but they go to him because he has a good bedside manner."

Wes rubbed his ear. "He's the one with the Hummer, isn't he?"

Anne nodded. "Abernathy likes his cars. We have a few ob–gyns like him who come to pay off their college fees. They usually don't stay."

Wes wasn't in favor of civilians driving Hummers. They had delusions of valor, he said.

Their doorbell rang and it was Tim Justice, who was in his early thirties and bald. He wore a black leather jacket.

"I've been listening to juju music in my car," he said.

"Which musicians?" I asked.

"Sunny Ade," he said.

"Ah, King Sunny," I said.

He had Sunny's Mesa/Bluemoon CDs. I told him I was more familiar with his earlier records, his Green Spot and African Beats days, before his brief collaboration with Chris Blackwell. He thought juju had a similar sound to blues.

He was no good at maintaining eye contact. He frowned at an imaginary point between us. I guessed he was popular with students. Wes and Anne seemed to like him. They called him "Just."

Laura Broussard arrived shortly afterward in a floppy red wool cap.

"It's so nice to meet you," she said, removing her cap and shaking her curly hair. "I was so excited to hear we were having a visiting professor from Africa. We had one from China last year and another from Australia the year before, and they were so much fun."

She twittered on. She had only been to Europe. She would just love to travel to other continents. She would go to China, Australia and South Africa.

Wes and Anne's daughter, Bailey, was teaching in Guatemala for a year. Laura said if she were in their position, she would be calling Guatemala all the time. Anne said Bailey would stop answering their phone calls.

She and Wes went to the kitchen to bring our dinner to the table as Laura asked if I'd read any books by Mississippi writers. I mentioned *Native Son*.

"That's set in Chicago, though," she said. "You have to read Eudora Welty and Faulkner, of course."

I'd never heard of Eudora Welty. I asked which Faulkner novel she would recommend.

"*Absalom, Absalom!*," she said, "*The Sound and the Fury*, *Light in August* and *As I Lay Dying*."

Her accent was strong. "*As I Lay Dying*" sounded like "AzAhLahDah." Tim didn't seem to have an accent, or perhaps he had one I couldn't identify.

"Add *Go Down, Moses* to your list," he said. "And take off *Light in August*."

"Why?" I asked.

"It's not one of my favorites."

"Why not?"

"I'm surprised a writer of Faulkner's caliber used the 'tragic mulatto' cliché to explore racism in Mississippi."

"I wouldn't say that," Laura said.

"That there's racism in Mississippi or that Joe Christmas is a cliché?" Tim asked.

Again I suspected that this was an ongoing argument. I also thought Tim was being confrontational for my benefit, which only made me suspicious of him.

"Joe Christmas is more than a cliché," Laura said. "Wouldn't you say, Wesley?"

Wes, who had just walked in, put a dish on the dining table.

"I say we should eat," he said.

They were like a family. Wes was the father, Anne was the mother, Laura was her chatty younger sister and Tim was their sullen son. We had pumpkin soup and rolls, followed by roasted chicken and potatoes with herbs, followed by cheese and crackers. I never thought a meal without pepper could be so tasty.

"I make my own soups," Anne said. "There's nothing better than a home-cooked meal."

She didn't buy vegetables from Walmart or Winn-Dixie. She went to a farmers market instead. I told her I'd never seen as many shoppers on motorized shopping carts as I'd seen at Walmart. She said obesity was the cause. Obesity and disability fraud. She was forced to buy her meat at Walmart because there were no butchers in Middlesex.

"I suppose that's one good thing to say about this place," she said. "Butchery is over."

"Bless your heart," Laura said with a smile.

After dinner, Laura confessed she wasn't familiar with any of the African women writers I was teaching and I told her I'd never heard of Eudora Welty.

"I don't have enough leisure time to read," Anne mumbled.

She was preoccupied with nibbling cheese. Her attitude

reminded me of Moriam's. I would have liked to find out about the job prospects for labor and delivery nurses in Middlesex, but there was no point. Moriam would never be interested.

Wes recommended I read Tennessee Williams' plays. He'd published essays on his works.

"There's a Tennessee Williams festival in New Orleans in the spring," he said. "His birthplace is Columbus. Let me know if you'd like to visit."

"Miss Welty went to the college there," Laura said. "It's Mississippi University for Women now, and co-ed. They have a symposium on her every year that's worth going to."

I nodded, though I had no intention of going anywhere for a while. I asked Wes about the other colleges and universities in Mississippi and everyone chimed in again.

"We have Mississippi State University in Starkville," he said. "They have a campus in Meridian."

"There's Ole Miss in Oxford and Southern Miss in Hattiesburg," Laura said.

"Alcorn State," Tim said. "Medgar Evers went there."

Why the constant references to black history? I wondered.

"Millsaps," Laura said.

"University of Mississippi Medical Center," Anne said.

"Jackson State," Tim said. "We have a few community colleges and private colleges, but Mississippi is at the bottom of the list for education."

"Ole Miss is highly rated nationally," Laura said.

She needn't have bothered defending her state. Mississippi had more colleges than any state in Nigeria.

Wes was keen to find out what Lagos was like. He hadn't been back in thirty years.

"I remember the airport," he said, "and the traffic. We drove from Lagos to Ibadan. I found Ibadan a lot calmer than Lagos."

"Ibadan is busy these days," I said.

I didn't tell him how much Lagos had deteriorated. Instead, I talked about the proliferation of Pentecostal churches there. He was under the impression that the system of government in Nigeria was based on the British parliamentary system. I explained that the judicial system was based on Britain's. Nigeria didn't have a jury system. We didn't have an electoral college either, but the government was like America's with an executive branch, a senate and house of representatives we called the National Assembly.

"What we call Congress," he said.

"Or a complete mess," Anne said.

"Where is Nigeria politically?" Wes asked. "Left, right, center?"

"It's hard to tell," I said. "We've only just got back to having a civilian government, but Nigerians, I believe, are by and large centrists like the British. If we had to choose between Republicans and Democrats in Nigeria, Republicans might win because of their stance on taxes, smaller government and religion."

"Jeez," Anne said.

I almost added that Nigerians were religious as hell and didn't trust governments, but she would probably say the same of Republicans.

"If it's any consolation," I said, "most of us here are Democrats."

I enjoyed their company but found them demanding, as academics could be. All Wes needed to say was, "This is where I stand. How about you?" I would have told him I didn't trust politicians, their parties or elections.

Laura was first to leave that evening. She was driving to New Orleans early the next morning. Her husband was an engineer from Louisiana. He was often gone for months, working on oil rigs. They went deep-sea fishing together. One of their sons was at Loyola University and the other was at Ole Miss. I was fairly sure that was what she said. Her accent was sometimes hard to understand.

As for Tim, I found it hard to engage with a white guy who tried so hard to be politically correct. He was originally from Nashville and his girlfriend taught at a school in Biloxi. He was going there for the weekend. They were in a motorcycle club. He offered to give me a lift back to campus and, as we walked to his car, he told me he'd never planned to stay long in Middlesex, but his job worked out for him in the end.

"It's good to have you here," he said. "I get tired of being the token in the department."

It was too dark to reexamine his features, but I'd seen African Americans in Middlesex who clearly had white blood. Why couldn't it be the other way around?

"You're black?"

"As Joe Christmas," he said.

I shook his hand as if we'd just met. "Why didn't you say?"

"It wasn't necessary."

Everything he'd said seemed sincere now. But how could he have mentioned it? By introducing himself with "Hello, I'm black"?

"I was wondering why you were giving Laura such a hard time, man."

"I always give Laura a hard time. Don't be fooled by her. She'll shoot a deer."

I laughed. "So long as she doesn't shoot black men."

Laura was troublesome. I found out once I started work. I hadn't noticed her manner at the dinner because I was thrown off by

Tim's, but she had a way of evading conversations she didn't want to engage in. No matter who she was dealing with, a student or colleague, she just twittered her way past them with a smile. Perhaps the art of avoidance was part of her Southern charm, but you couldn't pin the woman down, on any issue. I suspected she was a Republican.

Tim told me to look out for two characters in *Cat on a Hot Tin Roof,* Maggie and Mae. She was both of them combined. He admitted he was deliberately provoking her that night. For years, he had been trying to get her to acknowledge that there was racism in Middlesex and Laura would only say that people there didn't cross boundaries, or were used to certain patterns of behavior. He knew how pervasive racism was because of being, in his own words, a reluctant eavesdropper. White people assumed he was one of them, so they didn't always censor themselves in his presence.

I sensed the racism in Middlesex, in the air, in the water and on the campus grounds I walked. I saw it in the mansions on Confederate Drive and the shotgun houses on Martin Luther King Boulevard. I told Tim that if I started talking about it, I might never stop.

Within a few days of our meeting, he revealed that he was an army brat and had lived all over America. I noticed this with other members of the department who were from out of town. It didn't matter where they came from—Alabama, even. They would mention where they had lived to prove they were not originally from Mississippi. The people of Middlesex, meanwhile, were always proud to say they were born and raised there and had never left the state. Even Virginia would be too far up north for them.

I was right about Tim being popular with students, although I couldn't understand why. He was tough on them. They couldn't, for instance, get away with coming late to his classes or turning papers in late. He would tell them off and penalize them, yet they seemed to like him, calling out, "Hi, Professor Justice," whenever they saw him.

Everyone called me "Professor Karim" without difficulty, but half the books on my syllabus had not yet arrived. Mrs. Turner, the bookstore manager, was convinced there was a college-wide conspiracy against me.

"Professor," she said, "in all my years of running this store, I've never seen anything like it before. I ordered those books weeks ago and with all the follow-up phone calls I've made, you would think those books were coming all the way from Africa."

Mrs. Turner was in her sixties, with silver hair. I told her the books were probably coming from England.

"I'm telling you, Professor," she said, "I order books all the time, from all over the world, and I've never seen anything like it before."

"Let's hope they arrive soon," I said.

She leaned forward. "They don't want students here learning about Africa. But I'll get you your books, I promise. I'm looking forward to reading them myself."

"Thank you, Mrs. Turner," I said.

Other people called her Miss Arnelle, but I was extra polite to her. You didn't want to get on the wrong side of her. She had a prominent spot in the bookstore window for books on African American abolitionists and civil rights activists like Sojourner Truth, Frederick Douglass and Fannie Lou Hamer.

"Our children don't read them," she said. "They try and hide our history, so I put it on display. They still don't read them."

Browsing the books, and not just because Mrs. Turner was watching me closely, I had profound respect and appreciation for

African Americans who had made it possible for immigrants like me to whine about casual racism. It made sense that people whose ancestors had been forced to come to America were instrumental in driving its political maturity. It also made sense that Herbert Macaulay, the father of Nigerian nationalism, was a descendant of repatriated slaves. He would have been enlightened enough to devise a political strategy to oppose colonialism. Championing freedom would have been in his blood. But Lagos had long forgiven itself for being a slave port. Mississippi, despite its defensiveness, was still being shamed for its participation in the trade.

My class was actually a World Literature class. Wes wanted his students to have exposure to literature they would not normally read. He invited professors once a year, for a semester or two, and sometimes a whole year. Regarding my English Composition classes, I told him I'd taught British English, not American English, but had familiarized myself with the differences in spelling and grammar rules. He suggested I teach an Introduction to Composition class for freshmen who had low scores on the English section of the ACT examination, and an evening class for non-degree students who planned to apply to Certified Nursing Assistant training programs. Both classes were usually taught by instructors. I thought he was making a special allowance for me, so I could have a lighter load, but later found out that no one wanted to teach them.

In my first week, a student called Madison dropped out of my Introduction to Composition class. She was a shy girl and was almost in tears when she came to my office to tell me she couldn't continue. I asked why, and she said she had trouble understanding my accent.

"I see."

"I don't mean to be rude or anything."

"It's all right."

"I feel so bad."

"Don't."

I felt bad for her and later mentioned the incident to Tim, who took offense.

"Now, why would she say that?" he asked. "Honestly, some of these kids..."

Tim was intense. All I wanted from him was to find out how Madison could change classes. After much protest, he promised he would take care of her.

Most of the students in that class were white and male. My evening class for non-degree students, which turned out to be my most rewarding, had a good number of African American women with full-time jobs. Going through the class roster the first time, I mispronounced some of their names: T'Keyah, LaBreona, Sharquetta. I apologized for doing that and told them the same had been done to me in America. I should have left it at that, but made the mistake of saying I wished people would make more effort to get ethnic names right.

LaBreona said her name wasn't ethnic; it was French. T'Keyah said hers was African.

"My cousin name Kenya," she added.

She dropped her possessives and certain verbs when she spoke.

Sharquetta watched me with interest. I was sure they were all curious about their African professor, but I wasn't quite sure I measured up to their expectations in my chinos and jacket.

My best students in the class were Tisha and Tavarious. Tisha worked at a juvenile detention center, Tavarious at an office supplies store. He had eyebrows shaped like a woman's and called himself a "people person." Tisha had two young children she constantly talked about. During class exercises, she and Tavarious often got into arguments over grammar and punctuation rules. One evening, Tavarious yelled, "It's supposed to be a colon, not a semicolon." Tisha, who was older, told him, "You need to be quiet. You do not know what you're talking about." Tavarious shook his head and said, "We both grown," over and over. It was like watching my children quarrel. After class, I talked to them about being civil to each other, even though they were back to being friends.

My African literature class was predominantly white and female. My best students were Louis, who could pass for an Igbo boy, and Casey, who dyed her hair black to match her clothes. In my second week, I handed out notes and maps on Senegal and Casey presented a paper on Mariama Bâ before we read *So Long a Letter*. A week later, we discussed the book, but most of the class were too tired to contribute. One of them, Rob, could barely keep his eyes open and he conveniently sat at the back. I was surprised that so many of them worked part time, Casey and Louis at nearby restaurants.

Casey annoyed other students. They rolled their eyes and huffed whenever she answered questions. In week four, she and Louis developed a rivalry during our class discussion on *Our Sister Killjoy*. The previous week, I'd distributed handouts on Ghana and Louis had presented a paper on Ama Ata Aidoo. Casey thought the protagonist in *Our Sister Killjoy*, Sissie, was homophobic because she slapped Marija, the German woman who tried to kiss her. Louis thought Sissie had every right to slap her.

"Marija invaded her space," he said.

"Sissie could easily have turned her down," Casey said.

"What if Marija were a man?" he asked.

"That would be different," Casey said.

"Why?" Louis asked.

"Because," Casey said. "I can understand her slapping a man to protect herself."

"What if Marija was as strong as a man?" Louis asked.

"We don't know that," Casey said, "and it's still different than a man trying to kiss her."

All of my students said "different than."

"If a man tried to kiss me," Louis said, "I'd knock him out."

He won that round but lost the next when Casey said Sissie was racist.

"Wait, wait," he said, raising his hand. "How can she be racist?"

"She compared Germans to pigs," Casey said.

"Are you serious?" Louis said. "She was an African woman—"

"Ghanaian," I said.

"Sorry," he said. "She was a Ghanaian woman in Germany. She was just making an observation about their skin color."

"She could have compared them to something else," Casey said.

"To what? Milk?"

Casey's face turned red. "I thought she was racist in other ways."

"Was she racist when she, um, criticized Nazis?" Louis asked.

"No," Casey said.

"What about her views on colonialism?" I asked.

Casey hesitated. "No."

"You see?" Louis said. "Sissie wasn't racist. She was just mad."

"About what?" I asked.

"Everything!" he said.

I'd always believed the power of a book was in its ability to unite and divide, and *Our Sister Killjoy* divided my class along color lines. Even Rob, who was usually asleep at the back, joined in the discussion and I was sure he hadn't read the book. Most of the class sided with Casey, but I had to admit that if an African woman had any intelligence or pride, she would have to be mad about everything.

What I appreciated most about *Our Sister Killjoy* was that Sissie was a confident protagonist. If some of what she had to say offended readers, so be it. She was not addressing them. She turned them into eavesdroppers, and eavesdroppers sometimes didn't like what they overheard.

After class, Louis approached me, zipping up his sweater, and said, "Sorry, Professor. I didn't mean to get loud. It's just that Casey always has something to say."

"Don't you?" I asked.

He frowned. "Yeah, but Casey thinks she knows everything."

"Don't you?"

"Yes, but she doesn't know everything about Africa."

"Do you?"

He threw his hands up. "Aw, man!"

He could have been my son, but even so, I would never favor him in class.

"Keep talking," I said.

I had a student in my evening class who was so quiet I might not have noticed her. Her name was Andrea. She was older than my other students and probably in her mid-twenties. She performed terribly in class exercises. After completing them, the students would exchange papers with their class partners, who would mark them and hand them to me to review and grade. She always got Fs, yet on her homework assignments, she consistently got Bs.

One evening, she handed her class exercise directly to me because she didn't have a partner in class. I later discovered that she hadn't answered a single question. She had attempted the first two, but her answers didn't make sense. I realized she couldn't write. She'd managed to fool me, perhaps by copying answers from her class partners. I couldn't be sure because my students changed partners from class to class.

I gave her an F as usual. She didn't comment when she picked up her paper at the beginning of the next class. I said nothing to her, but for the first time, watched her during the class exercise. She sat next to Tisha and kept glancing at Tisha's paper. At the end of class, I compared her answers to Tisha's and they were identical. After class, I asked if I could have a word with her.

"How are you coping with this course?" I asked.

"I'm doing fine," she said.

"You got an F on the last exercise."

"Yes."

"What happened?"

She hesitated. "I didn't answer the questions."

"Why not?"

"I was tired."

I didn't know what she did for a living, but she wore skirts and blouses, unlike my other students, who showed up in jeans and tracksuits.

"I saw you copying Tisha's answers," I said.

She shook her head. "I wasn't copying."

"I saw you," I said.

She hugged her bag and swayed from side to side.

"Do you do your own homework?" I asked.

"Yes."

My gaze dropped to my pen. "I think you have trouble with writing. If that is the case, cheating on class exercises and getting someone to do your homework won't help."

She became tearful. "I'm not trying to cause no trouble. I just need to get through this class."

I wasn't sure her tears were genuine, but if I reported her, she could be thrown out of my class. If she didn't pass my class, she wouldn't be admitted to a CNA training program. She pulled out a Kleenex from her bag and dabbed her eyes. How she'd managed to graduate from high school, I didn't know. Wes had said the public school system in Middlesex went downhill after elementary school, and Tim had said football and cheerleading were more important than education in any high school, public or private. Still, I couldn't believe that she had gotten through high school without learning how to write.

"Do you have trouble reading?" I asked.

"No."

"Are you sure?"

"I don't have no trouble reading."

"Listen," I said. "I'm not here to make life difficult for you."

She nodded. "I'm just trying to get through this class. That's all I'm trying to do."

She had been trying for two years. It was her third and final attempt. I wondered if any of her instructors had noticed she couldn't write, but if I told Wes about her, she would have to drop out immediately.

I excused her. There was no point disputing what she'd said. She was a non-degree student, and the way I saw it, the end-of-semester exam accounted for most of her grade. If she carried on the way she was going, she would definitely fail my class.

Moriam stopped ridiculing me for living in Middlesex as she began to see how useful I'd been to her at home. It was snowing heavily in New Jersey now, and her commute to work took longer. She was never confident behind the wheel, but she was more worried about Taslim's driving. She often complained that he used the bad weather as an excuse for staying out late and was rarely home on weekends. I listened, or grunted now and then to pretend I was listening. She took offense if I made suggestions, such as when I told her to confiscate his car keys. She said that would mean he and Bashira would have to ride their school bus in the cold, and it was bad enough that she worried about them getting home safely while she was at work. I kept my opinions to myself from then on because she seemed on the verge of accusing me of abandoning her.

One Friday night, she called at around eleven o'clock to say Taslim had gone out to meet his friends. She'd tried his cell phone repeatedly, but he wasn't answering.

"Maybe he's on the road," I said. "Remember we told him not to answer his phone while driving."

"Can you believe it?" she said. "He promised he would be back on time. Honestly, I will deal with that boy when he gets home. He thinks I'm playing with him. I will ban him from using that car until he goes to college."

The trouble was that Moriam still didn't follow through after a threat. Taslim even teased her about that. Her first answer was always no, but if he pestered her enough, she eventually said yes.

As she went on about him, I grunted at intervals.

"What is 'hm'?" she asked, after a while. "Is 'hm' all you can say at a time like this?"

I switched the phone to my other ear. "You said he's not answering his phone."

"I told you that already."

"I heard, and I said he might be driving."

"So?"

"So let's wait until he gets home. We can't do anything until then."

"No," she said. "I want you to take care of this now, as a father and as a man. He never listens to me, whatever I say. What is this? Bashira is not this difficult. I thought she would be the difficult one and she hasn't given me any trouble since you left. Taslim is getting out of hand. God only knows what he and his friends are doing at this time of the night. You have to talk to him, Lukmon. A boy needs a man to control him. You can't just sit in Mississippi saying 'hm.'"

"I said I will take care of it."

"You never said that."

"I'm saying it now."

"All right, all right. But call him right now, *right now*, and tell him he can't drive around this late at night in the winter. You hear me? God forbid something happens to him."

The woman ought to make up her mind. When I was home, she'd wanted me to switch roles; now I was away, she wanted me to switch back. She wasn't helpless. She'd given Taslim permission to leave home. He would not dare go out otherwise.

I mumbled a goodbye and called him afterward. He immediately answered his phone.

"Dad?"

"Taslim, what are you doing out so late?"

"Uh, it's not that late."

"What do you mean it's not that late? Your mother has been calling you. She just called me and she was shouting. What is wrong with you? Don't you know she's worried? Where are you, anyway?"

"I'm almost home."

"Are you driving?"

"Yes."

"Why did you answer your phone, then? Didn't I tell you never to answer your phone while you're driving?"

"I saw your number."

"You must have seen Mom's number. How come you didn't answer her call?"

"She calls me for no reason. I thought you were calling about an emergency."

"Drop your phone, please, and find your way home."

"Okay."

"'Okay' what?"

"Okay, Dad."

There were times I was conscious of playing a role as a father and this was one. It wasn't that long ago that I was a teenager myself and out doing what I shouldn't. I was relieved Taslim was safe and really didn't want to call Moriam back, but I had to reassure her.

"Yes?" she said.

"I've just spoken to him," I said.

She started howling again. "You see? You see what I mean? No respect. No respect for me, that boy. This is what I've been going through since you left. He thinks he's a law unto himself in this house. I've told him, 'You get on my nerves one more time and I'll send you to Mississippi to live with your father.'"

"Well, he's on his way home to you."

"Foolish boy. He will see what I will do to him, driving around at night as if he has no one to answer to, going to meet his friends when it's snowing. What I will do to him, he will never forget..."

I kept quiet until she fell silent, then I was forced to speak.

"How is Bashira?" I asked.

"She's in bed."

"Tell her I will speak to her tomorrow."

"How can I tell her when she's asleep?"

"Tell her tomorrow when she wakes up."

Moriam was quite capable of handling Taslim. She knew as well as I did that shouting at him wouldn't work, yet she continued to. She would call to report him for not coming home on time. I would answer her calls, and without a hello, she would say, "Do you know what your son has done?" As if I had the power of prediction. One night I again told her, "Look, take his car keys from him this weekend."

"Who will drive Bashira around?" she asked.

"No one," I said. "He will be stuck at home with her."

"I don't know if I can do that."

"Why not?"

"It's not fair to Bashira."

"Do it anyway and he will behave himself. You'll see."

She didn't want to drive Bashira around. Taslim knew that, and he was taking advantage of her.

That weekend she took his car keys and he couldn't believe what was happening to him; neither could Bashira. They called me separately: "Dad?" "Dad!"

Bashira said she'd done nothing wrong. She didn't see why she should be punished because Taslim was suffering from senioritis. Taslim asked what he could do to get his car keys back and I said, "Obey your mother."

It was as simple as that. He apologized to Moriam, and the next time she called, she was back to making fun of me.

"Ghosts of Mississippi," she said. "How are you?"

Ghosts of Mississippi was the movie based on Byron De La Beckwith's trial for the murder of civil rights activist Medgar Evers.

That January, Byron De La Beckwith died at the age of eighty. Then, in February, Medgar Evers' son, Darrell, died. He was forty-seven. I listened to a radio report on Mississippi Public Broadcasting about both men, and apparently, when Medgar Evers' body was exhumed in 1991 for an autopsy that led to the third trial and conviction of De La Beckwith, it was found to be well preserved, as if he had been buried recently. I could only imagine what the experience had been like for his family to see him again, yet as a young man. That moment, when the past and present coincided, characterized Middlesex.

Once in a while I had a loss of temporal perspective in the city. There were no Confederate flags outside the public buildings, such as the court house or city hall, but I saw photos and posters of the flag indoors in private businesses. The CPA I consulted about state taxes had a mini one on his desk. Without solicitation, he told me about his great-grandfather who had lost property to the Yankees during the Civil War, as if it had occurred a year before. Tim later told me that Civil War reenactments were held at the mall and white folk gathered around to watch as black folk kept on walking.

The African American community in Middlesex was almost half the population and I gave Tim my honest opinion about them: they were not receptive without an introduction. Beyond the college, where I didn't have the benefit of one, I opened my mouth to talk and they stared at me as if my foreign accent spelled trouble. He said I shouldn't worry about that. They were like that with him and his girlfriend Erica. They assumed they were an interracial couple.

I had not seen a single interracial couple in Middlesex, but I'd seen biracial children—no adults. Once in a while, I saw Mexicans tending lawns in white neighborhoods and Choctaws who came from a reservation nearby. There were quite a few Asians in the city: Indians, Pakistanis, Chinese, Koreans and Filipinos. Tim said there was a Jewish community, which had dwindled over the years, and they attended a synagogue in town. Muslims had a center out of town that also served as a mosque.

He was helpful with information. So was Odell, the computer manager at the college. I didn't have to make appointments with Odell, as some of my colleagues did. He introduced me to his barber, Tommy, who pontificated about everything from the Old Testament to the presidential elections while cutting my hair. Tommy called me "Professor," even as his younger barbers made it clear they were not impressed by my qualifications.

At the college, Mrs. Turner continued to intimidate me. Whenever I visited the bookstore, she invited me to her church, Fifth Street Baptist, so I lied that I was Muslim to please her.

"It don't matter," she said. "We all worship one God. My nephew's Muslim, but he always comes home for Christmas."

She gifted me a pocket-sized New Testament, King James Version, after which she would say, "We missed you last Sunday," and I would answer, "Yes, Mrs. Turner."

Elderly women took to me because I sucked up to them. Mrs. Turner was the eldest of seven children raised on a farm. Her parents were sharecroppers. She went to a desegregated high school, where she was subjected to racial taunts on a daily basis. She attended Alcorn State University and met her late husband there. They had four sons, all of whom were Alcorn graduates.

Another elderly woman whose name I didn't know befriended me. She was white and worked as a cashier at a diner near the college. I went there when I was in the mood for Southern food. The first time we met, I was paying for my meal when she asked, "You military?"

I said no, noticing her front teeth were missing.

"You at the college?" she asked.

I told her I worked there and she said I was entitled to a discount if I showed my ID. The food at the diner was fantastic: fried chicken, sweet potato casserole and collard greens. She gave me inside information on the menu: "Liver and onion's on Wednesday," or "Catfish fry's on Friday." For this, I got to hear about her granddaughter's boyfriend who was arrested for "felony bad check" and several DUIs, her divorced daughter whose trailer was destroyed by a tornado, and her own trailer, which burned down when her daughter and granddaughter moved in with her. I was so disturbed by her string of bad luck, I told Tim about the fire in her trailer and he said someone there was probably cooking meth.

The woman was a great-grandmother. Her granddaughter had recently had a baby. Where they were all living, I didn't know, and I was too afraid to ask. She told me she earned $10,000 a year and bought furniture and clothes from the Salvation Army family store. She never once asked where I was from and had only this to say about the people of Middlesex: "They think they're good Christian folk, but they ain't."

I learned more about Middlesex through her and other people I met outside the college. They went "huntin'" and "mud ridin'" for sport. On Fridays and Saturdays, they drove to the casinos in Choctaw territory to gamble. On Wednesday evenings and Sunday mornings, they were in church. They lunched at Cracker Barrel or Chick-fil-A. Younger kids spent their weekends at the skating rink and the bowling alley with their families. Teenagers met at Waffle House or La Piñata at night, and found parking lots in which to drink and take drugs. At the start of football season, they toilet-papered their friends' homes. The man who told me this said TP-ing was an American tradition. I told him I'd never witnessed the phenomenon in New Jersey.

To me, TP-ing was an act of vandalism, but the point was, in New Jersey, American culture had seemed Westernized. In Middlesex, American culture was downright African, especially during football season. Young men painted on their eye black; young women cheered in their short skirts. There was much chanting and feasting in the form of tailgating. There were bonfires.

One aspect of these African ways I appreciated was that their youths were polite to their elders. They addressed their elders as "Mr." and "Miss" or "Sir" and "Ma'am," whether they respected them or not.

For me, the best place to observe Middlesex people of all kinds was Walmart on a weekend. Everyone converged there, from old African American men with Jheri curls to young Mennonite women with their headgear. Some people actually walked around in their bedroom slippers. I would be standing in the checkout line and a person behind me or in front of me would volunteer intimate details about their lives: their debts, their grandmother's hoarding habit, or their kidney stone operation. They were smug about being down-to-earth and showed off their lack of knowledge. I once put my plantains on the conveyor belt and a man asked, "Hey, what are those? Oh, I thought they was bananas. All I know is bananas."

A major entertainment event for them was a 1950s musical at the Little Theater. Pageants, ballet recitals and Pentecostal plays were held at the older, restored theater. I spoke to people who had no idea who Faulkner or Tennessee Williams were. I went to the post office; the service clerk had never heard of Nigeria. This was downtown, where half the businesses were closed. A UPS storeowner there told me the rich businessmen in Middlesex made sure franchises and businesses were kept out so they could control the labor market. He was against big government and taxes. On his wall was embroidered art, saying, "It's hard to be humble when you're from Mississippi" and "God writes the best stories." There was a poster of a gun, but it was too far away to read the caption. He was also a notary public and had a sign for that on his counter. As we stood on opposite sides of it, talking to each other, a woman, probably in her sixties, came in to get her gun permit notarized. She had a present for her granddaughter, wrapped in pink paper and tied with a matching bow. She wanted it couriered to California. After I left his store,

I went in search of *The New York Times* and couldn't find a copy anywhere, except at the college library.

I asked Tim about that one afternoon when we had lunch at a Thai restaurant near the college.

"It's the same way they watch Fox news," he said. "They don't trust any other source."

"Here's what I don't understand," I said. "Whatever they say, when you look at how they live, they're not that different from the rest of the country."

They had abortions, according to Wes's wife, Anne. They seemed to accept gays. There was a professor at the college who sometimes had lunch with his partner at the Thai restaurant and no one harassed them. Of course there were people in Middlesex who would attack, if not kill, them, and yes, there were people who loved their guns and Jesus, but you could find them in any American city.

"People here don't live up to their own values," Tim said. "They vote for values they can't live up to because they allow politicians to manipulate them. Make no mistake, the one factor that truly divides this country is race. They can deny it until they're blue in the face, but that's the way it is. You come from a country where the military can just walk in and take over the government. Well, it wasn't all that long ago that people here weren't allowed to vote. And let's not kid ourselves about the Founding Fathers. Writing the Constitution may have been an enormous task, but observing it was a lot harder for them. Racism is everywhere in America and it cuts across political lines. Liberals may think they're more progressive, but if Daddy doesn't have a job and Mommy can't feed the kids, they'll find someone to step on."

"The almighty dollar," I said.

"It's the lowest common denominator," he said. "And when Daddy can't make money, everyone else suffers."

"Mommy, too?"

"Sure, but they're in it together, the ones who wear the pants and the ones who would like to believe that Father knows best. Why do you think they all pack pistols around here? They're still stuck in that antebellum mind-set, petrified that if their men are not around to protect them, they might be forced to surrender their virtue. Virtue most of them already surrendered at sweet sixteen, mind you. They stand by their men on the Second Amendment and everything else, even when it affects them negatively, even if it kills them to. But hey, these are great-granddaughters of women who were complicit with Massa when he did as he pleased with slaves, so what do you expect from them?"

It became clear to me that racism was first and foremost an economic problem, which would continue so long as it could be used to rationalize the abuse of black nations. In America, its core purpose was to justify the exploitation of slaves and their descendants. Their oppression was consequential to that.

When Tim talked about race, he didn't always specify who he was referring to, but he didn't need to. Our conversation that afternoon reminded me of an exchange I'd overheard when I stopped to listen to an African American man at Speakers' Corner in London. The man was a member of the Nation of Islam and looked biracial to me. A woman asked why he spoke with such disdain about white people when he was, as she put it, part white. "Lady," he said, "the color of my skin and color of my eyes are the result of rape." It was the first time I'd seen someone publicly renounce their white blood. Where I was coming from, people had clung to any foreign ancestry, no matter how remote it was, and however it had come about. I knew a Lagos woman with the last name Cruz who claimed her father's side of the family was

Brazilian. In Mayflower School, I'd actually heard a girl declare herself a quarter-caste. She was from Port Harcourt, and her grandfather was an English sailor her father had never met.

In private, Tim often spoke as if white men were responsible for all that was wrong with America. I could see why it was expedient, but it just wasn't accurate, and who better than an African man to understand how unfair it was to be regarded as a perpetuator of rape and every other human-caused atrocity. Still, I didn't defend white men whenever he carried on that way. Their reputation was their problem. Another afternoon, he would tell me that black Southern women were some gun-toting sisters who wouldn't hesitate to pop a cap in a brother's ass, only to reinforce his view that race was the sole dividing factor in America.

He was the closest I had to a friend in America, and I could imagine Moriam's amusement that he looked white and talked about race and racism so much. I could sympathize with her now that I knew what it was like to avoid having such discussions for the sake of staying what she might call positive. I sometimes joked that he could get away with being radical while I could not, but there was only so much I could learn by reading and observing, so I continued to listen to what he had to say.

He was for affirmative action for African Americans, and resentful that white women benefitted from it. It was clear how affirmative action had helped me. Qualified as I was to teach African literature, I couldn't get a job without it. He described my experience in America as white, which surprised me until we talked about black poverty and incarceration; black businesses and the lack of access to finance. I didn't tell him this, but a lot of what he said was applicable to the majority of Nigerians. Nigeria was essentially the United States with a minority of rich people in place of white people. Those of us who left had expectations that there were more opportunities elsewhere, and the competition was less. Not only did we arrive in America with some advantage, we could return with a greater one. By leaving Nigeria, however, we were opting out of that system. We were basically saying it didn't have enough to offer us, and we no longer wanted to contribute to it. Yet, here I was, coming to the understanding that African Americans were in a situation similar to mine in Nigeria. So, I had to ask myself this question: How then could I justify committing myself to a system that exploited them?

I was curious to hear Tim's opinion on racism in Middlesex College, meanwhile. At work, he seemed to get along with the other members of our faculty, Laura included. He liked Wes. Wes was real, he said. Yet, he also said Wes was disingenuous to claim that Mississippi could be a blue state, knowing full well that white men had made sure it would always remain a red one.

Racism on campus was covert, he said, and I was more likely to encounter it in liberal circles, which made sense. I wasn't, after all, socializing with rednecks and having heart-to-heart conversations about race with them.

"You've heard the president talk about the soft bigotry of low expectations, haven't you?" he asked.

I said I had but wondered if the president were reminiscing about his privileged education.

"It applies to students," he said. "Watch out for that."

I said I'd already seen evidence of it with students in my evening class.

He said, "Now, for you, as an academic, to get anywhere, you must allow them to lay claim to discovering you and raising you. But don't expect to rise higher than them, and always remember to be as black as they want you to be."

"You're depressing me, man," I said. "Seriously."

It was hard enough living up to American expectations of what it meant to be African. I didn't even care if Tim was accurate. I just couldn't live in a place like Middlesex, with that level of cynicism, so I kept my word about not talking about racism from then on.

As a result, our conversations got more personal. He told me his parents got divorced when he was a child and he stayed with his father. He was an overweight kid and his father forced him to go on early-morning runs. In his late teens, he went to live with his mother for a while. He wanted children but didn't want to get married. His girlfriend Erica did. We weren't close enough for me to advise him not to marry her because it might mean the end of his sex life. He smoked dope. I didn't know how he could do that and teach. He said he'd heard Nigerian dope was good. I said it was so good it almost blew my mind.

Through him, I discovered more blues musicians. The only one I'd ever paid attention to was B.B. King. Now, I listened to John Lee Hooker and Muddy Waters. He wasn't a fan of country music but he recommended artists like Johnny Cash, Willie Nelson and Patsy Cline. I found them soulful; so soulful I was convinced they all had black blood.

We also talked about literature, and some other afternoon, I asked him why writers like Tennessee Williams and Faulkner were classified as Southern writers.

"The South claims them," he said. "Then there's the politics of who's labeled a regional writer. Have you read Truman Capote?"

"Only *Breakfast at Tiffany's*," I said.

"You should read his short stories. Capote grew up in Mississippi and Alabama, but he's not always classified as a Southern writer. Now, Miss Harper Lee? She's a Southern writer, through and through."

I'd never heard the term Northern writer, but perhaps the South needed to point out how much their writers had contributed to American literature. I spoke to people in Middlesex and could tell where Tennessee Williams' lyricism and Faulkner's weightiness came from. I looked around and could understand why animals and even inanimate objects were personified in Southern literature. The landscape was alive, like Maggie the cat. There were extremes, divisions and contradictions everywhere and the legacies of slavery and segregation were still fairly obvious.

What set Middlesex apart was its tyrannical form of unity. You "might-could" be different, but you dare not announce that you were. There was little room for self-expression. If you were vocal and you disagreed, there was no public space for dissent, or discussion of alternative ideas, except in safe, contained places like the college. Even then there could be repercussions for speaking out. Freedom of speech was limited, and this in a state that defended the Constitution. I couldn't understand it, but by early spring, when the tornadoes began, I'd progressed from a voyeuristic position to an acclimatized one and formed my opinion of the place. Middlesex suffered from its own dogged insularity, and in that respect, the city reminded me of myself.

The next African Literature Association conference was held in Colorado that year but I missed it because it took place during spring break and I was ready to go home.

The idea of New Jersey being home was new, and before I left, Wes asked if I would like to return to Middlesex College in the fall. Having taught there for half a semester, I was open to the idea. I even considered applying for a permanent position, but I didn't think Moriam would move to Mississippi. Nor did I think it was fair to ask that of her or our children.

They were all at the airport to meet me. Taslim drove and, according to Moriam, nearly crashed the car on the way there. I hugged them as if I hadn't seen them in years. Bashira was taller and Taslim looked as if he'd gained some weight. He had been accepted at Fairleigh Dickinson to study accounting. It wasn't Princeton, but, as I told him, having a degree from an Ivy League college was no guarantee of success.

We were still waiting to hear from Rutgers, and my advice to him was partly due to the fact that Moriam told me Dr. Aderemi's daughter, Anjola, had gotten into the University of Pennsylvania, and she was a National Merit Scholarship finalist. Frankly, the news made me sick, but my main problem was how to tell Moriam about my job offer.

We got home and she'd cooked enough to feed two families. The house smelled of Christmas and New Year. As we ate in the kitchen, she and the children rehashed what had happened in my absence, with a "Remember" this or "Remember" that, and laughed conspiratorially. They even laughed about the trouble Taslim had given Moriam, which made me wonder what the fuss had been about.

We'd just finished eating when he announced he was going out to meet his friends.

"You see?" Moriam said, proudly. "This is what he does. His father has just come home after two months and he wants to go out."

"Me, too," Bashira said, standing up. "I've gots to go."

She followed Taslim with a strut. She was enjoying the fact that he no longer had the SATs as an excuse for avoiding housework.

"Look at them," Moriam said, prouder still. "Typical American kids."

"Don't Taslim's friends ever come here?" I asked.

"They do," she said.

I was surprised. They'd never come to the house when I was there.

"Where is Bashira 'gots to going'?" I asked.

Moriam wrinkled her nose. "It can't pass Alice's house."

After they left, she gave me the latest updates about tender-headed Nia, who was planning a trip to Ghana in the summer, and Bisi the Gossip, who was facing a foreclosure. Moriam herself was watching her diet and exercising at the hospital gym. In our bedroom, I spotted a women's magazine she had been reading with a headline about spicing up your sex life. I hoped she might learn something from it.

The woman had a vibrator. She didn't even bother to hide it. She kept it in the drawer of her bedside table. She said it was a birthday present.

"From who?" I asked. "Nia?"

"Of course not."

"Who, then? Bisi?"

"No."

"Kim?"

Kim seemed a likely suspect. She was the nurse with the nose piercing. Moriam reached for the vibrator and so did I. We pulled it like a Christmas cracker and I yanked it out of her hand so fast she lost her balance and fell on the bed.

"This is spousal abuse," she said with mock seriousness. "I won't tolerate it."

She and her Lifetime Movie Network brand of feminism. She'd finally replaced me with a mechanical device.

"Look at you, barely off the boat and already behaving like a bad woman. I will beat the hell out of you if you don't tell me who gave this to you."

"Please," she said. "I've been working out. What can you do to me?"

I threatened her with the vibrator. She kicked and screamed and admitted that Claudette, the middle-aged, divorced nurse, was the one who gave it to her.

"Old slut," I said.

"It was just a joke! Claudette doesn't even date!"

"You believe that?"

"She's a Christian!"

"She's still a slut. *Oya*, use it and let me see."

I wasn't jealous. Let the vibrator do all the hard work. That was what it was meant for.

"Whore," Moriam said.

It seemed like the right moment to bring up the subject of going back to Mississippi, but she didn't let me finish. I only got to "Miss—" and her hand went up.

"I've told you before. I'm not going anywhere."

"I don't expect you to," I said, "but I've been there long enough to know you will be fine if I get a permanent job there. There are hospitals all over the place. Wes's wife is an ob–gyn and she has contacts. I'm telling you, you may not earn more, but we'll save more. We're throwing money down the drain on rent here. We can buy a house for less there."

"I'm not living in a village. That is not what I came to America to do."

"Middlesex is not a village."

"Really?"

"It's even better than some of the cities here."

"Thank you very much. I'm still not going."

"What if it's the only place I can find a permanent job?"

"Get a permanent job there first, then we will discuss that."

"You don't think life would be better for us there?"

"Lukmon," she said. "You've just come back and I'm happy to see you, but I'm tired. Please don't give me *wahala*. All

I've been doing since you've been away is trying to keep this family together. Now, you're telling me you want to go back to Mississippi."

"I'm just saying that if I do get a job there, I would like you and Bashira to come with me."

"Didn't you say the schools there were bad?"

"There's a good high school in Columbus."

"Really? Is that near Toomsuba?"

She once saw an online job ad for a nursing position in Toomsuba, and the name amused her. I told her she had no business laughing at it, coming from a country with towns that had names like Okitipupa.

"I'm telling you there is a school in Columbus that Bashira can attend in the eleventh and twelfth grades, the Mississippi School for Mathematics and Science."

"Ah, Columbus. That was probably the first place he discovered in America."

I shook my head. "You know what? Forget it."

"No," she said pointing at me, "you forget it, because I saw how much they were paying nurses in Toomsuba. You don't know what you're asking of me."

"I'm not asking you to do anything. I'm taking the job. I will tell the man when I get back. But if I do end up getting a permanent job there, I would like you to be in the same state I'm in. There's nothing wrong with that."

"There's nothing wrong with me staying here, either. I didn't come from Nigeria to live in a village."

"Stop calling it a village."

She hissed. "It is a village. A village of people who buy guns at Walmart. Didn't a Nigerian there shoot his wife?"

"So?"

"Didn't you say he shot her and got away with it?"

"What has that got to do with what we're talking about?"

She tapped her temple. "Maybe he shot her because of the racism he'd faced there."

"There's no point having this discussion with you."

"I'm not going anywhere," she said. "You complain that everyone here is racist. This one is racist, that one is racist. Who is going to follow you to Mississippi, so one day you may turn around and shoot me and say racism caused it?"

That was the end of our discussion, and any sex. Seriously. If she'd wanted to have sex with me right then and there, I would have turned her down. I was that furious. What kind of woman had I married?

I couldn't reason with her. I left her on the bed, and she did her best to ignore me from then on, talking to the kids about what had happened at home while I was away. It got to the point that they noticed. She would ask if they remembered some event or another and they would look at each other and say, "Nope."

New Jersey was colder than I expected, and people there seemed ruder—at least at a diner I went to with my family one evening. I asked for a steak with no gravy and the waiter, after a moment of confusion, said, "You mean without the '*au jus*.'" Even I, with my rudimentary knowledge of French, knew that was wrong, but I said, "Yes, please," and before I knew it, the guy was asking where I was from. "Hungary," I said. "No pun intended." He walked off without a word and Moriam spent the rest of the evening warning me that if he spat on our food, she would hold me responsible.

Later on, we had another argument, this time over money. The day she received her first paycheck, she sent ten percent of it to her mother, and I teased her that she was tithing. When I suggested I do the same for my sisters, it was a problem.

"What are you sending them money for?" she asked. "Aren't they married women?"

She went on and on about them. I began to miss the warmth and tranquility of Middlesex, and the predictability of my life there. By the end of spring break, I didn't mind going back.

In my literature class, I taught Buchi Emecheta's *The Joys of Motherhood*, and every single one of my students sympathized with Nnu Ego. I could understand their disapproval of her brutish first husband, Amatokwu, but not of her second husband, Nnaife. I asked Rob why he had no sympathy for him and he said the man was a loser.

"He blames everyone for his problems. She had a hard life, too, but she always worked and tried to adapt. He just kind of gave up on life after he lost his job. She was more...sad about how her life turned out, and her sons didn't help, especially the one who ended up going to America and abandoning her. Her life sucked."

"More than his?" I asked.

"Yes. She never caused what happened to her. He caused what happened to him."

Rob was a reservist as well as a waiter. He was always tired in class. Middlesex College had quite a few students like him, in the Reserve and National Guard. Some apparently joined just to get tuition benefits.

Our class discussions were casual, to encourage participation. All I required from my students was that they contributed a comment or two. For class papers, I expected proper literary analyses. My students had to pay attention to plot, character, point of view, imagery and other elements, and I marked their papers with a rubric. They weren't particularly challenging or demanding, so the class was perfect for brushing up my teaching skills.

In my evening class, Andrea continued to make good grades. I didn't watch to see if she was cheating or broach the subject of her literacy again, but as the end-of-semester exam approached, I noticed a change in her. She made an effort to say hello to me when she came to class and would stop to talk to me afterward.

Just before the exam, she gifted me a pen she'd bought from the office supplies store where Tavarious worked. It was navy blue with "For Professor Karim" in silver lettering. My first thought was that I hoped Tavarious had not seen it.

"I want you to know how much you've inspired me," she said.

"Thank you," I said.

She was an attractive woman and always made an effort with her appearance. I still wasn't sure what she did for a living, but she needn't have wasted her money buying me that pen. As I'd predicted, she did fail her exam and I finally told her she needed lessons in reading and writing, and would have to find help outside the college.

Earlier that summer, a high school graduate was found hanging from a tree in the front yard of his home. He'd played basketball, so I imagined he was fairly tall. The local news reports said he may have committed suicide and the coroner's report later verified he had.

Wes and I talked about him the day I confirmed I would be returning to the college. He said there weren't enough resources for teenagers who suffered from depression, especially in the African American community, where depression was regarded as a stigma. He also said the rate of teenage deaths in Middlesex was high in general. They died from drug overdoses and were killed in single-car crashes, gang shoot-outs and hunting-gun accidents.

I talked to Mrs. Turner about the boy when I saw her at the bookstore and she had a different take on the matter. She flapped her wrist dismissively and said, "That child didn't kill himself. I've known him since he was a baby. He and his mama came to my church every Sunday."

Out of respect, I thought I ought to get more information from Odell.

"They hanged him," Odell confirmed.

"Wow...Really?"

"Sure. He was messing with white girls. At least that's what I heard, and this isn't the first time it's happened. There was a man about three years ago. He had served time for sexually assaulting a white woman. He had some kind of mental disability. He went missing and they found him hanging in the woods. Mm-hm."

Who went all the way to the woods to hang himself? I thought. Why didn't anyone call the FBI or the NAACP and how come people didn't protest? And why, after all that white men had done in Mississippi, were white men lynching black men and not the other way around?

"You don't cross the line," Odell said. "Everyone knows. But young people, you can't stop them. He messed with the wrong girl, that's all."

I later asked Tim how white people could say the boy had hanged himself, while black people were saying he was lynched, and no one was talking to each other or doing anything about it.

"That's how they deal with everything here," Tim said.

"But lynching in this day and age?"

"I wouldn't be surprised."

"I don't understand. How can this not be all over the national news?"

"I told you," Tim said. "This is Mississippi. They keep their news local."

Taslim got into Rutgers. He called and said, "Dad, you'll never guess what has just happened." He sounded so afraid, I thought he'd crashed his car.

I shouted when he gave me the news: "My son!"

He chose Rutgers over Fairleigh Dickinson. The day after commencement I flew back to New Jersey. Middlesex was so hot I might as well have been back in Lagos. In New Jersey, proms were in the air now that the school year was coming to an end, and if the SATs had been stressful, they were nothing compared to the proms.

Moriam, who seemed to have forgiven me for agreeing to spend another semester in Mississippi, immediately began to pester me for money. At first I thought that all I needed to do was to give Taslim money to buy clothes to wear for the prom. Then I heard, "Money for the limousine," which I didn't mind. Then I heard, "Money for the postprom party," which I couldn't understand. Then I heard, "Money for the graduation party," which wasn't just a simple open house for family and friends, as Taslim would have had in Nigeria. His classmates were reserving hotel rooms and halls, and hiring caterers and DJs. They were pressuring their parents to spend thousands of dollars, as if they were getting married. I told him, "You will not bankrupt me because you've graduated from high school."

Moriam suggested he should have a barbecue. He said he wanted a real prom party. Everyone else was having one. He kept going on until I finally said, "You want a prom party? Go and work for one."

"Why can't I get any love in this family?" he asked, with a smile. "American parents are proud of their children's accomplishments."

"Are you going to Princeton?" I asked.

"Didn't you say Ivy League colleges weren't everything?"

"If you weren't admitted to Princeton on a full scholarship, don't give me stress."

Next, he sprung Cancun on us. He and his friends must have been planning the trip for months, but he thought the best way to convince Moriam and me to let him go was to casually slip it by us. We'd just had dinner in the kitchen that evening when he asked, "Hey, may I go to Cancun this summer?"

"Can-who?" Bashira said.

"See me, see trouble," Moriam said. "We barely have enough money to send him to a community college and now it's Cancun."

She was speaking with pride yet again—about how Americanized our children were. I was somewhat irritated that she would bring up Taslim's college fees. That was supposed to be between us.

"Maybe I shouldn't go to college, so I can go to Cancun," he said.

She shrugged. "Don't go to college. We'll use the money for a deposit on a house."

"How will you pay for the rest of it?"

"That is not your concern."

"Didn't you say your friend in Philadelphia was facing a foreclosure?"

"That is none of your business, either."

She'd obviously confided in him in my absence. The bigger the house, the bigger the debt. Bisi the Gossip was finding out and I hoped Moriam would learn from that.

Neither of us wanted to be buried in America and our aim was to retire to Nigeria and buy a house in Lagos or Abeokuta. We would be able to do that because we were earning dollars. We could never get a mortgage in Nigeria. There was no such thing there. The only Nigerians who got loans were rich people, who got richer by defaulting on their loans. The most we would get was a payment plan for two years and the moment we failed to pay, our house would be gone. Which financial institution in Nigeria would believe we could afford to buy a house if we didn't have all the money in hand? Which financial institution there would even trust that we would survive for ten to thirty years, let alone give us a mortgage for that long?

Taslim turned to me. "So, can I, Dad?"

"Can you what?" I asked.

"Go to Cancun."

"If you take a Greyhound bus."

"And then swim some," Bashira said.

We had celebrated her sixteenth birthday by going out to dinner and she'd seemed reasonably happy with that.

"I don't expect you to pay," Taslim said.

"How will you pay, then?" I asked. "With spit?"

Bashira slapped the table. "Hah!"

"I was hoping to borrow the money from you," Taslim said. "Then work throughout the summer to pay you back."

"He says he will work and pay us back," Moriam said, as if I hadn't heard.

She was trying to make me look like the difficult parent.

"What kind of work?" I asked Taslim.

"I dunno," he said. "I'll find something. Something's bound to come up."

"Is that okay, Daddy?" Moriam asked.

"Is what okay?" I asked.

"For him to borrow the money and pay us back."

Perhaps she'd given up on being Mama, but Baba was still going strong, and now that he had some money, no one could stop him.

"Why?" I asked. "So he can drink tequila and drive while intoxicated?"

Mexico was not America. If Taslim broke any laws there, the US Embassy would not come to his rescue. As for going snorkeling and scuba diving or whatever else he intended to do there, Africans were bound to get hurt participating in such activities.

"Ben's dad will be there to chaperone," he said, with an earnest expression.

"What about Riz's dad?" I asked.

"Riz hasn't asked his parents yet."

"I wonder why. Only American parents. Always trying to be best friends with their children."

"Come on, Dad. It's not like I'm having a graduation party."

"Are you your class valedictorian?"

"Huh?"

"If you're not your class valedictorian, don't disturb me."

"Never mind. I knew you'd say no anyway."

He fell silent and Bashira began to talk about Laurie, a girl in her class. She'd met Laurie's mother on sports day and the woman said, "Hey, Bashira! Laurie's told me all about you!"

"She was like going on as if Laurie and I are best friends," Bashira said. "I can't even stand Laurie."

"These kids are so rude," Moriam said, smiling again.

In Nigeria, she would have backhanded Bashira for talking badly about a parent.

"She wants me to call her Angela from now on," Bashira said.

"You cannot call her Angela," I said.

"Why not?"

"She is your elder. You will address her properly."

"She gave me permission."

"You see?" I said, turning to Moriam. "The woman hardly knows Bashira, and she wants Bashira to be on a first-name basis with her. Have you ever heard such nonsense?"

"Hey," Bashira said. "You and Mom call me by my first name, but you hardly know me."

She began to hum to herself as Taslim resumed his offensive.

"You know what happened in class last week? We were

talking about, uh, Dre's graduation party and this guy asked, 'So when's your party?' And I'm like, 'I'm not having one.' So he asked, 'Why not?' and I said, 'Because I'm a seniorita.'"

"What?" Bashira asked.

"A senior with parents who are recent immigrants to America," he said.

Bashira looked puzzled. "Oh."

Moriam laughed. "Did you make that up?"

"Yes," Taslim said. "So he asked, 'Is Riz having a party?' and I said, 'Riz is a seniorita, too.' So he says to Riz, 'Hey! Seniorita!' and Riz says, 'I may be a senior, but I ain't no Rita.'"

Now it was Taslim's turn to slap the table.

"I don't get it," Bashira said.

"He was..." Taslim said. "Oh, never mind. You have to have been there to understand."

"That was lame," Bashira said.

"These children are crazy," Moriam said.

"'I ain't no Rita,'" I repeated.

"Come on," Moriam said. "They all speak like that."

"Yeah," Bashira said, dancing in her chair. "That's how we do."

"Um, should he have said, 'I'm not a Rita,' then?" Taslim asked.

I ignored him. "We come here to live. You end up going to a good school. You have the best opportunities and you take them for granted. Someone asks why you're not having a graduation party and the first answer you can give is that your parents are to blame."

Taslim smiled. "I wasn't blaming anyone."

"What? Aren't we the backward immigrants in this house?"

"I didn't say that."

I shook my head. "This one being self-deprecating, the other one playing down her intelligence. No wonder they fit in."

If Taslim thought he could make me feel guilty by telling me that story, he was mistaken, and I wasn't the only Nigerian father refusing to give in to prom pressure.

The great Dr. Aderemi wasn't paying for his daughter's graduation party either. He told Moriam he was still paying for her sweet-sixteen party, not to mention her eighteenth birthday. He believed that teenage parties were a government ploy to keep the economy going and was living on Mylanta because of the proms. In fact, he went as far as to say he didn't want to hear the word "prom" ever again.

Moriam said he was just panicking because he knew what kids got up to at their proms, and somehow, during their conversation, she promised to ask Taslim to take Anjola to their school prom. I wished her the best of luck.

The day she asked Taslim, I was with her in the family room. Bashira was at Alice's house for the weekend. Taslim walked in wearing basketball shorts that ended at his shins.

"I'm not doing it," he said, folding his arms.

"Why not?" Moriam asked.

"Because I'm not in an arranged-marriage situation here."

"I'm talking about taking her to a prom, not marrying her."

"Mom, I don't want to take Anjola to the prom!"

I, too, was getting fed up with the word "prom." To me, the proms were an American coming-of-age ritual with clothes.

"Why not?" Moriam persisted.

"She doesn't want me to take her to the prom anyway."

"How would you know?"

"We spoke yesterday and she never mentioned anything about the prom to me."

When Taslim said "spoke," he meant communicated online. I was aware that Taslim and Anjola kept in touch that way, but outside of school, they didn't socialize. Did she intimidate him?

I wondered.

"Who are you taking?" I asked him.

"A friend."

"Which friend?"

"Dad, we're all going together."

"Who? You, Riz, Ben and Dre?"

He didn't answer. Moriam was watching him.

"What do you people do at these proms anyway?" she asked.

"Mom," he said. "A prom is not a secret cult."

"Do you drink alcohol?" she asked.

"Why would we do that?"

He was lying as if he had no parents. I'd had my first beer at the age of eleven and Moriam had had her first taste of alcohol at the age of ten, when she tried her father's schnapps.

"What about drugs?" she asked.

"Mom."

"So no one drinks or takes drugs at the proms?"

"I won't be doing either."

"What about sex?"

"Mom, don't start with the sexually transmitted diseases."

"I just want to know."

Taslim didn't take drugs. That I was reasonably sure of. The rest, I couldn't vouch for.

"Please take Anjola to the prom," Moriam said again.

"No," he said.

"Why not?" she said. "She's a well-brought-up girl from a good family."

"You take her to the prom, since you love her so much," he said, and limped out of the room.

"Didn't I tell you?" I asked.

She shrugged. "Don't mind him. He's not serious."

"He's eighteen. You can't force him to go out with someone."

"'He's eighteen' doesn't mean he can do anything he wants."

"He was lying, by the way."

"About what?"

"He drinks. He probably has a fake ID hidden somewhere in this house."

She looked around the room. "In this house? While I'm here?"

"Of course."

She snapped her fingers. "He thinks he can deceive me? He will see."

I had told her what I'd learned about teenagers in Middlesex, only to prepare her for ours, but she was determined to prove me wrong. She waited until Taslim had gone out that night, then she went to his bedroom to search for evidence. Why, I didn't know. If he had a fake ID, he would be carrying it. I didn't even know how she could go into his bedroom. Whenever I walked in there, I held my breath. Apart from the odor of damp trainers, the room always looked as if he'd dived onto his bed, fought with his sheets and flung his clothes around.

She came back minutes later, hopping as if the floor was too hot to walk on.

"See me, see trouble," she whispered. "Come and see what I found in your son's room."

I put my glasses on, thinking it was a fake ID, but it was a passport photo of a girl.

"Talk to him," Moriam said. "Talk to him before her father finds out and kills him."

The girl was white. I'd also told her about the boy in Middlesex who was lynched.

I had not spent as much time with Taslim as I should have. I did not talk to him the way I talked to Bashira. I was stricter on him. I sometimes put him down, yes, but that was only when he behaved as if he had no brains. He had brains. All I was asking was that he use them.

The next day, I asked him to come to Paterson with me. Moriam still went to the farmers market there once a month to buy meat, and I offered to step in for her.

"Man, do I have to?" he asked.

"Come on," I said, throwing the car keys at him. "You drive, and try not to kill us."

He drove with his mother's temperament. He got angry with drivers who cut in front of him, sometimes accelerating to overtake them. I'd never been to Paterson before. The houses there were smaller, with one-car garages. We passed a Catholic church, a cemetery with gray headstones and came to a stop by a building covered with vines. A boy walked his dog across the road.

"I don't know why your mother has to drive all the way here," I said. "Why can't she just go to Pathmark?"

"She says their meat is not halal," Taslim said.

"Who cares if it's halal?"

He checked the rearview mirror before driving on. "I wish I knew more about Islam."

"Why?"

"I don't know. Riz practices it."

"You can't eat bacon or drink alcohol if you practice Islam."

"Well, that's it for me, then."

So he did drink. He and Bashira ate bacon. Moriam still did occasionally, which was why I couldn't understand why she bothered to buy halal meat.

We came to another stop by a plaza with signs saying "Checks Cashed" and "We Buy Gold."

I seized the opportunity. "Why won't you take this girl to the prom?"

"Which girl?"

"Dr. Aderemi's daughter."

"Anjola?"

"I'm not saying you should, but I'm just wondering."

He checked the rearview mirror again before driving on. "She already has a date."

"Yes?"

"But don't tell Mom."

"Why not?"

"Because. Her dad thinks she's going with a group of friends."

"Who is her date? Anyone you know?"

"Demetrius."

"One of your friends?"

"Kind of."

"Greek?"

"No."

"What is he?"

"Human."

"I'm just asking to have an idea of the situation. Is he Hispanic? African American?"

"God…"

"Just tell me."

"African American."

I was prying into the Aderemis' lives but couldn't help myself.

We were approaching the farmers market and passed several grocery stores with Spanish and Arabic signs.

"I'm sure her father wouldn't mind," I said.

"Yes, he would."

"Dr. Aderemi?"

"Of course he would."

"Why?"

"Because Demetrius isn't preppy."

"What is that?"

Taslim sighed. "Who knows? There's always something with Nigerian parents. Something they don't approve of."

"Is that what Anjola said?"

"Dad, you're all like that. You're always sizing up people."

"How? When?"

"Admit it. You're not like regular American parents."

"What are regular American parents like?"

"Accepting!"

"They're not accepting. They're just pretending."

"Dad, you admitted you're a racist."

It was a false admission, but I'd given it voluntarily.

"I only said that because of what happened to Amadou Diallo."

He tapped the steering wheel. "No. Please don't use him as an excuse. If there's one lesson to come out of what happened to him, it's that you have to face your heart."

Face your heart. He was unexpectedly eloquent.

We passed a Turkish café and an abandoned Lebanese restaurant.

"It must be hard for you here," I said.

"Not for me," he said. "Maybe for you."

"In what way?"

"I don't know how you can live that way, putting up so many barriers."

"What do you mean?"

"I have all kinds of friends. I don't think about their race."

Neither did I. I thought about his.

"Is that why they don't come to the house when I'm around?"

"I don't want to deal with it. You might say something."

"I was joking. I'm not a racist."

"They may not know that, though. You see the worst in America. My friends and I are just trying to see the best, that's all."

"I'm sorry."

I was apologizing for America, not for my behavior. I was as fed up as he was with racial barriers, but how would hypocrisy help? Having spent a few months in the South, I found the North unduly self-congratulatory. How integrated was Manhattan, Brooklyn, or even Paterson? How diverse was our neighborhood in New Jersey? Of course, there were places where Taslim could get shot walking around, even in broad daylight, but we didn't live in one of them. He was more likely to get pulled over by the police driving around a neighborhood like ours at night. I wanted to tell him that giving in to our primitive urge to stick to our kind was normal, and safe, but I knew better.

"Look," I said. "Mom saw a photo of your girlfriend in your room yesterday."

He stepped on the brake so hard I held on to the dashboard. Now, he was the one apologizing.

"It's all right," I said. "So...why didn't you tell us?"

I expected him to be angry that Moriam had been snooping in his room, but he wasn't.

"I've told you why already," he said.

"Does your sister know?"

"No."

"Sure?"

"She would probably tell you if she did."

"What do you mean?"

"Bashira tells you everything."

"She doesn't tell me everything."

"Well, ever since you two had your book club thing..."

"You don't like literature."

"Yeah, well, there are plenty of things I do like."

I'd made one attempt to talk to him about hip-hop and given up. We could have talked about his soccer games, but I thought that would go to his head. He had enough encouragement from other parents after he played: fathers slapping him on his back and mothers saying, "Good game," and batting their eyes at him. Would they applaud him that way if he beat their sons in class tests? I doubted it. Would they be happy to hear he was dating one of their daughters? I wasn't prepared to take a chance.

"You should talk to me when you feel like it," I said. "I don't know why you don't. Your sister doesn't either. You're always with your friends. She's always with Alice and her other friends. She seems to talk more with your mother—"

"I talk to Mom as much as Bashira does."

"They both talk a lot."

"Bashira's more like you, though."

"How?"

"She's always going on about how white girls are stupid."

"She is?"

"Well, she does a stupid white girl voice."

I could imagine Bashira doing that, even though she had white friends. If she was reacting to their supposed appeal to the opposite sex, I was disappointed. If she was becoming cynical about race, it would be too much of a burden for her. The one consolation I had was that she would not be as vulnerable as Taslim was. He was protecting his girlfriend, and defending her people. People who were not likely to protect or defend him.

I watched the road ahead. The market was on a street lined with fresh fruit and produce stands and already crowded with shoppers.

"Stupid girls come in all shades," I said. "So do stupid boys. So, whatever you do, always respect your girlfriend and always use a condom. Sex is not so great that you must fall sick, and your mother and I are not ready to be grandparents."

Again I sounded self-conscious, but I didn't know what else to say.

He drove as if he were in danger of crashing. We crossed a railway line. A Middle Eastern woman pushed a shopping cart on the sidewalk. Two Hispanic men polished an electric-blue sedan at a car wash. He came to a stop by a halal meat store and I turned to him.

"What is her name?"

"Jen."

It would be, I thought. What was the matter with him? He saw his mother, still fresh, and not a line on her face. Didn't he know what was good?

"I don't care if you date an Eskimo."

"She's not an Eskimo, Dad, and that's an offensive term."

"It is?"

"Especially when you use it that way, as if you'll accept anyone. But yes, Bashira said it was."

I was already tired. Why was he lecturing me?

"We're talking about your girlfriend here," I said. "Have you met her parents?"

"No!"

"Why not?"

"Because it's not that serious!"

"I hope this isn't a case of Daddy grabbing a gun when he finds out."

"Her parents are not together."

"What are they? Separated? Divorced?"

He hesitated. "Divorced."

"What does her father do?"

"I don't know."

"How can you not know?"

"Dad, I said it's not that serious. We don't talk about our parents anyway."

"What do you talk about?"

"Wow. This is..."

"I'm just asking. What about her mother? What does she do?"

"She's a nurse. Please don't ask me anymore questions. This is seriously creeping me out."

There was no point. All this information I would have known in Nigeria, without asking.

"Listen," I said. "I don't want you hiding from anyone's family, like your Uncle Ismail. You're coming from somewhere. Always remember that. I don't care who they are or what they've got. Let their last name be Kennedy, even. You're a Karim, an Ahmed-Karim. You hear me?"

He frowned. "Yes."

"'Yes,' what?"

"Yes, Dad."

Love necessitated care; care necessitated caution. That was how Moriam and I parented our children. I hugged him and told him I loved him. Then I told him to check his side mirror more often and stop trying to overtake everyone on the road. There was no need to rush.

Moriam cried during Taslim's graduation. I was just glad he walked across the stage and collected his diploma without doing a cart-wheel or making a radical pronouncement against society. I was proud of him—so proud I'd invited Ismail, who never showed up. Perhaps he hadn't yet forgiven me for the July Fourth fireworks.

After the graduation ceremony came the prom. I took photographs of Taslim and his friends when their limo arrived, until Moriam grabbed the camera from me.

"Smile!" she said.

"Mom," Taslim said. "We have to go."

"Only a few more!"

"Mom, I said we have to go!"

"Get in the limo quick," I said. "Your mother is on barbiturates."

He practically dove in. After they left, she started crying again.

"What is wrong with you?" I asked.

"He's—"

"Pull yourself together," I said. "He's not getting married."

"These children," she said, wiping her tears. "They grow up so fast."

"Yes, and they can leave home fast as well."

"Look at me, crying over a child who couldn't even bring his date home. Why didn't he bring her here? At least let us meet the girl he's taking to the prom."

She couldn't wait to size the girl up. Now that we knew more about Jen's family, she was less concerned about Taslim getting killed by a crazy father. I actually thought the risk was higher in a divorced family, but I wasn't going to tell her that.

"That's his business if he doesn't want to bring her home," I said.

"Don't you want to meet her?"

"Please. So many beautiful black girls around and my son goes out with a flat—"

She raised her finger. "I won't tolerate that kind of talk in this house."

I smacked her backside.

"Don't touch me," she said. "Racist."

That only encouraged me. My hands were all over her.

"Leave me alone," she shouted.

Bashira, who had dismissed the whole prom as lame, was in the family room when we ran in.

"Dad!" she said. "Leave Mom alone!"

"Your father is a racist!"

"Your mother loves white people!"

"This is so disgusting," Bashira said.

"As for you," I said, pointing at her, "you'd better not bring a white boy home."

"What if I bring a white girl home?"

"Well, that would be between you and your mother."

"Why?"

"She's the gay expert in the house."

"Ah," Bashira said, raising her forefinger as Moriam had done. "Racist and homophobic."

Always the provocateur. She had a poster of D'Angelo on her bedroom wall. It was practically pornographic.

Why was I being accused of homophobia? Because Moriam had a gay colleague at the hospital, and she actually referred to him as such. His name was Matt. He was a nursing assistant, and white, yet he talked like a caricature of a black woman. He called her at home once in a while, and the way I saw it, they had for all intents and purposes adopted each other as pets. She was his little African woman and he was her little American gay. Since Matt, you couldn't say anything about gay people without her correcting you. In fact, if you mentioned the word "gay," she was ready with a rejoinder. All I asked was why she didn't mind Matt speaking in that voice, yet she got angry whenever her nursing manager, Nancy, called her "girl," and she said I was homophobic. I asked her to define the word. She said Matt's voice was part of his sexual identity. I said I had a gay colleague who spoke in his normal voice. She said he was probably boring, as if he didn't have a right to be. I told her gay men didn't exist to provide straight women with entertainment. So now I was homophobic as well as sexist, racist and possibly anti-Semitic.

We sat on the sofa for a moment to catch our breaths. She and her children were on the diversity bandwagon, and nothing

I could do would get them off.

"I done tire," I said to Bashira. "Bring home anyone you like."

"Bushman," Moriam said.

I actually felt more like a white man under attack. What was wrong with these people? I thought. Why were they so sensitive? Couldn't they take a joke?

After the prom came the graduation parties. Ben had his at a country club, Riz's was at an Asian fusion restaurant and Taslim was still refusing to have a barbecue in our backyard. He was looking forward to Dre's party now, which was the graduation party of the year.

Ben's father was an orthodontist, Riz's was a radiologist and Dre's was a music executive. I knew this because Moriam made sure I did. According to her, Dre's father was friendly with hip-hop artists who lived in the Oranges, and he and his wife were always on vacation in St. Barts. For their son's graduation party, they'd hired a famous DJ who was normally booked a year in advance. The whole week, all we heard from Taslim was "Dre's party," "Dre's party." Then we heard "the DJ," "the DJ," when it looked like the DJ might not make it because he was in Tokyo. Then we heard the party was on when the DJ landed in New York.

The day after the party, Taslim woke up at about five in the evening. He called his friends and I overheard him talking about who had hooked up with whom, and some guy Dre's dad had walked out of the house because he was acting like a fool.

He managed to drag himself to the kitchen table for dinner while Moriam and Bashira were out grocery shopping. I watched as he served himself lukewarm rice and chicken stew in a soup bowl. His hair was uncombed and his eyes were swollen.

"You must have had a good time last night," I said.

"I'm messed up," he mumbled.

He used a spoon to eat. He had the loudest swallow.

"What's wrong?" I asked, when he stopped abruptly.

"I feel sick," he said.

"How much did you drink last night?"

"I didn't drink."

"Listen, I know a hangover when I see one."

He pushed the bowl away. "I know, I know. You were seventeen when you got into university and you drank until you passed out. You could have choked on your puke and died."

"Just remember," I said, "this is not Nigeria. If you get caught here, there will be consequences."

He rubbed his temple. "Dad, can you please..."

"What?" I asked.

"Stop with the fatherly advice."

He looked embarrassed. I couldn't imagine talking to my own father that way.

I shrugged. "If you don't want my advice..."

Now he looked irritated. "You see? This is why I don't tell you anything. Anyway, I wasn't doing anything my friends weren't doing."

"That may be the problem," I said.

"Dre's father was watching us! We couldn't do much with him there!"

"You expect me to believe that?"

"Obviously, not everyone. But I hardly did anything. There's not much I can do in this house without someone jumping down my throat."

"Who jumps down your throat?"

"Mom."

"This same Mom who smiles, whatever you do?"

"She wasn't smiling while you were away."

"What were you doing to upset her?"

"Nothing."

"Is that why she was always calling me and yelling?"

"She yelled over nothing. All I'm saying is try and give me credit. I'm a lot more serious than you think. I'm not going to mess up my life on alcohol or drugs."

My pride got in the way. "I was trying to have a conversation with you."

He threw his hands up. "Great."

"Just be honest. How much did you drink last night?"

"Man..."

"Or is it drugs we're dealing with here?"

He had to be taking drugs to think he could get away with talking to me that way.

He pressed his palms together. "Dad, please just give me credit. That's all I'm saying. I may want to have fun, but I'm not a total idiot."

"Okay," I said.

If he didn't want to talk, I wasn't going to force him. He wasn't a kid anymore and I had my own problems.

He got a job within a week, delivering pizza. He used the Corolla, which meant that I was back to being the driver in the house. Moriam started talking about buying a third car. She said he would need one when he started college. I told her he could buy himself one, since he was a man.

One night he came back from work and announced he had something to say to us. I thought we were back to Cancun again. We were in the family room and he went off to Bashira's bedroom to get her.

"Why can't you children leave me alone for one second?" Moriam asked, when they returned.

"It won't take long," he said.

Bashira sat by Moriam and Taslim remained standing.

"What's going on?" Moriam asked. "Is your girlfriend pregnant? Is that why you're hiding her from us?"

"Mom, don't start."

"We warned you," Moriam said. "We'll see if you can pay for diapers with the money you earn from delivering pizza."

"I've been thinking about joining the Reserve," he said.

He was in his work uniform, a red cap and T-shirt. I thought he was talking about doing extra shifts.

"That's good," I said. "How much do reserves get an hour?"

"I mean the United States Army Reserve," he said. "Now, please don't panic. I've been thinking about it for a while. I've done my research on the program and I know it's the right option for me. I'm eighteen. I don't need your permission. I'll get tuition assistance, which will help. All I have to do is show up for training, after which I serve for a few years."

He waited for a reaction. I was thinking of Rob and other reservists at Middlesex College.

"I'm confused," I said. "How can you join the army when you're not a US citizen?"

"You don't have to be a citizen. A green card is enough."

"How can you serve in the army with a green card?"

"Dad, it's not like I'm going to be on active duty."

"Please tell him no one can guarantee that," I said to Moriam.

She was rocking back and forth. For a moment, I wondered if she already knew. Perhaps they all knew and the family meeting was staged for my benefit. Her joke about his girlfriend being pregnant was out of character. The Moriam I knew would be yelling her head off. As for me, I could laugh about being a stay-at-home dad. I could even laugh about moving to Mississippi and being muzzled there, but not about this. America was not funny anymore.

"How long have you been thinking about it?" I asked, trying to stay calm.

"Um, a while now, like I said."

"I'm sorry. You can't."

"Can't what?"

"Join the Reserve."

"Why not?"

"We're Nigerian."

"So?"

"We don't risk our lives to get an education."

He shrugged. "I've made up my mind."

"My friend, you probably won't qualify for the program at this late stage."

"Thanks for the encouragement."

"You're eighteen, Taslim. You can't join the army."

"I'm old enough to—"

I jumped to my feet. "You're not even old enough to drink! What is wrong with you? You think joining the army is a game? You think war is all bang, bang, and the hero survives, as they do in your stupid action movies?"

Moriam winced. "Lukmon, *ni suuru.*"

"*Kini*?" I asked.

"My father was in the army," she said.

"Please, leave your old man out of this."

"You guys," Bashira said. "Chill."

"Not a word from you," I said, pointing at her. "We're your parents, not guys, and don't you ever tell us to chill again."

Her voice quivered. "I'm just saying—"

"Out of here if you're going to cry," I said.

She walked away mumbling, "You told me to always speak my mind."

"Yes," I said. "Now, I'm telling you to learn when to shut up."

"*Wahala*," Moriam whispered.

"And you," I said to Taslim. "You'd better not even think of opening your mouth until I've finished what I have to say."

"Why did you have to talk to Bashira that way?" he yelled.

"She is rude and so are you."

"Lukmon," Moriam said. "That's how they all talk."

"They don't all talk like that," I said. "Maybe you should come to Mississippi and find out."

"Why didn't you just stay there?" Taslim said. "We were doing fine here! Mom went to work! She paid our bills! What did you ever do, except sit around correcting our English and whining about America?"

I gestured at Moriam. "See what a fool your son is?"

"I'm not a fool," he said. "I know what's going on. Bashira didn't have a birthday party and she didn't complain. I didn't have a birthday party and I didn't complain. I didn't even have a graduation party and I'm cool with that. I'm working and doing something to help pay for college and I'm the fool?"

I lunged at him and grabbed him by the collar. "If you say one more word..."

His voice was hoarse. "Make sure you don't leave a mark. You said it yourself. What do the police care? You're just another nigger to them."

Moriam stepped between us. I could easily have pushed her away, but I released Taslim's collar.

She turned to him. "You're threatening to call the police on your father?"

"He threatened me!"

"'He'?"

She slapped him. "*Oya*, call the police. Call them. Let them come here and arrest me. Tell them you're old enough to join the army, but you need protection from your parents like a child.

Go on. Call the police. I'm waiting for them."

She'd barely touched him, yet he fought back tears.

"Go and take a shower," she said.

He stunk of pizza. The smell made me sick. After he left the room, she faced me.

"You have every right to be angry," she said, "but you do not turn on our children that way."

I couldn't believe what I was hearing. "Am I the only one in this family who has sense?"

"Stop talking to him as if he's stupid!"

"He wants to join the army! You know why? Because he doesn't think!"

"He thinks, Lukmon. He just doesn't think like you."

I forced a laugh. "I leave him with you for a semester, a semester in your care, and he's sleeping with white girls and joining the army. Aren't we American? Aren't we really American now?"

"Stop blaming America for everything!"

"One year I stayed at home with him. One whole year, and he was all right. What do you hope will happen now? He will get money for his tuition? Is that what you want, so you can make more trips to the mall? Is that the price you put on your son's life?"

She shut her eyes. "May God forgive you."

"Use your brains! Use your brains for once! That's all I ask of him! He's telling me he wants to join the army! You're damn right I talked to him like that! I'm more worried about his life than you are!"

She shook her head. "You have so much anger in you."

Her television psychobabble pissed me off further.

"Where do you think it came from?" I asked. "The water? The air?"

"What are you talking about?"

I pointed at her. "I gave up work to play househusband for you."

"You're working now! You haven't been home for the past how many months?"

"I can't tell you how peaceful they were, except when you called."

"God is watching you, Lukmon. God is watching you."

"I hope He's watching all of us. I hope He isn't busy chasing money."

She slapped her chest. "You think I liked being the man of the house?"

"Spare me. You have no idea what it means to be a man."

"A real man would back down for his son."

"I did."

She was standing right there and she hadn't even noticed. She put her hand on her hip. "What you went through for less than one year, women go through all their lives and they are strong enough to take it. Yes. Yes."

"That's because they talk, talk, talk, like you. They can't keep their big mouths shut, going on about their problems, and some poor unfortunate bastard has to listen to them."

"You are the bastard."

"Yes, I am."

If I was a bastard, she was a bitch. She should have been at home more. She could have worked fewer hours. She taught Taslim that education was an expense. She interfered with my role as his father, even now.

"Me," I said to myself. "A nigger."

I couldn't let that go. He would be hitting me next. I headed for the bathroom. All I wanted to do was to scare the hell out of him.

"Where are you going?" Moriam asked.

Bashira was in the hallway and I brushed past her.

"Dad, Taslim's in there."

I banged the door open with my fist. The bathroom was steamed up and the shower curtain drawn. A Jay-Z CD was playing "I Just Wanna Love U."

From then on it was slapstick: I dragged the shower curtain to one side; Moriam ran in and jumped on my back; I shrugged her off and the curtain collapsed on Taslim; she fell to the floor.

"Mom," Bashira yelled.

I tried to hold Taslim still, but the shower sprayed me and he punched me to free himself.

"Taslim!" Bashira said. "Stop it! You'll hurt yourself!"

Moriam grabbed my legs and my knees buckled. Taslim slipped from my grip. I heard a crack followed by a thud. He was under the shower curtain. Moriam was pushing me aside and pulling the curtain from his face. There was blood in the tub.

"Bashira," she said, far too quietly. "Call 911."

Dr. Aderemi was working that night. He sewed up the laceration at the back of Taslim's head. It was superficial, he said, but about two inches long. The impact of the fall had knocked him out, but Moriam resuscitated him before the ambulance arrived.

Dr. Aderemi used the word "we" a lot. We were lucky. We had to run tests. We had to observe Taslim overnight.

He looked smaller, and younger, on the hospital bed. He wasn't talking and neither was I. I was afraid—too afraid to consider that he might be permanently injured. Moriam didn't seem to think that was the case because she tried to coax him to speak.

Dr. Aderemi eventually called us aside and we didn't stop Bashira from following us. She had cried all the way to the hospital.

"Has he been having any, um, emotional problems?" Dr. Aderemi asked.

I couldn't meet his eyes. Moriam hesitated.

"No," she said.

"I'm only asking because sometimes parents may not be aware."

"He's not having any emotional problems," Moriam said.

"So this was just an accident?"

"Yes," she said.

"He slipped in the bath."

"Yes."

I could sense Dr. Aderemi was watching me. I would rather have him than some doctor I didn't know asking us questions, but I didn't owe him an explanation.

"Okay, then," he said. "We'll continue to monitor him."

"I'll stay with him," Moriam said.

Dr. Aderemi shook my hand and patted Bashira's shoulder before he left.

"Help Daddy with my overnight bag when you get home," Moriam said, without looking at me.

As I drove back, I remembered how angry Taslim got whenever Bashira took her time to come to the car. He once shouted, "Get your butt in here," and I told him not to speak to her like that again. He never did after that.

"Are you okay?" I asked.

"Yes," she said.

She usually didn't talk when she was in the car with me. She would stare out of the window, her mind elsewhere. We were comfortable with that type of silence. This time, I knew she kept quiet because she didn't feel safe.

We got home and, as I packed Moriam's overnight bag, she reminded me about Moriam's eye cream.

"What's that?" I asked.

"She uses it at night," she said. "It helps her not to look tired."

I hadn't even noticed Moriam looked tired. Bashira found the eye cream in our bathroom drawer, but she hesitated before she handed it to me.

"Never mind," she said. "She won't care about this anyway."

I agreed. "Will you be all right on your own?"

"Yes," she said. "I'll clean up the bathroom. Do you think Taslim will be okay?"

I didn't want to lie to her. I still wasn't sure.

"Let's pray," I said.

We said *Al-Fatiha.* Then I remembered how I'd taught Taslim the Lord's Prayer when he was a boy, and we said that as well.

HOPES

Taslim never joined the Reserve. I often think about his hospitalization that summer of 2001 and wonder if my actions leading up to it were driven by a premonition. If he had joined the Reserve and been called to serve in Iraq, would he be alive today? That is a reasonable question. You could say my fears were irrational, and that what mattered in the end was what was going on within my family, not outside it, but we can no longer sit in our small corners and assume that events in other parts of the world will have no impact on us.

Moriam had her own take on what happened. She said I attacked him. She also said I had violent tendencies and had physically threatened her on several occasions. Taslim apologized to me, nonetheless, and I told him the matter was over, which was my way of saying I was sorry. So long as he wasn't joining the Reserve, I was.

After he was discharged from hospital, his friends Riz, Ben and Dre visited him at home. So did his girlfriend, Jen. Bashira's friend, Alice, came over, as did Moriam's friends. I'd forgotten how many she had: Bisi; Nia; Dr. Aderemi and his wife, Desola; her colleagues at the hospital, Matt, Claudette and Kim; and our former neighbors Cathy McFadden and Howard Ostrowski. For all I knew, she may have confided in them. They were her people in America and that was exactly what she would have done in

Nigeria to expose and shame me.

I wondered if she had gone as far as to tell them what I'd said about them—that Bisi was a gossip, Cathy a serial killer and Claudette an old slut. Even Howard looked at me accusingly. "Your son's a decent young man, Luke," he said. "You and Maryanne should be proud of him."

I had told Taslim I was proud of him, many times. What I hadn't said to him, or anyone else in my family, was that I was scared. I'd been unable to provide for them for a while. I couldn't protect them fully. They'd changed so much I could hardly recognize them and I had no control over a single one of them.

Perhaps I wasn't the man in *The Beautyful Ones Are Not Yet Born*, after all. Perhaps Moriam was Nnu Ego in *The Joys of Motherhood* and I was her brutish and loser husbands combined. Her friends testified how kind and considerate she was, and how hardworking and generous. No one came to visit me or vouch for my character. Ismail was still involved with his Long Island woman. Osaro was busy working on his second book, a novel titled *First Chapter*.

I went back to Middlesex in early August and my second semester there may have saved my marriage. Moriam called me one night and said, like some pioneer heroine in the wilderness, "I don't know what I'm going to do in the winter." She didn't think she could handle a snowstorm with Taslim and me away from home. I again tried to persuade her to come down South. The house was too big for her and Bashira, I said. For the first time, she said she would consider moving, but it took her several months to decide, and to get Bashira on board, by which time I had a permanent job at Middlesex College.

All this was well before September 11, the day that changed how I would see America. I was getting ready for a class that morning when the plane crashed into the first tower. I thought I was watching a movie trailer. Then the second tower got hit and I realized what was happening.

"My God," I said.

Immediately after the attack, there was a compassionate kind of unity in Middlesex. In fact, the only other time I would witness that kind of unity was after Hurricane Katrina, when Middlesex almost resembled a war zone. People came from as far as New Orleans to camp in churches. My barber, Tommy, who had once told me he didn't trust white folk, took exception to the national media. "They always want to show the division here," he said. "They never want to show when we come together." Post-Katrina, people in Middlesex blamed people from New Orleans for the rise in crimes. Following September 11, Muslims in Middlesex were singled out for reprisals. An Indian dry-cleaner in town had a fake bomb delivered to his door. He was a Sikh.

My family moved from New Jersey to Mississippi in the summer of 2002. Bashira had completed her sophomore year of high school and Taslim his freshman year at Rutgers. He stayed with us for a few weeks before he went back to New Jersey for a summer internship. That was the last time he would live at home. Bashira continued high school in Middlesex and started preparing for her ACT. Moriam got a job at a hospital and we finally bought ourselves a house. She qualified as a Certified Nurse-Midwife and we became American citizens about a year later.

During the Iraq War, Taslim graduated from Rutgers, but he didn't stay on the CPA path. He got an MBA from Georgetown University and today works for an international management consulting firm in Washington DC. Bashira was accepted at Emory University to study English. She started a blog, "One Muslim Girl," on which she often raged about Islamophobia.

At one point, I was worried that she was turning into a radical, but she insisted she wasn't. I warned her to be careful. The government could end up monitoring her. Her blog didn't last, anyhow. She grew out of being controversial before she graduated.

She got her MA and PhD in English literature and now teaches at a liberal arts women's college in Atlanta. She is engaged to a young man called Jamal. The poor guy drove all the way to Middlesex to ask for her hand in marriage. I told him his family ought to write mine a letter of request, according to Yoruba tradition. He asked, with a smile on his face, if an email would suffice because he'd made plans to propose to Bashira the same weekend. He, too, is in academia. His family is African American and, like ours, Muslim by mouth.

As for Taslim, I don't ask about his love life. He says he dates in all shades and colors. If I were a woman, I would stay well away from him, but they keep trying to change him, including his mother. Whenever she lectures him about marriage, he says we are responsible for turning him against the institution. He may be right. I don't know how Moriam and I manage to stay married, but we're in our fifties and in good health. Either of us could be sick or dead, as I told her the last time she nagged me for being cheap. She is still shopping. I can't stop her. Her latest purchases are fabrics for traditional wear. She is planning Bashira's engagement ceremony. Her mother and brother hope to attend, visa willing. So do my sisters.

Bashira, meanwhile, threatens to elope. The arguments between her and her mother over the engagement ceremony are, as she would say, epic. I have to wonder if they are due to her mother's impending menopause. Whenever Moriam gets irritable, I take her to New Orleans for a weekend. She loves Orleans. A weekend there loosens her up. She knocks back hurricanes. She was never a good Muslim to begin with and

I'm just trying to preserve my life at this point. In my family, we don't live that long. Both her parents are still alive.

To take pressure off Bashira, we read and discuss works by a new generation of African writers who are all over the Internet and acting like reality-show stars. I say they're a welcome development if they would only back their self-promotion with the substance of the previous generation of writers. Bashira says the previous generation had no choice but to use colonial languages and forms of expression, and the new generation is doing the same with globalization.

I have been in Middlesex for over ten years now, teaching at the college. The city is yet to recover from the recession that followed the Wall Street bailout of 2008. Downtown, local businesses close as hotel chains are raised on the highways. Everyone passes through Middlesex, but no one settles here, unless they're from around here originally. These days, I see more interracial couples in the city center. An African hair-braiding salon has opened on Main Street, according to Moriam. We have since discovered a small community of Nigerian doctors who live here, yet people still ask where I am from. I always tell them Nigeria, because what they're really asking is where my accent is from.

I was here when President Obama was sworn in. Actually, I was a visiting professor at Northwestern University when he was elected in 2008, and I went to Grant Park that night to hear him give his victory speech. I was here on Christmas Day in 2009 when the underwear bomber boarded Northwest Airlines Flight 253 and failed in his mission to blow up an American plane. I was here in August 2011 when the United Nations building in Nigeria was attacked by a suicide bomber and I've since followed the news on Boko Haram.

I have always seen Nigeria as a great big dysfunctional polygamous family, with mothers from different parts of the country and of different religious persuasions, and children all over the place. Everyone sucks up to Daddy, a fat, manipulative fellow who has his favorites. Daddy is running out of money. Some of his children still eat their fill; others have taken to pilfering from home and outside. Most go hungry, and now there are grandchildren to feed. If you are a member of that family, you would be frustrated that it fails to take care of its own.

These days, I see America as, not exactly a schoolyard bully—bullies know why they're disliked—but as an overconfident kid strutting around the schoolyard, having pissed off all but a handful of sycophantic followers by instigating and interfering in fights. Once in a while he defends kids who are picked on, so he thinks this gives him the right to do whatever he wants. If you care about that kid, you might want to pull him aside and say, "Hey, even your best friends don't like you. They will kick your ass at the first opportunity and in my opinion here's why."

For all the dialogue that goes on in America, you don't know what people say in private unless you eavesdrop on them. At the college, I continue to make sure students can express themselves freely in my classes. I have taught war veterans younger than my children and I'm in awe of them. Today we might talk about the premise of a novel, tomorrow about characters in the novel. We recently read *What Is the What* by Dave Eggers, set during the Second Sudanese Civil War. Next week we will discuss the politics of narrative appropriation and the lines between fiction and nonfiction. I will ask whether at eighteen or nineteen an American could be considered a child soldier. I might even ask what a novel like *What* means for African literature.

I have seen no evidence to suggest that literature can change the world. I once came to the same conclusion about God. Now, I am willing to accept that God is indeed the greatest writer. No other writer can replicate His narratives for each and every one of us, and our beginnings and endings. I listen and mediate in my classes because some of my students fought for freedom, so the least I can do is stand up for a right I believe in.

I haven't always. I remember the morning Moriam came home without Taslim, having stayed at the hospital with him overnight. She walked into the family room, where I was waiting, and I asked how he was.

"What kind of man are you?" she cried. "How could you do that to your son?"

She charged at me, slapping and kicking. I bowed my head and kept still until she was through. I didn't say a word.

Acknowledgments

Much gratitude and thanks to Markeda Wade, Sarah Seewoester Cain, Sue Tyley, Pam Fontes-May, John Fiscella and Michel Moushabeck.